HOME AGAIN

HOME
AGAIN

MATTHEW MCCONKEY

BROKEN TRIBE PRESS

Home Again, Second Edition, 2024

ISBN: 978-1-965412-20-6

Broken Tribe Press
Raleigh, North Carolina

www.brokentribepress.com

For Bees

CHAPTER ONE

1

I hit him so hard that he fell. He didn't even scream out it happened so fast. I looked around and made sure that no one was watching. I was in the clear. I knelt down and continued to beat that kid with the lead pipe until I could no longer raise my arm. After a few long minutes, he was dead and I was nearly out of breath; even thought I was having a cardiac event as my heart pounded against my chest.

I rolled him into the nearby ditch beside the side street. I closed the hood of my car in a hurry. I slammed it way too loud because I had gotten too caught up in the moment. I got into my car and headed for home, fast. I didn't turn on the lights until I got a mile down the road. I should have been scared out of my wits, but fuck it. I did what I came to do. I changed the future by stopping the past.

Let me back up for a minute. Let me back all the way up…if this story is worth telling I'll have to start at the beginning. It's confusing as hell so bear with me. So here goes…

I was sitting up in my office writing my newest novel, *Tricks of the Trade.* I call it "writing in my office," but what I was actually doing was surfing the Internet for Atlanta Braves baseball news. I really liked all that insider stuff on websites about rumors of trades and things like that. I should have been paying more attention to my work, but I sometimes got distracted. Not because I had ADD or anything like that, but because my work seemed trite. There was too much going on in my life for me to really write like I used to. I was once a captain of the writing world. Lately, I had been just getting by with my good name. Even that was fading it seemed.

My novel, which I had to write under the conditions of my contract with Bob Windom, wasn't that good at all. In fact, for the past several books, I had pretty much written them in a matter of weeks, not paying attention whatsoever to whether they were any good—if I'm being completely honest here, a lot of those books lately had been pieced together by *other* books that I had floating around in my hard-drive which weren't that good to begin with. But I salvaged what I could and made something out of the quarter books and half books that were floating. They weren't good even after I got them written and published. I didn't care. Writing, for me, had become something I wasn't interested in anymore. It seemed that I was too busy wallowing in my own self-pity and just constantly being in a state of nothingness back then to sit down and actually concentrate on creating something worthwhile like I had back in the day. Creating worlds that only you can see takes a lot of time and effort—time and effort had escaped me, become boring.

I used to be really, really good at my craft. So good, in fact, that a few movies were made based on my books. I gladly accepted the royalties from those horrible films, every quarter, and still to this very day. I didn't care if the movies were good or not because their creators always fucked them up. Why care? If people hated the movies then they would go read the book I wrote. That never changed. I used to go to the film premiers, to those horrid adaptations, but after a few of them tanked, I stopped going. What was the point? I didn't like the way the directors made them, and they sure as hell didn't ask me for my opinion.

The last several novels I wrote were a chore and this last one was no exception. I had phoned the last several books in and, like I said, I had pretty much quit thinking about my writing process altogether. You see, back when I was young and hungry, and when things in my life were going like a gravy train with biscuit wheels, I could lay out a great plot, with several great twists along the way that always left my fans wanting more. Hell, I wanted more. Bob Windom gave me some great advice one time: always leave them wanting more. And that I did for a while.

Around my thirteenth book, *The Snowman,* I gave up and just wrote for the sake of fulfilling my contract. Running out the clock, I called it. Did I care that my books and my reputation were sliding off the mountain that I was once king of? Nah, that was for narcissistic writers. Me, I was comfortable with taking the money and writing absolute shit. I blame part of that on the booze.

Looking back, I lost a lot of fans because of books like *The Snowman* and *Tinker Toys.* I just had too much on my mind and was drinking heavily here and there, to write good stuff anymore. And when I was sober and actually tried, I discovered that my prowess, my *talent,* had been used up. My fields of imagination had become nothing but a small lot of thinning grasses. I had gotten to a point where I just said *fuck it,* and rattled off stuff I knew wasn't good by *anyone's* standards, much less mine.

2

Awards weren't a big deal for me anymore because I had won countless accolades that sat collecting dust upon my mantle. I wasn't one of those who needed praise for my work. I believed that once I finished writing the novel or short or whatever, that was that. I never went back to read my past work. That never interested me as a writer. I think those who do are so wrapped up in vanity that they can't see anything else. Not me. Once I was done, I was done—no use in performing a postmortem.

It had been a while since I had won an award for my writing. Maybe the literary world had grown tired of my imagination and wanted new blood to take the top honors I had received over the years. Nope, that wasn't it at all. What happened was that I had stalled and sucked at my job. Newer and better writers were taking my spot. That was okay. I didn't care as much as I did when I was twenty. Who does?

I put out hits in the past, and I knew that my sales had slumped a bit, even without Curtis – my literary agent and best friend – telling me so. *Tricks of the Trade* was going to be my final book with Windom Publishing. I knew that. And it wasn't the final nail in my coffin because, after all, my great-grandchildren would be cashing checks from everything I did throughout my career. If Windom let me go, so what? I had other things in my life I was dealing with to be bothered by writing novels. Did I mention I was drinking here and there? Sometimes I like to omit that—one of many character defects.

As I was sitting in my office in dead silence reading an interesting article about the Braves' last game, a knock came at my closed office door. "It's open!" I yelled not taking my tired eyes off the computer screen. The door opened and in came Jennifer. "Dinner's on you tonight," she said. "Thought I'd tell you." I just waved my hand in acknowledgment, and my estranged wife went away, closing the door quietly behind her. *Dinner's on me.* Well, I haven't heard that one before, I sarcastically thought in my mind.

For a long time, so long in fact that I fail to recall the exact beginning, Jennifer had been placing "dinner on me". She went out most nights, leaving me and the kids to fend for ourselves in the kitchen. The one thing that my wife did well was cook. She went to culinary school at one point during the beginning of our marriage but decided to quit when she got pregnant with Samantha, our first child. She always said that she was going to go back and one day open a restaurant, but that one day never came. Too bad because the woman was a wizard in the kitchen.

Instead, she pursued a career in real estate. Why real estate? Who knows? Maybe it was a vehicle for her to meet new people, especially men. That's what I thought anyway. Maybe she just wanted to feel in control of something. *Why the hell did she even need a job in the first place,* I questioned myself many times. I mean, we weren't hurting for money. Hell, with all the royalties, book contracts, advancements, and movie deals that I had inked over the years, even our kids didn't really need to work for money. I had taken care of them all with my pen.

Jennifer leaving the house as night was closing in wasn't anything out of the ordinary. I had gotten used to it and so had the kids. Our kids, Samantha and Davey, weren't little anymore. They knew something wasn't right about their mother leaving and staying out all night. They were seventeen and fifteen, respectively, and knew which way the wind blew, so to speak. Yet I never told them a bad word against their mother— didn't see that as the right thing to do.

Did I ever wonder where she went? I guess in the beginning I did. I had some inclinations that she was about the town. I wouldn't hear about it from others, though. I had no friends except Bill, the old man next door whom I adored because he was as much of an Atlanta Braves fan as I was, and Curtis. They were the only two men I talked to and even then I really never got personal. So if Jennifer was out with some guy, how would I know? It's not that I cared anyway. I never really did because I was no better.

3

Jennifer and I had drifted so much and for so long that thoughts of her being with someone else didn't rattle me as it would a man who was actually in love with his wife. Hell, I was doing the very thing that Jennifer was probably doing. But in my case, it wasn't with some random, strange person. Marie Evans and I *had* a history, a deep one that transcended secret trysts and rendezvous. What we had was special, even if it lasted just one weekend a year every October.

I think the kids knew Jennifer was walking out on me on those nights. It made Samantha mad; I could tell. Davey, well, he was another case entirely. He would withdraw within himself. I think Jennifer's transgressions, although not completely known or obvious, weighed on the kids' minds so much that they affected them in different ways. Truth be told, I pushed her to do it. I showed her barely any love and I think, after a time, it had gotten to her.

4

In the dining room that night after I finished reading the all-important *Braves Report*, the kids and I sat at the table eating pizza mostly in silence. Pizza at the Matthews home was a staple "go-to" dinner that always yielded leftovers. I admit I was no cook and I knew the kids hated pizza because we had it three nights a week— every night Jennifer went out to do whatever and whomever. Me, I was fine with pizza. Sometimes I would change up the brand for a different taste. But it didn't matter to the kids because they began to associate pizza with their mother's infidelities—if they only knew mine.

We sat at the dinner table the night of the explosion that was years in the making. Most times, well... every time, at the dinner table we would all sit there in silence chewing our food while lost in thought. Although we sat together, our hearts and minds were miles away. Within arm's reach but unable to touch one another.

I sat at the head of the table, Samantha to my right and Davey to my left. Samantha sat there chewing her food and looking down at her plate, while Davey sat slumped in his chair with his earbuds in, listening to whatever it was that he listened to those days. I imagined looking at us from afar was like seeing a dysfunctional Norman Rockwell painting. The title of the painting could have been called *Family Tradition*, but clearly for all the wrong reasons.

I was sitting there chewing my pizza when I spoke to the kids, trying to break the silence that encapsulated our wonderful dining experience. "So, how was school today? Anything exciting happen?" I awaited an answer. Nothing. Davey didn't hear me and Samantha never looked up to answer. "No? Well, let me tell you about my day. I'm almost done with my newest novel." God, I was such a good liar. Hell, lying to myself daily in the mirror after a night of drinking or talking to Marie for some good old-fashioned phone sex had become second nature to me. Lying was something I was great at. "It's a novella. Yeah, putting the finishing touches on it. Should be ready by the end of this week. Pretty excited. Probably the best thing I've done in years." More lies. I was practically just writing words in hopes that they made sense at this stage in my career. It would all eventually catch up with me.

Something was off that night, especially with Samantha. I was used to Davey not listening or replying because of his music, but at least my daughter would always acknowledge me and my writing. Back in better days, before the world had hardened her, she would love to talk about my craft. And I took a lot of joy in talking to her about the mechanics of writing, about how to tap into imagination, and so on. But as she had gotten older, she didn't seem to care about that stuff anymore. Maybe the world had gotten to her, or maybe it was just my and Jennifer's dynamic that crushed her. Whatever the case, Samantha was different. I could see that night that things were going to be different from there on out. Sometimes you just know.

I looked at Davey and motioned for him to take his earbuds out of his ears and talk to me. "Davey, how's school?"

He replied in a low voice with a tone that made it clear he didn't want to be there. "Fine, I guess."

"Haven't seen any grades in a while," I said. "Still on that honor roll?" Davey shrugged his shoulders.

"Maybe, I don't know."

"Well, high school is difficult. You'll go through a lot of changes mentally and physically, but you'll get there. I remember when I was in high..."

"Where the hell is mom tonight?!" Samantha broke in violently.

"What?"

"Mom! Where's she tonight? Another home showing at eight-thirty at night?" Her voice was dripping with sarcasm and pain.

"Honestly, I have no idea. Probably had a meeting or something," I said, not wanting to tell her that she was probably out fucking some guy. There are just some things you can't tell your kids, even if they already suspect the truth.

"It's *always* something with her. All the time. I'm tired of it."

"I know," I replied, not knowing what else to say.

She was right, though. Jennifer's reluctance to be home had hit the kids hard. I gave her space; I would hole up in my office so we didn't have to breathe the same air in the house. But Jennifer ratcheted our distance up a notch by leaving for hours on end. Usually, she wouldn't come home until after midnight. I would see her pull into the driveway from my office window as I finished a bottle of Wild Turkey, still talking on her cell as she walked to the front door. I didn't mind, though.

Samantha did mind; she minded plenty. She resented Jennifer for not being there with us. It wasn't as if it had started recently. My wife's absence began several years ago and her not being there became the status quo. Samantha was more observant and vocal about it, but not so much with Davey. Little did *I* know, Davey watched *a lot* of our household goings-on. I would come to understand later that Davey's depression linked right back to me and Jennifer. Our marriage helped hasten what was to come of our son later on.

5

I never threw their mother under the bus. I always held my tongue when it came to her in front of my kids. I didn't want them to hate her because of something that I might have said. Unbeknownst to me, Samantha *did* hate her. She hated Jennifer for her abandonment of not only me but also her and Davey. I had unintentionally rallied her to my side. Samantha viewed me as the victim of Jennifer's behavior alongside her and Davey. But who could blame her? She didn't know the whole story from the jump, did she? "I know how you feel," I said to Samantha.

"Do you really? Because I'm beginning to think that you don't. *Your* wife, *our* mother, is out somewhere doing whatever she wants while having a family she barely sees. It's total bullshit!"

"Whoa!" I said trying to calm my daughter down. "Calm down. She has an important job." I was just saying that to defend Jennifer because she wasn't there to do it herself. It was the least I could do.

"Yeah, right. Like selling houses is finding cures for diseases. Please. Doesn't her absence bother you at least a little bit?"

"It does, but that's how it is when you work," I said as vaguely as I could. I couldn't just sit there and tell them it made no difference at all to me if she was there or not. I tried not to give the perception that there was something wrong between Jennifer and me. But who was I kidding; Samantha and Davey were growing up and not immune to the adult world. I should have just been open and honest with them instead of dodging the truth. Honestly, Jennifer could have walked in with a guy, taken him to our bed, and had sex with him while I was in the house and it wouldn't have mattered to me.

"Work? Why does she need to work? She's got everything she could ever want," Samantha pressed.

"Maybe she likes getting out of the house. Could feel..."

"Why do you keep defending her?" Samantha interrupted. "We're not little kids anymore, Dad. Davey and I see how you and Mom are. You practically don't even breathe the same air in this house. So if you're defending her because you think in some weird way that you're doing your fatherly duty to protect us from harsh realities, then you're mistaken." And that's what I loved about Samantha. She was articulate and to the point when presenting her case. She had a way with words, and over the years I tried to nurture her raw potential. However, she always seemed reluctant to be a writer when I brought it up as a possible career path. I think she thought she would have to be as good as I was, or at least as good as I *once* was. Honestly, she could have been better than me.

I sat there looking at the kids, both of whom were looking back at me, waiting for a rebuttal to Samantha's statement. She was right, though; they weren't little kids anymore and I had been treating them as such. I guess I had forgotten how old they were. As a parent, you never want your kids to grow up. You'd love for them to be frozen at a certain age so you could enjoy them for eternity. Time doesn't work that way, of course. Things change, people get older, and time marches on, whether you agree with its direction or not.

I sat at the dinner table trying to find the words to say that could accurately describe our marriage. At first, many words came to mind: sham, fraud, loveless, bullshit, insane, trapped, disappointment, and so on. But how do you sit there as a father and tell your kids how bad your marriage to their mother is? Did I owe them the truth? The truth about *our* marriage as well as *my* transgressions?

6

I wasn't ready to reveal all that to them at the dinner table. Not really the place for such talk. There are just some things that you don't tell your kids. M*aybe later*, I thought, *when I'm on my deathbed*. Those deathbed confessions are always the best, aren't they? That's when you know you're leaving for good and there's nothing anyone can do to retaliate against you for your sins. *Maybe when I am dying, I'll tell them about Marie*, I thought as I sat there. But, then again, perhaps I needed to get on their level and talk about what was bothering them. Perhaps it was time to just tell them everything. Show them what was behind door number one, skeletons and all.

I looked at them and prepared to tell them some adult stuff. I never thought that I'd be at a point in my life where I was telling my two children about my terrible marriage. I hadn't even told Curtis how things were at home and he was my best friend. I looked at Samantha and then at Davey, who still had his earbuds in, waiting for me to speak. "Now's not the time to talk about this. I know that..." I balked at telling them at the last second.

"You're going to let her walk all over you forever! And for what?! Keeping it all together here?! For us?! Don't use us as an excuse for staying with her! Just end this, for Christ's sake! This house is falling apart!" Samantha jumped from the chair and stormed out of the dining room. Davey and I sat there looking down at our plates of pizza. Samantha was right, though, and I knew it. Hell, Davey knew it. That was the most truth that had been spoken in this house in I-can't-tell-you-how-long. Good ol' Samantha.

I had used them as an excuse to stay married for years. The truth is that I should have ended my marriage long ago. But I always held back, fearing the psychological effects a divorce would have on the children. I guess the road to Hell *is* paved with good intentions. But, ultimately, holding it all together for them caused more harm.

Maybe there wasn't anything left for me to do there. The kids were growing up, obviously ready to handle anything that came their way. Or, at least, Samantha was. Davey was more fragile. He had issues about which I had no inclination until later. I mean, I saw some things with Davey that should have caught my attention early on. But you only say that shit when the bad stuff actually happens. Much like when you know the guy who lives down the street is strange, like *murderous* strange, and you don't say anything because you think it's in your head. And then he goes off and kills someone and you're like, "Damn, I knew there was something off about that guy." That's how I felt about Davey. I saw things, but didn't really "see" them, you know? Damn, I wished I had...maybe I could have saved him.

Davey was his sister's exact opposite. He was quiet, always had been. And you never knew how he was feeling because he always looked depressed, even as a young child. Sure, he had his moments as a full-blown kid, laughing and playing and stuff like that. But those times were sporadic at best. I do remember a time when he and I took a special trip, though. I'll never forget that.

7

I followed Samantha to the back deck, where she sat in a chair underneath the twinkling stars. I'd given her some time to cool off because if you approached her when she was fuming, you had no chance of talking to or reasoning with her. She just had to cool off and gather her composure. That's when I usually reached out to her. I guess we were the same in that regard. It had been thirty minutes, probably not enough time for her to calm down and think clearly, but I tried to talk to her anyway.

"Don't try to smooth this one over, Dad," she said gruffly.

"I'm not," I said as I pulled up a chair to sit beside her. "Man, it's a little chilly out here, right?" I remarked, noting the slight chill of early October. "Listen, I think it's time that you and I had a talk about this, father to daughter." I was going to do something that I told myself that I wouldn't do earlier. I just could not maintain the charade. I wanted Samantha to understand why things were the way they were. She was right; she wasn't a kid anymore. In one more month she was going to be eighteen years old, practically a grown woman. And she deserved the truth. No matter how harsh it was.

"Your mom and I aren't on the same level anymore. We never were, not really." I began to explain to my silent girl with her arms folded across her chest.

"Sometimes people get married for the wrong reasons."

"So what were your reasons?" She finally asked, interrupting the long silence that followed my words.

I sat there for a moment and wondered what they were. I had always kind of known what they were, but I was taken off guard by Samantha's question. I had asked myself that very question all the time back in the day, but to actually hear someone other than my conscience ask it was numbing. "Well," I forged ahead, "when I met your mother, I was at a mixed-up place in my life. I was nineteen, going on twenty, and felt as if I was choking on my own life. Your grandfather had wanted me to go to the same college as him. 'Be a lawyer,' he said. I tried college, didn't like it, dropped out, and hitchhiked across the South for the better part of a year."

"You never told me that," she replied after another long pause. "I mean I read it online on your website bio, but I thought that you were just making stuff up to seem more interesting to people."

"No," I said as I leaned back to look at the stars with her. "I did. I left home with a hundred bucks and a backpack to my name and just started walking."

"Why did you do that? Didn't you know how dangerous it was out there for a young kid?"

"Nah, I was nineteen years old; I was invincible. Nothing could hurt me. But I got to see a lot of places and talk to a lot of people and you know what the one thing that I got out of all that was? I found out what people are afraid of the most."

"What's that?" Samantha asked.

"Being alone. People have a fear of being alone, dying alone. And I had that fear, too. I just didn't know it until I realized that I was just like the people I talked to that year."

"So you met Mom and got married just to *have* someone? Sort of like a necessity-type situation?" Samantha asked piecing together my story's conclusion.

"Sort of. There was a girl before your mom though. I loved her immensely. We met a long time ago in school, in the fifth grade, and were boyfriend and girlfriend, best friends after that. She and I had a lot of history together. I asked her to marry me once on the night of our high school graduation."

"What did she say?"

I laughed before I spoke, still feeling the sting of Marie's response. "She said that 'we're just kids.' I mean, she was right, but damn I loved her, kids or not. I was a year older than you are right now when I asked her. And when she said no, we just kept on keeping on. I saw that I had no immediate future with her and that's where I got mixed up...pretty badly, I guess."

"You thought that you'd be together forever, right?" I looked from the stars and to Samantha, who I could tell understood me in some way. "I mean, that's how I feel about Randy. We've dated ever since freshman year and I have no idea what happens after we graduate. Bothers me sometimes when I think about it. I mean, I know that I want him in my life forever, you know?"

I chuckled to myself at the thought of how similar she and I were. "Yeah, I felt the same about Marie. But I knew deep down that Marie had other plans that didn't include me. It's a hard pill to swallow when you realize that."

"Whatever happened to her?"

"She went to Duke University, graduated, and became a professor at Fillmore College," I replied.

"When was the last time you talked to her?"

"A few weeks ago. See, I, um, we've never stopped seeing each other, even after I got married to your mother. We just had a connection so strong that neither she nor I could ever completely end things." And just like that, I finally confessed to someone other than my own reflection about Marie Evans.

Samantha was a bit stunned; I could tell. She sat there for a minute or two with her mouth gaping open, still trying to process what I had just told her.

"So you've been cheating on Mom this entire time?"

"If you want to call it that. I never saw it as that because I never stopped loving Marie, even though it wasn't reciprocated enough on her end."

"Does mom know?" Samantha asked, still processing it all.

I shook my head. "No," I replied to her, feeling that I had let her down. Samantha had thought I was the victim of Jennifer's abuse, but it was me who had, the entire time, fired the first shot. "I got married to your mom because Marie didn't want to settle down. And I knew that. Your mom came along, and we started dating and one thing led to another, and there we were. 'That next logical step,' as I called it. But I did ask Marie to marry me one last time before Jennifer and I got married... the night before, actually. If she had said yes, my life would have turned out differently. You and Davey would not have been born."

"Wow," Samantha said after a few moments of silence and profound thoughts about what I had told her. The things I told her I swore that I would take to my grave. But in rethinking it all, I figured it was best that she knew the truth—that I was not a victim as she saw me. "I don't even know what to say about this."

"Not much you can say. I'm not going to sit here and expect you to understand any of this. But I married your mother for the wrong reasons. And the only reason that I stay around is because of you and Davey. That's why I've held it together for so long. You were right. I didn't want you guys to think the divorce would be your fault. Hell, maybe I was just too scared to be alone, I don't know. Maybe a mixture of both."

"So the entire marriage has been a fraud?"

"I mean, parts of it were real especially when you guys were little. But over the years, I just put a lot of distance between me and Jennifer. I made her not love me anymore because I couldn't ever love her like I should have. Things have been fucked up for a long time, kiddo. It's all on me, I guess."

"Now this all makes me think about all the good times that we've had as a family. And now it all seems... fake."

"No, they weren't *fake*. All the Christmas Days, all the birthday parties, vacations, cookouts – all of that was genuine, Samantha. Believe that. Our relationship with you kids was at the forefront, no matter how we felt about each other."

"Have you guys ever talked about getting divorced?" Samantha quizzed.

"No. There's no need. We've come this long, why stop now."

"Aren't you afraid that she's going to run off with some guy that she meets?"

"No. I don't love her like I probably ought to, so that wouldn't hurt. I know that your mother has cheated on me, but I've also been with Marie once a year for decades now. How am I any different? I just wanted you to know that you can't blame your mother for everything because some of the reasons things in this home aren't right fall on my shoulders."

"I can't believe this. All of this...is just...bizarre. Me and you having this conversation. Maybe I wasn't ready to hear the truth."

"No, you're ready. It was my fault for trying to keep you a little kid forever. Being an adult isn't easy, kiddo. You'll see soon enough. Think you got everything figured out, and then something comes along and screws everything up."

"So where do we all go from here, Dad?" Samantha asked feeling out of her depth in the conversation and rightly so.

"Still moving forward, I guess. What else is there? I mean, if your mother finds someone else she wants to be with, then it's whatever. I know that when she leaves, I won't be alone because I'll always have you and Davey. My fear has been vanquished to a certain degree."

"What about this Marie girl? The love of your life..."

"Who knows? She'll never be tied down. I'll never have her like I once did. I guess maybe I never really did at all. Perhaps everything was just a teenage illusion that got me through my turbulent youth. She and I just... are, I guess. I just can't quit her. I've tried," I said for lack of a better explanation.

For the first time in a very long time, Samantha and I sat out there for what seemed like hours talking, laughing, and sharing things that I never thought possible. I opened up to her, and she in turn lowered her guard and talked to me about school, her goals in life, and her long-term boyfriend, Randy, whom I had respect for at the time. He wasn't a typical punk teenage kid. He appeared to have a good head on his shoulders and seemed to be going places. Up to that point in time he had not done anything to change my opinion. I was happy for Samantha.

8

I grew closer to my daughter out there. My main point was that I didn't want her to be angry with her mother for making me out to be the victim. I was no victim. I was an accomplice in crimes of love and betrayal. But can you betray someone that you have no affection for? *I* never felt betrayed by my wife. Maybe she did by me. Probably so. Rightly so.

How could I? Betrayal only and always comes when there is something to be betrayed. I loved Jennifer at one point, but not like I loved Marie. Marie betrayed me several times over. I had an immense emotional connection to her that she damaged at will, only to call me a few weeks after our October trysts as if to rub in my face that I could have her but only on *her* terms.

That was treachery. I had given her my heart countless times, only to have it returned to me in bloody shreds. When we were growing up, I tried to stop seeing her. But she would always reel me back in and then things would end badly again. It was an endless cycle with us. Almost like being on a hamster wheel that goes nowhere. Those were the dark times in my youth. Just when I thought she and I would last forever, she would change her mind and tell me that she needed a break. Typical Marie.

I was her fool and she knew it. She loved me when she wanted to, but she would never allow our relationship to thrive. She always said it was because she had watched her mom and dad's marriage fall apart and that she didn't want to go through that. That's why marriage to her was like a cross to a vampire—something to stay away from at all costs.

I understood her mindset and promised her that we wouldn't end up like her parents. But she was always too afraid. Just when I thought I had gotten over her from our latest break-up, she would slip me a note during class. They were always the same: *meet me behind the bleachers after school at the baseball field.* There, we would talk, makeup, and make out. A few months later, the cycle would turn around, and she would need a break and I'd try to adapt to being without her. Just as I was about there, she would write another note in class and catch me again; a dumb fish taking the bait, knowing better the entire time.

Even in adult life, while Jennifer and I were married in the first years, Marie would call me up and want to know if we were still on for our October meeting. And like a puppy dog, I always said yes. I could have turned her away and focused on my wife like I should have. But the thought of maybe having Marie once and for all was too great of a chance to pass up.

That crazy notion of someday having her was what really fucked up my marriage and writing career. If I could have told her no and stuck with it, everyone would have been better off. Why the hell didn't I just ignore her calls? I wished a thousand times I could have. Maybe things would have turned out differently in the end... for me, for Jennifer, for Samantha, for Davey, and even for Heather Parker in the final act of my life. If I hadn't answered the phone when she called, how different would my life have been?

Nothing ever netted after those October visits to her late father's lake house. The only thing that I was left with was emptiness as I drove away. She and I would have these extensional conversations and have sex, play board games, and listen to vinyl records. It was as if we were frozen in time back when we were in high school. It was funny how we never seemed to get beyond what we did when we were young. The years upon years of encounters were just a reconnection of sorts, a two-day weekend for us to gear down and love each other like when we were teenagers. It was a taste of what would never be.

After that, we would stay in contact off and on until the next October weekend. I vowed every time that I left that lake house that I would not be at her fingertips. I also vowed to be a better man to my wife, whom I had estranged myself from. But when I was alone up in my office pounding upon my keyboard and drinking, I would think of Marie and about how good it felt being there with her in that lake house. Being alone with thoughts of Marie was what sunk me. It always did.

My feelings for her hadn't changed in decades. I always had those pesky butterflies in my stomach when I would recall our times in the past—more so when she and I would meet in October after a year of being physically separated. A part of me wanted to be away from her, but a bigger part of me wanted to be with her, just as I had when I first saw her. That part always beat the other, every time. I hated myself for loving her but I could never walk away, not entirely. And, in the end not walking away cost me everything.

9

I was never honest with Jennifer. I had told her about Marie in the past and about how our relationship was and how I was weak when it came to her. But I never told her about the October meetings. As far as Jennifer knew, I was at a writer's conference as a guest speaker. It was a good cover and one that Jennifer never questioned because of my career.

I wanted to get away from Marie, but I could never do it. I had actually convinced myself in a drunken stupor one night up in my office that, when she mentioned our next October meeting, I wouldn't go. However, when I sobered up and her call came, I fell right back into those bad habits. I fucking hated myself at times.

Talking to Samantha about things helped a lot. I know that I had placed a ton on her lap, but it felt good to offload my secrets. It wasn't right for her to hate her mom for something I had set into motion years ago. I could not be the victim of Jennifer's actions forever and my daughter needed to know that her dad was not as squeaky clean as he appeared. The truth, I have discovered, is often nasty and full of caves and doors that weren't meant to be entered into.

I was damningly flawed. I knew that. But did I want to change it? Did I want to change my marriage with Jennifer? Not really. Over the last few years, I had consumed myself with my feelings for Marie. Once I saw Jennifer going out more, working, and taking those "weekend realtor's conferences," I became absorbed with thoughts of

Marie. I had gotten it into my head that Marie and I would eventually end up together. All I had to do was wait like I had been doing for years. Just wait.

It was crazy: I was married to a woman I didn't truly love and the one that I did love, I could never be with. It was a paradox of the worst kind: to have and to have not. I hated it. Sometimes I wished that Marie and I had never met. It would have made things a lot better for me. Maybe I could have been a better husband to Jennifer. Who knows? But what's done is done, and you can't go back to the past. If only I could have ignored Marie's calls...if only there was a way to get back to a point in time where I could have let Marie go. Maybe things would've been better. But you can't go back, right?

CHAPTER TWO

1

I went up to my office after Samantha and I spoke openly about life and all that comes with it. In talking to her, I could tell she was withholding something. I couldn't figure out what it was, but a father knows when his own flesh and blood isn't being forthcoming.

Samantha wanted to tell me something out there on the deck, but whatever it was, she elected not to utter the words. It was fine by me at the time because the evening had been too full of truth, more than I felt comfortable with. What is it about finally telling the truth that just exhausts you? Maybe it's the unloading of weight that has been holding you down for as long as you can remember.

I sat at my desk with the lights off, looking out the window. I looked out into the dark neighborhood, waiting for Jennifer to arrive. "For what?" I asked myself. It wasn't as if I was missing her. What did I care what time she came home? I never fretted over it before, so why was I then? Maybe *some* longing had crept in after all.

Maybe I would have been a better husband if Marie wasn't in the picture. I think having Marie in my back pocket for so long had given me a sense of invincibility to a degree. I had a wife. And then I had a woman whom I had loved dearly and madly for decades. My emotional connection to Marie Evans was what had taken my mind off my marriage, numbing me. I dare say that had it not been for Marie, my marriage might have been better. Perhaps Jennifer and I would have been happy, and maybe the kids, too.

2

I guess I had always thought Marie would one day just submit to me, and the two of us would finally spend our lives together like I thought it was supposed to be. But who was I kidding? I turned forty just two months ago, and my life as I knew it was ticking downward. All of my really, really good years were gone, usurped by kids and Jennifer and my writing career, which was silently slumping at the time.

I held out for years for Marie to one day say, "You know, maybe we should get married." I would have married her in a heartbeat. Or at least, that's what I tell myself I would have done. I would still have to take into consideration Samantha and Davey. I had to account for their feelings. How would they have taken it? But then again, look at what toll Jennifer and I had had on them. They were wearing out mentally, Davey more so than his sister. I never really thought about how Davey was feeling. I saw the wear on him over the years, more so in the last six months before he killed himself, but I never really *saw* the wear our family life had on him.

I knew Marie would never tell me what I wanted to hear. I knew she was perfectly content with our arrangement. Was I happy about it? No. But it was always good to have her in my arms once a year in her cabin by the lake if I'm being honest. It was as if, during that last weekend in October, she and I *were* married. That's what I had convinced myself of, anyway. It's funny what a man can trick himself into thinking.

I wanted to quit her, really did. But how could I? She was what I had always wanted ever since I was a kid. Marie knew how to string me along and keep me coming back for more— when I was a kid *and* especially when I was an adult. I tried to be strong and tell myself that when she'd call to make sure we were still good for that weekend in October, I'd just tell her no. "I'm going to stop being a sucker," I would tell myself over and over. But I never could. You have no idea how many times I wanted to walk away from her for the last time.

Yet, I was at her mercy. The prospect of her coming around that weekend in the cabin was too much to leave on the table. Each year I went to her hoping that it was going to happen— Marie finally saying that she wanted me every day, not just the once-a-year weekend. And each year I was disappointed leaving the cabin with her standing in the driveway waving in my rearview mirror. Every year was the same. It never changed. I never changed.

Being a sucker for a woman that I would never have, I neglected my wife, which wasn't right. I guess I started feeling a little differently because I had to break it down to my daughter. I wasn't a victim. I had sent Jennifer into motion by my actions alone. *I* was the one who had acted cold. *I* was the one who pushed her away all because of Marie, a woman I would never have.

Of course, that's the benefit of being able to look back at things. Retrospection is always twenty-twenty, perfect vision to see things that were imperfect. In looking back, you have the advantage of seeing how bad the decisions you made were and how horrible outcomes ensued.

3

I took time to survey the damage I had caused. And it all began the night when I confessed everything to my daughter. I never planned on telling Samantha anything about Marie and my state of being or my marriage to her mother. But there I was, spilling my guts to her. Do I regret it? No. I guess it had to be done. After all, fate's arrow had been shot from her bow long ago when it concerned my family.

I remember a picture that hung on the mantle above the fireplace of my house. The picture is a hand-drawn family portrait that Davey made when he was eight years old. It had four people, stick figures, all standing side by side, smiling and holding hands. They were outlined by a red-crayon-colored sketch of our home. I remember seeing it for the first time and falling in love with it. I loved it so much that I went out and bought a frame to place it in and later hung it above the fireplace. It was simple yet so profound. That's how he saw us then— happy and together and smiling.

The picture was a token. It was a token from Davey on how *he* then viewed his family. Little did he know, the family he drew on that white sheet of paper was a sham, an empty husk. He later discovered that the kind of family he wanted only existed in his drawing. I take full responsibility for that. We could have been great, but I let things get in the way— not just Marie, but other things that blurred my vision along the way.

4

There was a night I recall with dead clarity within which I put my heart out there. It was one of many times Marie crushed me like a bug underneath her shoe. I was with her on that last weekend in October, the night right before Jennifer and I were married. I made a last-ditch effort to get Marie to be my wife, but it was to no avail. I thought that it was necessary for me to ask before I committed myself to Jennifer— the last desperate act of a desperate man.

I wanted to make damn certain that I had no chance with her. I didn't, back then, *want* to be that guy who loved someone else but married a girl just for the sake of it. And the crazy part was that's exactly what I did. Women always make men do crazy, stupid things that make no sense. As soon as I said, "I do," I sealed the fates of Jennifer, Samantha, Davey, and eventually myself and Heather.

5

The night before my wedding, Marie and I were at her father's lake house. The sun was sinking into the west, giving way to the dark sky and stars. It was a tradition for the two of us to sit there and watch the sunset together on the back deck of the lake house that overlooked the enormous body of water before us. The entire scene was picturesque. It was one of the things that I loved the most about going there once a year. Being with her made it even more special.

After the sunset, we sat on wooden rocking chairs, bundled up with blankets from inside the cabin, sipping piping-hot chocolate, and looking out across the lake and woods that shadowed behind it. I remember the stars reflecting off the still water as I readied myself for what I had planned to do on my way to the lake house earlier that day. I know what you're thinking—I spent the night before my wedding with another woman. But you have got to understand something quite clear: Marie Evans was not just "another woman." I saw her as my destiny.

In my car, I drove with intention. It wasn't just another annual visit to have sex with Marie and do all the things we normally did when we were together. No, that night, there was a purpose to what I was doing. I had a mission.

I was getting married the next day, but I wanted to ask Marie one last time to marry me. I knew it was a gamble, but it was one I felt I had to make. I wanted to roll the dice one more time and see if I could break the pattern of snake eyes.

We both sat there in the darkness, silent. We sipped our hot chocolate, looking at the stars and the lake before us. We didn't talk much up to that point. I noticed she was *unusually* quiet. Marie was generally a chatterbox. I thought it could've been a good thing but wasn't really sure. Was it possible that she was concerned about me being married, and how would that affect our relationship going forward? Could Marie be more fragile than I had thought?

I swallowed the last of my hot chocolate and placed the mug down on the floor of the deck. I swatted the butterflies away from my stomach as I got ready to speak to her about the future, *our* future, and the future of me and Jennifer. It was funny, though. I swear to God I think she knew that I was going to bring it all up. *Good,* I remember thinking. At least she had some inclination as to what I was going to say.

"So," I started. "What's got your tongue tonight?"

Marie sat there, holding her cup of hot chocolate to her mouth with both hands. "Nothing. Just thinking, I guess."

"About?" I replied, trying to bait her the best I could.

After a few silent minutes, she finally broke into speech.

"You and this marriage thing you're doing. You know this is a huge mistake, right? You gotta know that."

I was stunned by her words. Was she being truthful about my impending marriage or was she concerned about us? At that point, I had no idea what she was thinking. Marie wasn't the easiest person to read.

"Why is it a mistake?"

"Because you don't love her. All this is going to do is head the two of you down a road to nowhere," Marie said, shaking her head. Thinking back on that statement, she was right on point. She predicted it right then and there. How did she know? Twenty years later, her prophecy came to pass.

"How do you know if I love her or not?" I asked as her words soaked into my mind. I knew she was right. She knew she was right.

Marie turned and looked at me, "Because you're here with *me* on the night before you get married."

She had a point. But I was there to try to sway her to me, once and for all. I knew that it wasn't going to be easy, not by a long shot. But I had to know where I stood with her. I knew that I stood somewhere, but not where I thought I ought to be. That was what made me furious. After all the history we had together, she kept me a safe distance away. Not too far because she still needed me for whatever selfish reasons she had.

I got up from my seat and flung the warm blanket from my body. Man, it was cold out there that night. But my blood was about to boil as I paced slowly on the deck. "You know, you say stuff like that, but you don't mean it. It's just your little way of getting inside my head."

"Getting inside your head?"

"Yeah, you do. You knew that I'd be here tonight. You always know. You know how much I love you."

"God, the love card again," Marie said with disgust in her voice. She hated hearing that I loved her. You see, Marie was a casual kind of girl. Emotions just got in the way. I knew *that* a long time ago—knew it that night before I got married. However, just like every lovesick person out there, I thought *I* was going to be that one special person who could finally fix her. Wrong.

"Yeah, *the love card.* We're going to have to either fix this or forget it. I'm getting married tomorrow afternoon, and I need to know where we stand."

"You know where we stand. Why do you ask questions you already know the answers to?" Marie asked.

"Look, I love you. I always have and always will. We've been together for a long time. Lots of ups and downs, right? But I gotta know before I get married to Jennifer. Is there ever going to be a future for the two of us, aside from these once-a-year trysts?"

Marie sat there not saying a word. She looked out across the lake and around at the swarthy forest that enclosed the lake house and the two of us. She was trying to think of how to respond to my question. She knew what she wanted to say, but she wanted to say it without the barbs and briars it was going to come wrapped in.

"I can't honestly tell you yes or no. I have no idea what life has in store for us. Or me, for that matter..."

"Then marry me!" I said rolling my proverbial dice.

"What?? Marry you??" The two of us stared at each other for what seemed to be years. And then her reply came as a whisper: "No." A "no." I knew that would happen but still had to know for sure. I could not have married Jennifer unless I knew the truth from the horse's mouth. And there it was, the answer to my burning question. "I love you, but not like that. You know my stance on marriage." She spoke lowly, almost as if she was ashamed of what she said.

"Because of your parents? When are you ever going to get past that? Here you've got this guy, me, right in front of you, madly in love with you ever since I first saw you. I can't keep doing this. This, whatever this is. It's not healthy for me anymore. Probably never was. Do you know how hard it is to love someone and *know* you'll never get the opportunity to have them?" I spoke from the heart.

"I'm not trying to be a bitch. I've just got some stuff going on. School, trying to line up a teaching job afterward, you know, regular life stuff. Marriage just isn't on my radar... don't think it ever will be."

"There's always going to be something. No matter what, right?" I said with hate in my voice.

"You've got it all right now. Your life is already on the right track. Why are you so high-strung?"

"Because of you!" I exclaimed. "I can have everything I want, but the one thing that I can't get is you. Why? I need to know before I leave tonight!" It was a simple demand, I thought. "Why can't I have you? What is it about me that you don't want?!"

"Because I don't want to be tied down and one day, when things go bad, and they will, not only would I lose a husband but also a best friend. I can't afford to lose twice like my dad did."

"You won't. We won't. We'll make it." I said, trying to make a case that would stand, anything that would sway her feelings.

"Yeah, that's what my mom said for years. See how that turned out? I'm not going to end up like my dad. Broken and beaten by life and marriage. You saw when we were growing up how things were at home. No, I'm not going down that route. I'm sorry if that bothers you, but marriage and Marie will not ever happen. It's not you, Jerry, believe that. If there was anyone on this earth who's worth marrying, it's you. But I won't. Can't." Marie explained. I could have sworn that I saw tears in her eyes. But that might have been the moonlight reflecting in them. I don't know.

Her words carried a lot of weight. She had seen things happen to her parents that had discouraged her about life and how to live it. I always knew how she felt, but I also always thought that I'd be the exception to the rule. I thought for years up to that night that she and I would end up married one day, living in a house with a white-picket fence in a suburb. I would be a writer and she would be a professor. We would have two kids and a dog named Bee-Gee. That was my dream. But, that night at the lake house, she crushed it once and for all.

I had tried, in vain, to sway her my way. But I couldn't get through to her. Perhaps I never could. She was devastated by her parent's divorce when she was a kid. That event had an effect on her *and* on her future decisions; especially when it came to love. She was guarded. Even as a young teen, she was that way. And the older she got, the taller her walls grew. I used to be able to scale them but just barely. Eventually, I couldn't anymore.

I knew, that night at the lake house, that her walls were just too high. I tried to climb them and break into her castle and rescue her from the clutches of self-doubt and alienation. I could not. The room she held herself captive in was well-guarded, reinforced with steel, and covered with thick ice. Marie would never be mine, except on the last weekend in October. Then I could have her all I wanted. Gluttony.

"Then I guess Jennifer and I will get married as planned," I said in a low voice, leaning against the deck railing, finally giving up.

"How's that going to affect us?" Marie asked, after another one of those silent pauses that we so often had.

"Us?" I asked with surprise. "I'll be married. There won't be an *us*. That's what I'm saying."

"I don't know if I can handle that," Marie said in a wounded voice. I knew she felt like a shot duck spiraling out of the cloudy afternoon sky. She wanted to be something different, I knew it. But she would never take those first steps toward it. Marie was so mired down in the marsh of her parents' dysfunctional marriage that she, herself, was truly frightened of the prospect of stepping into that arena.

"Then what are we going to do? I can't just quit you. But I'm going to have to learn how. I have to end this and move on. I can't be unfaithful to Jennifer, not right at the beginning of our marriage."

"I understand," Marie said, with tears streaming down from her eyes. I guess it wasn't the moonlight after all. She was as hurt by my words as I was by hers. There we both were, the products of our own creations; the sum of our decisions up to that point in our young lives. I stood there and looked down at her crying. I wanted to go over to her, to hold her like I used to. It was tough, but I stopped myself several times as she sobbed into her hands.

I knew that if I consoled her, I would never be able to walk away for good. Marie, like I've said a hundred times, had this hold on me that was hard to break. I thought I had finally quit her... yeah, right.

I left her crying on the deck. I walked down the steps and reached my car. I got in and sat there for a minute, thinking about what had just happened. Had I finally stood up for myself and broken off an unhealthy relationship with the love of my life? I felt differently sitting in my car on that cold night. I felt that a chapter had indeed ended and another was about to begin. I wasn't sure what was in store for me as I thought about Marie sitting and crying. I had to fight like hell not to get out of my car and rush to her and hold her in my arms. I wanted to, really did. It took titan-like strength to restrain myself from getting out of the car. I refrained, but it wasn't easy. Not going back to her that night was the hardest thing that I've ever done up to that point in my life.

I drove around aimlessly for hours, thinking and rethinking everything up to that point in my life. I had just gotten my first book published and was feeling pretty good about my position in life. I was about to get married to a very beautiful woman. What was there to be vexed about? Marie came to mind. She always came to mind.

I wanted her. I would have given up my career as a writer to just spend the rest of my life with her. I would have given it all away to be with her. But the wreckage of her parents' marriage was enough to discourage her from ever committing herself to anyone but herself. In all the years I had known her, I was her only sexual partner. She had deep trust issues, and when I told her that there wasn't going to be an *us* anymore, it hit her hard.

I was the only guy in her life. We had built something together over the years that I thought would stand the test of time. But I was wrong. I thought she and I would end up together, but it was pointless. She was too guarded and scared and I couldn't just sit there and wait for her to decide my fate. So I had to take action. I hated seeing Marie cry. The last time I saw her cry was when her mother left. I had comforted her. But that night at the lake house, I could not console her like I did on that other night when we were kids. I had to let her go. Reluctantly, I had to.

6

My wedding came and went as planned. My mind should have been with my wife. We were on our honeymoon, me and Jennifer, and instead of fully enveloping myself in our time together, my mind was adrift on what Marie was doing, how she was feeling. I had no contact with her after I left the lake house. And as far as I was concerned, I didn't think that I was ever going to again. I honestly thought for a while that Marie and I were actually over. Funny, the lies you tell yourself to get you through the day.

My mind wandered so much after the lake house episode that I dreamt of me and her together in various situations. I couldn't help myself. She utterly dominated my thoughts. What I wondered and feared the most was whether we had finally reached the end of our road. Was it the final time that she and I would be together?

I had been with her through all the ups and downs throughout our young lives. We had broken up numerous times in the past only to get back together. And then the break-up would occur again. It was hills and valleys with her.

The thing was, no matter how many times we would break up, we always found our way back together. But, this time, I wondered. I wondered if the stakes were higher since I did something that should have been the last nail in the casket: I got married, and that should have sealed off any connection that I had with Marie. For a normal man, it would have. But I ain't normal. I'm complicated.

Sharing a history with someone is powerful. It can ultimately override common sense. Marie had something of a spell over me, from which I couldn't free myself. I tried in vain. It was like she was the most powerful witch with the most powerful potions. She could make me do things I didn't want to do and feel things I hated feeling. I wanted to stay away from her, but I could not. I hated myself for that— hated myself for being with her while I was married.

I loathed myself for the way she made me feel, even if it was happy and especially if it was melancholic. I wished that she would just vanish and never return. Maybe move away to parts unknown. But I knew deep down that I would always think about her and wonder where she ran off to. I wished a thousand times that I would have gotten my number changed so she couldn't contact me. But I didn't because, in some twisted way, I wanted her to contact me, even though I tried to tell myself that she was a devil.

I wanted her gone, but I needed her near. It sucked. All she had to do was marry me and she and I could have lived together forever in this life. But she refused me. I should have grown up and told her to go to Hell, but I never could. I hated her but loved her at the same time. It was an impossible situation with her; I couldn't live with or without her. What was I to do?

7

What I did next was something I should be ashamed of. Mere days after Jennifer and I arrived back home from our honeymoon, I got a call from Marie in the middle of the afternoon. I was up in my office, drafting a book and Jennifer was at culinary school. This was before the house had two little ones roaming around. It was still and quiet.

The phone on my desk broke me from my work, scaring me. I looked at the ringing phone and checked the ID. It was Marie. I let it ring for what felt like forever before picking it up. "Hello," I said feeling nervous, trembling a bit, and speaking as though I had cotton packed into my mouth. I was both excited and afraid.

"Hey," Marie said over the phone. "Listen, I did not like the way we parted the other night," she said, spilling her words out quickly before I could hang up the phone.

I sat at my desk holding the phone to my ear. All the hatred that I had for her evaporated as I listened to her sweet voice.

"Yeah, me neither," I replied after a few moments of silence, leaning back in my chair and looking out through the window quitting my work at the moment.

"So... how's married life?" Marie asked after another pause.

"It's been less than a week. But it's good so far. Jennifer's a good one," I said. She was a good one. Even I knew that.

"That's good. You deserve someone like that. You always have. Look, I'm calling to um... to um, say goodbye to you," Marie said as her voice cracked over the phone. I had heard her wounded before, but that day there was something different, something odd about her. She never acted like she needed me before, but I swear to God that day she did. It was a game-changer for me. Shouldn't have been, but it was. It was the beginning of the end.

"Yeah, things have changed," I said, still bitter over her "no" answer to my marriage proposal.

"Yeah," Marie said. I could tell that she was crying but doing all that she could to conceal it. "I just want you to know… that I've always loved you. I don't know… but it's always been you from the start. I'm sorry I never told you the right way. But I'm telling you now. I guess that counts for something, you know?" The tears and sobbing had become more pronounced. She was mortally wounded. My marriage to Jennifer nearly crippled her. It was never my intent to hurt Marie. My purpose was to *marry* the woman sobbing into the phone. But she refused me, and I met Jennifer and that was that… the rest was history.

Marie had always been my first choice. Jennifer, my runner-up. I felt bad about applying labels to these women, but that's how it was. We all give and have labels placed on us for whatever reasons. Some are valid and others aren't. I gave Marie and Jennifer labels and probably shouldn't have.

"So, where do we go from here?" Marie asked in a quivering voice.

"Nowhere. It's gotta be over between us," I said, trying to freeze my heart that was in the process of shattering in her anguish. "I tried for years with you, but you just never listened."

"You know why I'm the way I am," Marie sobbed.

"Well, what do you want me to do, huh? Let life pass me by while waiting for a girl who I probably was never going to get. I couldn't do that anymore, Marie. You gotta understand that."

"So this is really the end?" Marie asked after another long pause as she sniffled.

I sat there in silence and thought about everything in a blur. I thought about all the times that she and I had shared over the years, both good and bad. How was I to just walk away from her? I wanted to, but God, I couldn't. Even marriage wasn't enough to drive us away from each other. I wanted to leave her alone and had since the night I left her lake house. But there she was, calling me crying and sounding so pitiful. The ice block that I had put in my heart had melted as I listened to her cry like the young girl I knew way back when; the innocent girl who could do no wrong.

We talked on the phone for what seemed like hours. She had finally stopped crying as we both figured out how my marriage to Jennifer wouldn't be an obstacle. She said that she needed me and like a fucking fool I bought it, even at the risk of jeopardizing my marriage with Jennifer. I never viewed myself as a gambling man, but there I was gambling the future on a woman (again) that, in the end, would never, ever be mine. I should have never even picked up the phone. Throughout my marriage, I thought a million times about how that phone call was the catalyst for what happened thereafter. I guess you could say it was the first domino to topple.

8

Had I not answered Marie's phone call after my and Jennifer's honeymoon, would things have turned out differently? Of course, they would have because I wouldn't have been sucked into Marie's world and been unfaithful to my wife. I don't blame Marie for my decision to cast my wife to the side like an old blown-out shoe. I did it, not her. But it wasn't just that one phone call on that one day. It was all the phone calls I took from her over the years. All I had to do... all I had to do was not answer any of them. Maybe things would have been different. Maybe.

Had I not picked up that fucking phone while at my desk that day, my life would've been better. I would've learned to live without Marie... Jennifer and I would have two kids: Samantha and Davey. They would both have been healthy and alive, and Jennifer and I would have been happy, too. Marie would have been a distant memory that would haunt me from time to time. We had too much history for me to ever clear her from my memory banks for good. But at least she would have been gone.

That phone call caused me to go back to Marie; it caused all my infidelity; it caused me to have hope that one day she and I would have a legitimate future; that call caused me to destroy my marriage to Jennifer; it caused me to drink and obsess over Marie so much that I put both my marriage and career on the back burner; it caused the eventual falling out of me and Samantha and the ultimate blow of Davey killing himself. All of that happened just by me answering Marie's phone call that day after we returned from our honeymoon.

9

Just when I thought I could quit Marie, she pulled me back with tears and a heartbroken speech during that phone call. I was a sucker for her and would continue to be for the next two decades of marriage to Jennifer. It wasn't right, I know. But I loved Marie more than Jennifer. I knew, deep down, that I could never love Jennifer as much. I tried but never could. And after a while, Jennifer knew it. After a while, the two of us just stopped. No more pretending. Our relationship just ceased to exist.

After I pushed Jennifer away, she began to forge her own identity without me. She was "Jennifer Matthews" in name only. She was married to me on paper, married to a slowly declining bestselling author. While I held onto my once-a-year trysts and every-so-often phone calls or emails from Marie, Jennifer was out there trying to find a connection with someone who returned her love. Looking back, I don't blame her. It was all on me.

CHAPTER THREE

1

Marie was a contributing factor to my mental demise. Everything that I had built over the years with my family and writing career was completely fake. I had married a woman who I didn't love as much as I should've. I still carried a flaming, red-hot torch for another woman who I would never have. I sincerely wished that she would disappear off the face of the Earth or maybe even die. I know that sounds morbid, but it's true. At least, in death, there would be no more phone calls or luring me to do and say things that make me hate myself. I've said that I hated myself for what I did to my family. And that's true. I never wanted to be the kind of person I turned out to be.

2

I got a call one morning from my best friend and literary agent, Curtis Phillips. He said that Windom Publishing, the publishing house that had taken a chance on me when I was a wide-eyed kid long ago, wanted to sit down to discuss the future since my contract was set to expire soon. *No big deal*, I thought, *just formalities*. Little did I know they were about to confirm what I already knew—that I was a washed-up has been.

In the back of my mind, I knew that being summoned to the mothership meant something was off. I was never asked to come and do a face-to-face with Bobby, the big boss, himself. Curtis did all the heavy lifting and face time for me. All I did was sign my name on the contracts, cash the checks, and half-ass write the books to fulfill my commitments to Windom. Should've treated Bobby better with better writing because he did, after all, take a chance on me. But on the B-side of that, I had made him a lot of money, too, so he got what he got. With modern technology, there was no need for me to be there in person. I did show my face at the office from time to time, you know, to keep up appearances and whatnot.

I knew that my books were slumping. I did. But I didn't care. Do you want to know why? I had made money at something that I never thought that I could make a living doing. I had everything paid for; my kids' kids would never have to worry because I had made enough for a generation of Matthews with my craft. So what if I was just mailing them in? I was still good. I knew that for sure. However, I had stopped trying and could see where the lines were beginning to get blurred. Did I think I was going to be let go by being called to Windom's headquarters? Absolutely not. In my mind, I was still a commodity, a product that was a household name that translated into money.

I had been very distracted by my personal life while writing my last several books. Marie, Jennifer and my relationship with our kids had each taken away from the creative genius I had cultivated over time. With all that distraction going on, I returned to an old habit that I thought I had shelved once and for all. I started drinking again. Not just a nip here and there, but a lot mostly here and there.

The power of the drink came and gripped me tightly. There were a couple of books, *The Power of Me* and *Settle the Score*, that I don't even recall writing. I had just re-signed a lucrative contract with Windom and I rewarded their confidence in me with two books right off the bat that were alcohol infused to their core. Ironically, they were also the last two good books I'd ever write. I remember being at a book signing one day and fans had brought me those books to sign. I couldn't honestly even remember writing them much less the processes of formulating the plots and narratives.

3

On all previous occasions when my contract was up, Curtis would hammer out a new deal, show up on my doorstep, come in, see the family and I'd sign the papers at the dining room table. This was before the Internet and before Curtis could email me the paperwork. Done and done, each time. No big deal. Never was. Being summoned to the publishing house itself in Atlanta struck me as odd. But still, I didn't think anything of it because I had not been to the mother ship in over a decade for anything business-related.

If I only knew what was coming, I could have prepared myself for the impending tailspin. I saw it coming, but that still doesn't really prepare you, does it? Knowing something is coming isn't the same as actually feeling the raw impact of it. I still felt I was a good writer, damn good, but the talent was locked up somewhere inside me. I knew Windom didn't think I was good anymore. I could hear that through the phone conversation Curtis and I had before my traveling to Atlanta. Curtis could never hide the concern in his voice.

When I came downstairs the morning before I left for Atlanta, Samantha and Davey were sitting at the table eating microwavable waffles and bacon. I came down and didn't see their mother. "Mom gone this morning already?" I asked Davey who just nodded without looking up from his plate. *Par for the course with Davey not making any eye contact,* I thought. I walked over to the kitchen counter and poured a glass of orange juice from the jug that sat on the counter. "You're all dressed up? Where you going?" Samantha asked as she finished up her math homework.

"I've been summoned to Atlanta to see Bob Windom. Contract thing," I said looking at my kids as I sipped the O.J.

"Very cool. Big payday?" Samantha asked.

"Hope so. Maybe another five-book deal, who knows? Could be the last one I ever get," I said in jest but secretly knew I may not see a deal at all. But I was cocky in front of my children. I hoped Windom couldn't do without me. Even if my sales had suffered because my writing had become terrible, I was still *the Jerry Matthews*, best-selling author. My name alone was worth something, right?

"Well, in that case," Samantha said, "I feel the need to ask for a new car since you're going to get this huge deal."

"Nice try," I said looking at the clock on the wall. "You have a car already. Sixteenth birthday ring any bells?" I said as I walked across the kitchen and tousled Davey's messy hair and knuckle-bumped Samantha. "I'll see you kiddos later today. Have a good day at school. And be careful, okay? Randy picking you guys up this morning?"

"Yes."

"Okay, tell him to drive safely, and seatbelts, don't forget the seatbelts, okay?! Love you guys!" I said, walking through the house to grab my briefcase and coat before stepping out the front door.

4

I walked outside into the cold drizzle of that October morning and in the driveway sat Jennifer in her car. I thought she had gone some time ago, but there she was just sitting with her car turned off, parked right behind my car. I walked over to her, and she rolled down the window almost robotically. She looked as though she had been crying, but I decided not to ask her about it because she would just lie anyway. Besides, I didn't care much to begin with. Why start now? "Thought you were at work," I remarked.

"Yeah, I was... but I'm not feeling so well at the moment," Jennifer said, staring blankly out the windshield.

"You sick or something? I heard from the DeVines that a stomach thing is going around."

"No, just um... not feeling up to it today. Look at you, all dressed up. Hot date?" Jennifer said finally, looking at me with those soulful hazel eyes. Something was wrong. This was the most we'd spoken to each other in months. It was strange.

I looked down at my suit, "Oh this get up? No, I've got to go to Atlanta to see Bob Windom. Contract thing."

"Doesn't Curtis handle that stuff?" she asked.

"Normally. But Bob wants us both there today for some reason."

We looked at each other in silence. Jennifer wanted to say something but she just couldn't find the right words. Her mouth gaped open like a trout. No words. You can't be married to someone for twenty years and not know when something's amiss. I might not have loved her like I did Marie, but I still cared for her well-being. I wasn't *that* cold-hearted for Christ's sake.

"You sure you're okay?" I asked, pulling away from her car.

Jennifer sat there, hands in her lap as she looked around the inside of her car and out the windows at our well-manicured home. She wasn't okay. I would later find out that she had some news that she was keeping from me. That chance encounter in the driveway was the beginning of it. The entire day was the start of it all. She could not find the words to tell me; like it mattered, anyway. There wasn't anything that she could tell me that would be a surprise. Hell, look at what I did to her over the years in secret.

When she eventually did tell me the truth, I wasn't destroyed by the news. A normal married man would be, but not me. I was too self-absorbed. I was too busy hoping that Marie would come around and say that she wanted to be with me forever. Plus, there was the Davey thing going on at the time when I was told. I didn't have time for Jennifer's problems. I barely had time for mine.

"Yeah, I'm fine. I'd better back out and get going so you can get to Atlanta, huh?"

"Yeah," I said looking at my watch. "I probably won't be back until eight tonight. Don't wait up. Not like you would anyways." That last part was under my breath.

"Okay." Jennifer rolled up her window, started the car, and rolled backward down the driveway. I stood there in the cold drizzle and watched her drive down the road. Something was strange about that whole encounter. She never talked to me that much. It was the longest conversation we'd had since we'd taken Davey to eat at his favorite restaurant for his birthday last March. I remember exactly how weird things seemed as I stood in the driveway and realized I hadn't felt that concerned for Jennifer in a very long time.

5

I sat in Windom Publishing's reception area in a rather comfortable chair, texting Marie about being in Atlanta. I had not talked to her in about a week so I was going through withdrawals, so to speak. As I texted her, I kept thinking about my wife's behavior that morning. The drive is hours from my house and my thoughts wandered on for those miles. Jennifer just acted differently from the normal fuck-you attitude she had always given me when I saw her. Rightly so, I deserved it. But still, I wondered about my wife. I wondered more than I had in years.

I asked Marie what she was doing. I knew it was a gamble because she was probably teaching a class at that time in the morning. But a few minutes later, my phone chirped and she sent back a text that read: *not much…grading papers. U?*

Sitting here at my publisher. Contract thing. Having a good day?

Not really. Up all night with a friend and I'm not built for late nights anymore, lol

I wondered who in the hell had kept her up all night. I instantly got jealous at the idea that some other guy was there doing things I did with *my* Marie. I didn't expect her to be celibate for an entire year between our meetings. I mean, I guess I always knew she had male friends and random sexual partners, although sometimes she hinted that she hadn't had sex with anyone but her toys up until our October meeting, but I never thought about it much. However, it was on my mind as I sat there.

Who were you with?

One of my students who graduated last year. He looked me up when he came back to visit some friends at the college.

Someone I need to be worried about?

Before I could receive her reply, Bob's new secretary Dana opened the door to his lair. "Jerry? Bob and Curtis are ready for you." I rose from the chair, turned off the phone and placed it into my coat pocket. I couldn't care less about Bob and Curtis. I wanted to know more about this dude who was with Marie and had kept her up all night. What was that all about?

I walked in and saw Bob, an old man in a gray suit, sitting behind his enormous desk. Both men stood up to greet me as I entered the room. "My God, Bobby, has it been this long?" I asked as I reached out to shake his liver-spotted hand. I didn't care how long it had been. My mind was still focused on Marie's late night with some unnamed guy. A younger guy.

"It has, Jerry, it has. Please have a seat. How was your drive in?" Bob Windom asked, getting comfortable in his chair again, although I noticed him ease down slowly. Not as youthful-looking as I remembered him. The years since I'd seen him last hadn't been kind to him. He looked thin, *too thin to be healthy,* I thought. And what was with the hand twitch? He didn't have that the last time I saw him. But that was years ago.

"Not bad. Traffic was a bitch though. How you been these days?" I asked, making automatic small talk but still thinking about Marie and her guy as I settled into my chair next to Curtis while patting him on the arm. Hadn't seen my friend in a while.

"Good, no complaints. Life's been good to me. I don't get to see my writers much anymore since all this new technology has come about. Everything is so impersonal these days. Well, I remember when back in the old days I would see my writers at least twice every three months. Now, I'm lucky if I ever see them at all. Started this thing called video chat. Now, that's pretty neat-o."

"Love that tech, though. I was surprised that you wanted to see me. Usually, Curtis drops by the house with the papers. Kind of flattering that you wanted to see your golden boy," I said.

"Yeah, we thought it would be best that we talked to you in person about this issue. Emails and letters wouldn't do for something like this. I guess there's still a certain way I like to do business even if it's old school," Bob said.

I sat there taken off guard over what Bob had just said. "Something wrong?" I asked feeling like I was about to get jacked.

Bob took off his glasses and rubbed his face and then put them back on. His mannerisms told the whole story for me. There was a change coming from the old man, I could see it a mile away. I felt it coming when I was informed that Windom wanted to see me in person. Right there in that office, I saw the storms forming off the horizon. "Jerry, you've been a great talent for us many, many wonderful years. You brought us back from the brink of ruin with all your books and stories. I owe you everything, I do. You single-handedly put Windom Publishing back on the map, and I can't thank you enough. You got us through some really tough times, kid."

"Why does this sound like a farewell speech?" I asked looking at Bob and then at Curtis to my left, who sat there looking down at the floor with no expression, hands folded in his lap. He knew it, too, I figured. My own best friend and agent knew why I had to come to Atlanta. He was just too much of a coward to say it. But I had already known in a way.

"Look, Jerry, I'm going to cut to the chase here, okay? When your contract expires after this novel, I've decided not to renew it. I wanted to you to tell you in person." I was floored by that statement. Absolutely knocked out and down for the count by his words. I thought for sure that I was going to get a pat on the back for a job well done for all the books I've written and be told that I was going to get another huge deal. I didn't under any circumstances deserve it, because I was fucking Jerry Matthews, dammit! I was being let go. I kind of suspected it, but then that was just a vague notion. It only played in the darkened theater in the back of my mind. But I was still upset nonetheless maybe out of automatic response.

"Can I ask why?" I asked, looking at Bob and then at my friend who offered no words whatsoever. But I knew why. It was my sales, had to be. I had gotten sloppy with my work.

"Sales," Bob replied quickly. "It all comes down to sales. The last five books have lost us money. We've put more into advertising and marketing your work and those books of yours didn't make us our money back. You've put us in the red."

I sat there and soaked in everything he had said. Hell, I did it to myself over the years. "So this is it? A long-term relationship is going by the wayside because of a *few* dollars?" I asked still feeling like I ought to fight it out. Maybe it was my pride. I don't know. But I couldn't just sit there and say okay. That would seem like I was cool with everything.

"More than a few dollars, Jerry. More like ten million in the last five years. You see, when it was brought to my attention by our sales department that you were beginning to dip, we thought it would be a good idea to put out a better advertising machine for your work. And every time that we did that, your book failed to get anywhere close to breaking even with our initial investment. Your books have declined to the tune of fifty-five percent over five years. Frankly, we just can't afford to do it anymore. Readers of yours are leaving, and readers are money. Especially these days with all the competition out there."

"Then scale back the advertising dollars. I'm a household name by now. You don't need to push me out like I'm a newbie," I argued, my pride on the line. Bob was suggesting I couldn't write anymore, but that wasn't the case. Well, not the *entire* case. I was too distracted to write, that was it. I could still write with the best of them.

"Doesn't work like that," Bob said. "With all the money we've lost with you, anything that we pay you for a deal won't cover us for our losses. Your fan base has slowly left you. You've become a risky investment. Numbers don't lie. Unless you want to invest some of your own money into your book to cover any losses we take?"

"You're my agent; anything you want to add?" I turned and asked Curtis, who had been very quiet during the proceedings.

"I've tried to negotiate a deal, but Bob's pretty firm on his position. When we looked at the numbers, your marketability isn't like it used to be. His profit margins for your work aren't anywhere close in the plus column anymore," Curtis said, finally looking me square in the eyes.

"So this is it, then? This is how I end my relationship with Bob Windom?" I said looking at the old man across from me. Was I mad at him or myself? It's one thing to quit, but it's another thing to be let go because the bosses think you can't perform anymore. I could write... I just was on an extended hiatus.

"This isn't how I wanted things to end, Jerry. You know that. Or at least you should. We had a good run and now it's over. Don't think that this decision came lightly. It didn't. Curtis and I discussed this for several months. Your last book will be the very last one with Windom Publishing," Bob announced from his desk.

I sat there with the old man looking at me and my best friend staring back down at the floor. I had forgotten all about Marie's text. My losing the contract was a much bigger, more pressing issue. My life's work, my career, was slowly slipping away into the abyss, and the sixty-seven-year-old man at the controls didn't see my potential like he had when he first signed me. Was I washed up? I wasn't, but I knew that whatever creativity that I had was somewhere inside of me under all the booze and other bullshit. The bigger question was did I even really care? My pride hurt, but other than that no.

The numbers that I never knew about until that afternoon in his office were the deciding factor that got me let go from Windom. I knew that I was cooked. I could tell that my writing was bad. I didn't care to leave money on the table because I was going to be okay in the future. *So what if I didn't produce a good book anymore*? So what? Then again there was my pride. I was good at what I did. Damn good. I think that's what bothered me the most. They thought that I was just slipping. Little did they know that I had things going on inside my mind that prevented me from being as good as I knew I truly was.

I should've told them that I was distracted and that my next book would be a blockbuster, if I really, really tried. But I thought better of it. Telling Bobby and Curt that I was mailing it in would make me seem like a vampire, reaping money from an old man who had been paying me good money to keep him and his company afloat. I saw myself as a thief sitting there, taking money I didn't deserve. So I kept my mouth shut.

6

I had forgotten all about my concern for Marie's *up-all-night* thing with one of her former students. My focus was on being dumped by my long-term publisher. We had, I thought, a really good relationship, one that would last long until his son eventually took over the business. But I was apparently wrong in that assumption.

Who was I kidding? I was a fucking thief, taking Bobby's money while handing him utter shit.

And what about Curtis? How long did he *really* know about Bob's plans? He was supposed to have my best interests at heart, but as I walked out of the Windom Building, I wondered. Had he betrayed me, forsaken me because I couldn't make him as much money as I had in the past?

Curtis Phillips and I met at a critical time in my career. When I was a fledgling writer, trying to get someone, anyone, to look at my stuff, I found it difficult and rather trying at times to keep a lock on my dream of becoming successful. This was before the Internet made writers what they are today: A dime a dozen. Had the internet been around as prominent as it is now, my writing career would have begun with published work long ago. But I was born a little too early and had to go at it the old-fashioned way.

The day that I met Curtis was at a writer's convention in Atlanta. I guess you could say that's where my career began. I traveled to those writer's conventions to sell my manuscript and snag an agent. An agent was someone who was a must because back then publishers absolutely refused unsolicited material. So if I didn't have representation, then how in the hell was I ever going to get my foot in the door?

Atlanta was hot that day. I was milling around the Grand Hotel, the site of the writer's convention, looking for someone to partner up with and take me to the promised land. I knew I was good enough. But I needed the right person with the right connections.

At the convention, I ran into similar idealistic writers and hopefuls who travel around from convention to convention, much as I did. They were searching for the same connections as me but to no avail. I could see in some of their eyes that this was their last convention and if they didn't find what they were looking for, they were going to abandon ship. Not me. I had a dream that could not be extinguished by the word "no."

I walked about the hotel's main floor, through droves of people chattering and talking about their trade with strangers. They shared a common trait: they were *all* hoping to achieve success, other than just having a family member tell them how good they were.

I had gotten past standing and talking about writing. I was a man of action and had a plan. I was going to find an agent to look at my material. It was the same plan for every convention that I attended over the last several years. I was batting .000 in the last ten conventions I had attended. At one point I was beginning to think I was never going to get what I wanted. I had dreamed of becoming a published writer for so long that the mere thought of what it was going to be like for me when I did achieve success drove me to keep going. No matter how many times I was told I wasn't good enough.

I remember standing off to myself in a corner, alone with my thoughts. I looked at all the wannabe-published writers talking and mixing it up *with* published writers and publishers who had come to the convention to speak on behalf of their industry. Some of those writers I had seen before and even read some of their stuff. *Mine was better*, I often thought. So if *they* could get a deal, then why couldn't I? It all came down to one thing: who you knew. And I knew no one.

I stood in the corner, arms folded across my chest, listening to random talk, when a well-dressed man around my age walked over to me. "

Everyone's trying to make a connection out there, right?" Curtis remarked about the floor of wannabes. I remember he was wearing a buttoned-up white shirt with a blue tie pulled down a shade.

"Yeah, sad thing is those recruiters out there ain't intending on helping any of those guys. Even the publishers are here for an ego trip, just like the writers. They think they have this secret, but in reality, it's not a secret to how they got to where they are. It was nothing but luck. That's the truth," I articulated, feeling a bit bitter. I was a little jaded by the entire process and hated the elite publishing world. They all looked at themselves as if they were gatekeepers.

Curtis laughed, "Yeah, it's a game of chance. Like blackjack. You only win if you get dealt the right cards. It's all in how they fall."

"Yeah, well I've been at the table for years now, waiting on my winning hand," I replied, looking at all the nameless, yapping wannabes.

"You don't seem like the others out there," Curtis observed.

I shook my head, "I'm not. They're out there kissing ass to get where they want to go."

"Then why are *you* here?" Curtis asked.

"I'm looking for an agent. I know my material is good, and I don't need tips and tricks from the insiders. I just need a rep to sell my material. Seems you can't do anything anymore without an agent."

"You're right. Publishing houses are very greedy with money these days. They've spent so much trying to find the next big thing, and they've all about lost their asses in their searches. So they're more cautious these days."

"Yeah," I said. "I can't even get an agent to look at my stuff."

"Why not?" Curtis asked.

"I have no idea. Every time I contact one, they just send a form letter back to me saying that they are not taking any new clients. And they say this without even looking at my material. To them, I'm just another letter."

"Most agents are dicks. Chasing money, not giving a shit about the writer. You wait, sports agents are getting in on this idea of milking the talent for whatever they can for a bigger piece of the pie. Over the next ten to fifteen years, you'll have agents getting hundreds of millions of dollars for their players just to get themselves a huge cut. Literary agents are the same. All these hopefuls out there are after money and so are the agents. The industry has changed since the creation of the blockbuster. Everyone wants a piece."

"How do you know that?" I asked the stranger.

"Oh, I'm an agent," Curtis said frankly. "I used to be a lawyer at my dad's firm but decided to strike out on my own after he and I had a falling out. Now I troll the conventions for talent." A smile slowly etched across his lips.

"Any luck yet?" I asked not even thinking about asking him to look at my stuff.

"Yeah, a few I think are worth it. But I look at character more than anything. That tells me all I need to know. I mean, Hell, all these guys are writers, but *who* are they, you know?" Curtis said.

"Yeah, character means a lot. Comes through in their writing, too."

"It sure does. You seem like a good guy, not wanting to play bullshit games. What do you write?"

"A little of everything... drama... horror... comedy... young adult. Just whatever I feel like," I responded.

"*I* represent a little of everything. Actually, I don't have anyone on my roster yet. You want to get out of here and go to dinner someplace? Maybe I could take a look at your material, provided you got some with you..." Curtis asked, trailing off.

"I keep a manuscript in my car," I said dryly, feeling that my time had finally come.

CHAPTER FOUR

1

Curtis and I went to a place called The Captain. It was a surf 'n' turf kind of place, really upscale and much nicer than anything I had ever been to before. I was used to fast food back then. Curtis treated me on his own dime. I refused at first, but he insisted, saying he was going to write it off as a business expense. Who was I to argue? I had no money to spend at a place like this. The prices on the menu the nice blonde girl handed us were enough to make me feel even more uncomfortable than I already was.

2

About halfway through our dinner, Curtis wanted to see my manuscript. He had asked a lot of questions, like where I came from, where I wanted to go in life, what my hometown was like, you know, the usual bullshit. I handed him the crudely stapled papers that had been well-traveled and very well-handled. Although it was old and torn in places, my manuscript was still in decent condition, passable for Curtis's review. The clear tape on some of the page rips gave it character, I thought.

For about an hour, Curtis read and thumbed through my manuscript while I ate lobster and steak like a king. I watched him as he took his red pen from his shirt pocket and made notes to himself here and there on my papers. I was kind of nervous watching as he did it, but who was I to argue with him? He was treating me to a nice dinner and was reviewing my book. It was as close as I had ever gotten to having an agent look at it.

As he finished the last few pages, he placed the manuscript down on the table and sipped on his iced tea that had been refilled thrice since we had arrived. Curtis, I later learned, was a man who loved his tea. He finished off his steak that he had been gnawing on as he read my book and looked at me as he chewed the final piece, "Not bad. I think you got something here," he said.

"You really think so?" I asked, trying to be as reserved in my response as possible. I had never been told that I may have something before. So my nerves were a bit all over the place.

"Yeah. I can work with this. Your mechanics need work, and sentence structure needs to be cleaned up substantially, but all in all, I think I can get this published within two months. You got anything else you're working on? Publishers like to know that they're not dealing with a one-trick pony," Curtis said.

"A few things in the first draft stage," I said. "Couple of short stories and parts of full-length novels."

"Good. Get those going passed the first draft stages. At least finish one of them so I can shoot our prospective publishers a follow-up when they publish you."

"You think I'll get a deal?"

"No doubt. Your stuff's refreshing. The market is soft right now so you shouldn't have any problem getting a deal. Keep in mind, though, it won't be anything huge. I'll make sure you get something good, long-term. As long as you can deliver the goods."

"I can," I said enthusiastically. "My imagination is always going. I've got a lot of writing ahead of me."

"I think I'll take this to Windom Publishing. Bob's a small-time house that used to be big-time, but several contracts have sunk him over the decades. Paying out more than he's bringing in. He's trying to bring his house back from the brink. You might be the guy to do it. Ever heard of Steven Budding? Yeah, he was the one who got this huge deal from Bob but then lost his feel and never recovered his fan base. Bob lost millions on him. Ever since then, Bob's been searching for his diamond in the rough."

"And you think I can do it for him?" I said, wanting to jump from my chair and scream out in victory.

"I believe so. This book is really good. As soon as I shop it around, I'll drop it on Bob. I want to get the absolute best deal for you."

"Why not just take it straight to Bob if you know he'll take it?" I asked, trying to figure out Curtis' strategy.

"Because those publishing guys all travel around in the same circles. Once I circulate this book around, everyone will be talking about it, and Bob will want it. He'll outbid his competitors and will win because we want him to. We choose the outcome, not them. Bob's a good man. Better than those other bastards out there in the industry. Fucking vampires."

"You're the boss. I'm just glad that you liked it," I said, feeling as if I were a twelve-year-old kid having someone read my stuff for the first time.

"You and I met for a reason. You're going to need me as much as I need you. So, ready to sign on with me?" Curtis asked, picking through his loaded baked potato. Of course, I was ready to sign with Curtis. Hell, I would have signed with anyone at that point in time. But Curtis was right, we met for a reason. Everything in the universe had lined up perfectly for us to meet, to have dinner, and for him to accept my work. I was so excited that the rest of the night was a blur. It was one of the most surreal moments of my life.

3

For the rest of my career, Curtis had guided me through everything. He had taken care of the contract stuff, which allowed me to just focus on my work. We had a strong bond of trust. I never questioned him on anything because he was out getting me the best deals he could. Movies, books, whatever; Curtis was on top of it all.

He had convinced Bob Windom to take a chance on a twenty-year-old kid with a five-book deal. At the time, a deal that big for a writer so young was unheard of, and it put the publishing world on its collective toes. Soon I was cast into the forefront of the literary world as its next big thing. And Curtis was behind it all. He always knew best.

However, with the turn of recent events up in Windom's office, I wondered if Curtis had my best interests at heart. I had a lot of questions in the aftermath of my release. If Curtis knew about it beforehand, then why didn't he tell me, or at least warn me about what Bob was thinking? Honestly, I felt blindsided by both Bob and Curtis, two men I had trusted without any qualms. I probably deserved it though. Look at what I had become over time.

And why would I not trust them? Curtis had taken a chance and signed me on. From there I made him rich and gave him a powerful name that both known and unknown writers tried to woo to represent them. Curtis had become a major player in the publishing game. And even with all his notoriety and power, Curtis always remained grounded in reality and never allowed the industry to change him, no matter how much success he achieved.

Bob also took a chance on me as a young, unknown writer. Curtis told him I could revive Windom Publishing's name if he would just sign me onto his wilting roster. Bob, who was willing to try anything to get back on track, signed me and held his breath. My first book was a best seller and made his initial investment into back threefold. He was happy, I was happy and so was Curtis. We all made money and found success through each other.

When I was told that my sales were lagging, and my fan base was waning, I understood it was due to the quality of the writing I had produced. My head hadn't been in the game, to say the least. I was okay to just fade to black. I was headed in that direction anyway.

What pissed me off was that it was implied that I was not the same writer who had made the best-seller list with my first five books. To think that I couldn't sit there in my office and hammer out another bestseller was insulting. If I wanted to, I could have created a masterpiece that would have knocked the literary world on its ass. But I simply didn't want to because of all the fogginess in my mind. I was too bogged down in the swamp.

I knew what the problem was: It was me. I didn't lose my trade or forget how to make a reader forget their troubles for a little while. I knew how to tell a story and most importantly, how to write one. Curtis never knew what was going on inside my head. He never knew about Marie or my marriage or my on-again-off-again drinking. Even though he was my best friend, there are some things you can't even tell your friends. Some things you just keep hidden. I've often heard there are a few sides to people: a private side, a public side, and a secret side. I had them all.

4

On that day I was informed I was going to be released from my contract, I found myself at The Captain, sitting in a booth alone, slowly eating a bowl of potato soup. I was stewing over things in my head, trying to figure out where I was going to go from there. The end of my contract didn't exactly mean it was the end of me as a writer. And what was I worried about? It wasn't like I needed the money. I was rich beyond my imagination, with ample enough money saved up. My kids and their kids would be okay financially, thanks to my writing prowess. But it was a pride thing. I was a writer, not a has-been. I sat there and tried to figure out how to come back. I knew I had been mailing it in, but Bob and Curtis thought I was losing it.

I wasn't really even thinking about writing another book because of all the distractions going on in my life. But by God, sitting in there in Windom's office I had a fire lit under my ass, and I wanted to prove to them and to myself that I was still as good as I once was. *But you wait*, I told myself at The Captain, *just you wait.*

As I sat there, my phone was blowing up with texts, not from Marie but from Curtis. He wanted to talk to me. I didn't really want to speak to him because I felt that he should have told me sooner about what Bob had planned for my future. However, the adult thing to do was talk to him face to face. I at least owed him that. I texted back to him and told him that I was sitting in a booth at The Captain. He replied, saying he'd be there in a few minutes.

I finished up my potato soup and sat there like a losing pitcher in the World Series, thinking a mile a minute. My thoughts were rushing around so quickly that it was difficult to latch onto one idea. I had an array of emotions as I sat there waiting for my friend. I felt angry, hurt, betrayed, and demoralized at all once. I wanted answers and the only one who had them was Curtis, the gatekeeper. And then there he stood, right in front of my booth. "Can I sit?" he asked.

I responded with a simple hand gesture, waving to the booth seat across from me. I wanted to say, "Get the hell outta here," but I was trying to be an adult. It was still hard for me, though.

"I know you're mad, and you have every right to be," Curtis said, seating himself across the table.

"Mad isn't the adjective I would use… maybe *betrayed*," I replied.

"I didn't…. Look," Curtis began to explain himself. "I didn't betray you, Jerry. I tried to help you out as much as I could. Bob's plans were made well before I knew about them."

"And you couldn't turn him around?" I shot back, wondering to myself why I had just asked him that. I didn't care that I was slumping because I knew I could snap out of it…if I wanted.

Curtis leaned back against his seat and looked around the restaurant before he spoke, as if trying to search for the right words, "Bob's son, Arnold, is taking over his father's company. There's a sea change coming, not just for you but for Windom's entire roster. You were the first to fall. The others are on their way out as a part of Arnold's 'Great Reconstruction' of what his dad built. I don't know if you noticed, but Bobby ain't in good health. I think he's dying. He hasn't said anything, but I get that feeling, you know? He's different."

"How long did you know this was coming?" I asked.

"A day, really. I got a call about it *a day* before I called you. I had a feeling that he wasn't going to renew your contract. There was some talk between me and Bob and Arnold for a few months about all of this. But I thought they'd give you another two-book deal and be out after that.

"Your sales have dipped quite a bit over the last few books, and Bob's son is dropping all the dead weight as the transfer of power takes its shape. You really thought I was withholding information on you?" He asked without hurt in his voice. Curtis was such a pro.

"I didn't know what to think," I replied considering my true feelings, knowing that Curtis had always been square with me. I guess deep down I should have known Curtis would never turn on me. I got so mad and caught up in the emotions that I wasn't thinking straight. He wasn't the one to blame. I was.

"We've been through a lot together, you and me. And for you to think that I would just turn on you is pretty fucking stupid." He was right. It was pretty fucking stupid. "Arnold is pulling the strings now. He phoned in his decisions on who to keep and who to cut from a golf course. He's a grade-A pecker if I've ever seen one."

I sat there for a few moments, looking at my iced tea sweating down the side of my glass onto the table. He was right; there was no way Bob would have let me go on his own. He might have reduced my contract money but wouldn't let me go outright. When I had time to think about it, I remember Curtis predicting years ago that Arnold would one day own the company and drive it into the ground. So far, that prognostication was coming to fruition. "Are my numbers really that bad?" I asked, ready to hear the absolute truth because, in all honesty, I didn't know how bad they really were.

Curtis sat back, and I could tell that he didn't want to enlighten me. "Like I said in Bob's office, your marketability is off quite a bit. Your sales have tanked with the last few books. Even the most hardcore of your fans are losing interest. I troll the Internet, and people are saying you've lost that edge you used to have. And when Arnold was checking profit and losses at the house, your name came up as one not to renew. You and I both know Bob would have re-signed you out of loyalty because that's just how he is. But Arnold's an entirely different kind of animal. Loyalty to him is disposable. So... what's going on with you?"

"What do you mean?" I asked knowing damn well what he meant.

Curtis sat there, gazing at me. "Your last few books have been horrible. What's the problem? Something that I should be concerned with? Look, I'm not asking as a writer-agent relationship here. I'm asking as a friend. A concerned friend."

I sat there in my booth seat and picked at what was left of my food. Across from me was my friend of many years, the one man who picked me out of thousands and changed my life by recognizing my talent. I had to tell him the truth, much like I had to spill the beans about Marie to Samantha that night. "I um... I've got some issues."

"Okay," Curtis said leaning in, "What? Talk to me."

I was still hesitant but felt that I owed Curtis the truth. "My marriage is falling apart. Has been ever since we said, 'I do.' I've been drinking off and on... and there's this other woman in my life that I've been waiting on forever it seems."

Curtis slowly leaned back against his booth seat. "What?" he asked, stunned.

I nodded. "Yeah. There's so much going on that you don't know. I don't even know where to start."

"Whatever it is, has it messed you up to a point where you can't write?"

This time I shook my head, "No, not really. I *can* write. I'm still really good. I've been phoning the last few books in because there's so much going on that I've just lost my passion. I've got too much going on," I said tapping my index finger to the side of my head.

"Are you and Jennifer getting divorced?" Curtis asked.

I sat there for a minute before I answered, "I don't know. What's the point? The woman I want I'll never have. I mean, Jen and I have come this far, right? Probably should though."

"Who's the other woman?" Curtis asked, still shocked.

I sat there and looked at him, not believing I was about to tell him about Marie Evans. "There's this woman who I've been seeing for twenty years now...."

"A mistress?"

"No," I said, quickly defending her honor. "It's not like that. She and I met in the fifth grade and were friends and dated off and on. We've got a lot of history together. She was the woman I wanted to spend the rest of my life with and have a family with. But she would never settle down. So, she and I meet once a year in October for a weekend at her father's lake house. Have been ever since I can remember. I can't help myself. I love her," I said slowly.

Curtis was wide-eyed and sat there, not knowing what to say. My big reveal dumbfounded him. "Does Jennifer know about this? I'm going to assume not."

"No. And even if she did, it wouldn't matter. We've not been what you would call a 'happily married couple' for a very, very long time."

I could tell Curtis was having a difficult time processing what I had just told him. He looked like my daughter had when I told her about Marie. "So what are you going to do?"

"About?"

"You and your wife?" Curtis responded.

"Nothing. Same thing we've always been doing, I guess. It just sucks that I've been the way I've been over a woman who I was never destined to have. Look at where it's gotten me."

"Good, God," Curtis replied. "I don't know what to say, man. I thought your life was just... awesome. It always seemed that way."

"Far from it. Sorry to disappoint you," I said. "I'm as fucked up as the rest of the world."

"Where do you see yourself a year from now? Hell, six months, even?" Curtis said, asking perhaps one of the best questions I'd heard in a while.

I looked around at the people who began filling the restaurant. The place wasn't huge by any means, but it wasn't small either. About a hundred people and the place began to get cramped, uncomfortable. I had to think a bit about Curtis's question. Indeed, what was in store for me in the future? I had no idea. "No clue," I replied. "But I want you to know this: I'm still a good writer. I want you to get me another contract with whoever's out there."

Curtis held up his hands and shook his head. "Listen, word of Windom cutting you is going to hit the streets quick. And other publishers will see you as damaged goods. They've got access to the same data we do. You're too risky right now," he said bluntly.

"What?" I was surprised that publishers weren't lined up outside of The Captain, waiting with a contract in hand for me to sign. I was still Jerry Matthews, right?

"The publishing industry is taking a beating right now because of the Internet. They won't sign anything risky right now at all. And you are very risky. Once they find out that Bob let you go, they'll all wonder why he let his best writer go. And then reality will click and they'll say, 'he must be washed up'. All they have to do is read your books, man."

"I'm not washed up!" I said, loudly defending my pride. "I'm not."

"To them, you are, okay?" Curtis pointed out. "You're a relic. Times are changing out there, man. Unless you're a sports figure, political figure, or a movie star with an interesting bio or a reality star, no publisher wants a deal. Your name hasn't been on the bestseller list in a long time. You think they don't troll the papers and look at that? However, there is an alternative."

"Such as?" I said, soaking in Curtis's words.

"Self-publish on the Internet. You can do that. Takes no money and if it does it's just for ads and the media push. You've got the funds to do it, too. You want to get back into the spotlight? Go that route. You've got the name recognition."

I sat there and thought about it for a few moments. "You think that would work?" I asked, not knowing much about self-publishing.

Curtis nodded, "Yeah, because at some places you would retain seventy percent, which is a better deal than Windom or *any* publisher would give you right now. I'm telling you as my friend: the publishing world as you know it has shut down around you. It's happening to me, too, for that matter. It's getting harder to find prospects because the good ones are self-publishing, cutting agents completely out of the equation. In a few years, agents will be a thing of the past."

I sat looking around, thinking about what Curtis was saying. It was hard for me to believe that publishers wouldn't be tripping over themselves to snag me. But Curtis was shooting me straight. If he says the publishing world has changed, then it has. How would I know? I'd been in the same place for years and had no idea what the outside world had to offer. I knew what it was when I went in, but now? No way. "So," I started, "what now?"

"Finish the last book for Windom and start over."

"Is going the self-publishing route a good idea?" I asked.

Curtis nodded, "Yup. You can make it. But you're going to have to want it and stop phoning it in. If you can't do that then you'll never get back. Self-publishing will be good for you. And anyway, it's really your only option if you want to keep writing. You still have name recognition to pull you through. It's a good investment in yourself. Get your life together and stop the drinking."

5

Hearing Curtis talk made me feel that everything was going to be okay. Maybe getting dumped by Windom was a good thing after all, a wake-up call. I sat there and thought about how much had changed since Curtis and I first came to The Captain decades ago, when I was unknown and Curtis was looking for prospects.

We were older, wiser, and more successful than each of us ever thought possible. Who would have known, way back when, that we'd be sitting in the very same restaurant where it all began, talking about the end and a hopeful new beginning. Life is a circle, and you always end up where you began. So much had changed, but at the same time, so much was the same. Curtis and I still had a very special connection, as if we had been friends at another time, in another life. Hard to describe what Curtis and I had. He was like a brother to me. Hell, he was my best man at my wedding. And shame on me for ever thinking he would betray me. I felt like garbage for thinking him capable of that. He just wasn't that kind of guy.

6

Curtis and I sat at our booth at The Captain and caught up with each other for another hour and a half or so. Although we were great friends, we were both too preoccupied with work and life to just sit and chat like gossiping teenage girls. Most of our spare time was to catch our collective breath and relax from the rigors of life. We just didn't have time to spend with each other. We both knew it.

Despite this, though, Curtis and I found some occasions to golf or even catch a baseball game together over the years. But those times were few and far between. He would be on vacation and I would be off someplace doing a speaking engagement, or I'd take some time off from my book and he'd be closing deals. We really enjoyed each other's company, but getting together to do things was extremely difficult; it was almost a Herculean task.

Technology has become our best ally over the decades. We went from the telephone, or what the hipsters call landlines, to email and instant messaging and then to texting. Texting has become our go-to method of communication. Important stuff was sent either through an email or a phone call, but everything else was through text. Funny—that was my and Marie's approach to communication, too.

7

It was around seven o'clock on that fall evening when Curtis and I stood outside The Captain. The night had settled in and a definite chill was in the air, thanks to the faint breeze that blew in from the south. I put my hands in my coat pockets while Curtis lit a cigarette and blew smoke into the air. "I thought you quit," I remarked watching his gray smoke blow to the right.

"I did. But the kids at home have shot my nerves so bad that what used to be a means to take the edge off is now a habit that I can't break."

"Try drinking. It fixes everything," I laughed. But I knew all about the evils of drinking.

"Between smoking and pussy, I don't need any more vices," he said. We both laughed.

"So, heading back home?" Curtis asked me as we stood there, watching people mill about the shops on the sidewalks.

"I don't know. I probably should. Thought I might walk around the district. Haven't been down here in years. I don't know," I said as

"I don't know. I probably should. Thought I might walk around the district. Haven't been down here in years. I don't know," I said as I looked up at the streetlights lighting the big city, casting their fluorescent glow onto the pavement.

"Okay, you sure you don't want to ride with me to get your car?"

"Nah, it's a four-block walk. I need it."

"Alright then. Hey, I'll text you or something in a few days. Finish up that novel and get back on track. It's been really good being your agent for all these years," Curtis said, hugging me.

"You bet. Thanks for gambling on me," I said with my chin resting on his right shoulder. "Okay. Be careful going home."

The next and final time that I would see Curtis would be at my son's funeral.

CHAPTER FIVE

1

After Curtis and I parted ways, I stood there for a moment and looked around my surroundings. It was cramped with shops and eateries on either side of the street and flooded with people walking around talking to their friends or spouses or kids; some had heads down, eyes fixed on their phones texting while walking nearly into other people. Everyone was wearing something warm to block out the chilly night air as fall was knocking on the door.

I looked at my watch and decided that I could mill around a bit in the city before heading home. There, Samantha would probably be with Randy watching TV or listening to music, and Davey would be out of sight in his room doing whatever it was that Davey did behind his closed bedroom door. Jennifer might or might not be there. With our interaction earlier that morning, I wondered briefly what was going on with her. But I didn't dwell on it much. Would I be missed if I was a few hours late coming home? Nope. Kind of depressing when you think about it.

2

I walked down the sidewalk with my hands in my coat pockets through a sea of people. It was nice to be able to just walk without someone recognizing me and wanting to talk about my work. I had experienced that before. At first, it was awesome, but as I got older it became more of an inconvenience. At one point, it had gotten where I could not actually go anywhere without being spotted. These days, I blended into the woodwork. It was good.

Nowadays, I could walk around and no one would even shoot a glance my way. Was it because I was a relic? Or was it that this society doesn't read anything that isn't on a blog, and writers like me aren't celebrities any longer? I mean, I liked not being hassled, but walking around in Atlanta on that chilly fall night, I got the feeling that I had become a face in the crowd— just another guy walking with his hands in his pockets.

It's a complete and utter paradox. Here I was, hating being bothered in public and always dodging strolls like the very one I was on. But walking and looking at these nameless people ambling right past me without even a nod gave me chills that were unrelated to the cool breeze. It was bullshit, I know. I wanted people to let me be, but the farther I walked down the street, the more concerned I felt. Had I become some nameless guy no one knows? I remember back in the old days, hell, even five years ago, I could have walked these streets and been noticed by at least twelve people within a ten-minute period. That night... not one single person!

Maybe I *had* become somewhat of a recluse. Okay, yes, I'd become a recluse. It wasn't like I'd set out to do it, but rather it just happened. I think, after my last book, I slid into a personal slump (exacerbated, no doubt, by Marie's absence) and didn't get out much to do interviews for magazines that liked to keep up with me. Maybe my reluctance to get out there contributed to my sales declining over the years. I don't know for sure, but it was a distinct possibility.

The hardest part of being a human is coming to the stark reality that the problems that have vexed you are by your own doing. I sabotaged my career by just mailing it in and expecting everyone to still care. I realized, walking down that sidewalk, that the reason my numbers were down and the reason I wasn't being noticed on the sidewalks anymore was *me.* And *knowing* and *owning* this reality made it a bitter pill to swallow.

When you open closet doors and talk to the skeletons that stand behind them, you begin to find out things that you never wanted to admit, never wanted to see or hear. But once you finally admit your actions, you are compelled to open other doors that hold even more secrets and more skeletons—rooms full of bones from the past. My first door to open was discovering that my career wasn't in decline because of Bob or Arnold Windom but because of me and me alone. I was to blame, not them, not my fans, and especially not my family.

Lately, when I would write, I wouldn't put that much into it because my fans, with their unwavering loyalty, would buy anything that I published. I knew this and used it to my advantage. Sure, my bestsellers were all because of my fans, but that was it. The writing declined somewhat throughout my career, and the reviews got worse with my last two to three books. I didn't care because people were still reading my stuff and providing for my modest lifestyle.

But I had gotten lazy and it really took me getting fired and walking down a sidewalk in Atlanta where no one knew me to realize that *I* was the problem, no one else. Perhaps I knew I was the problem all along. Of course, I did. Who am I kidding?

So I confronted the skeleton in my closet. I realized that to get back on track, I needed to get fired up like I did when I was younger. Back then I wrote gold and put effort into my words. And people knew it. Lately, I had just typed aimlessly on a keyboard, in one drunken state after another, not remembering any words I had written.

I remember an interview that I once did for my then-most-recent book, *Curtain Call.* I was asked about certain passages in the book by a guy at a rock radio station in SoCal. He asked me about this and that and about why the main character, Steve Harding, had to kill the old man at the end. I sat there racking my brain, trying to figure out what the hell this fucking guy was talking about. Did I write that? I had no clue. Honest. I did what good writers do: I made something up for the interviewer, and from what I could tell it sounded intelligent even if I don't recall anything. It all sounded like the truth.

I had told Curtis earlier while we were eating how my last book for Windom, *Tricks of the Trade,* was going to be me back to the basics. I lied. It was the same bullshit I'd been turning out for years. For a brief moment, I thought about going home, tearing it up, and writing the best damn book of my career. Then I smashed that idea to hell and told myself, "Why would I give my best book to Windom? Fuck 'em." They were going to get the usual.

3

I grew tired of walking and the night had gotten darker and colder than it had been when I first began my stroll. I happened upon a bookstore, not a big chain, but a quaint one run by a sole person for nothing more than the love of literature, no matter how dead it was becoming. I loved these kinds of bookstores because, when you went inside, the little bell attached to the door would ring, and you could instantly smell both old and new books. I opened the door and warmness consumed me. I looked around the rather large store and saw people standing and reading or sitting down in comfortable-looking chairs, some sipping hot beverages while playing with their phones or checking out a book they might consider purchasing. A real hipster place that's for sure.

I walked around the store and scanned the titles of books and authors I had never heard of. A few I had, but only a handful. I mean seriously, how many authors does the average person know? There had to be hundreds, if not thousands, of authors sitting on those wooden shelves I'd never heard of before. That was the appeal of the bookstore to me – its promise of adventuring into something new.

I walked around looking at random titles of different genres. Then I stumbled upon my section. There they were, sitting among others in the general inventory of known and unknown writers. I stood there and fetched my very first novel, *Days of Rain and Sun*. It was a new edition paperback, unlike the first edition hardback from long ago. It was the book that garnered the first of many awards.

I had been writing it ever since I was in high school, constantly tweaking it, rewriting it, shelving it, and swearing to God above that I would never work on it again. But I always found myself gravitating toward it because I knew what a good story it was even if I couldn't get it right.

Days of Rain and Sun was the manuscript that I gave Curtis to read at The Captain on the afternoon when we met at the writer's convention. He loved it and for good reason. I had spent years perfecting that book, almost driving myself to the brink of insanity. It was good, and even I knew that anything that I did as a follow-up was not going to be as good. I was right.

Days of Rain and Sun was about a veteran coming back home after a war and having to get acclimated to regular life again. Of course, it was an uphill battle because his wife had an affair with his best friend, and his young children didn't know him. His family had all but died off while he was away. He was a stranger in a strange land, and after years of trying to get back what he had lost after the war, Dave Combs, the main character, says "Home ain't no place for a soldier" before committing suicide.

My work got so much positive feedback that veterans would approach me on the street to tell me how much on point I was. I was even asked if I had served time in the military. When I said no, they were shocked. People said that I had an insider's understanding of what soldiers who had returned home felt, their full range of emotions. But I actually just placed myself in a combat situation and tried to flesh it out way back when I was just a wide-eyed kid trying to get published. I had no inside scoop. After all, I was just a kid when I wrote it.

Days of Rain and Sun was hailed as a literary masterpiece and up there on many critics' top-ten lists. Being young, I was floored by all the praise that it and I had gotten. I wasn't ready for all the pressure that eventually came with being an acclaimed writer. I never saw myself in that way. All I wanted to do was just write, and maybe make a good enough living so that I didn't have to work like a regular stiff. All I wanted to do was to write books and be happy. Where in the hell did I go astray? Oh yeah, Marie Evans.

When *Days of Rain and Sun* waned in popularity and after all the praise died down, a reporter from *Topple Magazine,* a writer's magazine, asked me what my plans were for my next groundbreaking novel. It was the first time that I had ever been associated with the word "groundbreaking." I knew what all the people had said about the book, but "groundbreaking"? Come on, were they for real? I was just getting started. And that's around the time when I was *just getting started* with drinking.

I was uneasy having all those questions tossed at me by news outlets and Q&A sections at writer's conventions. What's your follow-up going to be? Is it going to be on par with *Days of Rain and Sun?* Are you worried about the sophomore jinx? Those questions haunted me everywhere I went. The pressure to beat my first novel was set into motion by the people who now expected it.

The pressure to write another home run book came at a price. Sure, I had hundreds of book ideas floating around, but which one could I hang onto that would be as good as my first? After running through the list of possibilities, I finally settled on my next book, *Hometown.* I picked up a copy and thumbed through its pages there in the bookstore, something that I had not done since I wrote the damn thing. It was a complete nostalgia trip just reading some of the lines. The crazy thing was that I almost recalled writing those words as I stood there, marveling over my own work.

Hometown had great expectations tied to it way before I even published it. Everyone expected each of my books to blow the previous one away. And *Hometown* did just that. It bested *Days of Rain and Sun* and was another highly acclaimed piece of work. Did I know it would be so successful as I wrote it? No, I just sat down for six months and wrote and wrote and wrote up in my office. Sometimes I was sober, sometimes not.

When I finished, Curtis looked at me and said, "This is fucking gold." And that was the sentiment, so to speak, from all the critics. Two books into my career and I had accomplished what most writers can't do in a lifetime of work: back-to-back masterpieces.

Hometown worked so well because it was another one of those emotional returning-home stories. This one wasn't about a soldier, but about a guy named Sam coming back to his hometown after becoming a successful writer. He returned to reconnect with friends and family he had left behind. The most acclaimed part of the book came in the parts where Sam and his father, Steve, reconnected after years of silence just before he died. It was my masterstroke.

It was an emotional part of the book that required me to recall feelings about my father. It was emotionally the most difficult book I had ever written because it was loosely based on my relationship with my dad, which was up and down over the years. Using those feelings as the backdrop to my writing, I could tap into the basic dynamic between most fathers and their sons. It hit home with my growing number of fans, and it set me apart from the mediocre writers. I was being mentioned in the same breath as F. Scott Fitzgerald, Stephen King, and Charles Dickens. It was crazy to be up on their level, but there I was standing on top of Mount Olympus with all those titans of writing, just two novels into my career to boot. Movie adaptations of those books came and did fairly well.

4

I went over to the seating area in the middle of the bookstore and sat down in one of the available chairs. Others were sitting, minding their own business, engrossed in their phones and books and magazines. I could have been naked, wearing a clown wig, and no one would have noticed me. Is that what our society has become? *Maybe*, I pondered as I sat there, thinking people didn't recognize me anymore because they're so self-absorbed. But that was only wishful thinking.

I pulled out my phone and checked it for any messages. Nothing. I wondered why Marie never texted me back. I mean, what did it matter, really, in the grand scheme of things? She wasn't my wife or anything, so why was I jealous of her being with someone else? I shouldn't have been, but I was, to tell the truth. I was jealous.

Marie and I had an understanding. I was married and she was not, and she could do whatever she wanted, just as she wanted. That was the thing about her not being tied down: if she wanted to go someplace to spend the weekend, she could. If she wanted to have multiple sex partners within a week, she could. I could too, but what was the point? I only wanted Marie. Jennifer and I had had no sexual contact in a long time, maybe years. That didn't stop her from finding someone else. And why not – Jennifer was a sexy woman who could have anyone she wanted. Eventually she did, but at a price.

I sat in the bookstore, holding my phone and people-watching. I must have seemed a little creepy, but then again no one noticed me watching them. I sat there, wrestling with myself on whether I should text Marie. She left me in the lurch with her non-response. But then again, she didn't owe me anything because of our arrangement.

I will say again that the arrangement we made wasn't my idea; it was hers. I was never happy with it. However, if I wanted to be with Marie, the ultimate love of my life, I had to play by her rules. And I have ever since we were kids.

5

Feeling odd and suddenly out of place, I got up after about ten minutes and walked across the bookstore to the exit. Suddenly, my phone vibrated with a message from Curtis. I clicked on the message icon and unknowingly found myself fully enthralled by my device, just like all the other drones.

As I began to open his message without watching where I was going, I was immediately hit in the face by the opening of the bookstore's glass door. I crashed down onto the carpeted floor, dropping my phone with Curtis' unread message to the side. Standing above me was a vision of beauty. The woman who hit me with the door as she was entering the bookstore was – you guessed it – looking at her phone, checking a message.

"Oh my God, are you okay?! I didn't mean to do that! I'm so, so terribly sorry!" She exclaimed as I sat there on my ass, holding my mouth and nose, both stinging with pain. I felt the flow of blood and checked with my hand. Nothing. I even ran my tongue across my teeth, yup, they were still there. Thank God.

"I'm okay, I'm okay. Not your fault," I said, getting up and picking up my phone. I looked at this woman with her blonde hair pinned up, wearing black-rimmed glasses and a baggy sweatshirt. It was total serendipity how we met in the bookstore. That night, I came face-to-face with my future, or glass-door-to-face with my future.

"God, are you sure you're okay? I wasn't watching where I was going. I... I was checking messages on my stupid phone," she said, looking at my mouth and red nose that still felt like it was bleeding.

"You're fine," I said holding my nose. "I wasn't watching where I was going either."

"Is there anything I can do? You want some ice?" She asked as others entering and exiting the store stopped for a moment to see what the commotion was about. Then after a few dull seconds, they went right back into their phones, tablets, and real books. They lost interest in the two of us.

"No, I think I'll be fine. Just a little pop. My arm caught most of the blow. Had it not been for that, it could've been worse," I replied while looking at her. God, she was beautiful, standing there looking back at me. It was funny, almost as if we had met someplace before, another time, or maybe in another life. There are times in our lives when we meet people who we instantly connect with. It's unexplainable but the feeling is there—you just can't place your finger on it, but it's like your heart knows when it meets its match.

"I'm really sorry about this. I feel terrible," she apologized.

"Look, neither of us was watching where we were going. I blame these damn phones," I said, raising mine.

"Me, too," she replied, biting her lower lip nervously. "Have we... met someplace before?"

She asked me that as if she wasn't sure she should've voiced her thoughts. Later, Heather would go on to say that she felt as if we both had met someplace in the past but, for the life of her, could not recall exactly where. Standing there, looking at each other, we experienced an unworldly connection. I couldn't explain it then, nor can I now as I remember that day with absolute clarity.

"I was about to ask you the same thing," I replied, forgetting all about my thumping mouth and throbbing nose.

"I'm Jerry Matthews," I said extending my hand. She shook it.

"Heather Parker. You live here in town?"

"No, actually I'm just visiting. Had a meeting earlier today."

"What do you do?" Heather asked. We both moved out of the way of the people coming in and out of the bookstore.

"Um… I'm a writer," I said lowly, assuming a girl her age wouldn't even know who the hell I was. But I was wrong.

"Jerry Matthews? *The* Jerry Matthews?! *Days of Rain and Sun, Hometown*? Oh my God, I just slammed a door into one of the best writers in history!" Heather shouted.

"That's me. You a fan of my work?" I asked, surprised because girls her age didn't find my stuff that provocative. Or did they?

"Yeah, we studied your first novel in my lit class last semester. Professor Lopez had it as required reading," Heather replied.

"My work is being studied in *college*? Wow. I never knew about that," I said in amazement. I guess I had made it after all.

"Yeah, next semester we're reading *Hometown.* I can't believe that I hit *the* Jerry Matthews. Crazy!" We both smiled and laughed it off and then stood there for a few moments of awkward silence. I wanted to say something, anything, to keep the conversation going but was unable to catch any of the mile-a-second thoughts that came screaming through my mind. I tell you this though—it was the most I had smiled in a very, very long time.

For some reason, I didn't want that moment in time to end. Neither did she—must have been that cosmic connection we had felt.

"This is going to sound dumb and if it does, I'm sorry. But why don't you let me buy you a cup of hot cocoa? I know this little coffee shop down the street here that serves some of the best stuff you'll ever drink," she said, folding her hands within each other at her waist and standing on the tips of her toes. It was so cute that she was so nervous. Hell, I was nervous, too.

I stood there, astounded. Did she want to buy me a drink because she felt that she should since she hit me with the bookstore door, or because I was a famous writer that she had been studying? But those notions quickly vanished because she flashed me a smile that I had never seen on anyone before. Not on Marie and not on Jennifer. It was a smile that plainly told me, "Hey, there's something between us here already and I want to know what it is and why I can't walk away." I had that feeling, too. I smiled back—hard not to.

It's difficult to quantify love. But you know when you have it and when you feel it. It hits you like a ton of bricks falling from above. Samantha once asked me what it feels like to be in love. The only answer I gave her was how I felt about Marie, without mentioning her name. However, standing there with a woman who was half my age in a bookstore, I wished that I could tell Samantha what love feels like because I felt it at that moment, something stronger and more profound than what I had ever before experienced.

Heather and I met by chance. What were the odds? But it happens every day, they say. That door hitting me was the best thing to happen to me in a long time. Its smack to the face woke me up from the slumber I had allowed myself to fall into. And that lull was broken by a beautiful college student who looked at me as if she had been searching for me her entire young life. "Yeah, I'd like that," I replied to her offer.

CHAPTER SIX

1

Heather Parker and I sat across from each other in a coffee shop called Cup O' Joe. It was a trendy place where, by the looks of it, a lot of hipsters and college students frequented. The place was sort of small, but not so much that you couldn't get comfortable or get lost among the woodwork, nor was it too small to feel crowded with just a handful of people. To paraphrase Goldie Locks, this was just right. And why wouldn't it be? I was there with a very attractive woman—a very attractive *younger* woman.

Heather seemed to fit in but, as for me, I seemed out of place. (I often felt out of place in those days.) She and I sat there with our piping-hot cups of cocoa under a low-lit lamp that hung from the ceiling at our table. The dim environment seemed to set an intimate tone between us. *Was this a date?* I wondered. It certainly felt like one. But then again, we had just met and a date didn't seem appropriate. We were just two people talking and having a hot cup of cocoa in a coffee shop. That was it. That's what we both told ourselves, anyway.

"So, what's it like being a famous writer?" Heater asked me while I gingerly sipped my huge cup of cocoa.

"Well," I began. "It's not what you'd think it'd be. Certainly not what I thought it'd be," I said. This wasn't like a magazine interview because if I had received that question from a reporter, I'd lie and say it was an awesome experience. I've said that in the past, but Heather's face put me at ease like I could lower my guard and just be plain. I liked that. I hadn't been just plain in a long time with anyone. Hell, there were a lot of things she did that I liked, and I had only known her for less than an hour.

"Have you ever heard that saying, 'art imitates life'? Well, it does. My life has anyways."

"Been bad?" she asked, putting the oversized cup to her mouth while looking at me, penetrating my soul with her eyes behind those sexy, black-rim school-teacher glasses. Ironically, Marie had a pair but only wore them at home while she was reading. They were sexy on her too, but on Heather, they were out of this world.

"Not really bad, but not the way I thought it'd be, you know," I said, relaxing some. "When I was a kid, I had this preconceived notion that being a writer was going to solve any future problem I might have. But it didn't. You take my being a writer away, then I'm just as confused and fucked up as everyone else," I said, looking around at the hipsters in their backward baseball caps and college sweatshirts. The crowd was a lot younger than I was and I felt out of place, like a relic, sitting there with Heather.

"You seem ill at ease," Heather noticed as she slowly placed her cup on the small table.

"That's a good way of putting it," I said. "What about you? What's your story? Besides hitting strange men with doors."

"Well," Heather started as she moved a few pieces of her hair from her eyes. "I'm a college student. Have no idea what I want to do with my life." She laughed in a way that I'd never heard before. It seemed so full of life, honest. "My dad has been pushing me to be a teacher and that's what I'm going to school for, but I hate it. Hate the thought that I'll be trying to teach kids stuff they should know with a state-accelerated curriculum."

"Damn. Well put. What do you really want to do?" I asked, sipping on some more of my hot cocoa.

She sighed and looked out of the window next to us and then back at me. "No clue," she laughed. "If I did, things wouldn't be as complicated as they are. Seems that I'm just spinning my wheels at twenty-two years old."

"Sometimes doing your own thing is hard. Especially when it goes against your parents," I said, speaking from experience.

"Yeah, tell me about it. But I guess I have time to figure it out. I read in your bio online that you're married with two kids. Marriage all it's cracked up to be?" The thing about Heather: She might be twenty-two but fuck did she talk like I did. She seemed older. She seemed like ... I don't know, an old soul.

I chuckled a bit at her question. "Yeah. But what they don't tell you on my bio is that my marriage started decaying from day one, that my son is incredibly introverted and my daughter, I think, is sexually active with her boyfriend which drives me up a wall. Which I can only suspect will result in a baby by the time she's eighteen."

Heather, I could tell, was sorry that she had brought up my family. "I'm sorry, I didn't know it was a sore spot," she said, looking like she had offended me.

"It's not... it's just how life is," I replied. *Yeah, how life is*, I thought as I sipped my cocoa with a girl half my age. Christ, I had a daughter who was just a few years younger than Heather. What was I *really* doing, sitting at this table with her? I wondered what my true motivations were as we talked. "You got a boyfriend?"

"No. He and I broke up because he was too controlling and abusive. I just couldn't deal with him anymore. Too many tears and bruises, I guess. He just put his hands on me one too many times." Heather put the cup up to her lips again and sipped again, scanning the room, perhaps for her abusive dickhead ex-boyfriend. "I feel that my soulmate is still out there, somewhere, just waiting for me. Kind of a romantic that way, I guess. Sounds corny maybe."

"No, it sounds right. I'd like to believe in soulmates."

"You don't?"

I sat there and considered her question by thinking about Marie and my wife. Betwixt the two of them, I considered Marie my soul mate. But can you feel that way towards someone who doesn't feel that way towards you?

"I want to believe, I do. But lately, I don't know."

"Did you think you and your wife were soulmates?" she asked.

I shook my head quickly. "No, nowhere close. I knew it, too though. The girl who I wanted didn't want anything to do with me and eventually my wife, Jennifer, and I just sort of happened. I had this, um, fear that I was going to live my life alone. And when I met Jennifer, I just sort of settled. Stupid reason to get married. However, a reason nonetheless."

"Loneliness is not a stupid reason. It's bred out of fear that motivates us to do things that we normally wouldn't do, like end up with people who we ordinarily wouldn't be with. It sounds like you were scared at the time."

"Maybe. But I screwed her out of being happy. I took that away from her. I robbed her of years, her best," I replied, trying to remember when exactly Jennifer and I had been happy last. My brain could not remember any particular times that our happiness was authentic. Perhaps it was as far back as our honeymoon in South Carolina. Perhaps not even then. Not really.

"So, umm," Heather began as she changed the subject, "any new work coming out soon?" she asked while flashing her gorgeous smile.

"Yeah, something that isn't very good. It'll be my last one with Windom Publishing. I was told today that my contract wasn't going to be renewed. That's why I'm here in Atlanta."

"Oh my God, that must be... you must feel horrible."

"I did, but they were right. I'm not as good as I used to be. It's hard to write masterpiece after masterpiece, especially when you don't care anymore. I've been writing for the sake of getting paid for my last few books. I just basically mailed it in, so to speak." I said leaning back in my chair.

"I think your stuff is great. I have a copy of every book you've written. I became a fan since we started studying you in class this semester. I think you're really, really talented."

"Thank you," I said. "I'm going to begin work on a comeback novel, though, that should be as good as *Days of Rain and Sun.*"

"I can't wait," Heather said, staring at me through her lenses.

2

Two huge cups of hot chocolate and three hours later, Heather and I were laughing and sharing stories at our little table like we had known each other for years. It was like we were best friends catching up on old times; like Curtis and I would when we got some face time. I don't know. There she was, a perfect stranger to me, yet it felt like we had known each other all our lives. Sounds strange, I know, like something that I would write about, but I swear to God, it was like that. Just like in the movies, when a boy and girl meet.

It was the strangest feeling that I ever had with anyone, ever. I never had that sort of simpatico with Jennifer, not even with my lovely Marie. The butterflies I used to get when I would talk to or see Marie were nothing compared to the swarm inside my stomach while talking to Heather. It was a feeling you get when you go really fast down a hill and your stomach drops. That's how I felt with her on our first night together.

There was an x-factor that defined our connection. What it was and where it came from was a complete mystery. We both felt something but didn't dare tread too deeply on the subject during our first meeting. It was there, though, and it was undeniable.

Heather told me in the coming weeks of our budding relationship that she knew something was up when she saw me lying on the floor of the bookstore. I wanted to tell her the same but held back. How does a forty-year-old man tell a twenty-two-year-old girl that there's something between them? You don't. You can't at the risk of sounding utterly ridiculous.

"So, how old are your kids?" Heather asked.

"Davey is fifteen and Samantha is eighteen. Well, eighteen in a little bit."

"Wow, you've got kids almost as old as I am!" Heather remarked. Her observation struck me. Here I was, talking to a girl who didn't even know about life, and she could've been my daughter's friend or something. When I thought about it, sitting there in the wake of her comment, on the face of it, it felt wrong. But I couldn't help myself though. I mean, here was this very vibrant girl talking to me, who had bought me a cup of hot cocoa and spilled her life story to a total stranger. Well, I guess I wasn't truly a stranger because she and her classmates were studying *my* work. Nonetheless, she didn't *know me,* know me. Only one person really knew me: Marie.

We discussed a lot in that coffee shop: politics, crime, sports (Heather was a Braves fan through and through), religion, and other topics two people use to keep the conversation going. Time dripped from the clock that hung on the wall at the far end of the coffee shop and as I looked at it, I wanted the hands of time to stop moving for the moment. Just for a little while anyways. I wanted this time with Heather to never end. It was the best I had felt in a long while and I wanted that good feeling to last. It was perhaps the best conversation I had ever had with anyone in my entire life.

When she made her remark about my kids being nearly as old as she was, I withdrew and she knew it. I had forgotten about being forty, and there she was reminding me that I had kids practically her age. I had a mixed bag of thoughts racing through my mind. I was too old for her to be talking about life, and the deep connection I felt with her didn't strike me as creepy. I wasn't thinking about her sexually. I was struck by this young woman on a level that I had never been upon before—not even with Marie. There was just something about her. An X-factor. An intangible.

I never thought about being forty much. Most men my age and some younger than others, go through a mid-life crisis where they go out and buy a car, join a garage band, or cheat on their wife with a younger woman. And all for what? A chance, a second chance, to feel young again, to feel that fire and to abandon the silly notion that old age is for losers. Of course! The mid-life crisis is all about looking back, assessing where you came from and where you're going. If a man has arrived at his midpoint in life and doesn't like where he has ended up, he gets it into his head that he can go back, *time be damned!* But you can't go back.

That night, I hadn't made conversation with Heather in a feeble attempt to feel young again. Age had never bothered me because I was intelligent enough to not let it. Curtis had gone through a crisis when he turned thirty-six: he cheated on his wife with a nineteen-year-old intern at his agency, bought a convertible, and colored the gray out of his dark hair. But the thing he would later admit to me was that all of that didn't make him feel much better. It was a short-term distraction from an ongoing problem. For reasons unknown, Curtis didn't like where he was in life and tried to make himself feel like he was winning again. And why do men, like Curtis for example, feel like they were winning in their youth? Simple: they all had momentum.

The big difference, for me, was that I wasn't trying to take Heather to a hotel and have sex with her in an attempt to feel young again. I enjoyed talking to her because, like I said, there was an unworldly connection between us, the x-factor. We both knew it when she hit me with the glass door at the bookstore. It was our destiny. Heather, she told me later on in our relationship, knew that I didn't have any foul intentions with her like wanting her sexually or seeing nothing past her looks. She felt the same way I did. She couldn't place her finger on it, but there was something about me, spiritually, that she was drawn to.

Knowing that I wasn't trying to have sex with this woman to prove to myself ageless made me feel a little better about her calling out my age the more that I sat there and thought about it. But what she said was true. I did have a daughter who was a stone's throw of Heather's age and that in and of itself did seem a little disturbing. However, in talking with Heather, she didn't seem like any twenty-two-year-old adult I knew. I wish that I could accurately pontificate what I felt inside when I came to Heather, but words could never touch my feelings—not really.

I had talked to people her age, and they all seemed disconnected, using verbiage that only their generation knew. Heather wasn't like that at all. She spoke like I did, with insight and a keen sense of self. As our relationship blossomed, I eventually revealed to her that I knew she was an old soul when we talked at that coffee shop. Didn't take too long to say that to her, either.

"I didn't mean that you're old... I'm sorry, I shouldn't have said it like that." Heather fumbled on her words of apology.

"It's okay. It's true."

"You don't look forty. You look like you're in your late twenties. Very handsome," Heather said sheepishly.

"Yeah, we Matthews men age well. Like a fine wine. Thing is, I have never felt my age. Even when I was a kid, I felt older than I was. My friends used to make fun of me because I thought of things on a totally different plane than they did. I never knew where my maturity came from but it was always there early on."

"Me, too! My friends used to call me 'old woman.' In high school, I didn't party, drink, or smoke weed like they all did. I was always at home studying, listening to music, or reading," Heather said, revealing another layer of her soul. "I was a very boring teen." We both laughed.

"What kind of music do you like?" I asked.

"Oh, let's see... The Killers, Kings of Leon, Foo Fighters. They're my favorites. You?"

"Bob Dylan... R.E.M... and U2. I like Foo Fighters a lot, too. Saw them in concert a few years ago."

"Wow, between the two of us we've got some pretty awesome music," Heather replied.

3

Heather and I talked until the coffee shop closed and the owners had to basically throw us out into the night. When we emerged from the low-lit café, the evening air had gotten considerably cooler than it was when we first went inside. It was October, after all. Heather and I walked down the sidewalk, closely side by side, which wasn't nearly as busy as it was hours ago. There was hardly anyone walking around and most of the shops were in the process of closing for the night. The streets and buildings had nearly gone to sleep.

She and I walked closely, still talking about things like favorite movies, best childhood memories, and life in general. Nothing too profound on that first night, which we later considered our official first date. We just talked about topical things, much ado about nothing really. We were feeling each other out, so to speak. I did, however, learn a lot about her because she, just like me, was transparent, and didn't hide behind her rough edges. I loved that because it was refreshing for me to meet someone that genuine. And she was. She was more authentic than anyone I had ever met.

Heather and I walked down the sidewalk, talking and laughing without a care in the world, against the variable breeze that swirled around us. Before we knew it, we were standing by a red car parked on the side of the street next to the bookstore where we met. It was her car. "Well, this is me," Heather said, looking at me. "Hey look," she said, pointing to the bookstore door. "We met right there." She giggled.

I looked and smiled a bit. "Yeah, we did. I'll send you the doctor's bill later." I rubbed my nose and she laughed. I glanced at my watch and saw that it was late, practically midnight.

"I'd better get going. I've got a long drive ahead of me." It was one of those instances in life where you get to a juncture and cannot put thoughts into words. I wanted to say something but couldn't commit to anything worthwhile. I didn't want to leave. I didn't want the night to end. I didn't want to go home. She was the same. Heather bit her lower lip, also trying to think of what to say, eyes behind those black-rimmed glasses looking around the quiet street. But like me, she didn't say what was really on her mind because she didn't want to sound crazy. Great minds think alike.

I loved her. I know that might sound crazy and stupid, but my heart melted as soon as I saw her from the floor of the bookstore, that serendipitous event that would forever shape our future together. I couldn't just tell this enchanting girl, nearly twenty years my junior, that there was something special between us. I could not admit it, even though I profoundly felt it, felt it so much that I trembled at the thought of it. I couldn't risk looking stupid in front of her. At the time, I couldn't allow myself to think she could possibly feel the same way about me.

"I had an awesome night. Thanks for buying me hot cocoa. It was really good. And that café was perfect." I said, feeling like a bumbling teenager on a first date standing on the girl's front porch.

"No problem," Heather replied. "It was the least I could do. I mean, I did almost break your face." We both laughed.

"Yeah… well, it was very nice meeting you, and I hope you figure out what you want in life."

"Yeah, I hope so, too," Heather said, looking at me as if she didn't want that night to end there at her car underneath a streetlight. I smiled at her and turned and began to walk away up the sidewalk reluctantly, plunging my hands into my coat pockets and immediately thinking about how I was walking away from my destiny. God, what a night, I thought to myself.

Something told me to look back at her and I did. She was standing there, watching me walk away. "What?" I asked from a distance of twenty or so feet.

"I don't know," Heather replied simply. I stood there and looked at her under the light. She was angelic, standing there with her hands in her pockets, waiting for me to walk back to her. And I did as if I was drawn to her like a moth to flame.

"You okay?" I asked, already knowing what it was that she was feeling because I felt it too. Nonetheless, I couldn't work up the courage required to articulate what I was feeling. That sort of thing only happens in movies and cheap paperback novels. We smiled at each other.

Heather looked around the empty street and then back to me. Our eyes met and locked in a hypnotic trance. "I don't know. I, um, really liked talking to you. I've never been able to talk to anyone like that before. Especially someone I just met."

"Me neither," I admitted. Even with Marie, back in our golden days, I never had that dynamic Heather and I shared. "You're a pretty awesome girl, you know."

"Same here. Not the girl part though." We both laughed, breaking the tension between us. "Can I call you sometime? Maybe text you?" Heather asked, biting her lower lip again as if she was bracing herself for rejection. How could a guy reject someone so beautiful and so full of life and promise? A guy couldn't. I didn't.

"Yeah, sure. Give me your phone." I took her phone and added my number to her contacts. "There. Anytime you want to talk, call or text me, anytime," I said, trying not to get lost in my fast-moving thoughts.

"You sure? I don't want you to feel weird, as a married man and all...".

I cut her off right there, "Listen, my wife and I are only married on paper. It's not a marriage and never was. I don't even know what the hell you'd call it anymore. I don't want *you* to feel weird about calling me."

"I'll try not to. I've never talked to a married man before," Heather said with blades of honesty in her voice. She smiled nervously at me, brushing her blonde hair out of her face.

"Well that's okay, I've never talked to a twenty-two-year-old girl like this before. I guess we're even," I joked.

"This has been a strange night. Not a *bad* strange, but... a *great* strange," Heather said.

"Yeah, I just came to Atlanta to get fired from my publisher and ended up getting nailed in the face and taken out to a coffee shop by a beautiful girl. *Strange*," I said with a smile on my face.

"This is going to sound crazy but..."

"Crazier than asking a total stranger for his number? And chatting him up for hours in a coffee shop? Just kidding."

"Can I hug you before you leave?" she asked. It was the simplest request I had ever gotten from anyone in my life. I never had anyone *ask* for a hug before. But it fit the scene we were in: Two strangers in love underneath a streetlight on an early October night.

I moved closer to her and we hugged. It wasn't one of those friendly hugs, but one that was tight and full of passion fueled by a sense that we had met some place or time before. Could it have been that Heather and I were souls who had traveled through time and space only to meet once again in Atlanta on a chilly October night?

As we embraced, I could smell her intoxicating perfume and her honeysuckle hair. I had this weird sensation that I had smelled her before. It made those pesky butterflies in my stomach stir with sharp ferocity. They say smells can trigger memories of times long forgotten. Her perfume and hair took me back to a time that I couldn't recall for the life of me, but I knew that I had smelled that smell before. But when and where? I couldn't say, still can't. Maybe it was in a past life. Maybe she and I were together long ago. When we pressed our bodies together, I knew it was right; it felt familiar. I had felt her touch before; long ago, I was sure of it.

Was there such a thing as a past life? When we die, do we go to Heaven or Hell? What really happens when the lights upstairs finally go out for good? I don't believe our souls just stop. I don't. The soul is a very strong energy that cannot, even in death, be extinguished. Was it possible that Heather and I were together in another life here on earth or some other plane of existence? Why did she seem so familiar to me? Why did her perfume and hair smell so familiar? Why did this time under the streetlights seem so... right?

What if I had lived thousands of lives, without knowing it, and in each one I'd been with some version of Heather? Maybe that's why things seemed so natural between us. *What happens after this life?* I stood there and pondered. I wouldn't know, of course, until I actually died. I wondered where I'd be then. Would I even remember being alive in a new life? However, I could be just plain wrong. Perhaps there's nothing at the end of the light tunnel. *So much to think about,* I remember thinking while holding Heather. *So much to think about.*

We stood there in a passionate embrace for an eternity until a passing car broke the spell. We let go of each other and stared into one another's eyes. "That was nice," I said softly, trying not to ruin the ambiance.

"Yeah, it was," Heather replied. "I better let you get back," she said softly.

I nodded my head, "You going to call?"

"Yeah, you bet," Heather said faintly and smiled.

4

I drove home that night with thoughts of Heather and Heather alone. I had forgotten all about Marie's non-communication as I drove down the interstate in a trance, thinking about this young woman and what the future held between us; if anything. Was I stupid to think a twenty-two-year-old woman in college wanted to be with me? *What if it was destiny at play here?* I thought driving what seemed to be endless miles back home. I don't know. But I will tell you this—I was like a deer in the headlights when my mind zeroed in on her. She was all I thought about.

I thought for an instant that she only wanted me for my fame. But then again, it wasn't like I was a rock star in popular culture. I was just a writer, nothing more, and a fading one at best. I wasn't as celebrated as I once was, not like years ago, back when she was ten. God, that thought made me feel uncomfortable. I hit my professional stride when Heather was ten. I felt creepy about that. I did.

Heather was a special person and you could just feel it coming off her in waves. At least I did that night. I had never met anyone like her in my lifetime. Was it fate that we met at that bookstore? Had everything in my life and in Heather's led us both to Atlanta at that same, precise moment? Had fate drawn her bow and shot an arrow dead at us, going through Heather and into me? I certainly thought so as I drove down the road, not paying any attention to my surroundings. The yellow and white lines on the road whizzed by, and roadside landmarks went unnoticed, as my thoughts were on Heather. Honestly, I don't truly recall getting home that night. I was utterly intoxicated by this young lady.

I had ventured to the big city that day to get fired and, in another instant, found myself getting smacked in the face by a woman who would become my future. It's funny how life is. Just as one window closed, another opened wide. As I drove, I wondered what the future had in store. No way in a million years did I expect to meet a girl like Heather, but for decades I thought I had with Marie. Marie was a distant memory, though, as I drove home.

I snuck a quick peek at my phone before I got into my car that night at Windom Publishing's parking lot before I left Atlanta. I wanted to see if Marie had texted me back. Nothing—nothing from anyone that late at night. No kids texting to see if I was okay, no estranged wife checking in on me. I was a bit stunned by my children's silence. Jennifer, not so much because I was used to us not talking, after almost a decade's worth of short answers and silence. I expected her lack of communication.

Marie's silence hurt as well because I hung onto her last word every time. I hated that and, like I said before, I hated myself for allowing it to get to that point. But I was her fool, her sucker to the bitter end. I always was and I just could not help myself because I had loved her for so long. It's very difficult to just quit loving someone, let alone someone you've held onto for years. It was like trying to quit breathing. You do it and you die.

Marie had poisoned me from being able to commit to a wife whom I probably shouldn't have married in the first place. I was never right after Marie decided to be just a secret, once-a-year couple. I should have turned her down, but it was one of those take-it-or-leave-it kinds of deals that I was too weak to refuse. Having her for a weekend in October beat having her no days of the year. It was a "happy" medium that I thought I could deal with, but as the years rolled on, things wore me down to where everything around me—my empire—crumbled, and all I could do was play the fiddle as I watched it all burn. I watched everyone get hurt. I hurt everyone.

5

What if I could go back in time? I wondered on my way home that night. What if I could go back, knowing what was in store for me, and fix the hazards? Wouldn't that be nice? Perhaps I would get another shot in my next life. Would I do things differently? Yes.

Heather had given me something I had not felt in a very long time: a sense of being. I never had it from Jennifer; I mean I could have, but I never grew our marriage as I should have because of

Marie. Heather seemed to be another chance for me to be what I always wanted to be: happy. Maybe Heather *was* my second chance.

As I drove home that night from Atlanta, I thought about what it meant, in the grand scheme of things, to meet someone like Heather Parker. I wondered, in a myriad of fog, how two people from different generations could have such a connection. We both felt something as soon as we looked at each other in that bookstore. It was something cosmic. That's the best way I can explain it. Being a writer, you'd think I'd be able to spice up that description a little better. Normally I could. However, Heather had left me nearly speechless.

I never had that kind of kinship with Jennifer. For years, I'd thought Marie was my "one and only," but after meeting Heather, I started to think my relationship with Marie was merely a consequence of an unbreakable habit and an unwillingness to let go of the past. Funny what a few hours of driving down dark and winding roads alone will cause you to think. Letting go of the past meant letting go of Marie and owning my failing marriage. Heather had already made me feel I could do both.

I didn't *want* to place a whole lot of stock into Heather, I mean Christ, she was just twenty-two years old after all. But it was too late for that kind of thinking. I was already hooked, even if that small part of my brain told me not to be. What twenty-something college student knows what they want? However, at twenty I thought that I knew what I wanted. Well, I *did*, a matter of fact. I wanted to be with Marie forever. Was it possible that a girl like Heather wanted me? And why me? Then I began to think about our connection that seemed so magical. Our connection was profoundly strong, even though we had only known each other for a handful of hours.

Time seemed to stand still for the two of us back in Atlanta. It was as if fate had ceased the hands of time to give us enough time to talk and get to know each other in that coffee shop. It was the best time I had ever had with a woman, including Marie and Jennifer. For a little while, I had forgotten all about being a washed-up writer. For a little while, I had forgotten about Marie. For a little while, nothing and no one else mattered to me, except Heather.

CHAPTER SEVEN

1

Over the successive weeks as October drew to a close, and before my annual weekend tryst with Marie, Heather and I talked on the phone daily, sometimes for hours on end. And when we weren't talking on the phone, we were texting. We never ran out of things to say to one another, constantly diving into conversations both deep and trivial in nature. Never had I talked to anyone as worldly as she, even though she was younger than me. Everything was in a very good place between us. The best things in life sometimes come out of nowhere, hitting you right in the face with a glass door in a bookstore.

2

The more I talked to her, the more I fell in love with her. It was never my intention to fall in love again. Marie had been my North Star for so long that I didn't even entertain the notion that there could ever be another. There was just something about her that seemed right, pretty much as it was with Marie back in the good ol' days. I had that pang of longing in the pit of my stomach. With Marie, I had begun to wonder whether there really were ever "good ol' days." Or were what I deemed "the good ol' days" simply an illusion that my misled heart had given me? Probably.

3

How were things around my home during my budding relationship with Heather? Normal, I guess. Whatever passes for normal at my house. Samantha was becoming more and more of a ghost in the house. She was spending most of her time with Randy, which was fine with me. I knew she loved him. I would only object to their relationship later on when Samantha told me about her future plans. But for now, at that point in my world, she and I were fine. We always seemed to be for the most part back then. That's why our falling out broke my heart. I never fully recovered from that blow because we fell out hard. The best way I can describe it is that I was a boxer in a ring. When Samantha and I had our relationship-killing fight, it was like I was knocked to the ground and got up, groggy on an 8 count. And then, after what happened with Davey, what was left of me in the ring was knocked to the floor and left unable to get up again. Heather had to pick up and carry what was left—which wasn't much.

Davey was his usual self around the house, too. I couldn't tell if he was having problems or not. He would come home from school and dart into his bedroom and sometimes not even come out for dinner, which was usually either pizza or burgers. I wanted to try to bring him back to the Davey I knew from years ago, but that wasn't going to happen. He was too withdrawn, too cold to thaw, and I was too wrapped up with Heather to fully comprehend what was about to happen. I wish I'd been more cognizant of what was happening to him. But I wasn't being a good father to my son. I know that now— doesn't help to know in the present tense.

It's not that I didn't care about Davey—I did, very much so. The effort it would have taken to break him from his funk was something I was just too lazy to do when it came down to it. So was his mother. She was just as much to blame as I was. But I guess I blame myself more because I was home more than she was. I saw the signs, at least I tell myself that I did. So I just let Davey be Davey. I wish that I would've done more. Maybe I could've prevented his death. Hard to say what a little forced intervention would've done. I blame myself more than anyone could ever imagine. I failed him as a father....

Jennifer, just like everyone else in the house, had become a memory, a ghost that haunted our home. I was okay with it because that had been the norm for years. After I found out why she was more distant than usual, I looked back and began to see what had been going on the entire time. Sometimes the answers are right in front of us, staring at us. Sometimes you see the forest but not the trees.

Jennifer was falling apart and was slowly becoming an emotional cripple, not by me and not by Davey's eventual death, but by something that had happened in her life. Her second life, I called it, her hidden life. I got my first glimpse of it the day I talked to her in our driveway before traveling to Atlanta. I knew something was amiss then and afterward when her secret was revealed, everything clicked. It was all right there, staring at me. I had seen the forest but totally missed the trees.

4

I sat in the living room one uneventful afternoon, watching the Braves playoff game on the big TV. It was a businessman special against the Dodgers. For the baseball illiterate, a "businessman special" is when teams play during the middle of the week, usually one o'clock. An odd time for a team that usually plays during evening or nighttime hours. TV networks had dictated the playoff times of teams these days, and I was all right with that. Hell, the Braves were in the playoffs and I was happy.

Anyway, I sat there with nothing to do, nothing pressing at the time, and the house all to myself. The kids were at school and Jennifer was doing whatever it was Jennifer did. The last time I saw her for longer than a minute, she had been crying in her car in the driveway before I left for Atlanta. I briefly wondered what had been wrong. And then I tabled that wonderment as Freddie Freeman crushed a two-run double off of Kershaw in the third.

I got up from the couch to get a Coke from the fridge when my cell phone chirped. I walked through the dining room and back to the living room to pick it up. It was Heather. "Hello."

"Jerry, what's up?" said asked in her sweet voice.

"Hey, not much!" I said excitedly. "Just watching the game."

"They winning?"

"Down by one in the third. Freddie just doubled in two runs against Kershaw."

"Good." It was neat to have a girl in my life who loved baseball and the Braves as much as I did.

"How's your day?" I asked, getting myself comfortable on the couch.

"Fine, I guess. Just finished up my world history class. I hate that class. So boring. I think it might be because of Professor Morgan. His voice is so monotonous that you literally fall asleep in class."

"Yeah, sounds about right. I had a teacher like that in high school. One day he's up there teaching and keeps looking at me. I turned around and looked, and everyone else in the class had their heads down, sleeping. Any more classes today?"

"No, thank God. I'm done for the day. I've got some biology stuff to go over for an exam this Friday, but other than that it's going to be a very quiet week on the homework front."

"Yeah, I've got homework but it's actually *work*, work."

"When do you think your novel will be finished?"

"I don't know. I don't care really. It's my final book with Windom. Why give them something great? I'm conflicted, I guess. I want to finish with Windom on a high note, but I think this novel was doomed from the start. I wasn't really invested in it. It's parts of different novels and shorts that I had started writing years ago that I'm patching together." A lot of that was the drinking mixed with the fucks I didn't give. I owed Bobby Windom my life, really, and didn't want to mail it in like I had in the past. *But what the hell,* I told myself day in and day out while trying to write this new, contract-ending novel, *I'd given him trash with the last several novels. Why stop now that I'm leaving?*

"Well, when you're out of your contract, start on something else. Show them that you're still that great writer."

"I don't know," I said, not wanting to jump into the writing game again so quickly. When Bob implied I couldn't write anything good anymore, I left his office fired up and wanted to write the next great American novel. And I had every intention to actually do it. I did. But as time passed, my energy had waned. Getting back into my office and trying seemed too hard. Maybe after the playoffs. If the Braves lost, then maybe. (They did lose, by the way.)

"I read a quote from you the other day. You said: A writer always writes; they can't help it," Heather said.

I didn't know where or when I said that, but it sounded like something the young and hungry Jerry Matthews would have said, back when things were awesome and good and new. The Jerry Matthews of now was a dimmer, more cynical man, often hungover. I was a relic for passersby to see. I was okay with that. "Yeah I might have said that, but that was probably a long time ago. When I feel good again, I might write something. I mean I've got something on the hard drive. It's not much, but it's good. Maybe I'll dust that off and work on it. Who knows?"

After some more idle chitchat, Heather asked me the question I wanted to hear. "When do you want to get together?" She asked.

"I don't know. Soon. Seems like we haven't seen each other in years."

"Weekend is good for me, you?"

"Should be. I don't think there's anything pressing I've gotta do. I pretty much make my own hours, you know?"

"Cool. I know just the place we can go," Heather said with excitement in her voice.

"Where?"

"Can't tell you. You'll just have to wait. It'd ruin the surprise."

"I can do that," I replied as Brian McCann cranked a towering homerun over the right-field fence, putting the Braves in the lead.

5

The weekend came and led me to Atlanta to see Heather Parker. It was our second date (only if you count our coffee shop night as a date), and over the days prior, Heather kept silent on what she had in store for us. I wondered what the girl had planned. Was it a dinner for the two of us; a movie; a road trip or something that I had not even thought about? It really didn't matter because just being with her would be fine with me. I needed to see her, rather than gaze at the pictures she sent me on my phone.

All I knew was I had driven hours south to see a girl who I barely knew, but somehow knew all too well at the same time. Did I love her at that point, even though I hardly knew her? Yes. On the surface, I should have been ashamed of myself for stepping out on my wife. But I had committed that treason years ago with Marie. And what of Marie lately? Hadn't texted or talked to her since my Windom trip. That said all that I needed to know.

With Heather, I didn't see it as *betrayal* either because there was something different with her. I guess you could make the case I was rationalizing what I was doing. And you might be correct. Who's to say? It felt like I had known Heather for centuries. The connection I had had with Marie was pretty much null and void by comparison. Besides, Jennifer was off with some other guy. I never saw her actions as treachery. I simply didn't care. Hell, I had driven her to it. If anything, she deserved to be happy for everything I put her through.

There was something about Heather that just seemed right. Not just in my mind, but in my heart and soul. Maybe that's why it was so different. Marie had me for so long that my feelings had gotten manipulated over the passing decades. I held dear to those feelings that she was *the one*. Hell, I had even fucked my own marriage up, wrecking a woman to whom I had verbally committed in a formal ceremony over my feelings for Marie. It was all my choosing, though. I can't place the blame at anyone's doorstep but my own. Sometimes I sit and wonder if I had the opportunity to take it back, to fix our marriage, would I?

On the surface, I had destroyed what could have been a perfectly good marriage, and for what? Holding out on hope that Marie, the true love of my life, would eventually wake up from her self-imposed sanction against marriage to take my hand? It was silly to think that, after twenty-plus years, Marie was ever going to commit to me. She never was. Never planned to, either.

Jennifer should have left me a long time ago. I wouldn't have blamed her if she had. I expected her to, but she stayed, I think, for the most part, because of our children and in some part for the comfortable lifestyle I had afforded my family. I mean, she could have taken me to the cleaners through a divorce, but she didn't. I often wonder why she didn't when I thought about how I treated her throughout our marriage. A normal woman would have, but I think she was holding out in the hope that I would eventually snap out of whatever funk I was in. However, after all those years, I think she just gave up, almost like I had with Marie. With Marie, I still had a—albeit faint—flicker of hope that she would call me up and announce she was ready to settle down. Jennifer perhaps had hope, but it was about as bright as a burning match in pouring rain.

I had begun to look at Heather as a new beginning, even though we had only known each other for a very short time, in this life. But things felt different with her; I felt as though I belonged and was wanted. It was a confluence of feelings that I had never experienced before. With Marie, I felt as if I belonged, and with Jennifer, I felt as if I was wanted, in the beginning anyway. But Heather was the first woman with whom I experienced both feelings.

Where is my relationship with Heather going? Another question I posed myself while driving south. Who was I kidding? Questions like that had run through my mind over and over again, back at home up in my office, around the house that I haunted like a ghost, out in the backyard, and all points in between. I turned Heather Parker around and around in my mind a million times.

In the end, man is judged by his actions and his actions upon others. I had made Jennifer Samantha, and Davey's lives bad. It could have been better and I know that. I was the reason that it got sideways. I was at the controls, no one else.

6

That evening, just as the sun was about to dip its golden rays into the horizon, I pulled into an empty gravel parking lot surrounded by towering pine trees. It was a local park, miles from Atlanta, in a neighborhood where Heather had grown up as a kid. I parked the car and sat there, looking around at the still landscape. It was beautiful with the sun's last flickering rays touching everything in the park.

Just as I was about to text Heather to see where she was, her car pulled into the lot from the opposite direction. I got out as she parked beside me. She got out, smiling at me. "Hello," she said as she walked around to me. I stood there, watching her move with such elegance that I thought I was dreaming in daylight, dreaming with my eyes wide open.

"Hey," I said, stricken by her beauty. It had been weeks since I had seen her face in person, and I had forgotten how pretty she was with her blonde hair, black-rimmed glasses, and a baggy sweatshirt, a different one from the day we first met.

"Is the venue okay?" Heather asked.

I looked around. "Are you kidding? This place is amazing. And you used to come down here as a little girl?"

"Yeah, all the time. My parents live just over that hill, at the farmhouse about two miles from here. I used to ride my bike down here and play all the time. Beautiful, isn't it?" Heather said, admiring the landscape.

"Yeah, it sure is." I looked around at the place where Heather frequented as a child.

"Trouble finding it?" she asked as she went around to her trunk.

"No, thanks to the good ol' navigation on my phone, I found it with no problem," I said, unable to take my eyes off her. "So, what's the big secret?" I asked, watching her pull a huge blanket and flashlight from her trunk.

"There's a place right above that hill, just past the pine trees there. I used to sit and look at the stars, sometimes with the telescope I got for Christmas when I was fourteen. Up there is the best seat in the house. And according to the weather reports, it's going to be cool and clear. Great night for stargazing. I hope it doesn't sound too cheesy," she said, looking at me with a sly grin. Cheesy or not, there was no way I was going to miss a night like this with a girl like her.

"Wow," I replied, floored by her simple plan for the evening. "I love it. I used to do the same thing back where I grew up. Of course, I lived in the city so I couldn't see the stars from my backyard that well. But that never stopped me from trying. I remember going to spend the weekends with my grandparents—they lived way out in the country, and it would get so dark, it was like you were blind. But man, when the moon and stars were out, it was something else."

"I just thought it would be cool to watch the stars. Paul used to think I was so childish for always wanting to do it." Heather recalled, mentioning her ex-boyfriend. Heather had spoken about Paul a few times during our many phone conversations. I could tell by her tone that she didn't like talking about him. But she did reluctantly. After all, no matter how horrible a person he was, he was still part of her past. I would meet Paul later. Things didn't end very well.

"It's not stupid. It's the best thing out there to do. I don't think people appreciate what we have to look at on a daily basis," I replied.

"Me neither," Heather said, grabbing me by the arm. "We'd better get to walking because it'll be dark soon."

7

She and I found her spot on top of the hill that overlooked the entire park. It was one of the most beautiful vantage points I had ever seen in my life, something out of a painting that I'd seen once—a great panoramic view. Heather unfolded the blanket and flung it out and laid it down over grass that was already gathering the nightly dew. From where we sat, leaned back on a huge fallen oak tree trunk (that had been there for decades, Heather had informed me), we could see the dark sky displaying all its twinkling and shimmering stars already. It was awesome. Darkness was slowly pushing away the light. The temperature was changing and crickets began their musicals. It was a perfect setting.

That scene will forever stay etched into my brain. When I lay dying on the living room floor of my and Heather's new house, my mind flashed thousands upon thousands of mental images saved over my lifetime, like a hard drive. That scene there on the hill under the stars was one of them. It went quickly past my eyes, but I could see it in my time of dying. If not for all the pain, I would've smiled.

My arm was around her and she was snuggled close to me. Even though the night was cool, we were warm from our sweatshirts and body heat pressed together. We didn't talk much as it had gotten darker. We sat quietly watching the stars show themselves, twinkling like tiny dancers in a cosmic play. It was grand.

I used to do that kind of stuff with Marie, back in the old days when we were younger. But I swear to God it never felt anything remotely similar to what Heather and I were doing that night. It just seemed so *right*, being there with her and watching something up in the sky like that. To this very day, I can barely put into words what that moment meant to me. I loved Heather. I did from the very beginning, if I'm being completely honest here; despite what I had tried to tell myself before.

"What are you thinking about?" Heather asked softly after some time had passed.

"Just about how good this is. Just... wow. This is amazing," I replied, trying but failing to explain it to her. As a writer, it was my job to paint the blind reader a picture of what was going on. On that night, I couldn't paint it. No brushes. No paint.

"Thank you for coming. I didn't know if you would," she said, lying against my right side with my arm draped over her, keeping her warm and close.

"Why?" I asked, scanning my eyes across the night sky.

"I don't know. Maybe I thought you just thought I'm a stupid dumb kid or something."

"You're twenty-two years old. The *most* mature twenty-year-old I've ever met. You're not a dumb kid. You're a very attractive and intelligent young woman. Any guy on this earth would be lucky to be sitting here with you right now like this. I'm just glad you decided to spend it with me," I told her, trying to build up her confidence. For some reason, Paul had pulled her down. I guess some guys are dicks like that. I was a dick like that with Jennifer. I knew of what I spoke.

"You're sweet, you know that?" Heather told me.

I sat there, holding her and thinking about how wrong she was. "Listen, I ain't sweet. Far from it."

"Because of your wife?" Heather asked with her head on my chest, gazing at the sky.

"Yeah, that's some of it, I guess. There are other things, too. Stuff you don't know about me."

"You're not some closet serial killer that gets ideas for his books by killing people, are you?" Heather quipped.

I didn't say anything and just sat there until I heard her laugh. "Not funny," I said, nudging and tickling her.

"No, I'm a very complicated man."

"Well, we're all complicated," Heather replied.

"Yeah, but I've done stuff that I shouldn't have," I said, thinking about a few of my missteps.

8

As I sat stargazing with perhaps the most amazing woman I'd ever met, I felt a pang inside my stomach. It was something that told me I could tell her anything, stuff that I had held inside the far reaches of my soul. I had spilled some of it to my daughter, to Curtis, but not a *full disclosure*. I mean, there was just some stuff that you can't tell anyone, for fear of destroying their impression of you.

Heather made me feel at peace and comfortable enough to tell her anything. Although I had only known her for a few weeks, I felt that I could tell her everything. And I did. "My marriage didn't work because of all the things that I have done. I pushed her away for so long that she went looking for love and affection in other places. I really fucked her up. Bad."

"Why did you do it?" Heather asked, not taking her eyes off the dark sky and twinkling stars after soaking in my words.

"A woman. I um...I was in love with this woman from my childhood. We dated off and on, were best friends, and all that. We met in the fifth grade and since then she's had a hold of me. I've never gotten completely away from her. We just had so much history together that I always thought we'd end up together one day. I thought she and I were destined to be together, you know?"

"She didn't feel the same, did she?"

I shook my head as I held Heather close on the cool October night. "No. I asked her to marry me the night before I married my wife, but she rejected me. Tough pill to swallow. Should have ended it right then and there, but I just couldn't bring myself to do it. I walked away from her, thinking we were through, but she called me after I got married and back from my honeymoon, and I fell for her all over again. Just hearing her voice made me fall again. I wish to God that I would've never answered that phone call. Because I had at that point I think, broke it off with her and moved on. As much as I could, you know.

"She and I have this arrangement every year on the last weekend of October, we go to her father's lake house and spend the weekend together. We've been doing that for as long as I can remember. Since we were both able to drive." There was a silence after that. Heather and I were both lost in our separate thoughts. I felt naked sitting there because there I was, baring my soul. I was stripping myself down to my simplest form, admitting things I had repressed. I hated myself for loving Marie and had said that numerous times in the past. It was the truth. The truth was I wish I had been better for Jennifer.

"Why didn't you quit seeing her?" Heather asked.

I took a few moments to reply because I was thinking about all the past October weekends with Marie, "Love is a strong bond. History, too. We had both. Or at least I did. I couldn't quit her, even if I tried. I was addicted and clung to a false hope that she and I would end up together. After all those years, I was still the same stupid kid as when I first saw her. One look was all it took."

"So almost twenty years, you've loved the same woman who never fully loved you back, and you jeopardized your entire marriage and family?" Heather concluded.

"Yeah, that's it," I said flatly. "I didn't want to get married to Jennifer. I guess I wanted to be *wanted* by someone because all Marie wanted was me on her terms. And I hated her for that, hated her for making me into the monster that I have become. After I started seeing the toll it's taken on Jennifer, I started drinking and then that's when everything began to slip. Over the years I got so consumed with both Marie and my own self-loathing that I neglected my kids, too. I tried to be the best father, but as they got older, I checked out."

"Why didn't you just divorce Jennifer? That would have been the best solution. Shouldn't have put her through that if you didn't love her," Heather said.

"When you have kids involved, it ain't that easy. I stayed because I didn't want them to be screwed up by a divorce. Really didn't want to see Jennifer bringing guys in and out of their lives. But in trying to protect them from *my* bullshit, I created more problems for them than I anticipated. I never wanted to hurt them, but in the end, I have. There's so much that I broke and can't fix," I said, watching a falling star streak across the sky in a flash and fury.

"You don't wear a wedding ring. Why?" She asked, rubbing her fingers against mine, where my ring should have been.

"A ring is a symbol," I said. "I didn't deserve to wear one because my marriage isn't a marriage, and it wasn't from the beginning. It was just a vehicle for me not to be alone. I used her and pushed her away over a woman who rejected me. And that's the bare, honest-to-God truth right there. It's really fucking terrible when I say it out loud, you know?" I said, knowing the errors of my ways. It's funny when you see the big picture, you begin to realize how much of the problem you created. All the bullshit and turbulence that had ensnarled my life, and set into an unstoppable motion that ruined Jennifer, Samantha, and Davey's lives. I was not the victim Samantha thought I was, but instead the predator. I was the cause.

"Do you still talk to her? Marie?" Heather asked.

"Yeah, I texted Marie a while back, but she never replied. I've always talked to her; that's my problem. At first, when Jennifer and I got married, I took her calls reluctantly because I was then trying to be a real husband, but I eventually got weak and became consumed by how much I loved Marie.

"Then we started talking all the time again. That was the M.O. of our relationship. She was a taker, I was a giver, and she knew it. That's why it's so easy for her and so hard for me. She knows how to play me, and I've allowed her to do it."

"Do you think you can leave her alone? I mean, do you ever see a life where you can just stop?"

I sat there for a minute or two, considering what she asked. "I want to, I really do. I can safely say that right now, I feel like I can. For the first real time."

"Why is that?"

I held Heather closer to me, tighter. "Because of you. I feel like we've got something that transcends anything that I've ever known. With Marie, I never felt like this as I do with you. Even with Jennifer. I feel right with you...like I belong here. And I know that sounds crazy, but that's how it is. I know we've only known each other—"

"I know," Heather cut me off before I got long-winded as I tend to do. "Feel the same. I've never been in this much love before, in such a short amount of time. And I wanted to tell you how much I loved you a few weeks ago. It hurt to hold it inside. But I didn't want to scare you away or make you think I was crazy or a stalker. But it was love at first sight."

I was stunned by what she said. Those butterflies in my stomach fluttered once again. I stood up from the tree trunk and, in the process, Heather rose with me. I looked at her dead in her hazel eyes and asked, "What did you say?"

Heather looked at me in my eyes for a few seconds and smiled, "I'm in love with you. The heart wants what the heart wants." I stood there, looking at Heather, and my heart melted like ice on a sidewalk in the summertime.

"I'm in love with you, too," I replied. We looked at each other deeply and then we slowly both began to lean toward each other. And when our lips locked, it wasn't a simple kiss shared by first-time lovers. Our kiss was full of passion and sent me into a world that I'd never been in before. I got lost in her kiss as my eyes closed and my hands on her shoulders trembled a bit. I had never felt like that before; it was uncharted waters for me.

After we stopped kissing and pulled back to look at each other I spoke. "Do you think you can handle being with an older man? This could get messy. I mean, I'm a handful." I half-joked.

"Do you think you can handle being with a twenty-two-year-old woman? Because I can be a handful, too." Heather asked with a lovely smile etched across her flawless face.

"Touché," I replied, looking at the love of my life. For the rest of that night, until the wee hours of the morning, we sat against that tree trunk and watched the stars. If I had died right then and there, I would've done so a happy man. It was magic.

CHAPTER EIGHT

1

Some time had elapsed since Heather and I had our second date at the park. And within that time frame, something exciting happened to me; I began to *smile* and *feel* a little bit more. Most importantly, I began to write again and drink less and less, until I was no longer finishing a bottle of Jack in a single night.

I was writing good stuff again—not that bullshit I was turning into Windom, but good stuff. Stuff like I used to write when I cared and when things were right. I was feeling like my old self again.

When I sat down behind my desk to read over the novel that had been floating around in my hard drive for some time, I decided to cull the entire thing. The manuscript read like a child had written it, and it was all over the place with subplots going in all kinds of directions. It was the usual stuff that I was phoning into Windom. Meeting Heather had jarred something inside my head. I had my drive again. And that drive turned on the lights inside my mind, once again, getting those creative juices flowing. I was smart enough to know that when the lights come on up in your head and the power that makes the gears move, you go with it and ride it for as long as you can because you don't know when it will stop.

2

My work on that first draft was typed and fleshed out with no emotion, no feeling or professionalism whatsoever. After Heather and I met and our souls connected, I became something better. It was like a light in a dark basement had turned on, and in that light, I could see things that I had abandoned in the darkness—my true self, the person that I used to be a long time ago. I liked that guy. I wanted to see more of him.

I erased the entire novel in my computer and decided to overhaul months and months of worthless work. Honestly, what I had written couldn't be called work, maybe more of just sitting there and hoping in earnest that something good would come of it. But after meeting Heather, I felt better, felt more...*alive.* So, taking my new emotions, I decided to return to it with a new set of eyes. And so I began a journey that would run me through several sleepless nights of work. It was exciting to feel that way again.

At the time as I stroked the keys, I had convinced myself I was writing the next American masterpiece. I would only later learn I had overestimated an ability that had left me some books ago. It really wasn't my ability to write; it was that I had trashed my good name with all those horrible books. My fans, growing smaller in numbers, especially after word hit the streets that I wasn't under contract anymore, began to not even care if I had anything out or not. I was attempting a comeback, but the question was, would anyone care?

3

The funny thing about having talent is that everyone, myself included, had come to expect good things from me. Like every book or story I penned would turn to gold. And, for the most part, they did. I cranked out book after book and made hand over fist in money, especially in my early days. At one time, I was the most popular and widely read author in the United States. But once I started thinking that anything and everything I wrote would be eaten up by fans, I began to get sloppy with my craft. And when I got sloppy, I didn't care as much. So Jack Daniels and I had become good friends.

You can tell, in the books I wrote, where my care dwindled. It was a slippery slope that took no time at all to hit rock bottom. And when I did, I crashed and didn't realize the toll it had taken until I was called to Atlanta to be released from my publisher. God, looking back at how distracted and depressed I was, it was a wonder that I could even write anything. The last three books were disastrous, I knew that and didn't need an online message board to tell me.

The deep dark truth of the matter was that I wasn't the way I once was. I knew that I had taken my eye off the ball and allowed myself to become self-involved with my inner demons. Things around me had suffered greatly: namely my marriage, my children, and my career. And after I allowed things to get in the way of my goals, everything fell. Marie was the root cause of all my sorrow. I let her consume me, my life, so much that I didn't care enough to keep all those before-mentioned things afloat.

4

In all honesty, I didn't know that I could get back on the horse and become a great writer again. It was a daunting task I didn't know I was up to tackle. But meeting Heather changed all that. Meeting her had flipped a switch inside of me and made me come out of the darkness that had consumed me for so long. Having her by my side, I thought I could fly and touch the sky. These wings of mine weren't wax, and the sun be damned.

Having a person like Heather in my life had given me something that I hadn't had in a long while: purpose, a sense of being. With her in my life, I could thaw my feelings that had turned to ice over the years. My imagination flickered back on, and my mind began to turn like it used to. Soon, I found myself in my office reading over the novel I had almost finished way back when. It was horrible, nowhere close to the standards of my peak career. It was going to be my comeback. In all reality, I shouldn't have had a comeback. I should have never left in the first place.

5

The words flowed like they used to. My fingers had a difficult time keeping up with my thoughts. Scenes from the novel spewed from my mind as the characters talked, and my attention was focused with laser-like concentration that I used to have back when writing was new and fun for me. My comeback novel was in full swing. I was feeling great.

When I decided to take a break one night and lean back in my chair to gather myself, I had written over twenty thousand words of a novel that was to surely launch me back into the forefront of acclaimed literature. Looking at the owl clock that hung over the mantle in my office, I saw that my twenty-thousand-word marathon had taken me nearly twelve and a half hours. Not too bad. I was writing again but not under a contract. Curtis was right: With the Internet and self-publishing, I could be a big name again. All I had to do was hit a home run. I was digging in the batter's box.

6

The story I had become enthralled with was about a kid who grew up in a small town with four best friends. My book dealt with their lives together as they grew up and apart after they all left for college, only to be brought together by a friend's fatal car accident decades later. It was a story I wrote from the heart because I wanted friends like that when I was growing up. But I never had the experiences I wrote about. Never had the loyalty my four main characters shared. I longed for what I transferred onto the pages of my novel. Sometimes writers do that—we project our pains, fears, hopes, dreams, and our personalities onto the paper and into the characters that we create. Ask any writer and they'll tell you that most if not all of their characters have a characteristic or two of themselves.

7

Growing up, I had one best friend: Steve Maddux. Steve and I met in the fourth grade and became fast friends. We had the same taste in music, girls, and baseball. And to boot, he lived a block from my house on Shady Grove Lane. I can't count the days that I would hop on my bike and pedal over to his house. And from there, he and I would just let the day surprise us.

Sometimes we rode our bikes through our small town. Some days we would shoot hoops at the basketball courts in the park. Some days we would hang out at my house and play video games and read comics. And some days we would play a simple game of catch in his backyard while his dad mowed the lawn. Those were *the good old days*. I haven't had times like that since then.

Steve was around when Marie first captivated my attention. And as we all grew older, Steve would pick up the pieces of my shattered soul and try to put me back together again. He did it successfully every time only to have to do it once more when Marie would break my heart again. I can't tell you how many times Steve fixed me back in those days. God, I wonder where my life would have gone if I had Steve around throughout adulthood. No telling. Someplace different, I know that.

During our sophomore year, just as I was getting settled into my turbulent high school career, something happened to me that changed everything. Steve's untimely death was one of the most difficult things I had ever faced up to that point in my young life. Even now, I get a lump in my throat when I think about him.

He was such a huge figure in my life and made an everlasting impact on me. I dedicated my first book to him because he always encouraged me to write and pursue it as a career. He believed in my work and future before I did. Had it not been for him, there wouldn't have been a Jerry Matthews, a best-selling writer. There would have just been a plain guy in a plain town named Jerry Matthews. *Would that have been so terrible?* I often wondered.

He would read my work, give me his thoughts, and challenge me to do better. Sometimes I hated him for having such a low opinion of my writing, but he was right. Steve made me a better writer by pushing me. I owe my talent to him because he was the only one who saw my potential and made me better. Had it not been for Steve, I may not have been as good as I was or as sharp. I could have easily given up, but he told me, "Never."

Steve died in a car accident on his way home from a baseball game where he pitched the school's first no-hitter. It was such a great day for the guy. I was watching in the stands, having no idea that I was about to see my best friend make school history. And I didn't think about what he was trying to accomplish until the ninth inning when he struck out the last batter for the feat. The crowd rose to our collective feet and screamed and cheered as Steve's teammates poured onto the field to congratulate him. They hoisted Steve up onto their shoulders as if he were a king. And for a little while he was.

I'll never forget that image for as long as I live. I have the newspaper article about Steve's no-hitter in a picture frame hanging on my office wall. I look at it from time to time, thinking about him and getting that lump in my throat when I remember him being carried off the field in triumph by his teammates. He will always be captured in the black-and-white image of forever youth. Who knows what he could have done if he had lived past that day? *Great things*, I imagine.

8

I had written about half of my new novel—well, the first or second draft anyway—and sat in Heather's living room, sipping on some hot chocolate and looking out her huge bay window as rain streaked down the panes. She had wanted to read what I had been writing. At first, I told her no because I wasn't ready for outside eyes just yet. But as I began to feel better about my craft once again, I decided to let her read what I had gotten down so far, albeit reluctantly.

It was strange to me because, out of all the books I had ever written, Jennifer never wanted to read any of them. As far as I knew, she had never read *anything* I wrote. That made me sad because it was like she didn't care. Maybe it was only the money she cared about. Who's to say, really? I don't know. Maybe she just didn't "get" my writing. Maybe all I was to her was a cash cow, a good lifestyle. No clue.

I wished I didn't need a comeback. But there I was, needing one to jumpstart my career again. It was entirely my fault. Who else was to blame for taking my eyes off the ball? I had just gotten lazy, plain and simple. When you're a writer and get lazy like I did, fans begin to leave; even the hardcore ones stop buying and start slamming you on their blogs. It happened to me in droves.

Meeting Heather had cleared the cobwebs from my brain. Quickly, the wheels inside my head began to turn, getting my brain to think like the writer I had been back in the old days. And you know what? It felt good. I felt alive, electric even, as I sat alone in my office, hammering away at the keyboard like a man possessed. And as far as the drinking? I had scaled back to hardly any.

9

After several cups of hot chocolate and several paces around her apartment, Heather finally took her eyes away from my laptop and closed it. She looked at me with tired eyes behind her black-rim glasses and just stared at me.

"What? Was it that bad?" I asked, not knowing what she was thinking. Heather sat there and looked around the room with her mouth slightly open as she thought about what to say.

"Wow. This is really dramatic so far. I mean, wow," she said, with a look of being blown away by my written words.

"You think it's a hit?" I asked nervously because I didn't know.

Heather nodded. "Yeah, I think this book is the best you've ever written. The characters, the plot, *the town*... you've made them all come alive on those pages. I have no idea how you do it."

I stood there looking at Heather who sat on the couch, legs crossed with the closed laptop in her lap.

"So, this is my comeback then?"

"You never left," Heather replied as I stood, looking at her while holding my mug of hot chocolate. Thunder cracked across the sky outside, rattling the walls of her apartment.

10

A few days later back in my office, I was in the middle of writing the last third of my novel. I had sat in my office for what felt like days, only coming out to use the bathroom down the hall or to grab something to eat. *What Is and What Will Never Be* was engrossing me in every way. I hardly drank anything, barely ate, and never left the office unless it was truly necessary. I hadn't done that before. Not even with my first books, when I was a fully-fledged writer, did I give my complete attention to a writing job. But there was something about this book, though. Maybe there was more on the line this time around. Perhaps it was because I hadn't written anything of honest personal value in a long time and I had forgotten what it felt like.

Perhaps it was me proving to myself that I was still a good writer. And by the way, the words rolled off my fingertips, I still was. Hell, I was better than I was when everything was new. The artistic explosion that was going on inside of me was exciting and different. I owed it all to the girl of my dreams, Heather. Had it not been for her, my book would have never been written—at least, it wouldn't have been that good. Not in a million years.

However, during my Great Awakening, I did neglect some things around the house—namely, my kids. Davey was still Davey of course, introverted and withdrawn becoming more so by the hour, barely even being seen in the house. Samantha would see me walking down the hallway in the same clothes that she had seen me in the day before. We would stand in the hallway and talk a little, but before long I was sequestered back in my office.

11

I remember a day—importantly—a conversation, that occurred just before Davey's suicide. I was in my office, leaning back in my chair with my eyes closed, thinking. Not of the book or anything in particular, but just thinking thoughts that came and went like fireflies in the night sky. I was rattled out of my contemplative state by a knock at the door. I opened my eyes and yelled out for the knocker to enter. The door slowly creaked open, and in came my daughter. "Got a minute?"

"Of course, come in. I've got lots of minutes. I was just resting my eyes. What's up?" I asked, looking at Samantha walk across the room and sit down on the couch opposite my desk.

"Nothing much. Just thought that I'd actually visit with my dad instead of bumping into him down the hall on occasion."

"Yeah, I've been pretty preoccupied lately, huh?" I said, looking at my daughter. She seemed to have something on her mind. Father's intuition.

"Yeah, maybe. I've got one parent off the reservation and don't need another one to go."

"You're right about *that*, kiddo. It's just there's been a lot going on with me lately, I guess. I've been too scattered," I said, chuckling.

"Why?"

Samantha was talking to me not like my child but instead as an adult. She cared about me. She cared about my feelings, too. That was the dynamic Samantha and I always had. We were two of a kind. "It's been a strange few weeks for me. Umm..." I began to think back a bit. "Well, first off, I was let go from my contract at the publisher."

"Oh my God, what does that mean?" Samantha said with concern in her voice. Up to that point, I kept my Atlanta trip a secret. No need to tell people that my contract wasn't getting renewed. Why rock the boat?

"Well, it means that I'm a free agent. I sent in my last novella, *Tricks of the Trade*, to them and that was it. Poof! No longer the great writer I once was."

"So what are you going to do since you're out? Uncle Curtis going to get you a new contract someplace?"

I shook my head, "Nah, I'm on my own. But thanks to the internet, I'm going to self-publish the book I'm working on right now. With my name recognition, I should be able to bounce back. Plus, I'll be able to make more money this way, too. I just got to get back to good again. It's kind of a semi-retirement."

"'Back to good'?" Samantha repeated with an incredulous look on her face.

"Yeah, I stopped being a good writer a long time ago. I practically gave up because I had so much going on inside my head that I just couldn't write anymore. Didn't really want to. So... I just sat and wrote complete and utter shit and tried to pass it off as my next great work. Lost my fan base along the way."

"How are you getting your mojo back then?" Samantha quizzed.

"Well, *that's* an entirely different story," I began. I was going to level with Samantha just as I had regarding the state of her mother's and my marriage a while back on the deck. She handled the truth about Jennifer and me so I felt as if she could handle the truth about me meeting the love of my life, Heather. "I met someone," I said, lowering my head and eyes so I could not see my daughter's reaction. I did, however, keep Heather's age a secret.

After a few moments of silence, I slowly raised my head to see Samantha's face. And to my surprise, she wasn't shocked. Sure, she was a bit stunned by my news, but not shocked to the point that it shook her to her very core. "You love her?" Samantha asked plainly

Without any hesitation, I spoke. "I do... very much," I said, with some guilt, which probably came from telling my child I was in love with a woman who wasn't her mother. I had some trepidation when I exposed my secrets to her about Marie, but opening the closet and telling her about Heather was something else. Heather was altogether different. I loved Heather with everything that I had in my heart and soul. I loved Marie, too, but my feelings toward Heather destroyed what I thought was love for Marie. Heather was real and tangible to me, whereas Marie was some rainbow that I chased—but never reached—for years. Marie was more a myth than reality. Most importantly, Heather loved me back.

"Told Mom yet?" Samantha asked.

I shook my head, "No need. We're not really married anymore anyway. That's... that's on me. And something else, too, kiddo. I know that I've not been the best dad to you and Davey. That's on me, too. I got selfish and thought about nothing about my problems and never really thought about my kids. I'm very sorry. I know that that doesn't fix years, but I want you to know that I'm deeply, mortally sorry."

Samantha sat there and looked down at her shoes. We sat in silence for what seemed hours before she spoke.

"It's okay. We're a family. We'll make it through somehow. So, is the other woman Marie?"

"Nah. Her name is Heather, and she is amazing," I said, thinking about her as I spoke, seeing her face and hearing her sweet laugh inside my head. Saying her name aloud caused me to slip into total nirvana.

"So...," Samantha said after a few more awkward moments of silence. "What's going to happen now? How does all of this work?"

I could tell that she was kind of apprehensive about the future and state of the Matthews family; what was left of us, emotionally, anyway. What was left in the weeks to come would be nothing more than empty husks in Davey's wake.

"I don't know. But what I do know is that I want to spend the rest of my life with her."

"Like married?"

"Yeah, like married, maybe. How would you feel about that?" I asked, seeking some sort of approval from her.

Samantha shifted a bit as if she was uncomfortable with the question, the notion that I would be with another woman in real life.

"If that's what you want, then I'm good with it. You and Mom were done years ago anyway. It's not going to destroy my perception of what life is like. People get divorced every day. You guys probably should have done it a long time ago. Maybe things could've been different... for all of us." Samantha spoke in a tough tone. But inside I think she was falling apart at the seams. Samantha had Jennifer's hard outer shell, but inside she was made more like I was. And as I sat there looking at her trying not to break down and cry in front of me, I could tell my daughter was weighed down by the load of life I was putting on top of her.

I nodded in agreement with her wisdom. I should have ended what Jennifer and I had way back when, but I stayed for the ride because of Samantha and Davey. But look at the cost. Look at the toll, not only on myself but also on Jennifer, Samantha, and Davey. Look at what they had to pay. Was it worth it to stay, just maintain the kids' illusion of a perfect marriage? Nope. Our marriage had jaded Samantha. She was very hard when it came to the affairs of her mother and me. She wasn't a fan of her mother. And eventually, she would end up hating me just as much. That's on me, too.

12

In the early stages of my marriage to Jennifer, especially after the kids could think and form opinions for themselves, it was important that I gave them the perception that their life was grand and that Jennifer and I were in love. I mean, on the outside Jennifer and I were the perfect couple. We had a nice house with a near-perfect lawn in a fantastic neighborhood. It was a perfect setting, better than anything that I could imagine on paper.

To the outside world, Jennifer and I seemed to have the best life. She was knock-out gorgeous with her dark locks curled and a terrific smile. She was beautiful. Any guy in his right mind would have been the luckiest man in the world to have such a stunning woman by his side. In an odd sort of way, Jennifer resembled a young Jenny McCarthy. How I got her, I still don't know. Blind luck, I guess. But ain't that the way it always goes? The guys with the best girls don't want them, and the guys who dream of girls like that can never get them. Not me. I had her. And what did I do? Let her go all because she wasn't Marie. Why did I stay? The kids. It was always the kids. Perhaps that was the lie I told myself to get by all these years. Sometimes we pretend things are better, wonderful even, when in reality they are awful. The best lies you'll ever tell are the ones you tell yourself.

To the outside world, everything was fine in the Matthews abode. My family and I appeared to be a well-adjusted, normal American family living the American Dream. No one would have ever guessed that within our four walls, I didn't love my wife, my son was a depressed introvert on the edge of suicide, and my daughter was planning to derail her future by running off to live with Randy. Behind our closed doors, our home was full of broken promises and lies and heartbreak. And all of it was caused by me and my actions.

"You didn't come in here to talk about my life. What's up with you?" I asked, noticing quirks my daughter had when she was nervous or anxious about something. She would always rub her index fingers and thumbs together, clear her throat several times, and look about the room nervously. All these things she did since she was a kid. Back then she would do them because she had done something wrong, like the time she accidentally broke the utility window by throwing a baseball at Davey. I sat there and wondered what she had done wrong this time.

"I've been thinking about my life lately and um..., I'm not sure that the things I wanted awhile back are the things that I want now."

"Such as?" I asked, leaning across my desk with my arms on the table, giving her my full attention. I was kind of scared because I had no idea what she was about to hit me with. I knew something was coming because she was anxiously rubbing her thumb and index fingers together.

"Well," Samantha began. "I know that you wanted me to go to college and everything, but I'm thinking about taking some time off after I graduate. Kind of, you know, to recalibrate myself, I guess."

"Recalibrate? What's going on with you? A few months ago you were all gung-ho about going to college and now you're telling me you want some time off after graduation?" There it was. She didn't want to go to college. She wanted to hang back and be with Randy. I had a feeling that she was going to put off going to college a few months ago. I guess she had finally summoned up enough courage to inform me of her plans.

There was something more at play and I knew it. She didn't know that I knew what was really going on here. I was going to tell her outright, but dammit, I couldn't say it aloud. It broke my heart when I found the evidence of her secret that she was trying to hide. I was going to confront her about what I had found in her bathroom a while back, but I didn't. I guess I didn't want that fight just yet; maybe it wasn't what I thought it was. What I wanted was for her to be honest with me. What she gave me were spoonfuls of lies.

"Yeah, Randy and I..."

"Oh, there it is, 'you and Randy.' I knew that *he* had a part in this. He talk you out of going to college?" I asked. And here it was: The past met the present and future. The same sort of conversation had gone down between me and my father decades ago. In *his* office, no less. I'll be damned if the past doesn't repeat itself. I was never good at history mostly because I never learned from it.

"No, he supports me going to college. Dad, we want to get married," Samantha said. Those words nearly stopped my heart and turned my insides into jelly.

"Married?" I asked as I reeled from her sucker punch. The image of what I found in her bathroom on the vanity sink loomed larger than ever. I was getting madder and madder the more she talked.

"Yeah," Samantha replied, biting her lower lip and nervously awaiting my response.

"You're eighteen years old, Samantha! You've got your whole life ahead of you! Why would you want to ruin it by getting married at *eighteen*?" I was a hypocrite, saying all this to her. I was dreaming and wanting to be with a woman four years older than my daughter, and here I was, giving her hell about marriage. Then I wondered what Heather's parents would say when she told them about me. Probably something along the same lines as what I was telling my own daughter, I'm sure.

"Because he's the guy I want to be with forever. I love him," Samantha defended.

"Love him? You're still a kid!" I said as I looked at her. Truth be told, she wasn't a kid anymore. She was practically an adult and wanted to be treated as such. But for me to have a discussion with her about a life-changing decision was making my head spin. Although I knew the day when my daughter wanted to get married would eventually come, I wasn't ready to have a conversation about it. I just didn't think it would have happened this fast. I had plans for her. I guess much like my dad had plans for me.

"I'm old enough to know what I want, and Randy is it."

"Listen, most marriages end in divorce and I could only imagine that those percentages are higher the younger you are. Just think about what you're talking about!"

"I have, Dad!" Samantha said digging in for a debate. "I've thought about this for a while now! I'm ready to do it."

"Well, I can safely say that you're not!"

"Who are you to say what I *can* and *can't do*?"

"I'm still your father, and you still live in this house! So... house rules!" I quipped. I was losing her, but I couldn't stop myself. My fatherly rage was growing. It was as if I had stepped back into the past, watching myself fight with my father about not going to college and living according to my own terms. I didn't understand his reasoning then and didn't until Samantha and I started shouting at each other. Then I knew what my dad was trying to tell me.

Samantha sat there, more tense than I had seen her in a very long time. I could tell that she was hurt by my lack of support for her impending marriage to a boy who, all of a sudden, I didn't approve of. I had met Randy a few times and, from what I could tell, he was a nice boy, clean-cut, with a bright future ahead of him. Now, he wasn't good enough for my daughter. He had ruined my plans for her.

"That's how it's going to be?" Samantha asked.

"You're not giving me a choice. You want me to support and go along with a fucking stupid idea! Nope, ain't going to happen!"

"I didn't come in here asking for your support, Dad. I came here to tell you I'm doing it!" Samantha said, bringing down the Hammer of Thor upon me. She popped up and stormed out of my office, slamming the door behind her. I sat at my desk in a state of bewilderment. I had lost Samantha, and I knew it. It was over. I couldn't stop it. In my rage, I wanted to confront her about what I had found. But I held back. I knew why she wanted to forgo college and get married. The proof was sitting on the bathroom vanity.

I stopped myself from screaming louder than I did. I nearly went into full rage mode but I had caught myself at the last minute. I didn't say anything that I couldn't take back later. And believe me, I've done that a lot in my life. So before the fight could get more amped up, Samantha stormed out of my office. It was probably for the best though because it could've been worse. In the end, I had lost my daughter. We would never be the same.

13

As the night crawled on, I sat in my office cooling down from my and Samantha's argument. She was right about one thing, what was I waiting for with Jennifer? I mean, if my kids are ready for a change in the household, then why didn't I just pull the damn trigger and leave to be with Heather? Hell, Samantha was planning on getting married and leaving. What had held me back for so many years from pulling up stakes and moving was always the same: the kids. I never wanted to put them through the hell of a divorce because I believed that Jennifer would rake me over the coals and play the kids against me as much as she could. I didn't want the kids to learn to hate me. But in the end, no matter how hard I tried, they ended up hating me anyway, but for different reasons.

Maybe it's time to move on, I thought, sitting slumped in my chair and staring blankly at my computer screen. Just then, my cell phone chirped from beside the monitor. I reached for it and looked at the I.D. It was a text from the one and only Marie. My hands trembled and butterflies I thought were dead reawakened in the pit of my stomach. I had not talked to or texted Marie since Heather waltzed into my life, and that was the way I wanted it. Things were quiet... until that moment. I had even forgotten about the text she sent me about spending time with her former student. See? I was getting over her. Progress.

Her text signaled that it was that time of the year again: the last weekend of October. Reluctantly, I opened the text and it read: *It's that time of yr. We still on??*

I sat there, shaking slightly and hoping that I had it in me to not reply. All I had to do was not text back and delete her message from my inbox. That's it—one simple and complete move. But I was helpless, much like I was so many times in the past. She was my weakness—well, one of them anyway. The kids were my biggest. More lies? Instead of leaving her alone, I responded: *you bet. See you there.*

Was I going to throw everything that I had with Heather away? I had already done that with Jennifer, and I had learned from my mistakes from the wreckage of my past. I was going to vanquish the demon known as Marie from my life so I could move on. I wasn't in love with her anymore because Heather was my destiny—at least I felt that way. I knew Heather and I had met for a reason. Everything happened for a reason.

I wasn't going to meet Marie at the cabin at Lake Harden for a weekend of sex, talking, and bonding. I was way past that. I was traveling up there to finally tell her that I was done and that I had met my soulmate, Heather. Marie had always hooked me like a fish from the lake, but things were different this time. I no longer needed her in my life. Heather was my true love and with that kind of love, I could do the unthinkable: finally break it off with Marie. At least those were my intentions while traveling up to Lake Harden.

CHAPTER NINE

1

The long drive to Lake Harden to see Marie for what I considered the final time was gut-wrenching, to say the least. I had made that protracted excursion every year with excitement and nervousness, hoping that this was *going to be the year* every time. However, that particular drive up to the lake house was different. Things had changed substantially in my life since the last time we had gotten together. I was there to end it all... finally.

I was no longer the stupid kid, from way back when, who clung to Marie's words as if they were spoken from Christ himself. No, I was feeling better and had, for the most part, liked myself lately. Heather had helped me in so many ways but, most importantly, she broke the spell that Marie had over me. I could see better, clearer with Heather.

I was not going to see Marie, have sex with Marie, or catch up with Marie. No. I was on a mission to pry myself away from her, to vanquish the monster I had allowed to ruin my life. But, we all know that I was ultimately responsible for doing that, not Marie. At the end of the day, it all falls on me.

2

I could have just blown her off when she texted and asked if we were still on for the last weekend of October. I could have ignored her, but I discussed it with Heather, and she told me that I needed closure.

She was right, showcasing a wisdom far beyond her twenty-plus years. I needed to see Marie in person to tell her that my time with her was finished once and for all. What a long and strange trip it had been....and what had it cost? Everything.

I never would have been able to go there to break it off with Marie had it not been for Heather, my emotional rock. She convinced me that, for me to begin the extensive repairs my life needed, I had to address and destroy my demons, one by one. She was right, of course. Marie was one of the biggest obstacles I had to face. But I later learned that it was *me* who was my biggest obstacle. For some reason, I was never able to get out of my own way.

All I ever wanted to do was to be with Marie and live happily ever after. That was the master plan for as long as I could remember. It was all that I had ever wanted, but it wasn't what *she* wanted. Her reluctance was what had gotten me into the stew that I was in.

I had gotten married to the wrong person for the wrong reasons. I pushed my wife away and thought of nothing but Marie day in and day out. Marie wasn't the cause of all my problems, but she sure was a major part of them. Toxic to thought and touch, she should have had a Surgeon General's warning attached to her.

3

I was ready to release her grip on me. I was ready to close the book on us and walk away knowing that she wasn't the person I thought she was. Heather was the real deal, the best thing I had ever felt in my life. And for me to be with her fully, I had to pry Marie's grip on my mind. It wasn't going to be easy, but it had to be done.

A year ago, I would not have even entertained the notion of driving to Lake Harden to break it off with Marie. There was no way that I would have thought about it. With every yearly visit, it was my goal to sway her to come and be with me exclusively. And every time I left the lake house, I came away with nothing. I just never could get her to say, "yes" to me. That three-letter word was all I wanted to hear her say. It proved to be the most difficult word in the English language for her to say.

4

I had been ready for a life with Marie for a long time. And that was me, waiting for her to validate my existence. My family and career should have been all the validation I needed, but Marie was the one thing that would ultimately complete me. I think that's why I longed for her—partly because I loved her madly and partly because she was my ultimate goal. She could've been my cash payout at the casino. I never could beat the house. Eventually, you just have to leave with whatever you still have and try your luck at another casino. With Heather, I had hit the jackpot.

Marie was my everything and had been for years. It was going to feel strange not to have her anymore. But did I ever really have her? No, it was just a thing to her, an insignificant little thing we did every year. It meant nothing to her, but it meant the world to me. It wasn't her fault for leading me on over all those years—it was mine. I gave her permission to walk all over my heart. I let her do things that I hated myself for, but, of course, in the end, the blame lies on me.

Although it was too late to fix the core devastation of my marriage, children, and career, I had to try. Trying meant shutting my feelings off towards Marie and leaving her where she belonged— in the past. My future did not have Marie in it. It was time to exorcise Marie, my demon.

5

I had many lingering questions for Marie, though. One of those prickling questions was why she never texted me back that day when I got released from my contract by Bob Windom. Another question was why she kept me at her beck and call. Why did she drag me through hell and abandon me in my self-imposed purgatory?

I wanted to just close my eyes and forget about her, forget all about the good times we had as kids, all the conversations that ultimately led to nowhere. I wanted to take a deep breath and exhale all the feelings I had for her, but that was all just wild thinking, not something I could actually do. If it were that easy, I would perhaps have done it long ago.

Had it not been for Heather giving me the confidence to end things with Marie, my drive to Lake Harden would have been just like all the others— going there, seeing her, falling in love all over again by the sight of her, her voice, and her touch. I was better, mentally, driving up there for the final time. I was armed with something I'd never had before— true love that went beyond comprehension. Heather's love was my armor and realization was my sword as I drove to battle the wicked witch at the lake house.

It didn't have to end like it was going to. Our history could have been rewritten if she'd only allowed me inside her heart. I often wondered what I had meant to her after all these years. Was I just a guy, someone to fawn over her, build her up, give her what others couldn't when she was younger? Had I been the Dr. Frankenstein to her monster? How much fault did I place on myself for making Marie what she was? Had I been the one who turned her into, well... her?

All these existential inquiries that I had concerned me. I had ruined everything in my home and wondered if I had turned Marie into someone who I hated over the years. *Nah, I couldn't have,* I told myself. She had that coldness embedded within her DNA long before I showed up. Her mother was the root cause of Marie being Marie. I didn't know much about her mother, but from what I gathered, her mom was a very cold and callous individual. Marie wasn't quite that extreme, but she certainly channeled her mother's energy.

6

That drive to the lake house was longer than normal. Maybe it was the anticipation of what I was about to do. I was going there to end everything with her, lay it on the line, and walk away. That was the plan. And when I finished with my task, Heather was waiting for me back in Atlanta. All I had to do was end that chapter of my life with Marie. I had no idea what was in store for me when I arrived at the lake house and how life would throw me a devastating curve ball that I thought I could hit.

7

I drove up the hill and the towering lake house was directly in front of me, unchanged from last year and all the others previous. The sun was in the process of taking her final bow just behind the still lake. I parked my car beside Marie's in the driveway that was surrounded by trees bursting with colorful red, yellow, and orange leaves, signaling changing seasons. The tree leaves were not the only things that were changing. I was changing; everything around me was changing. Life was changing.

I sat in my car for a few moments and gathered my composure and tried like hell to knock my nerves out. I had a flask of hard liquor in the glove box and wanted to open it up and take a swig. But I refused to because I knew what would happen if I did. Alcohol and I didn't mix well, never did. Why did I have it in the glove box? I don't know; maybe for situations like what I was about to walk into. Courage perhaps? Liquid courage, most likely.

Looking at myself in the rearview mirror, I took a deep breath and readied myself. I got out of the car and the cool October air greeted me. I shut the car door and made my way across the gravel driveway up to the cabin, where I ascended the front porch steps.

I walked around the porch, which ran alongside the house, and finally, I reached the back deck that overlooked Lake Harden—beautiful as always, unchanged since last year and years past. Sitting in a chair drinking hot chocolate and talking on her phone was Marie, vibrant and elegant as ever. The woman never changed. Sure, there were signs of some age, here and there. Her hair had some faint streaks of gray and crow's feet were visible, but other than that she was pretty much the same from the last ten years. She saw me, smiled and told whomever it was goodbye, and placed her phone down. "Jerry, I didn't hear you. Kind of scared me," she said, getting up and coming over to me for a hug. God, she still smelled the same. That smell I thought about when I tried to go to sleep some nights in bed. It was a perfume that Marie had worn ever since high school called, Revenant.

"I thought you'd be out here. Didn't mean to scare you," I said, hugging her back. The one thing that I noticed instantly was that I didn't get that feeling that I did when I first hugged Heather in Atlanta. Nowhere close to it. There was electricity there and used to be with Marie. But on that day, it was long gone.

"Hot chocolate?" Marie asked as we walked to the two chairs that sat in reserve for us.

"Of course," I replied, sitting down in my chair as she poured my cup of hot cocoa. When I sat down, my eyes were quickly drawn to the picturesque landscape before us; the sun was sinking behind the lake, just off the horizon. It was awesome, always was.

"Sorry, I've been so hard to get a hold of. School has kept me busy," Marie said, getting herself comfortable.

"I bet," I said dryly.

"So what's up?!" Marie asked, pushing me like I was just a buddy from high school.

"Nothing. Same old, same old, I guess," I said, wondering why in the hell she was acting like that. She was acting nervous, that I could tell. You can't be with someone for so long and not pick up on something like that, no matter how hard they try to conceal it. "You?" Marie was off that night. I could immediately tell. She was different.

She shook her head slowly as if she was really trying to think about her recent history. "The same. Still teaching at the same school. How's the writing biz?" She asked.

"Um... I got let go from Windom," I said, recalling that bite of reality vividly.

"Oh no, I'm so sorry, Jerry. I had no idea," Marie said, trying but not succeeding in sounding heartfelt.

"Well, we haven't talked in a while, so how would you know? It's okay though, I'm self-publishing this epic novel I'm writing. I'll be right back on track soon. It's perhaps the best thing I've ever written."

"Glad to hear you haven't given up after being dumped by Windom. I read the reviews for your last book and the critics were... pretty mean."

"What did you think about my last book?" I asked, knowing the answer to my question. She never read anything I wrote.

"I haven't read it yet. Been too busy and too tired to do anything extra. But I'll get around to it though. Books are always there," she said, and I couldn't help but wonder if she had even bought any of my books. I'd never know.

"Yeah, let me know what you think about it. It'd be nice to hear a kind voice in this cruel world," I said, knowing that she had no intentions of reading my work.

"You'll get back. Every artist has their slumps to work through." Marie said, lighting up a cigarette between her full red lips.

"I thought you quit," I said. Marie blew smoke into the air as the sun sunk lower.

"I did for a week but teaching wrecks your nerves. It's either this or cocaine," she laughed. I laughed out of habit. "How's the wifey and kids? Samantha has to be at least fourteen now, right?"

"No, Sam just turned eighteen. *Davey* is fifteen," I replied. She should have known their ages, for God's sake. She'd been around me when they were both born. I called her on both occasions to tell her the news. The more I talked to her, the more I began to wonder why in the hell I was so madly in love with her in the first place. Heather had successfully taken the blinders from my eyes and I was seeing Marie, *really* seeing her, for the first time, and I didn't like what I was seeing there on the back deck.

"Oh, that's right," Marie said, laughing. "Man, I totally forgot. Is Jennifer still avoiding you? How in the hell do you make *that* work?"

"You'd be surprised what you can do when you want to. Jennifer and I haven't made anything work in a very long time."

"I have no idea why you've stayed as long as you have with her. My ass would have been outta there a loooong time ago," she said, exaggerating the "o" sound.

She should've had some vague notion that she had a starring role in my life's shit. But she was too vain to figure that out. I was getting mad sitting there listening to her. It was like she was trying to provoke me. Maybe this was always how Marie acted, and I was just too pussy whipped to notice. But that night, things were different. I saw the way things really were.

My blood was starting to boil at her remarks. I wanted to just leave, but I also wanted to tell her it was over, that we were through. And by the way things felt, I wondered if she'd even care. She certainly acted like she didn't. Marie was off, like she had something on her mind. I would later find out what it was.

"Yeah, well, when you got kids in the mix, things ain't as easy as you'd like them to be. You have to take into consideration how divorce will affect them," I said.

"Yeah, that's true. I can't tell you how many kids who come from broken homes end up strange. I have two in my class right now who are messed up. Total introverts. Do you think your two are going to end up that way, living in a broken home?"

I shook my head, "I don't know. Samantha is strong, but Davey is really weak. I can't even get him to smile anymore. I'm beginning to think there's something wrong with him, mentally. I don't know though. Maybe it's my fault, you know? I haven't been Father of the Year material. I wonder, though, how Jennifer and my marriage will affect Davey in the long run."

"Maybe he sees your marriage for what it is: a front. That can't be a good thing for any kid to see," Marie said, hitting the nail on the head. She had her good points and observations at times.

"Yeah, I think you're right," I replied thinking about how all that started because I allowed myself to get mentally consumed by a woman who was to never be mine. Instead of providing my kids with a typical childhood where they saw their parents together, they only ever saw Jennifer and me on separate occasions. Togetherness was rare, and family time was nonexistent.

"But they are getting to the age where they should understand things, right?" Marie asked, blowing smoke into the almost night.

"Yeah, that doesn't mean it makes any more sense. Age and experience don't fix everything," I said, looking out across the lake.

"Nope," Marie replied, blowing more smoke into the dusk chill. "I told you getting married to someone you didn't care about was going to cause you problems." And this statement, as thorny as it was, was right. She did tell me that marrying Jennifer would lead to nowhere. She knew that I was marrying Jennifer for all the wrong reasons—hell, so did I. But what was I to do? All that knowledge and what happened—the inevitable.

"You sure did," I replied.

"But you live and learn, as they say. Can't be all bad, you got two kids out of the deal, right?" Marie pointed out.

"I did," I returned.

"I mean, look at me. I'm forty years old and have done it all, but what do I have to show for it? A professor at a college and an afterthought to everyone that I've ever known. I have no family since dad died, no kids, nothing," Marie said, showing me a side I hadn't seen in decades.

8

As we sat overlooking the lake, Marie began to sound like the old Marie, the one who I loved madly when I was young. It was kind of scary how she could switch from being and sounding like a bitch to a profound person with useful insight. Classic Marie.

"It's my fault though, I was the one that said I didn't want to be tied down," Marie said, running a hand through her hair.

"Retrospect," I began, "is difficult. You see all your missteps, miscues, things that you should've and shouldn't have said. Things you should've done and things you wish you hadn't. Life is like taking the test before you've learned the lesson."

"Yeah, you need to put that line in your next book," Marie quipped as she laughed. "I've been taking a very hard look at myself lately and I got to tell you, I don't much like what I see. I let time slip away so much that it almost got me. Twenty years... gone. *Whoosh!*"

"What's that mean?"

"What it means is that I um... feel like it's time for me to settle down and stop acting like time and its rules don't apply to me. Why am I any different from anyone else? I'm not. I made the old-woman mistake: I thought I'd stay young forever."

I sat there for a minute and listened to what she was cryptically saying. Was the great Marie ready to be married with a family? That was a profound realization spewing from her mouth.

"So what are you going to do about it?" I asked, dreading her response. I had traveled to Lake Harden to finally break it off with her forever, but was it possible that she was going to reach out and say she wanted *me*, after all the years that had passed? How was I going to deal with that? I had Heather in my life now, and I was happy without Marie.

Marie took a drag from her waning cigarette and defiantly blew the smoke into the air. "I met this guy awhile back, a former student of mine. He and I had this connection and we both knew it. I can't explain it. But as soon as we saw each other, we just knew. I want to spend the rest of my life with him," Marie said in a low nervous voice.

I sat there in shock, completely and utterly amazed by her reveal. Was the woman who had told me that she never wanted to be tied down, *wanting* to be tied down all because time was slipping away and her own mortality caught up with her? Was I angry? Yes, I was because it wasn't fair. It wasn't fair to me because I had sacrificed everything because of her. I had waited for *years* for the day that she and I would finally be together. And sitting there on that back deck looking out across the lake for the umpteenth time, she drove a knife into my heart and began to twist it as she smiled at me.

"You love this guy?" I asked, still reeling from her words. My voice sounded dry and empty.

A few moments passed before she answered: "Yes." We sat there in silence, hearing nothing but the sounds of the nocturnal creatures that moved around the forest. Somewhere an owl hooted. I was completely knocked off my game by her confession. I always knew that maybe one day she would find someone else, but that thought had taken refuge on the outskirts of my mind.

For years—decades—I thought Marie and I would end up together, spend our lives together. But things had changed. "I didn't want to tell you," Marie said, staring out across the lake and refusing to look at me.

"I thought about canceling this weekend and just leaving you alone, but I just couldn't do it. I wanted to be honest with you," she said as her voice cracked. It was one of the few times that I saw Marie hurt and sad.

I sat there, feeling all kinds of emotions. I should have been mad as hell, and I was initially because I felt that she had made me bring a terrible fate upon myself and my family. But I couldn't blame her for everything because I knew in my heart that I had been the purveyor of my misfortune. Silence was the only refuge I had, sitting there on that deck.

I was mortally wounded by her truth, by her words. I sat bleeding, staining the wood beneath me, soaking the grain of the wood. I had come up there to end things, but Marie had beaten me to it. It wasn't fair, and it wasn't how this was supposed to go. *I* should've been the one who walked away. Not her. Not that night. She had no right to be the one who pulled the trigger.

"You mad at me?" Marie asked with some trepidation in her voice after a few moments of silence.

"I don't know," I said, looking down at the floor. "I should be. I gotta know... how come you never wanted *me* like that?"

Marie sat there and searched for her answer to my question. Was it really a search for the right words, or did she already know? I wondered. "I don't know. I never had that connection with you. I loved you, but not like I love him," Marie finally replied. I sat there, hearing her words, but my mind blanked. Here she was, the love of my life— well, the former love of my life—telling me she didn't *love me.*

9

I had waited for so long for her, dreaming my nights away as a youth and as an adult for the one day when she and I would be together forever. And those dreams and misty illusions I held close to my heart had disappeared into thin air.

Those thoughts of love and happiness had fueled me for so many years. I loved her—insanely I did—but even I felt different when Heather came into my life. Just as Marie had changed, so had I. So how could I rightfully be mad at her for doing exactly what I had done? I came there to break it off with her and exorcise the ghosts of our shared past, but she beat me to it, quicker on the draw. "I understand," I said, breaking the silence between us.

I was numb because this was a conversation I never wanted to have. I was ready to tell her what changes I had undergone, and that I was moving on without her. But being on the receiving end of all that hurt a bit, not because I still was in love with her, but because it was an end. An end to what was and what never will be.

We sat for what seemed hours as the moon moved slowly across the sky with each passing minute. We sat there, processing what was said, both considering how to break up, although we were never together in the first place. It was a day I had in the past feared the most, but sitting there in the chill of the October night, I wasn't that fearful. I was overcome with a sense of freedom from the shackles that had bound me to her for as long as I could recall.

Heather had given me the strength to break free from Marie, and Marie herself had allowed me to go peacefully into the night without any fuss. We both had found love. And even though it was not with each other, it was still love, unfiltered and unbridled.

10

We eventually began to talk, catching up on times past in our lives, separate though they were. She and I laughed into the night recalling events from our youth, people with whom we went to school, good and bad times we had. And then we talked about parts of our lives that the other was not privy to. We eased into all of this, into everything.

In talking with her, not hoping that she would tell me that she wanted to marry me and make me the happiest man on the planet, I began to see why I fell in love with her long ago. Even though she was older, Marie was still that girl from long ago who I could not take my eyes off. She was still stunning in her beauty and age had not defiled her features in the slightest. Even now, when I close my eyes, I can see her back when we were kids. Back when things were wide open and no futures were written yet—back when everything was right, when things were simple.

It's difficult to describe what a woman like Marie can do to you. There are plenty of women out there like Marie and any man who has fallen under their spell can surely tell you: Once you fall for them, you fall hard, sometimes never fully recovering from the plunge you took. I was a success story, one of very few I'm sure in this world, who took the hit she dished out over time and survived. My survival through love's hot-as-hell flames was made possible by not my guile or strength or willpower but by Heather. She alone had rescued me and salvaged what was left. She cleaned me up, put me back together, and made me new again.

Marie was the type of woman who could kill you from the inside out. She could fill your heart up with love and then, at the drop of a hat, rip it out of your chest. She practiced that method scores of times, and all I could do was smile and hope that she'd come around because there was something about her. I knew, even when I was a kid, that she was the type who could burn you alive with her love if she ever took it away.

She had taken away her love for me that night at Lake Harden. But let's be honest here. She really never loved me in the first place. I mean, she loved me, but didn't *love me*. Had I not had Heather in my life and Marie revealed her true feelings to me, I perhaps would have driven my car into the lake off the bridge three miles from where we sat. Heather's love made it possible for me to break away from Marie's bewitching spell and survive the harsh truths that she had told me that night.

Had it not been for Heather, I would have wanted to kill Marie for making me do the things I did to Jennifer and my children over the years. But it wasn't her that caused the pain—it was me.

Another thing that Heather made me realize was that the pre-Heather me would have blamed Marie for everything. That wasn't the case. She never forced me to cheat on Jennifer with her. She never told me to push Jennifer away. Marie never told me to stay put and wait for her to one day come and sweep me off my feet. I did. It was me the entire time. I thought the one in control of my well-being was Marie, but in my self-exploration of my mind and soul along with Heather's help, she made me realize that *I* was the one pushing the buttons in my life, not Marie.

"How's this going to be now?" Marie asked hours later as we kept the hot chocolate and stories coming on that cold night. It was like the last episode's farewell of a long-running TV show where the cast watches clips of the highlights and talks about them. A retrospection, for lack of a better term.

"What do you mean?" I asked, knowing full well what she meant. I wanted her to say it.

"You got this new girl and I got this new guy. What do we do now?" Marie asked, sipping on her hot cup of cocoa as the night grew considerably cooler.

"I mean, we can't do *this* anymore," I said. "I'm not cheating on Heather. She means too much for me to do that."

There was a bit of silence before Marie spoke. "I thought so. I can't do that to him, either. Wouldn't be right."

"So this is it," I said what we both were thinking, feeling the cold reality that Marie and I would never be anything anymore. "I mean, if we remained friends, that puts Heather in a situation that she doesn't need to be in. She knows how I felt about you, and if we still communicated, then she would always wonder. She'd always tell me that she didn't, but I'd know better. It's just human nature."

Marie nodded her head. "I can understand that. I just hate losing you," Marie said as her voice began to crack under the stress of the situation. She wanted to cry.

"We've got a lot of history together, you and me. But we can't continue. Wouldn't work."

"I guess I knew that, coming up here tonight," Marie replied. "I knew that things would be over. Have to be, I guess."

"Heather knew that I was coming up here to break it off with you. There's no reason for me to keep talking to you after tonight. It wouldn't be... right, I guess. It just puts her in a precarious position, and I don't want that."

Marie nodded in agreement. "I know...I know. You're a good man. Always were. Will thinks I'm here with my aunt, cleaning up the place. He'd freak out if he knew that I came up here with you."

"You didn't tell him about us?" I asked, wondering why she didn't fully disclose our history to him.

"No, I didn't want him to be eaten alive by jealousy. And he would be. I mean, he knows we dated back in high school and that you're a famous writer but I haven't told him about us meeting up here every year. It'd drive him crazy. He'd just see you as competition. I want to keep this one, you know? I don't want anything fucking this up."

"You realize that you're going to have to tell him eventually because you can't have a relationship that has secrets buried in it. Never works," I said to her, advising her as a friend should.

"I know. I just have to find the time. And the courage. I don't want to lose him over something like this."

"But you have to tell him you and I were here and that nothing happened because we were both breaking it off. It might hurt, but in the long run, he'll be okay. Friendly advice: no secrets," I stated.

Marie sat there and looked at what was left of the night. It had gotten into the wee hours of the morning right before dawn. She knew I was right about telling him. Secrets in a relationship can surface and create havoc, no matter how deeply you think you bury them. Secrets, I have come to learn, have a way of surviving time itself.

11

We both stood in the gravel driveway as daybreak was about to shatter the dark cloak of nightfall. I was tired, cold, and stiff, but better yet, vindicated and free. I had finally extinguished my torch for Marie. It was over, decades later, finally over. We stood there, face to face, two feet apart, gazing into each other's eyes one last time. A cold breeze picked up causing gooseflesh to pattern itself on our skin.

We both stood silent, searching for the appropriate words or phrases that two former lovers would give in their final act. We were no more lovers, no more friends... no more anything that had a future. We had been reduced by time and love of others to mere casual acquaintances from a long time ago and maybe not even that, after we parted ways. Time and history were the only things that bound us together but, even that fades as memories and long-forgotten dreams wither away.

"It was a long, strange trip, wasn't it?" Marie asked, biting her lower lip, trying to hold back the waterworks. I give her credit. She was tough not to cry right there. I think she went down hard after I left. Just a hunch.

"Indeed, it has been," I replied. "So, what's in store for you down the road?" I asked as if I was tying up the loose ends in a novel.

"Maybe get married... a few kids... keep teaching the young minds of America. You?"

I stood there for a minute, shivering from the sudden cold chill that tingled my body through my coat.

"Set Jennifer free... try to be the best dad I can be... marry Heather... finish that Great American novel. I guess just try to be a better person in the second half of my life. Try to fix everything I've broken over the years. Probably will take the rest of my life to do it,"

"I truly hope everything works out for you. And for what it's worth, I'll miss you," Marie said. The tears she tried to dam up came flowing down her cheeks. Marie was something I hadn't seen before: Authentically hurt.

I stood looking at Marie as if seeing her clearly for the first time. I stood before a wounded woman who was no different than the girl that I first met decades ago. She was stripped down to her bare emotions, which had gotten the best of her. I hadn't seen her cry since I was a kid when she talked about her home life. Seeing Marie in that state, weakened and sincere, caused me to tear up myself. It was hard to say goodbye even though it had to be done.

"You, too," I replied with a big lump in my throat. "Can I have a hug for old time's sake?" Before I could wait for a response, Marie quickly leaned into me and the two of us stood enthralled in the embrace that we were sharing. Suddenly, the cool October breeze from the towering trees didn't make me shiver. Marie's body heat kept me warm as mine did her.

For that moment in time to never be lost, she and I were one, just as I always had hoped we'd be. However, the circumstances were different, but that did not underscore the raw feelings she and I experienced on that early morning. It was the last time I ever touched her, smelled her honey-scented hair and her perfume. It was the famous final scene between us. We were no more. It was over....

I look back on our encounter and like to think of that scene in the driveway under the dim night sky as a Norman Rockwell painting: Two former lovers sharing their last embrace on a cold October night by the lake. That painting would have hung in my office as a reminder of what had been and then ceased to exist.

After she and I said our goodbyes and after the tears, I got into my car and pulled away from her for the last time. Marie stood there in the driveway, watching me as I drove away. The dark image of her in my rearview mirror grew more distant with every revolution of my wheels that carried me away. It was just around the curve when Marie was no longer in my rearview mirror. All she was was a memory, a ghost of a past that I left standing behind me.

CHAPTER TEN

1

As the calendar flipped to November, I felt as if I was seeing things differently, in more ways than I had before. Had Marie's spell finally been broken? It seemed so. After I left Lake Harden, it was as if a black cloth had been lifted from my eyes. And after all those decades of darkness, there was light. How beautiful it was. At the same time, it was sad. I mean there was just so much history with the two of us dating back to when I was literally a child. I had quit her finally, but her impression on me was nonetheless everlasting.

In early November, I recall sitting there in my broken abode, thinking about what Samantha had said to me a while back in my office about the prospect of just ending things with her mother. Why was I even hanging on, lingering around a house like a ghost? All I was doing was haunting the place anyway. Our marriage was over. All I was doing was prolonging the act of actually getting a divorce.

I had no real value at home to anyone. Jennifer was off with other guys trying to find Mr. Right while Samantha was too involved with planning to marry her boyfriend. And Davey, poor Davey. What about *him*? November was going to be the worst month of my life; however, I didn't know it. How the hell could I? We all have moments in time that change us, define us; events that tell the world who we are, where we're from, and what we've seen. November was the month that broke me—what was left.

2

I had decided that since I was turning over a new leaf, you know, with finally breaking it off with Marie, maybe I should begin to clean out the rest of the skeletons in my closet. My marriage was a sham, but I still had my kids. Was it too late for us to have a good, healthy relationship? Samantha was pretty much done with me because of my lack of support for her impending marriage, and Davey had withdrawn completely for reasons unbeknownst to me. Looking back, I should've known what was going on. I was too stupid and too preoccupied with other things to really, and I mean *really*, do anything to help my son. That was on me.

3

Samantha had begun to move her stuff out of her bedroom. I had walked by it one day, peered inside and saw that barely anything remained. The bed was gone as well as her dresser, nightstand, and desk. The only things that were left were the posters and other wall décor she had accumulated over time. She was doing it, really doing it. I wasn't going to stop her. As difficult as the thought and action itself was, I had decided to just let her go. She needed to find her own way. That meant me standing by watching, much like my dad did when I did the same thing.

My dad had tried to stop me once, and the result was nothing but years of silence and resentment. I wanted to jerk Samantha by the arm and smack the fuck out of her and hopefully bring some sense to her and make her realize this was a bad idea. Samantha had my genes, and I knew how that would end. So I just stood by and let her do what she was planning. It was the best option.

I was still raw and not happy about her moving out and throwing her life away, but what could I do? I wondered if my past actions, the neglect of my marriage and kids over the years, had played a part in her decision. They probably did.

I wanted to be a dad to Davey again. Sure, Samantha and I had always gravitated more towards each other, as Davey did with

Jennifer. That was just how things operated in our household. No one seemed to mind, I guess. There were times that I tried with Davey, but he and I could never really find that common ground to work on. So we just drifted apart: he in his world and me in mine, only seeing each other when we had to. Honestly, I never knew how much he loved me, or even if he ever did. After his death, I got a few questions about my son answered in the form of a girlfriend that showed up at his funeral: Davey with a special someone. Who'd have thought?

4

Feeling that things were finally looking up for me, I decided there in my office that I was going to reach out to Davey. And the best place to do that was in the one place I knew I'd find him: his bedroom. It wasn't just a room in the house; it was my son's getaway from us and the rest of the world. It was a place where he could do and say whatever he wanted, and no one was there to tell him to stop.

He was in every sense of the word, a king, in that room. But I wanted to talk to my son who I felt I didn't know anymore. I wanted to hear his voice, something that I hadn't heard in quite some time. I wanted to establish some sort of communication with him. I felt that I had to. I had a faint voice inside my head telling me that I needed to get back with Davey. Before it was... before it was... was what? Too late? Yeah. It already was too late. I just didn't know it yet.

I found a stopping point in my novel towards the climax and walked out of my office and down the hall to Davey's bedroom door. It was closed, as usual, and the low thumping of music was heard emanating from the inside. He was locked away. I raised my hand and knocked on his door a few times. The music stopped and I could hear Davey walk across the floor and twist the door knob, "Yeah?" he asked, looking through the crack of the door with watery red eyes.

"Hey," I was going to ask him if he wanted to come into the kitchen and grab a pizza with me, but I noticed he had been crying. "You okay?" I looked dead in his red eyes and saw that he was distressed. It was all over his face. I'll never forget that image of him.

I didn't realize it then, but he wouldn't be alive much longer after this. Not much longer at all.

Davey realized I could see his eyes and he quickly rubbed them to wipe away his tears. "Yeah, just woke up," he said dismissively.

"Um...I'm going to throw a pizza in the oven; you want to split it with me?" I invited.

Davey shook his head, "Nah, I'm good. I just want to lie down here and get some rest. Tough day."

"You sure? I mean, I'd like to talk to you a little bit... see how you're doing. Doesn't seem like we've talked much lately," I said, trying to reach out to my son the best I could, trying to be his father.

Davey stood there in his doorway, looking down at the floor and then around everywhere but at me. "Nah, like I said, I'm tired. I think I want to go to sleep. Maybe next time, okay." I stood there and looked at him as he slowly shut the door in front of me and locked it tight. I could tell he was in bad shape back then but didn't know to what degree until he killed himself. If only I had known then what I know now, I could have grabbed him by his arm and forced him out of his bedroom. Maybe I could have saved his life. Maybe we both could have faced whatever it was that was bringing him down into despair and beat it together. I decided to just turn and walk away as his music turned up a little bit louder.

5

With nothing going on in the house, I decided to do something I had not done in a while: go sit outside on the front porch. It was a gloomy November day, chilly with a gusty breeze blowing from time to time, but all I needed was my Braves jacket and a cup of hot chocolate.

I sat in a chair I had bought some time ago at an antique shop as a mere porch decoration. It was stiff and felt like new, but that was all because no one, to my knowledge, had ever sat on the damn thing. I sat there and made myself comfortable, watching the cars pass by on the street. There weren't many cars that passed because the end of the street led to a cow pasture, essentially a dead-end. Most people who traveled up and down my street were those I knew from living in the neighborhood for so long. Sometimes people would wave and sometimes they wouldn't; the same went for me.

In the spring and summer, and even in early fall, I would sit at my office desk and watch people walk up and down the sidewalks. Like the cars, I knew the people too, and had known most of them ever since we moved into the house. There was always this sense of familiarity with everyone in my neighborhood that I had grown accustomed to. The neighborhood was like an old shoe to me; it fit.

I wasn't a shut-in by any means. I would mow the lawn, plant flowers, landscape, wash my car, and do other suburbanite chores. Just because I was a famous author didn't mean I had to live like a hermit. All my neighbors truly knew about me is that I wrote books, and I severely doubt most of them ever read them.

However, there were a few on my street who had read my work because there had been times while clipping my hedges when people approached me with one of my books in hand, requesting an autograph and Q&A session. I gladly signed their books and talked to them for a while. The funny thing is that I haven't had that happen to me in such a long time that I kind of miss it.

Back in my career's heyday, man alive, people *wanted* to know who I was, talk to me, shake my hand, and get my autograph—even have their picture taken with me. It was awesome back then. But I got lazy and let things get in the way. It struck me how quickly a person could become a faded memory.

I never recovered from the fall I took. Even the comeback novel I had worked so hard on and believed in so much wasn't enough to get me back, at least not all the way. Sometimes a person can't come all the way back. Sometimes you have to settle for whatever you can get.

6

As I sat on the porch, hands in my coat pockets, Jennifer's car came into my line of vision, and she turned into our driveway, talking away on her cell. She looked at me for a bit and told whoever it was that she was chatting with goodbye. She sat in her car for a few moments as though she was trying to muster up the courage to get out. I think seeing me outside on the porch kind of threw her—it wasn't my normal routine. To tell the truth, just seeing each other was something out of the ordinary.

Jennifer got out of her car, buttoned up her coat, and walked up to the porch. "Up by three today. What's the occasion?" she asked with a prickly, smart-ass tone that I had gotten used to over the years. She was a different Jennifer Matthews from the one I had encountered on the day I was let go from Windom. I sat there, looking at my wife and thinking about what to say to her. I had no intention of talking to her about anything. The two of us were way past talking and hadn't talked about anything worthwhile in years.

When it came to Davey, though, I felt I had to break the ice somehow to discuss our child who appeared to be in dire straits. "I think Davey is sick," I said, wondering if that was an appropriate way to describe what was happening to our son.

Jennifer stopped and turned to look at me with her hand on the doorknob. "Then take him to a doctor."

"He's um... he's not got the flu or a cold, Jennifer," I began, looking around the front yard searching for an answer to Davey's problem to just pop up out of the ground.

"Then what is it?" she asked, seemingly irritated— or even bitter—by me even talking to her. And why not? Look at what I had done to her over the years. That was the longest conversation we'd had in a long time there on the porch. It felt alien.

"He's out of it. I mean I tried to get him out of his bedroom today. He was in there with the light off, and I could tell he'd been crying his eyes out. I think something is bothering him... something bad," I said, finally turning my eyes to my wife, who stood at the front door looking at it and not me.

"You're serious, right? Have you bothered to *look* at the condition of this house in the last several years? It's no wonder he's acting the way he does! It's no wonder that Samantha's—."

Jennifer stopped herself from saying anything else. I rose from my chair, slowly keeping my eyes glued to my estranged wife, "Samantha's... *what*?" I already knew our daughter had left.

Jennifer stood with her hand on the doorknob, wanting to go in, but for some reason, she didn't twist the door knob. "Nothing, never mind." She stood there, looking down, and then spoke again before exhaling into the cold air, "Samantha's leaving, you know that right? Seen her bedroom? There's nothing left here for anybody. We're all done. It's a fucking ghost town here." And with that, she walked into the house and closed the door behind her. She didn't slam it like a normal mad person would have. I don't think she was mad. I think she was too tired to be angry. I think we all were, at that point.

7

I sat alone on the front porch as daylight turned to twilight, thinking about things in general; seems that's all I did there for a very long time. Jennifer's words about our daughter stung. I had caused a great deal of pain over the years by shutting out everyone—my wife and kids. Sitting there on the front porch, I knew that the future my kids, my wife, and myself had to look forward to had been destroyed by my past actions. I had been emotionally unavailable to them all. Did that cause Samantha to run away? Absolutely.

I never got Marie and I lost Jennifer. I should've been in love with Jennifer but wasn't. I only used her so I wouldn't be alone. I thought that she would be a consolation prize for not getting Marie. She deserved so much better than that.

My actions over the years pushed her down so much that she began to forget about me altogether. She went on and had multiple sex partners, hoping she would eventually run into Mr. Right. Maybe she did a few times, only to run him away by the insecurities I had planted inside her head. And that intensified her hatred of me. I, in turn, hated myself for causing her so much anguish.

Samantha was a carbon copy of her old man. We had the same sense of humor, the same intellect, and thoughts about life. But somehow, I let her slip through my fingers. Somehow along the way, I stopped being a dad who used to push her on the swing set out in the backyard. I stopped being her special guest at tea parties with her dolls and stuffed animals. Somewhere I just stopped.

Samantha's desertion hurt the most because I was closer to her. She was a daddy's girl and was the light of my soul. And when I wondered why she did the things that she did, I knew it was because I stopped being there for her. I had abandoned Samantha in our own house. I will be forever sorry about that misstep.

Davey's attitude, like that of his mother and sister, was a direct product of my bullshit. I managed to pull him down, too. I never meant to hurt my kids. But I had. I think that was Davey's problem: He had seen and felt over the years how cold our house had gotten, and he just couldn't stand it anymore. *I* was his problem.

I remember back when times were good; when he and I would go to the park and hit baseballs into the outfield. He had a good eye and a swing like Ted Williams. I always tried to get him into baseball, but it was something he wasn't too interested in. That was okay; I enjoyed our time out on the field anyway. Those were good memories....

Davey was the type of kid who was really into schoolwork. Most times back when he was about the house early in his school career, I'd see him at the kitchen table doing homework; not because he was assigned it, but because he asked for it. I remember asking what he wanted to be when he grew up on a fishing trip. A writer like his dad. Can you believe that? A writer. Surely, that changed over the years.

Looking back on that as I sat on the porch, I felt the pressure of the situation push against my chest in the November night air. I had sacrificed everything for a woman who I thought I would eventually get. I just thought things would turn out differently for not only me but also for all of us. I could sit back and let the things that I've done dictate the futures of my kids, or I could try like hell to rein them back in and show them that their father still cared about them.

Taking a deep breath and blowing out hard, seeing my breath, I decided right then and there that I was going to be a better person to them. I had to be. But little did I know, the future of Samantha and Davey was already written. And the author of their destiny was me and my past actions. Samantha was gone and Davey wasn't long for the world. The chances of me being their hero had evaporated into thin air.

CHAPTER ELEVEN

1

I was burning through my latest novel, *What Is and What Will Never Be*, and felt that this book was truly the best I'd ever written. I'd already submitted *Tricks of the Trade* to Windom and was glad that book was out of my house. That was the last thing I would ever write for that publisher and I was pretty sure that the critics wouldn't like it, and neither would my scant few remaining fans. I would lose more after that book hit the shelves. I didn't care. I had another book, a *better* book, that was going to knock their socks off. At least that was the plan. *Fuck it,* I thought. I felt good about my writing again.

It was some of the best stuff that I had written in a very long time. Whatever mojo that I had lost long ago had seemingly come back to me with a vengeance. I felt young again, almost as I did back when I began my writing career. During those times, I wrote some of the best stuff that any kid my age could have written. God, I wish I had those old stories I used to write by hand at the kitchen table when I was a kid. Most of them I recalled, others I didn't.

2

Sitting at my desk in the office, putting the final touches on my new effort, my comeback book, I stopped typing on the keyboard and leaned back to look at the final sentence. I had made it. I completed something that I was proud of, for a change. The book wasn't like the others when I finished. When I began my slump, I would finish a book and just send it straight to Bob Windom. From there they would do what I called a "hatchet" edit, and by the time I got an author's copy, it barely resembled what I had written. That tells you how bad I had gotten—a ghostwriter was on call for my books at Windom all because I had gotten lazy and didn't care anymore. Most of the time, I was drunk and didn't remember writing many of those books.

My comeback novel wasn't like that, though. It didn't need a ghostwriter, nor was I drinking. I was sobering up—I wasn't drinking anymore. I was fucking awesome at my craft once again, and that was something that I had not been in my writing for a very long time. I mean, as soon as I finished writing the final word of this book, I knew that my creation was going to blow up in the writing world. All my old fans that had strayed would come flying back to me, and I would once again be a best-selling author, not a relic of yesteryear or an answer on *Jeopardy!* that no one knew.

I should have never even put myself into such a predicament in the first place. I should have cleared my head long ago and stayed focused on what was important. But I didn't. I let too many things get in my field of vision that impaired me. But none of that mattered as I sat there looking at the fruits of my labor.

I had finished off my newest book, broke it off with Marie, met my soulmate, Heather, and decided that I was going to mend all the fences with my kids. Where did that leave my wife? Nowhere. Too much irreparable damage. The best thing for us was to get that divorce and officially move on with our separate lives.

CHAPTER TWELVE

1

I had finally completed all my final revisions on my comeback book a week before Thanksgiving. It took me less time than I thought it would. The words just seemed to flow out of me. It was like seeing an old friend again. I had recaptured the magic of my talent once again, and after I concluded the book, I sat back in my office chair, taking it all in. I was finished with everything!

Things around the house were the same, except for the fact that Samantha was gone. Her bedroom was empty; even its walls were bare. All it was now was a sad, empty bedroom. I avoided looking in when I passed by. Eventually, I closed the door. It hurt too much to see her not there. I remember passing by when she was younger lying on the floor on her stomach playing with toys. Later, when she got older, she'd lie on her bed and do her homework with music playing. Closing the door forever spared me the pain of walking by.

Samantha had gone to live with Randy and his parents, which brought me some sort of relief. At least I knew where she was staying, rather than not knowing. She was safe, I knew that. Randy's parents were good, salt-of-the-Earth people. If they accepted my daughter into their home, then they had my full support. I still wasn't on board with my daughter tossing her future out the damn window, but I also felt that a little time apart may do us both some good. I held out hope that she would come back but I also had to be realistic.

2

I had tried in earnest to draw Davey out of his bedroom to no avail over the last few weeks. We would both stand at his bedroom door, talking like a landlord and tenant when the rent's due. I tried; I really did. But even I realized it was too late. I mean, what parent just throws their hands in the air and gives up on their kids? I didn't plan to, but in the end, I did because Davey was beyond my reach. My only hope was that he would snap out of his depression and get back to being good again. He never did. He just got worse and worse.

3

Jennifer came and went. I wish there was more to say about her during that time, but there wasn't. I had no idea what was going on with her. It wouldn't have mattered even if she would have told me because there was nothing I could do about it. Sometimes things just happen. And sometimes people are pushed into things. She had a battle raging internally and externally. I didn't know it all at the time, but later, everything was revealed. Then it all made complete sense.

4

Back to me. It was a good feeling to write something I was proud of. Critics always said my first decade of writing was my best. And they were right. During that time, I could harness the magic and funnel it through my fingers as my brain and fingers worked as one. It was also in that formative decade that I began to win awards and receive critical acclaim for my work.

Soon I would become a household name with book clubs and group discussions. Later the movies would come—TV movies, mind you—but I didn't care. It was neat just to see my work on the screen, no matter how much they fucked it up.

At one point during my career slump, I was going to retire and never peck another key on my computer. But when you're a writer, whether a short-story writer or a full-blown novelist, you can't ever just *leave* the craft. Believe me, I tried to no avail. That's why I halfway did it for a long time.

5

I remember a cold, rainy day in Atlanta during October some years ago that made me realize that maybe I was down for the count. This was when I was drinking heavily and had Marie on my mind, twenty-four-seven. I was at a bookstore doing a promotional book signing of my latest abortion, *The Time in Our Days*. It was a shit book. I could only muster up about forty-thousand words during about three month's worth of writing. It was one of those books that I had just written to give to Windom. It wasn't good at all and when I was sober I read about a quarter of it. It was all I could stand to read.

Back in the good old days, I could fly through a hundred-and-fifteen-grand word count like nobody's business. For several years, it had gotten harder and harder to even muster forty thousand. I could have easily quit back then. But I still had to fulfill my contract or pay back the money that was already given to me through deferments. And fuck giving the cash back.

I was fully aware that my books were getting worse drunk or not. My editors were constantly sending shit back to me to fix and revamp entire chapters because they were not coherent. I fought them vehemently, but they would remind me each time that I had a deadline and if I didn't get something that they could print before my release date, I'd have to owe *them* money for holding them up. Then came the ghostwriters. My books were always published in May, and with each book over the last decade, I would push the May deadline. Always just under the wire. The last several books were ghostwritten. I think that *The Time in Our Days* was Windom's last straw and he ordered everyone afterward to be rewritten by his in-house team of book doctors; that's why the last several books are coherent but not good. No matter how good the book doctors were, they lacked my imagination and direction. They could reword everything, change some scenes but they could never capture what I could do sober-minded and especially when I cared.

In that small mom-and-pop bookstore that rainy and cold day in October, the line of my fans had grown notably short. I think I counted around twenty people, probably devoted fans who would read anything I wrote, no matter how terrible it was. Each one bundled up in their cold-weather gear, clutching my newest book that I was promoting, seeking an autograph with just my name or a personalized message. To them, I was a rock star. To me, I was just plain over it.

I had signed all that I could sign and the last fan, a kid of eighteen, approached my table not with my newest book, but one from the vault: *Days of Rain and Sun*, my ultimate masterpiece. I knew it, and the critics knew it. Had I never, ever written another book again, that novel alone would have stood the test of time. Even now, it still is regarded as one of the Top 50 most influential books of all time.

"*Days of Rain and Sun*," I said, looking at what was a rare first edition. "I haven't seen that edition out and about in a long while." I noticed the dust jacket was in a protective cover. This kid must be a big fan, I thought to myself.

"Yeah, this one is my favorite. I love the characters and plot. I've never read anything as thought-provoking as this. I really connected with it. It's what made me want to become a writer," the kid said, still clutching the book in his hand.

"Thank you. It's by far *my* favorite book. I've never written anything that good since, I don't think," I replied.

"I know. I'm still a huge fan and all, but what has happened lately?" The kid's tone changed a bit from our initial greeting. He seemed personally hurt by my declining abilities.

Here was a kid that no question was a fan of my work, so much in fact that I had inspired him to become a writer with just one book. He wanted answers on why I wasn't as good as I once was. *Good question*, I thought to myself. "It's like the last few books or so have been just... mailed in. They lack that—," the kid said snapping his fingers trying to summon the thought that had temporarily escaped his mind, "—sense of sincerity. It's like the books are cold lately."

The critics from coast to coast had ripped on me with each book. But there stood an eighteen-year-old kid who just gave me something that I hadn't been told up to that point in my career, at least not by a fan: My writing was cold. It *was* cold. I never could place my finger on the exact problem with my work. I knew that it wasn't good, but there stood this kid who told me the bold-faced truth about what my work was now: cold.

I lowered my head down and looked at the table, knowing he was right. I felt ashamed, sitting there trying to pass myself off as a writer. I wasn't a writer anymore. I was just a guy running out the clock to collect my money. Up to that point, I never once had a fan that came up and said such hard-hitting things to me. What balls on this kid.

I knew it sucked, sucked badly. But no one in my fan base had told me that to my face. Everyone just patted me on the back and smiled and wanted my autograph and a picture with me. Or at the very least they had the common courtesy to talk shit about my work on the internet but never to my face. My fans just wanted to talk and be a part of my legacy so they could tell their friends at work or school that they "met Jerry Matthews last weekend and let me tell you... he was such a down-to-earth kind of guy."

This kid shot me with complete honesty and made me feel like I had become a con artist, taking advantage of fans' money and giving them nothing but a book that wasn't worth the paper it was printed on. I was passing them slop. This kid wasn't taking it. He paid his hard-earned money to buy a book because he was a fan of my work. I owed him.

"Yeah, my work hasn't been where I want it to be lately," I said knowing that was a complete and utter lie. Maybe not so much a lie as perhaps the truth. I wasn't where I wanted to be so how could I expect my work to be?

"You're my favorite author and always will be. I just want you to hit a home run with the next book. I want to be involved with the characters you write again like in *Homecoming*. That's been lacking lately. It's like you just put out books to be putting out books. It's what I would call being on autopilot."

Damn, this kid was spot on.

I was stunned by this kid's bravado. Here he was, a pimply-faced kid critiquing my work like he was some well-to-do critic from New York City. He was the type of fan who had helped me earn a living doing what I once loved. And what had I been doing for him in return? Just taking his money.

When Windom released me, I was bitter. I had gotten what I wanted, alright. I wanted to be done but under *my* terms. But the house had beaten me to the punch. They released me, telling me that I wasn't good enough to hang around anymore. I wanted out. And that's what Bob did: he gave me what I wanted. That made me mad. And it was in that madness that I wanted to write something like *Days of Rain and Sun* again. I wanted to show the world, my fans, and especially myself that I was still the writer that I always was.

"What's your name, kid?" I asked as I reached for the book he was holding.

"Abe. Abe Aziz."

I turned to the first blank page of the book I came to and wrote the following inscription:

To Abe, thanks for setting me straight on my work. Here's to getting it right the next time for sure! I'll write the next one for you, buddy! Your friend, Jerry Matthews

I gave the book back to him, "Just wait until the next one, Abe. Just you wait," I said as I flashed him a hesitant smile. But that was some time ago, and my drive had waned considerably since.

Soon after Abe, I went home and buried myself in thoughts of Marie and booze. I wasn't going to hit a home run with the next book and didn't even get off the bench to swing the bat. The next book was *Tricks of the Trade* and it sucked. I had lied to Abe. I'm sure I let him down.

6

However, that promise I made to Abe was complete now, so as I sat in my quiet office, I wrote my dedication to him. I had completed what I thought was the comeback novel of a lifetime. Even Heather thought so. Thinking of Heather, I reached for my cell and called to surprise her with the good news. If anyone would be happy about the news of my finished novel, it would be Heather.

"Hey," answered Heather after a few rings. Immediately I could tell something was wrong. Normally Heather had a cherry, upbeat voice but her tone on that day was different. I'd never heard it like that and knew something terrible had happened. "What's wrong?" I asked, forgetting all about my entire reason for calling her.

CHAPTER THIRTEEN

1

"Um... I got an unexpected call from someone today," Heather said in a cracked and frightened voice.

"From?" I asked feeling my stomach go into knots. At first, I thought maybe she had gotten the sad news about a family member of hers who had died, perhaps her mom or dad. But I was wrong.

She cried a little, sniffled to fight back the tears. "Paul... Paul Hanson," she replied weakly.

I sat there at my desk, wondering who had reduced her to pieces like that. "Who's that?" And as soon as I asked it, my mind clicked, and I remembered her telling me a little bit about Paul but I couldn't remember anything remarkable enough to think it merited Heather being so upset.

A long pause on the other end of the phone as she wiped the tears from her eyes and tried to collect herself. "He's my ex-boyfriend—a very bad guy."

"How bad?" I asked, leaning on my desk with my elbows. Heather had never talked about much about her past. Apparently, this Paul Hanson was a huge part of her history. So much that she was rocked to her very core when he came calling. And by the way her voice sounded on the phone, I could tell that whatever they had had went sour in the worst way. He was one of those *can't-let-go* kinds or *If-I-can't-have-you-no-one-will kinds* of people. The subject came up a while back when we were trading stories about the past. Paul came up, reluctantly, and she didn't give me much in the way of a portrait of the guy. From her tone and some of the stuff that he had said to her during their relationship, I knew that he wasn't a great guy and one that she didn't like to talk about. So I left her alone about it.

Another long pause before she answered my question. And then she finally spoke to reveal the hidden parts of her past to me. "Paul and I used to go out together as you know. But I never told you about some of the stuff that he did to me. If I did I can't remember. I've tried to forget that part of my past. Sometimes those memories are there like a splinter in my finger.

"We met in the eighth grade and were together up until six months ago. I, um... I just couldn't take him anymore, you know? I had finally reached my breaking point. I didn't know what else to do; had no more options at the time," Heather said, almost trying to justify her finally leaving him six months ago. I could tell that she was scared of even talking about the guy.

"What happened?" I asked, thinking that this was just another high-school fling that had finally petered out much like all high school romances do over time. Something told me in the back of my mind that this wasn't an ordinary high school fling, though. This was something that produced demons—long-term debilitating ones.

Another long pause as she readied herself. "He used to hit me, hit me hard. It started in the eighth grade. The first time he did it, it was after a football game that the school lost. He had thrown three interceptions that had cost them the game. After that game, he was so mad. I tried to calm him down, but he flew into this rage... and then he punched me several times... blackened one of my eyes... nearly broke my eye socket," Heather spoke, shaking as she told the tale. I pictured the violence and fought back tears.

"What about your folks? What did they say?" I asked after she sobbed briefly. I wanted her to get it out, but I allowed her to do it at her own pace. The last thing I wanted to do was force her into a conversation about a past she was still running away from.

Another long pause. "I, um … told them that Paul and his friends were fooling around at his parents' house, tossing a football around when one of them went long and caught the football crashing into me. They bought it. As the beatings went on, so did my lies. I eventually got to the point where I could lie and believe it myself," Heather admitted as she laughed darkly at her own admission.

"How did you finally end it with him?" I asked, stunned by her story. It was something I hadn't expected her to say.

"About six months ago, I just left and moved into the city and into the apartment that I'm in now, actually. I left my friends and never told them where I was going because I was afraid they would slip and tell him where I was. The only people that knew where I was were my parents and I told them that they didn't need to tell him where I was. How he found me I don't know. I'm not on social media or anything. There shouldn't have been any trace of me where he could have known how to get into contact. Totally off the grid. But then he called. And the damndest thing: I had changed my number."

"What did he say to you when he got you on the phone?" I could tell that she was gripped with terror as she thought about the phone call from a voice from her dark past.

"He wanted to know why I left him. And he said that if I didn't come back, he'd kill me. And that he had found my number and that it wouldn't be much longer until he found where I lived." Her words chilled me to the bone. "Thing is… he'll find me and when he does… I'm afraid of what he'll do." Heather said, finally breaking down on the phone. I let her cry. It was all I could do for her.

I didn't know exactly what else to do, honestly. I had never been in that situation before. Her past was like something that I had written years ago in one of my novels. But Heather's dark and frightening past wasn't fiction. It was real life in its rawest form. Had she been one of the characters in my book, I would have given her the power to murder the abusing son of a bitch with an ax and bury his remains in the nearby forest. End of story.

"He's not going to find you," I said, trying to offer words of comfort. "And if he does, you've got me to protect you. I'm not going to let anything happen to you." I assured her the best I could.

"You ain't here...," she sobbed. "He could show up here any minute and kick this door down and kill me," she said through her tears. She was right. I wasn't there. I was at home, safely sitting behind my huge oak desk, basking in the afterglow of completing my novel that was going to win back my fans and attract new ones. On the other end of the phone line, Heather was falling apart.

Trying to figure out how I could help her, an idea sprang into my mind. I had a place where she could stay, a place where no one would find her, a place for her to feel safe and lay low for a bit. It was a cabin out by Lake Harden across from Marie's father's cabin. It was in a completely different town but on the same lake. Jennifer and I had used the cabin a few times in the past, but I hadn't been there in the better part of twelve years, maybe longer. It was taken care of by Elmer Duckworth, who was a grandson of the guy that we bought it from those years ago. I paid him to tend to the place through all the seasons as necessary as I rarely visited the cabin.

"Listen, Jennifer and I have this place up at Lake Harden that we stayed at some summers ago. I can make a call and have the place ready and cleaned up if you want to stay there. Which I think you might want to do. At least for a bit, you know."

Another long pause. "I don't want you to get into the middle of this. I didn't mean...."

"I love you. And when you love someone, you get in the middle of everything in their life, okay?" I said truthfully.

Another long pause on the phone. "I just need you tonight," Heather said. "I just need you here with me." Her voice had a hint of pleading in it. I ran my fingers through my hair and looked around the office. There wasn't anything keeping me there anyway.

2

When I arrived at her apartment, she threw her arms around me and buried her crying face into my chest, wetting my Braves t-shirt. I held her close and tight as she wailed. She was as emotionally wounded as I had ever seen a person. I finally pulled her from my chest, wiped her eyes, and walked her to the couch. We both sat down and held each other, looking out through the huge bay window that was across the living room at the rain streaking down the panes.

She held onto me as though I was going to float away much like a kid hangs onto a balloon. I wasn't going anywhere. I was there for her, holding her trembling bones as they seemed to rattle like one of those medical skeletons that hang in the biology classes. She kept crying, her face buried in my shoulder, letting it all out in a flood.

I sat there and didn't say anything. What could I say? What words could I offer her that would make things okay again? There was nothing. The only thing that I could do was sit there, hold her tight, and let her cry throughout the night. Sometimes the best thing you can say is nothing.

3

When the first break of daylight poured through the blinds of her bedroom, I found myself in her bed, half covered under her blankets. Heather was sprawled across the bed, one arm draped over my chest as her face lay silently and peacefully on her pillow. We had had sex that night for the first time, and I could still feel the sticky sweat that had dried on my body.

It had been a little hot in her apartment. Heather had the thermostat up to 75 because she was always cold. I, on the other hand, was always hot. When we got into the bedroom later that night, we both were so hot and sticky, I didn't mind much. Lying there on her bed, naked and exposed under her bedcovers, I was still warm, but too lazy to uncover the rest of the way. I just lay there and stared up at the ceiling.

I hadn't come to Heather's place to do her. I came there to comfort her in her dire time of need. But like most sex, it just kind of happened. Not before she spilled her past, revealing more and more pieces of a terrible history. I was captivated by the things that she said—horrified, actually—and sympathized fully at her every word.

We had talked about in-depth topics before, but that night in her apartment, she had got emotionally deeper than I ever thought she'd go. The road she took me down was a winding one, full of dangerous switchback curves and black ice. When the trip was over, I looked at Heather differently; not in a bad way, but I felt so sorry for her. I wished that I could have eased her pain. I wished that I could've stopped Paul before he got started.

With most people, you find out things about them as you go, and I thought that would be the same flow of the game with my relationship with Heather. She was twenty-two and didn't have that much life experience, or so I thought. As she revealed more about her past, I began to put its pieces together and figured out why she seemed older than her age, wiser beyond her years, an old soul if you will. After some of her tales, I realized that she was older because she had a tough time growing up and that mentally matured her.

Heather, while I knew her, never walled herself away from difficult emotions. She wasn't that way, at least not with me. When we talked, she was open and candid; very forthcoming. Not that I pried into her personal life. She would offer up some past story or tale of her childhood that helped me understand her. Most stories and recollections were happy tales, but when she began to tell me about some of her dark times, I sat in awe of her, the woman I considered my soulmate.

4

Heather told me many things that night. Things she said that she had never told anyone, not even her best friend, Macy. She was selective about who she talked to and told me that although she could've confided in Macy the things that bothered her, Macy would never quite grasp the gravity of Heather's problems.

"With you," she said. "It's different because you know how life is and have been through the fire and brimstone."

Heather told me about her father, a recovering alcoholic. She told me about all the times that he came home drunk and could barely make it through the front door. (I could relate.) And when he did, he would stumble and yell and laugh throughout the dark and quiet house, while she and her mother attempted to sleep. Oftentimes, though, there would be no sleep for Heather. Things would usually go haywire when she would go upstairs to sleep for the night. Downstairs, Roger would cuss and beat his wife—Heather's mother— into tears, showing proof of his rage the very next morning.

Then Roger, upon seeing his wife in her black and blue state, would feel ashamed of himself and try to be good and apologize profusely right up until the following Friday night, when he would come home drunk once again. Thus the cycle would repeat itself. Heather likened her childhood during that time to being a hamster on a hamster wheel: always running but never getting anywhere.

When was the breaking point? Heather said that one Friday night, her dad came home late. He had been late before, but that night, he was unusually late. Heather's mother, Stacy, would pace around the house and call his phone to see where her drunk husband was. No answer. In the back of Stacy's mind, she wondered if he had an accident on the way home from the bar. Would she have cared? Heather didn't think her mother would have wanted her dad to die, but as she confessed to me, her mother wouldn't have been broken if he had. At least the Friday night beatings would've stopped.

Roger had been in an accident that Friday, alright. It turned out better than it should've, given the drivers involved. Roger and the other driver, Denny Gline, must have had angels in their respective passenger seats. Roger, who was loaded to the gills and swerving badly on the country road leading to his house and coming from the opposite direction, swerved one way, Denny the same, and *BAM!* They collided head-on.

When the ambulances, police officers, and fire department arrived on the scene, the officials thought for sure both drivers were dead. Instead, they found Roger and Denny on the side of the road, kneeling and praying together. Denny, a priest, had taken a knee with Roger next to the ditch as the remnants of the twisted metal and busted glass lay in the road. Both were bruised and cut and bleeding, but there they were, thanking God for sparing their lives.

After the accident with Father Gline, Heather went on to say that her father got himself clean. He came home and emptied every bottle of beer and liquor in the house. He patched up things with her mother, got them all into church—Father Gline's church as a matter of fact—and became a pillar of the community. His days of terribleness had come to an end.

5

Other stories included Heather's bout with depression after her older brother, Steve, was killed in an accident while out with his best friend, Kyle. The two had been deer hunting in the woods for some time. And as the story was told from Kyle to her family and then from Heather to me, Steve must have gotten hot while crouched in his sniping position in a nearby thicket. He took his orange vest off and laid it on the ground. Moments later, Kyle recalled, he saw something stirring around from his vantage point in a thicket of briars and bushes. Not once thinking it was Steve, Kyle aimed and took a shot at what he thought was a deer. Kyle was utterly horrified when he ran upon the thicket to find his best friend lying on the ground, dead.

And then her stories came around to her ex-boyfriend, Paul Hanson. She told me things that shocked and appalled me. I could not believe what he did to her. I mean, how could anyone be that cruel and mean to such a wonderful person?

I was on the verge of tears as she recounted her memories of all the beatings, verbal abuse, and sexual assault that she endured from the prick from the ages of thirteen to twenty. I hung my head as she told me horrifyingly unforgettable stories that shaped her adolescence: Seven long years of torment.

I asked her why she hadn't told her parents, much less the police, about Paul's actions. She said that no one would have believed her because Paul was this good-looking, church-going, popular quarterback of the football team. He was a straight-A student and served on the student council. He did all kinds of volunteer work in the community. Heather said that if she'd told people about what he was really like, they would've branded her a liar and a drama queen.

Then Heather showed me something that I hadn't noticed in our time together. She rolled up her long sleeves and held up her wrists for me to see. Although time had healed most of the scars, on her left and right wrists were vertical valleys made by her dad's straight razor on Halloween when she was fifteen years old.

I sat there, stunned at the notion that this enchanting woman had once attempted suicide. Her depression, she told me, had gotten the best of her. When she said that my thoughts quickly turned to my fifteen-year-old son, Davey. Only he wouldn't slash his wrist and bleed out. He chose a different method of delivery to end his life.

On the night Heather attempted suicide, she had just returned home with a pounding headache from where Paul had hit her several times in the head for disrespecting him at a high-school Halloween party at a mutual friend's house. Of course, Paul had been drinking. And when Paul drank, he got violent and took all his frustrations out on Heather. Sometimes, Heather told me boldly, when he was drunk, Paul would do two things: rape or beat her, sometimes both. On that particular night of her suicide attempt, Paul had done both.

Paul dropped Heather off at her house after threatening to kill her if she told anyone what he'd done to her. Heather swore to him her secrecy. She opened the passenger side door and hadn't even gotten all the way out when Paul slammed the gas and sped away, almost sending Heather to the pavement. She stood there, collecting herself and watching as Paul's passenger side door swayed open and closed as his red taillights disappeared down the street.

Heather walked up to the door. Wiping the salty tears away from her eyes, she noticed her house was dark and empty. No one was home. She dug into her pocket, fetched her keys, and unlocked the front door to go inside. Heather told me that, once she was in there, she walked right over to the couch and sat down and cried so much that her eyes felt as if they were going to burst right out of her head.

She sat there alone in the dark living room crying, thinking about how she had to get away from Paul. She entertained the notion, she admitted, of running away and never being seen or heard from ever again. However, a different idea struck her violently amid her sadness. It was the ultimate way out.

Suicide. And the more that she cried and the more she felt the pain from her headache, the more Heather gravitated toward doing it. She said her mind raced wildly and the thought of ending the pain forever was grotesquely appealing to her. Before she knew it, Heather was in the bathroom, filling the tub with water while she undressed.

She said that she had stopped crying enough so her vision was not as blurry. She walked over to the medicine cabinet and opened it up. There on the third shelf right next to the vitamins for men and the Band-Aid box was her dad's shiny silver straight razor. She reached in and took it from its place, closed the door, and walked back over to the nearly full tub.

Heather said that she didn't recall getting into the hot water until she realized the sensation against her skin as she leaned back in the water. It was relaxing sitting in the tub, she said. Heather had been taking showers ever since she was ten, so soaking in a tub was kind of foreign to her. She said it felt wonderful.

She lay in the tub, head propped up against the back edge while the rest of her young naked body was submerged under hot water. Under the water, her right hand clutched the razor. Heather said she lay there and thought about how much better things were going to be. And that the one selling point for her death would be that she would never, ever feel Paul's hands hit her anymore. No more rape. No more being called stupid, a bitch, or a slut. Those thoughts alone were enough to make her do it, she told me.

6

Heather sat there on the couch and collected her breath. The rain outside had gotten harder, and the wind pushed the heavy drops of rain violently against the bay window in her living room, causing a constant *tac-tac-tac-tac* sound.

I sat there facing her, my hand on hers for comfort. I knew that going back down those roads of a dark past could be treacherous and painful. Heather bravely forged on, though, wiping tears from her eyes as she tried to smile the pain away and show me that she was stronger these days. She was, more so than she'd ever care to give herself credit for.

Heather went back to her story, squeezing my hand for strength to finish speaking. She said that all she thought about was how alone she felt, how isolated she had become within herself since being with Paul. The two of them had history, and Heather knew that the future wasn't going to be any better than the past or present.

She said that she wasn't waiting for Paul to have his moment like her father had the night he almost killed Father Gline. She wasn't as patient as her mother was to her father back in his drinking days. Nothing was binding her to Paul. The only way out, the only feasible way to get away from him and his wrath, was to kill herself. Suicide was the final solution to her problems because Paul would never in a million years just let her walk away. She knew his secrets.

She didn't remember how long she had been soaking, but it was long enough for the water to cool. Heather said that she just sat in the water and sort of blanked out, thinking of nothing really, empty thoughts. Her head still hurt, pounding and throbbing to her heartbeat. Paul had hit her hard several times, perhaps the hardest that he had ever struck her, she said. She thought that she might've sustained a concussion.

Paul had been hitting her in the head a lot more often to hide his blows. Hitting her in the face was going to attract too much attention, and then maybe someone would find out what he was doing with the Parkers' daughter. So, Paul began to hit her in the head as hard as he could—and no one knew about it.

Heather interrupted her Halloween story to recount a time when he literally knocked her out. She said she saw stars as she fell to the floor. She said she had a dream, while unconscious, wherein she was walking through a meadow. All was calm and serene, and the sun brightened up everything. The grass, she said, was a soothing green as well were the leaves on the trees that towered above her. For just that moment, she said, she felt no pain.

When she came to, lying on her back on her bedroom floor, she felt the tips of his boots crush into her ribs. As she tried to roll away for protection, his boots kicked and kicked her sides. Heather said that she tried to crawl away, but it was no use. Paul towered over her, a kid of thirteen, laughing manically, calling her obscene names. Heather said she began to think of that very moment while soaking in the tub and about how small she felt as she tried to crawl away on her bedroom floor while her parents were at the grocery store.

The tears in her eyes welled up and streamed down her cheeks while we sat on the couch and a thunderclap shook the walls of her apartment. Heather squeezed my hand a little tighter for more strength as she marched onward with her Halloween story.

She told me that in the tub, the thought of that night crawling away from Paul's boots flashed in her mind like a vivid home movie. She began to cry in the tub, her tears rolling down her cheeks into the bathwater.

Her grasp on the razor became tighter as she slowly lifted the instrument out of the water, raising it out of the bath. Heather said that she could hear Paul's laughter ringing in her ears, echoing throughout the walls of her mind. She wanted the laughter to stop. She wanted the pain to stop. *She* wanted to stop.

Heather held out her left hand, opened it wide, and took the razor. With a furious whip, she cut a bloody valley vertically down her tender white wrist. Almost as soon as she did it, blood sprayed out, gushing into the water. She said the bath water looked like areas of the ocean where people lured sharks with blood and meat.

Then came the pain, the awful pain that came with the bloodletting. But it was nothing compared to what Paul had done to her over the years, she admitted. Then, changing hands with the razor, she drove an identical bloody valley down her other wrist, but it wasn't as deep as the first one because her hand had grown incredibly weak and shaky, making her unable to grip the razor as tightly as she wanted.

Again, blood spewed out, followed by a blinding flash of pain. Her hands twitched and went numb as the razor fell into the water, resting on the bottom of the tub.

She told me that the vertical slashes on her wrists hurt like hell and burned like fire. At first, she wanted to place a towel and compress the wounds to stop the bleeding, but then her mind grew weak and her thoughts began to comfort her in her time of pain and sorrow. Heather said that this was when she began to fade away, seeing the bathroom grow further and further away from her sight. As badly as her slashed wrists hurt, it was no comparison to the ways that Paul had hurt her; she had a high pain tolerance. I had no doubt.

Heather said at some point, one she could not recall precisely, she closed her eyes as her life filled the tub and fell into a slumber, teetering somewhere between life and death. She didn't remember seeing a bright, white light as some report. Heather said that it seemed like only seconds had ticked passed between her eyes closing and her mother screaming and pulling her bloody and naked body out of the tub, clutching her, yelling at the top of her lungs for Roger to come to the bathroom. Her parents had gotten back home two minutes after Heather did what she did. A few minutes later they would have found Heather dead in the tub according to the EMT later on. They were lucky.

Heather could barely open her eyes. Her mother's face swam before her, crying and holding her, telling Heather it was going to be okay and rocking her on the wet, bloody bathroom floor.

After several blood transfusions at the hospitals and some quick decision-making by the responding medics at the Parker home, Heather's life was saved, but barely, not before she marked herself for life with her dad's straight razor. Her wrists were constant reminders of a night that she tried to get away from Paul. And what about Paul afterward? Well, he showed up at the hospital, crying his eyes out, swearing that he'd never leave her bedside. But did he blame himself? "Absolutely not," Heather said. Sometime after she'd been released from the hospital, Paul went right back to being Paul. On the outside people saw Paul as the doting boyfriend who tried to recuperate his knock-out gorgeous girlfriend. But the Paul people didn't see, weren't allowed to see, Paul was angry that Heather had tried to leave him this way. After she got back to being psychically healthy, Paul went back to hitting her again, raping her again.

Heather's parents pestered her for months about why she'd attempted suicide. She gave an annoyingly unclear but typical teenage response: "I don't know." But that excuse wore thin as she was counseled by Father Gline. Eventually Heather gave them a better lie. It was over school and the pressures that she felt about being a girl and a good student. Her parents and Father Gline bought it. After all, this girl seemed to have it all, what else would make her try a stunt like that?

All of Paul's concern and tears and public heartache were nothing more than a pony show, a performance that could've gotten him an Academy Award. But that was Paul. He didn't want people to know the real reason that Heather was in the hospital, wrists bandaged and groggy for days on end. He didn't want people to know just how much of a maniac he was for driving his girlfriend to nearly kill herself.

Heather would have died that night. That was her plan, after all. It seemed to be the only way for her to escape Paul's hell. Death was far better than living another day with Paul Hanson.

7

Heather sat on the couch as the rain smacked against the window, looking off in the distance, remembering the time following her suicide attempt. She said that she was numb for months. Numb from everything. She had done something that few dared and many teenagers secretly pondered. Heather stood on the edge of death and would have died if not for her parents coming home early and finding her bleeding out in a tub of red water.

Had her mother come into the bathroom a few minutes later, Heather would've never bumped into me at the bookstore. I would've never gotten the chance to know this wonderful person. I would've never been strong enough to let go of Marie.

Heather looked at me with watery eyes and squeezed my hand again, though not as tight as before. "I'm sorry," she said. "That was just a dark time in my life." I looked at her and wanted to say something to break the silence between us. I mean, what could I say after all I'd heard? So I said nothing. I tried to process her story, but it wasn't easy.

Nothing I could say would come out right. It's like when someone dies and you go to the funeral and you see the family. Normally you say, "I'm sorry for your loss." That's about it, the staple phrase that everyone says. Sitting there with Heather on the couch during the storm, I just looked into her beautiful eyes and said nothing. Instead, I drew her close and we sat there, listening to the wind and the rain and thunder outside. It was all I could do.

8

I looked over to my shoulder and saw Heather, who was also naked, asleep under covers. I lay there in bed and stared up at the ceiling, listening to the soft, faint breathing coming from the young woman whom I loved. I thought about how lucky I was to have met Heather and how things were looking up for me. I had finally quit Marie after decades of her holding me emotionally hostage, I had written what was quite possibly the best novel I had ever written, and I had found my soulmate. All I had left on my list to get right was to bring Davey back from the depths of despair and free my wife to allow her the closure that she needed. I also hoped Samantha would eventually come around so we could get back to good.

Everything, I thought lying in bed that early morning, *is looking up*. That was until I got a call from my daughter... then everything changed.

CHAPTER FOURTEEN

1

It was a call I never thought I'd receive but should've expected. What a parent fears the most came to pass for me. As I lay in the bed naked with Heather, my cell chirped out loudly on the nightstand. It broke the silence in the bedroom, and I jumped at the unexpected ring. I rolled over and took the phone and looked at the ID on the screen. It was my daughter. My gut told me something was wrong right away. My gut was correct.

I answered the phone with profound trepidation and Samantha's sobbing on the other end of the line. "Samantha?" I asked, fully awake and aware that some trouble had befallen my home. I didn't think that she was calling to mend our previously broken fences. She wasn't like that, too headstrong. Too much like me in that regard.

"It's Davey... he's... dead," Samantha said, her words punctuated by sobs.

I sprang to my feet, startling Heather. "What?!" I asked terrified of what Samantha was about to say again. I went nearly numb.

"He's dead... Dad! Davey is dead! Oh God!" Samantha sobbed.

I stood there naked in Heather's bedroom and, for a moment I thought I might still be asleep, and this entire phone conversation was nothing more than a nightmare. A nightmare would end, but Davey's death would always leave a mark much like Heather's slashed wrists. I will never forget where I was when I heard the news.

My mouth went dry and my mind wandered back to when times with my children were wonderful. I remembered Davey taking his first steps in our living room; I remembered Jennifer and me walking him to his first day of kindergarten; I remembered playing catch with him out in the backyard when Santa Claus had brought him a new baseball mitt under the tree. Man, he was so excited, and after he opened it, he wanted to go outside and pass baseball with me. It was sleeting outside, but we didn't care. It was just me and eight-year-old Davey playing a game of catch. Sublime.

My mind journeyed to other moments in Davey's life—quick flashes like someone flipping through a photo album. Thoughts went by fast, but slow enough for me to see the images and smile a bit. I know, smiling at a time like that, you must see me as uncaring, but it was quite the opposite. I smiled because the memories that passed before my eyes like flash bombs were of times I'll never forget. They are forever etched into my mind.

2

I remember Davey's first school dance in the seventh grade. He was so nervous. When I took him to the dance, he pleaded with me to drop him off a block away from the gym. I was hesitant at first, but I could see the need for his independence. Besides, I saw his other friends walking to the school as dusk descended upon the town and thought, *what the hell? Why not?*

We sat in my car at a stop sign just before the left-hand turn on the street that would lead us to the school. I remembered what it was like being a kid and all the nerves that went with a first dance.

"Get out here. Straight to school. I'll pick you up at the parking lot when the dance is over. Nine o'clock," I said.

"Thanks, Dad!"

Davey opened the passenger side door and bolted up the sidewalk where he caught up to his friends. Together they walked as a group of three towards the school.

Three hours later, I sat in the dark parking lot among the other cars. Davey emerged from the side door of the gym with a girl, Amy

Gonzalez, I later learned. From my view in the car, I could see the two of them laughing and bumping into each other playfully as they walked out into the cold night air.

When I saw Davey, I swear to God that it was as if I was watching a replay of my past. Long ago, there was a dance, a school dance that Marie and I exited side by side, talking and laughing much like my son and his girlfriend were. I don't recall that night with her much and had not thought about it in decades, but when I saw Davey, I saw my history repeating itself. *Hopefully, he'll be better off than his old man*, I remember thinking.

Davey and Amy stood beside my car talking, and I pretended to be texting someone as if to give the perception that I was a busy adult with better things to do other than to spy on thirteen-year-old kids at a school dance. In the corner of my eye, I watched as Amy leaned in to kiss his cheek before turning and walking away. Davey stood there for a moment and was dumbfounded as he rubbed his fingers across the fleshy part of his face where Amy's lips had touched him. I blew the horn to break him out of his trance, sending him jumping nearly out of his Reeboks. I laughed.

Davey shook the cobwebs from his mind and got into my car. He sat there and looked out the window for a moment before buckling his seatbelt.

"Have fun?" I asked, already knowing the answer.

"Yeah, not bad. Played some good songs," Davey said in a very matter-of-fact way.

"Dance with any girls?" I prodded as I tried in vain to pull out of the congested parking lot.

"Yeah," Davey nodded, looking out his window and hoping to catch an extra glimpse of his girlfriend.

"Was one of them that girl you walked out with?" I asked, finally allowed by another car to get into the line of creeping vehicles.

Davey responded, "Um... yeah."

It was the sort of dismissive reaction you'd expect from a teenage kid trying to evade his parent's questions. Eventually, I just stopped asking altogether.

3

I heard Samantha on the other end of the phone sobbing uncontrollably. I asked where her mother was.

"Not here and won't answer her phone," she said. She also proceeded to scream in pain through her tears, why in the hell her parents weren't at home.

I had no answer to her question that was packed with hurt and sorrow as she wailed loudly.

"Did you call the police?!" I asked loudly, but not realizing that I was speaking with such a vicious tone. I honestly was scared and was trying to talk through my daughter's sobbing. I began to pace the bedroom naked, running my hand through my hair nervously while the other one clutched the phone. I was shaking, too, as though my heart had fallen into my stomach. My mind felt out of control. All I thought about was Davey's life flickering around inside my brain like flashes of lightning. At that point, my mind felt like a steel ball in a pinball machine being bounced around here and there.

"Yeah, they're on their way... I need you here!" Samantha shouted in a voice that I had never heard before. Her voice was riddled with loss, sadness, and fear. She needed me. She needed both of her parents. She needed her family.

"Oh my God! I'm on my way there!" I shut the phone off and quickly scrambled for my clothes like a teenager does when he's been fucking his girlfriend and her parents show up earlier than what was expected. Heather sat up in the bed and asked me what had happened. I didn't stop to tell her, I just kept moving; putting on my boxers, then my pants, my shirt, and shoes.

I finally told her that Davey's dead—which I couldn't believe I was saying out loud—and that I needed to get home. I rushed out of Heather's bedroom and apartment so fast that I didn't even tell her goodbye or I love you, nothing. The only thing that I had on my mind was my dead son. And how did this happen? I had absolutely no clue. All I got was a frantic call from my estranged daughter.

4

I arrived at my house in record time after speeding the whole way there. "Dammit," I said as I punched the gas harder down the highway. Usually, it takes me nearly two hours, depending on traffic, to get to and from Heather's house. On that sad day, I got back home in an hour and some change.

I pulled onto our street, our quiet, maple-tree-lined street, and saw something that made my heart sink lower into the pit of my stomach. There in my driveway was an ambulance and two cop cars; my wife's car was nowhere to be seen. I pulled over on the side of the street and slammed the car into PARK, not even thinking about turning it off. Too much was flying around inside my head for me to think of something like that.

I didn't notice the neighbors all standing outside on their lawns, gawking and pointing and talking among themselves in small groups about the commotion. Nothing like this had ever happened in my neighborhood, not since *we* had lived there anyway. I ran across my yard and up to my front door where I was instantly met by a police officer. "You can't go in there," he said, putting his hand on my chest to stop me.

"This is my house!" I shouted, paying no mind that it was a policeman I was shouting at. At that moment, Samantha saw me from the living room and rushed over and hugged me tightly, so tight that I thought she was going to break my ribs. The officer knew right then that I belonged and slowly stepped away, letting me and Samantha have a shared moment. It would be the last tender moment we'd have.

The two of us walked, arm in arm, to the living room where she cried loudly. I stood there, holding my daughter and looking around the room. I could hear men talking down the hallway. I let go of Samantha and walked in the direction of their voices, toward Davey's bedroom. *Oh God, no!* I screamed inside my head.

In Davey's room, two paramedics stood over a body covered with a white sheet, lying on the floor, with another officer writing out a report on his black clipboard. I stood in my son's doorway and peered down at the 5'9" hump underneath the sheet. What lay beneath scared me because it meant that Davey was dead and this had all not been some horrible, horrible nightmare. I was frozen with fear as one of the medics turned to me, "Mr. Matthews?" I didn't reply, unable to take my eyes off my son's covered corpse. My mind was blank as I stared down at the white sheet.

I remember my mouth being dry, my heart pounding and my stomach churning. I never wanted to throw up so badly in my life. I remember my hands were sweaty and shaking. I remember feeling as though I were in a movie and that none of this was real. I mean, how could it be real? I had just spoken to Davey a few days ago. Right? Right?

"Can I speak to you for a minute?" the medic asked, walking me out of the door, acting as though I had a choice to speak with him.

As we stood in the hallway, I didn't take my eyes off that white sheet on the floor. I couldn't see all of it but I knew it was Davey. I couldn't look away. For the life of me, I couldn't.

"Mr. Matthews," the medic began somberly. "Your son is dead. I'm so terribly sorry." He paused for a bit to read my face, which was still looking into Davey's room. "We found a bottle of pain meds beside him on the floor. Hydrocodone. Might've been the culprit. We don't know."

Those were my pills I had taken for the broken ankle I had suffered in late April after I got drunk and fell off the deck stairs. Hurt like a bitch. But I thought I had tossed them. I guess I didn't.

"He must have taken the entire thing. Who knows how many. Do you know how many were left in the bottle, Mr. Matthews?" the medic asked in an attempted calm voice.

For paramedics, breaking news such as a loved one's death was never easy. No matter how many dead bodies they saw, the news still hurt. And this time it hurt badly. It was like I had been sucker-punched with a roundhouse kick to the face. I didn't answer his question about the pills. I just stared at the white sheet on the floor. I was blank.

When Samantha called and told me that Davey was dead, I thought he might have died in a car accident out riding with friends or something. As I drove at top speed back home, I dismissed that possibility because Davey didn't have any friends—none that I ever saw, anyway. He never texted, never went out to the park, never had friends over, nor did he ever go to his friends' homes in the last six months; that I know of. Of course, for a while there, I was locked away in my office drinking and writing shit and thinking about Marie.

And then it hit me about ten miles away from home: Davey had killed himself. It was my worst fear come true. I had been worried about Davey for a while, but just chalked it up to our home being a dysfunctional family dynamic that was fucking with his head. Hell, it fucked with all of our heads. And I caused it. I was the root cause of it all. I just told myself that he was fifteen and that his hormones were going all haywire and compounded with our home life, maybe he was just in a funk.

I knew better though. I had told myself a lie... again. I told myself on several occasions that Davey would just snap out of it. I said it over and over, trying so hard to convince myself, to sell myself the lie. Deep down, in a distant place where I couldn't ignore the truth, I had known that Davey wasn't mentally healthy. As much as I tried to dodge it, the truth was I caused it. It was my greatest failure.

His death was my fault. I caused it in a roundabout way by allowing my home, *our* home, to fall into disarray. For everything that I had ever done, Davey's death was the absolute worst outcome. I stood there in the hallway with the medic looking inside the door and only seeing the lower half of the white sheet. "I'm very sorry, Mr. Matthews," the medic said, patting my shoulder as he moved back into Davey's bedroom.

I stood there, blank. I say blank because that's the only way that I can describe my initial reaction to my son's death. Later, I would go through five stages of grief. In the hallway, I was numb to anything and everything. Numb to the white sheet lying on the floor. Numb to Samantha's crying that I could hear all the way to Davey's bedroom. Numb from... everything. Comfortably numb....

5

I sat on the couch with my daughter, holding onto her while she cried, as the medics carted my son out of his bedroom and through the house. They rolled him out of the living room, through the front door, and loaded him into the ambulance. After a few more questions from the police officer, he left too. Soon, the entire spectacle at my home was gone and in its wake were two spiritually broken people and memories of my dead son.

Then the stillness of the situation came and washed up in our home. It was eerie, the silence. We both sat there next to each other on the couch and didn't say a word.

CHAPTER FIFTEEN

1

Some time had passed. I didn't know exactly how much, but darkness was settling in our town and around my heart. I hadn't moved from the couch as I sat stationary on the left side, hands idle in my lap while Randy, Samantha's boyfriend, came to see about us. He talked to me for a few moments as he held onto my crying daughter there in the living room. Whatever problems the three of us had were tabled until a later date. At that moment, we had more pressing concerns. What could he say, really? What could *anyone* say? He said the usual staple stuff: "Sorry." "I can't believe this happened." "If you need anything, just ask." "I wish I knew the right words." I don't even remember answering him. I just sort of tuned him out... everything went blank.

Life around me hadn't stopped, unlike Davey's. My cell phone rang and vibrated so much that it became just part of the usual noises in the home, much like the ticking clock on the wall. I swear I never heard the clock tick unless I stopped and listened to it. And then when I would hear it, I wondered why I couldn't hear it unless I stopped and listened. That's how I felt with Randy. He talked, but I didn't listen. He had become the clock on my wall, background noise that you couldn't hear unless you stopped and just listened to it.

I missed many phone calls but didn't care. Most were from Heather who texted, leaving voicemails and missed calls on my phone. Two were from Jennifer. I didn't answer any of them. I just sat there, silent on the couch as Randy and Samantha finally wandered out of my field of hearing and vision. I don't even remember if she said bye or if I heard the front door shut. I was left alone in the house, and then I heard the clock ticking.

2

The house was dark with no lights on at all as the day finally submitted itself to the night. I had sat on the couch for hours, just blank, like a sheet of paper on a desk waiting to be written on. The thoughts that I had floated around in my skull like butterflies fluttering around in a field: aimless and weightless, being carried here and there by a light breeze. I tried to catch my random and cursory thoughts but to no avail. There were too many of them.

It was like being in one of those game shows where they put a person into a glass box, much like a phone booth, and then pump air and cash into the box. The object of the game is to grab as many bills as you can as the money blows harshly within the glass encasement. That was me, in my mind. I was trying to reach up and grab a floating thought, only to have it dart and dodge away from my hands.

I had listened to the ticking of the clock for hours before Jennifer came through the front door. She had been crying because I could hear her sniffling as she walked through the living room. I didn't see her, just her shape, her womanly outline in the shadows. She already knew what I had known for hours now. Our son was dead.

For a few moments, she stood there looking down at me through the darkness. The only light that penetrated the Matthews home that evening was from the open blinds in the living room. The street lights outside were bright enough to spill their artificial light inside our home. Not much, but enough to see what I wanted to see.

I sat there as Jennifer sniffled here and there. She wanted to speak. Not me. I was still feeling blank, numb. I wanted to just sit there as the days and nights passed me by. And if that was the case, then so be it. My son was dead, so what did I care? Jennifer stood there, not moving much before she opened her mouth. "Jerry...," my wife said. She stopped right there because she didn't know what else to say. We had never encountered anything like this before. Jennifer didn't know what to say and I sure as hell didn't either. It was such an empty feeling to possess. I mean, how do you talk to someone about the death of a child when you haven't spoken in what felt like years? It was hard. Everything was....

3

I could feel Jennifer's pain as she stood there holding her handbag down to her side by the strap thinking about what to say, what to do. Hell, I would be in that shape soon after I finally got myself off the couch and back into reality. But for now, I just sat there, looking into the darkness. No ticking clock anymore. "I ignored her calls all day... I shouldn't have." Jennifer said with stark realization. She dropped her purse onto the floor as she sat down slowly on the recliner across from me. Just like me, she sat in silence, hoping that I would at least engage with her about our mutual loss. I couldn't though. I was too far gone from reality, chasing those fluttering thoughts.

I think the most frightening thing about sitting in that dark house was its stillness. Jennifer and I hadn't been in the same room together in years, but there we were, sitting and thinking to ourselves, brought together by Davey's suicide. I wondered very briefly as I caught one of those elusive fluttering thoughts if Jennifer was thinking what I was thinking. How could she not be? Just as much as I was to blame for the way things were in the house, she was too, to a degree.

She had detached herself from the kids. She could have had a better relationship with them but didn't. As for me, I didn't care if she ever talked or touched me again. But our children? She should've spent more time with them and not cast them aside to go do her own thing. I at least was at home and tried to spend that quality time with them. Well, not always. I have to be honest here. Sometimes I like to paint myself better than I actually was; one of my many flaws.

She and I sat in that dark living room until the following morning arrived. It was an overcast and rainy start and would be so for several days as a slow-moving system stopped over Georgia. The weather, the dark clouds, and the overall gloominess of it all matched my mood and would do so for a very long time. There was no reason for sunshine. Our son was dead.

4

As the light, gray as it was, poured into our broken and battered home, I caught a good glimpse of Jennifer's face. She had been crying throughout the night with hard tears and a dry heaving that sounded like it strained her insides. She would later say that she thought she had broken a rib or two.

My eyes caught Jennifer's. It was the first time in a very, very long time that our eyes locked. I honestly don't think it happened during our marriage much (maybe in the early days). It wasn't an eye-lock like you'd get when someone attractive looks at you and you catch them but can't seem to look away because you're just too damn captivated. No. My eye-lock wasn't the sensation of being captivated. It was the sensation of being curious. I was curious about what Jennifer was thinking.

I had said that I went through the five stages of grief. I did indeed. However, I didn't go through them in order like some people do. It was like buckshot, hitting them all over the place, nothing directly, and each one of them practically every hour. Even after Davey was put into the ground, I was raw.

Jennifer sat there, looking down at the floor as the gloomy outside light began creeping into our living room. We didn't speak from the time she sat down earlier, hours ago, the previous evening. What time had she gotten home last night? No clue. I had no idea what time it was and I only heard the clock from time to time. Tick... tick... tick... tick, background noise. Time and the meaning of it were of no consequence to me. Perhaps nothing was at that point. Dawn was breaking the night outside. I was still trapped in the previous day's events.

I could see what the news had done to her. She was exhausted. Her eyes had big, black shadows under them. God, I wondered how long they had looked like that. They weren't there before. But then again, what was my definition of *before*? Matter of fact, when was the last time that I even looked at Jennifer? I mean really looked? I couldn't remember. When did she get those crow's feet in the corner of her eyes? She had the beginnings of aging but I never saw it before. But back then when I did look at her, she was young. God, I wondered, how long had I not noticed the clear signs of her aging? There were streaks of gray in her hair. How much time had passed? How much time had we lost?

Her dark brown hair was a mess. She usually kept it pinned up like a sexy school teacher in some teenager's wet dream, but that morning, her hair was down and had a disheveled look, as though fingers had been running through it for hours. She had that nervous thing about her. It was a tell, I told her years ago. When she was in deep thought or worried about something I could always tell because she would run her fingers through her hair as if doing so would provide the answer. Maybe she did it for peace of mind like those who chew their fingernails down their nubs. Perhaps it was just because.

The clothes she had on, her "house showing" clothes, consisted of a white blouse and a blue skirt that went a few inches below her knees. They were wrinkled and not as pressed as she would normally like to wear them outside the house. Nevertheless, she looked good sitting there in her depressed state. I know that I shouldn't have made such an observation, but my God it had been a long time since I had *really* seen Jennifer. I saw the woman who I married years ago sitting there and felt a sudden pang of macabre appreciation for her.

She was beautiful, no question about it. Anyone out there would be lucky to have her. But I really never did. Should have, I guess. In seeing her at that moment, I knew she wasn't well. I knew Davey's death would eventually take its toll on her; as it did the rest of us. Then there was something else off about her, something that didn't concern Davey. She still had that haunted look she had when I saw her out in the driveway that day I went to Atlanta to see Windom.

I'd been married to her for a very long time, so I knew something else was on her mind. I knew the day I saw her out in our driveway right before I was let go from Windom. Sometimes you just know when something is off. No matter what people will tell you, married folks, especially those who have been for a long time, share a sort of telepathy. I knew something else was burning down in her life, that secret life that I knew nothing about.

Our phones rang and rang but neither one of us wanted to answer. It didn't seem right to move on to doing normal stuff like eating, walking around the house, or even answering a phone. Not since Davey was dead. Normal stuff was gone.

Just as my thoughts began to flutter like butterflies in my mind again, Jennifer shattered the silence with a daunting question: "What are we going to do now?" She looked at me, broken.

I returned her stare. How was I to answer that question? "I don't know. I guess we need to make the funeral arrangements. I think he's at Conrad's Funeral Home already," I replied, merely guessing that our son's body was already taken there. I realized I had made no effort to call the funeral home to make arrangements. I was too overcome with emotions. What kind of father was I? Even when it came time to plan my own son's funeral, I had forgotten. I had failed as a father in every respect.

I shook my head, trying to rattle my brain to clarity. I got up from the couch, and my back popped. My legs were stiff and as I stood up, my body cried out as I stretched my bones. How long had I sat on the couch? I couldn't say. Hours I knew for sure, but how many? Perhaps close to sixteen; enough for the sun to set and rise again.

I picked up my phone and cycled through the missed call message icons and the text icons. Most were from Heather, some were from Samantha's phone and a few were from Randy. Either way, I scrolled right through them to clear them off my home screen and opened the Internet to find the number for Conrad's Funeral Home.

I walked slowly into the kitchen, away from my estranged wife as she began to cry again. I found the number and called it. Several rings later, a man with a monotonous voice answered:

"Conrad's Funeral Home."

"Hi," I said clearing my throat. "My name is Jerry Matthews. Um... my son died last—"

"Mr. Matthews, yes. I've been expecting you. We are very sorry to hear about your son. What you're going to want to do is get to the hospital and sign some paperwork. From there we'll call and get the release and go pick up your son. As soon as we get him to the funeral home here, we'll start the prep on him and whenever is a good time we'll need you and your family to come by here so we can begin planning his funeral." he said in a soft and sincere tone.

"Thank you. I'll be in touch." I said hanging up the phone.

My stomach churned like the steel wheels of a locomotive tearing down the tracks. I had to do something just then that I never, ever in a million years thought I'd have to do. No parent thinks that they will outlive their children, and that thought alone made me cry. I placed the phone down on the kitchen island and stood there as the rain began to fall outside. It's not natural for parents to bury their children. It was supposed to be the other way around.

I looked out through the kitchen window over the sink and listened to Jennifer cry loudly, calling for Davey as if he was just in his bedroom playing video games or reading a book. I half-expected him to come running out of there, asking what she wanted like he had in times past, back in the early days when things were good and magical. Hell, I even walked out of the kitchen and to the hallway leading into his room, thinking I might catch a glimpse of him. I didn't see him. God, I was hoping that I would one last time; even a ghost would have been okay.

I went into the living room and walked over to Jennifer and crouched down in front of her. She looked off to my side, wiping the tears from her face. I took her by her trembling hands. It was the first flesh-on-flesh contact she and I had in years and it felt foreign, not like it did with Heather, not like it had with Marie. It was almost like a shock. But I had to. I had to help her gather her composure and talk to me for just a bit. She and I, the parents of the late Davey Matthews, had a lot of work to do. And we had to do it together.

CHAPTER SIXTEEN

1

We talked for a bit longer in the living room, sharing many tears and a hug before we walked out of the house and got into her car in the early morning. It was still raining. Soon we were driving down the street, *our* street, our quiet little street where nothing bad ever happened. We drove together towards the outskirts of town to the hospital where our son lay in state, waiting for us. I couldn't tell you how long it had been since the two of us were in the same car driving.

We didn't talk as I drove. Jennifer was in no condition but, then again, neither was I. I had been up for hours and could feel it. The emotional hell I had been through at that point made me feel as if I hadn't slept in months. Jennifer, I could tell, had the same symptoms as me. We were both tired, both very sad, and both not wanting to see our son lying on a table dead.

As I drove down the road, my mind began to wonder, as a writer's mind often does. When you're a writer, your mind freely roams wherever it likes and there's nothing you can do to stop it. I don't remember driving or even arriving at the hospital to see our dead son. I cannot say, for sure, how we got there or for that matter, when we left. I was on autopilot, in a daze. Jennifer was the same up until she saw Davey in one of the back rooms. She went in to see him while I stood at the counter where the nurses' station was, fumbling around with paperwork. I don't recall filling out the papers, or if I even did it correctly. I couldn't focus on much as Jennifer screamed and cried as she looked at our dead son from behind me. Eventually, I finished with the papers and slowly went back to where Jennifer and Davey were. And when I walked in, I saw Davey on his back, mouth open, eyes closed as Jennifer leaned over him sobbing and kissing his face. I stood there and looked at them and cried too. It was all I could do. I just stayed back and let Jennifer have the moment, as many moments as she needed, with Davey.

2

In that room, I thought about Davey, finally pinning down one of my floating thoughts, capturing it with an oversized net, and then falling to my knees to inspect it. And what I found was a memory from two years ago, back when I first thought things with him weren't right. I wish I'd done more, but at the time I just thought he'd snap out of his funk. If only it was a funk—a funk you can snap out of. Depression, you can't just snap out of it.

A couple of years ago, I decided to take Davey with me to Atlanta to watch a Braves game. The Braves had hosted the Reds in a three-game series, and on that idle Wednesday, it was a rubber game. Not only was it a rubber game, but it was also a businessman special, meaning that the game was to be started at one o'clock in the afternoon and that seats for general admission would be good; a little pricey, but good nevertheless. I had escaped to Atlanta several times in the past to watch the Braves during their businessman specials. I liked mid-week afternoon games because the stadium isn't lined wall-to-wall with fans. You can actually sit there and enjoy the ball game with a few seats empty flanking you on both sides and in front of and behind you. Those were my favorite games to go to.

That morning before we traveled to Atlanta, I was in the kitchen eating Honeycomb cereal, bowl in my hand as I stood leaning up against the kitchen sink, looking around. Samantha had already run out of the house when Randy called her to tell her that he was there to pick her up for school. I wasn't crazy about a kid—although he was almost seventeen, or so I was told—driving my daughter—a year younger at the time—around, but she *was* getting older. What could I really do? Ever since Randy had gotten his license, he had come to pick my daughter up every day for school. She drove and had a car herself, but she always liked riding shotgun with her boyfriend.

I stood there eating my cereal, formulating a plan. I was going to see Davey walk through the kitchen, backpack hanging off his shoulders, head down, eating an apple, and ready to get into my car so I could take him to school. Sometimes he would hitch a ride with Samantha and Randy. It all depended on how Davey felt that morning or if he got up in time and ready before Samantha darted off.

Davey was slowly approaching the age where getting his license should've been a huge deal. But it was quite the opposite. He never brought it up like Samantha did. Before she was fifteen, all she talked about was getting her learner's permit, and then it was all about her driver's license. Davey wasn't like that. He didn't even speak about getting his learner's permit.

As I finished off my last bites of cereal, I saw Davey enter the kitchen right on cue, backpack and apple in tow. I put my bowl into the sink and cleared my throat and spoke to my son before he walked out of the kitchen. "Hey, uh... you got any big tests going on today?"

Davey stopped and looked up at me. He seemed so... tired. Even back then, early on in his ever-deepening depression, he had the look of a man who was working eighty hours a week and sleeping four hours a night. My son looked exhausted. I knew that something was wrong. I hoped that I was wrong; maybe just seeing things that really weren't there, but it turned out that I was right all along. "I don't think so. Not until Friday," he replied.

"Um..." I started, still leaning casually up against the sink counter. "The Braves are playing at one today, and I thought I'd go and if you wanted to, you could skip school and we could make a day of it," I said, presenting an offer most kids perhaps couldn't refuse.

Davey stood there, looking at me and then down at the floor. "It'd blow my perfect attendance record this year," he said bluntly. I was crushed by this. I really wanted the two of us to go to a ball game, eat hot dogs, drink Cokes, and reconnect.

I nodded and lowered my head in defeat. "Okay, yeah. I'll meet you out in the car. Let me get my keys," I said, turning around to look out the window. I was kind of devastated because I felt that I was losing time *and* connection with my son. The truth of the matter was I was trying to be the dad to him in the way my own father wasn't to me. Then I quickly realized something startling: I had become my father over time and was trying to back-peddle years and years of discord between my son and myself. Sometimes in life, you become the people you dislike the most. You don't notice it until you're already rooted in it. Then it's nearly impossible to break the cycle.

3

For years, I had not been the greatest dad in the world. Sure, I made money—lots of it—for doing what I like to do. And I gave my family members a good chance to do anything they wanted. But somewhere along the way, I had gotten introverted, so consumed by everything in my life that I systematically shut everyone else out. It started with me being unhappy in my marriage because I couldn't have the woman of my dreams, Marie. I allowed that to sink me into immense bouts of depression where I would be a ghost within the house for days, sometimes a drunk spirit.

Davey, back in his younger years, always wanted to be by my side, but I was always *too* busy, *too* inebriated, or thinking about Marie and what life would have been with her. Sometimes I would come out of my office, getting free from the shackles of my self-deprecating thoughts, and make myself available, but only on *my* terms. I had become *that* kind of father. Just like my own.

The kids and I would go outside and play together, maybe some kickball, maybe a little horse or around the world out on the basketball court; or we'd look at the stars at night on the back deck through Davey's high-powered telescope. Then, just as quickly as I got out of my funk, I would retreat into my turtle shell and hide until I felt like being around people again. Who paid the price? My family.

As Davey got older and began to see me for what I was, he began to hide in *his* shell, too, just like his old man. He would make himself unavailable to me, his sister, and his mother. Davey had two parents: one gone and the other tucked away in an office inside but might as well have been gone, too. I had failed my son but was too fucked up in my head to realize it at the time.

Or maybe I did realize what I was doing; I don't know. Maybe I knew it the whole time but didn't want to do anything about it. The thing about the past is that as more time passes, the fuzzier your memories become. And with all that time that does pass, you bend its narrative to better suit you. That's what I had done in the past, on occasion. Haven't we all?

When I did try to get myself fixed, stop drinking as much, and stop loathing myself over never getting Marie, I was never able to reel Davey back in. I had pushed him so far away that when it was time for me to bring him back in, I couldn't. I was ready for Davey, but Davey was past being readily available for me. I'm sure he hated me for not being around, even though I was cooped up in a room just a few feet from his. I might as well have been a thousand miles away.

I had offered many adventures for him and me to take in the past, just something to get us back on some sort of father-son track. He rebuffed them all. Hikes in the woods, shooting basketball in the driveway, passing baseball in the backyard, watching baseball games, going to the movies, playing board games and video games were all things that I would offer him. He never accepted any of those proposals because he didn't want to be around me since I dictated the times that he and I could be together. I think Davey might've seen it all as an insult. He might have been right.

4

I took my keys off the nail in the wall next to the backdoor and walked across the kitchen and through the living room, out of the house. I got into the car where Davey was sitting, started it and backed out of the driveway. As we drove down our quiet street, Davey spoke, breaking the silence, "Were you serious about me ditching school and going to a Braves game with you?" he asked in a tone suggesting I wasn't serious. I was serious, though.

"Yes," I replied, making the left-hand turn off our street. "You and me, two guys at a game. The weather's nice, too. Seats will be good because nobody wants to see the Reds, and it's at one."

Davey sat in the passenger seat, thinking about my offer. I knew he was thinking hard on it too because Davey, just like everyone else in this world, had a tell. His tell was that he drew his lower lip inside his mouth and rubbed his tongue against it. He was thinking about the pros and cons of spending a day with his dear old dad, something he hadn't done in ages. Although I couldn't say I remembered the last time we hung out together, but damn it, I was trying.

Davey sat in silence and pondered, and I grew a little tired of his sluggish response. If he wanted to go, then he would have jumped all over it like a normal kid. His silence and reluctance to speak told me everything that I needed to know. He didn't want to go with me, and he had lost interest in baseball altogether. It was funny; it was baseball that we talked about all the time when he was growing up. Baseball was our perfect bonding agent. Over time, it had corroded.

As we approached the school, Davey shifted in his seat as though he was about to confess something. I had abandoned any hope he wanted to join me at Turner Field for the game as we got closer to his school. Hell, if he didn't go, I'd probably just drop him off at school, go back home and sit and do nothing until the game came on TV. However, Davey said something I'd never thought he'd say: "Yeah, let's go. It'll be fun." A thin smile etched across my face as I took the next street down to the right to drive away from the school.

"You okay with giving up your shot at perfect attendance?" I asked, making sure that he really wanted to do this. Davey looked out his window and then at me. God, he hadn't looked at me like that in ages. It was like he was ten years old again.

"Yeah, I'm good," Davey said with a smile showing all of his white teeth. "School will be there tomorrow, right?" My thin smile turned to a full-blown *cheese* as I reached over and rubbed his hair playfully. He shrank back, grabbing my arm and pushing it away as he tried not to laugh. For a moment in time, we were back to the way we used to be, back when things were good. Back before things got heavy.

5

The car ride to Atlanta was two hours from where we lived in Georgia. We had the radio on, but neither of us really paid much attention to it. It was merely background noise. We had taken the back roads, electing not to travel the congested interstate. Normally, I'd just use the interstate, but that day, I wanted to be adventurous.

I fired up the GPS, put in the address to Turner Field and selected alternate routes. I got this one route that came up parallel to I-75. It was a series of back roads and secondary highways. I sat back, and let the technology guide us as my son and I did something that we had not done in a long time: talk.

We had a couple of hours to sit there and talk about anything that we wanted. No interruptions; no one asking anything from us. It was just me and him, together passing the countryside at a cool forty-five miles per hour toward our ball game. I felt great behind the wheel, better than I had in years, I must say.

At first, Davey and I talked about life, and what he and I thought the meaning of it all was. When he asked me what I thought our purpose was, I sat back in my driver's seat and smiled again. This was what I had always wanted: my child asking for my opinion on a subject that had been thought upon by the most educated philosophers. Everyone on this planet, rich and poor, black and white, young and old, has asked, "What is the meaning of life?" And there was Davey, asking me my thoughts.

"I didn't know you thought about stuff like that," I said, my left hand on the wheel and my right arm in my lap.

"I do, quite a bit," Davey replied. "I just can't come up with a good enough answer as to why we're here."

"What do *you* think it means?" I returned, easing my foot off the gas because of the sudden speed limit change to thirty in that part of the county.

Davey sat there for a moment and then spoke. "I think there isn't one. I think we're just here. I've read every philosopher's opinion, and I don't buy into any of them. I mean, I get their point, but in the end, it's *their* point, you know?" My son said in a grim fashion.

"Maybe there isn't. But I think there's something to life, though."

"What do you think?"

"I think that we're here to do a job, directed by whatever higher power you subscribe to, and once you do that job, you die. Maybe it's like making someone who needed a pick me up laugh, or becoming a millionaire and sharing your money and it touches someone who turns their life around all because of you. And then afterward you die of natural causes or in an accident once you've completed your job."

"So you think we're put here on earth to do a job but don't have any idea what it is. And when we do this job, we die right afterward?" Davey added, summarizing my theory.

"Right. Yeah, you've got it. I think as soon as we're born, we've got this future written out for us but we have no idea what it is. The only thing we do know is that we will die eventually."

"So you think no matter what, you can't shake what you're to become?" Davey asked.

"Yup," I said. "You're born to die, son. That's your future written out for you. That's the ending you get to know. People will say, 'Ah, your future is in your hands, so do the right thing.' But that thinking can't be further from the truth."

"So you think we have no free will?"

"No." I believed that then as I do now. "Free will is nothing more than a fantasy made up by people to give us some sort of control in our lives. Nothing could be further from the truth."

"If you stand in front of a moving train and then decide to jump out of the way at the last second, that's free will, right?" Davey asked.

I shook my head, "Not really. What if you were meant to have a change of heart at the last moment and jumped to the side of the oncoming train? You see, life is like a play and we're the actors. We're in this play, but we don't know the ending. Well, we know our character *will* die eventually...."

"So we're blindly following a script that we don't know the words to or the scenes until they pass?" Davey interrupted quickly.

"Exactly," I said feeling as if I had gotten my point through to my son. Davey sat back and looked out his window.

After we had driven out of the small town, where the speed limit picked back up to a quick fifty miles an hour, Davey began again. "I think you might be right, Dad. We have no idea what the future holds—the script, in other words."

"I don't think so. Other people have a different take on life. You'll hear more about that kind of stuff when you get older and get out into the world more. Then you'll be able to apply your own beliefs to what you think. The thing is, no one is right or wrong, because you can't prove any of it. All you can do is think about it and observe and then form your own opinion."

"Man, I had no idea that you were so... so...."

"Deep?"

"Yeah, deep. Since when did you become a philosopher?"

I laughed. "I've always been one, son. My entire life has been like a play. Bad scenes and all."

"When did you decide you were going to be a writer?" My son asked. I had gotten that question from a slew of reporters over the years but never from my children. To them, I was always writing so it wasn't something that they had much interest in. It was merely what Dad did. But when Davey asked me that question and even though I'd heard it hundreds of times over, it seemed fresh and inviting, especially coming from him.

"I don't know," I replied not giving him the staple answer I had given in interviews in the past. "I think when I was around ten or so. I was always writing these short stories. They weren't any good really. But a teacher found one I had left on my desk by accident in fifth grade one day and she read it. She loved it and thought that I should enter into the school's annual writing contest."

"And you won, right?" Davey asked, thinking he had the rest of the story figured out.

"No, hell no. I didn't even make it to the final fifty stories," I said, thinking back to a time that I could barely even remember. "Even though I didn't win the contest, my teacher, Mrs. Staple, told me not to give up and that if I tried really hard I could be an honest-to-God writer one day. She was the only one who really believed in my stuff.

And over the years I always sent her the final draft of my books up until she died."

"Wow. My own world-famous dad couldn't even hack it in a middle school writing contest." Davey said with playful laughter. I laughed too as we passed a small green sign on the side of the road that read: Atlanta 70 Miles.

6

Davey and I talked like fathers and sons are supposed to talk. You know, like what you'd see on TV in one of those warm and gooey family sitcoms, where the kid wants to know all about his dad because he thinks his dad is cool as hell. Yeah, we had that moment in my car that day. It was always one of those days that stood out most in my mind. Out of all the praise, and all the acclaim that I've received over my career, that day driving to Atlanta to see the Braves with my son is number one on my list. It was my favorite memory.

As we neared the big city, with its towering buildings standing tall and proud, Davey asked me about my own family—namely, his grandparents. Talking about my parents wasn't an easy thing for me and one subject I had avoided ever since I could remember. They were brought up a lot as I was coming up in the literary world because people wanted to know what my roots were, how I was raised, and what my parents thought about their one and only son.

My kids didn't ever see their grandparents. My mother, Claire, was dead and gone by the time I was nineteen. One night she went to sleep and never woke up. To this day, I still wonder what killed her. My father, Ernest, and I were going to have an autopsy performed, but he decided against it at the last minute. I was for it because I wanted to know, wanted some closure. Dad, on the other hand, didn't want Mom cut open. I never forgave him for that. I still hold a grudge against him for that decision. He had the keys to find out why my mother died but elected to forgo the post-mortem and bury her instead. I hated him for taking that away from me. And over time, I became more and more bitter about it. Every grave visit to her plot made me madder because, although I could've known what was wrong with her, my dad refused to know. Maybe he was scared, but that doesn't make it any easier for me to stomach if he was.

Claire Matthews was a beautiful, vibrant, outgoing, and always chipper woman. I rarely saw her in a bad mood. If she was, she hid it well, like some mothers do, I guess. She was one of the best cooks and best field medics—always treating my cuts and scrapes that I'd get out there in the yard or ball field or on my many bicycle wipeouts—this side of the Mississippi.

All my friends adored her and one time at a camp while out with a few of them, Jake confessed that he always found my mom attractive and wanted to do her. I didn't recoil at his confession because I understood why. Claire was a very sensual woman who looked like one of those gals straight out of a fifties pin-up calendar. Her brown hair was in swooping locks down to her shoulders; she always had ruby-red lips and was an incredible size four. If she wanted to, my mother could have been a model instead of settling down and raising a family.

She was a well-educated college grad and never used her smarts or degree for anything useful, which was a shame because the world missed out. Instead, she got married at twenty-five to my father and gave up on all the dreams she secretly held close to her heart. It's not that my dad beat her down or anything. Far from it. He *wanted* her to go out and do something besides taking care of us and the house.

He wanted Claire to stop being Claire. He told her time and time again that she needed to go be a teacher. She held a bachelor's degree in Education but never used it. I once heard her say to one of her friends on the phone long ago, when I was little, that she was just in college to appease her dad. Having a degree was just something to keep my grandfather off her case. We've all been there, haven't we? Doing things to please another, even though we die a little on the inside by doing so.

My mother could've been one of the best teachers any school system would have seen. But it was okay by me because she was always there for me growing up, holding the home together. She was the glue that held the family together. I'll never forget all the things she said and did over the years, and it hurt like hell when she died. There were so many things that I wanted to do with her, so many more conversations that I wanted to have with her. I wanted my mother to see what her son had become when he grew up. I feel now, as I did then, that a lot of stuff was still left on the table when she died of something unknown.

My father, Ernest Matthews, was a good man. He was a good dad, too. I was fortunate—I didn't have rotten parents like some of my friends had. Most of them had come from a broken home.

Dad and I shared a passion for baseball, especially for the Braves, since I could remember. Baseball was our one true connection. No matter what was going on or how distant we could become with each other, baseball and the Braves were something he and I could always talk about. At least we had that.

I remember my dad and I taking a father-son trip to Atlanta here and there—not too often because he was always at his law office—to watch the Braves back when they were terrible, year in and year out. I always treasured those times and look back on them fondly. I still have a few of the ticket stubs from the times we went, even a picture or two with me and him, arm-in-arm and smiling for the camera. I haven't looked at those pictures in years, but I can see them vividly like it was just yesterday in my mind's eye.

Ernest Matthew was a lawyer. He had a private practice in our town where he dabbled in practically everything. He made a lot of money to support me and my mother, and we had everything we needed. Back then growing up, I really didn't want much. Give me some comic books, some Nintendo games, and a few Stephen King novels I was set. And of course, the TBS Superstation where I could watch the Braves play almost every night.

But Dad wasn't always available. He worked a lot, long days that went well into the night. I asked him one time why he worked so long.

"Those people are paying me to help them, and I've got to give 'em my best."

That was verbatim and those words, direct and sincere, never left me. When he was home, it was awesome. I'd like to tell you that this world-famous writer comes from a broken home where his father beat him, and his mother was a drunken whore. That would be a real feel-good story: a boy coming up through immeasurable odds to become a famous literary chapter in the world of literature. That's not how it happened; sorry to disappoint. My family was good, and great most times, and I certainly appreciated the gravity of the situation of where I was during those days. But then Dad and I had a falling out some years later…we fell out hard.

"Well," I began to talk to Davey about his grandparents. "Your grandmother, Claire, died when I was nineteen years old."

"She did?" Davey said, shocked. "How?"

I shook my head as the tall buildings grew taller and taller with every mile as we got closer to downtown Atlanta.

"Don't know. All I know was one night she went to bed and the next morning my dad, your Grandpa Ernest, couldn't wake her up."

It was still painful after all those years to talk—much less think—about. I avoided the conversations about my Mom and Dad because things hurt. They hurt a lot.

The past, even though years and decades back in the rearview mirror, was still painful. Thinking about where I was when I heard the news is much like when people talk about where they were when the planes crashed into the World Trade Centers on 9/11. You will always remember. I do on both accounts.

"No autopsy?" Davey asked. He watched way too many cop shows on TV for his age.

"No, Dad wouldn't do it. Didn't want to cut into Mom's beautiful body. We buried her without knowing if it was a heart attack, a massive stroke, or whatever."

As I spoke, my mind escaped back to that period in my life that was a defining moment for me—one of them anyway. A watershed moment.

"What about Grandpa? He still alive?" Davey asked unlocking doors I hadn't opened in many, many years. Why would I? Too painful to even turn the knob. And what would happen if I opened those locked doors in my mind? Chaos and heartache.

That's it. The ghosts of my parents and their memories were locked away behind closed doors—locked rooms, and here was Davey just going through, jiggling the door knobs until they popped open.

My mother was dead from an unknown killer. There was *some* closure to that. Not much, but at least she wasn't my Dad. Ernest Matthews had Alzheimer's and he was in the fifth stage of the mind-altering disease where he had forgotten such things as how to dress appropriately for the season, where he went to high school and college and law school, and even where he grew up and where we lived. Most frighteningly, he had forgotten who I was over time.

When I would visit him—I know not nearly often enough—he would call me Tommy, who I assumed was a friend of his back in his early days. We would sit there, and he and I would talk about the days of old, his and Tommy's past, mind you. I didn't mind playing along. It was nice to be someone else for a change. I never corrected my dad; I just let him continue thinking I was his friend Tommy.

Dad was going off the rails as his mind was all over the place and nowhere at the same time. I couldn't stand to see it anymore, couldn't bring myself to see my own dad at his weakest. Maybe it was because I never fully forgave him about Mom; maybe it was because I was scared that the dad I knew was long gone. Perhaps it was because he didn't even know his own son anymore. To him until the day he would eventually die, I would be Tommy Harnish.

Hell, he had even forgotten the huge fight we'd had that made me leave home for a while. That fight had been brewing for some time, and it came right on the heels of Mom's death. I still had some pent-up resentment, and the hurt from Mom's absence made my fury worse. It was a typical father-son fight. But what wasn't so typical was I never came home until years later. And even then, I didn't really want to. Sure, I'd write to Dad and call to check in every once in a while, just to put his mind at ease that I was still alive, but I swore I'd never come back home—especially after every phone conversation ended with us yelling at each other and one of us hanging up.

That was the cycle of the two Mathews' men. Looking back on it now, I missed a lot with him all because of my stance on him trying to control my life at the time and the resentment for him not finding out about what killed my mother. I did eventually return home when I was married to Jennifer, only to find my dad losing his mind. It was noticeable, even back then. I knew what his memory loss was attributed to. I remember standing in the doorway of the front door when I rang the doorbell and him answering it, standing there with a confused look on his face, trying to figure out who I was. It wasn't because I was gone too long and had put on some weight and had a beard—it was because his mind was rotting from the inside out. It was a slow burn for him.

At least my mother was dead, and there was some finality to that. My father was dying a little every day while wide awake. There would be no going to bed before telling me goodnight for the final time, and never waking up to a brand-new day. Dad had wasted away in the prison that his mind had made. Every day, he became progressively worse. Eventually, he would be a shell of his former self.

"Yeah, Grandpa's still alive. He has Alzheimer's. He um...," I said, not ready to talk about this, especially to my son. I mean, I hadn't spoken about the situation to anyone, not even Marie. It wasn't a family secret, but it wasn't something I volunteered to discuss either. I was fine with letting his memory be just that—a memory.

I choose to remember my dad in the good times, not the ones where he couldn't remember being a lawyer for more than forty years. Living in the past had protected me from living in the present because I couldn't bear to see my dad systematically torn apart by his mind that was being erased like a hard drive in reverse. His cognitive decline scared me because I thought maybe I'd wind up just like that—alone and unrecognizable to even myself.

"He, um..., can't remember things all that well," I managed, trying to find the right words.

"I know what Alzheimer's is, Dad. What was he like back before he got all coo-coo for Coco Puffs?" Davey asked.

With both my hands on the wheel, I ran over a million things in my head. I didn't talk about Dad, Mom, or my past to much length.

But there was Davey, inquiring about his family's history. I guess he had a right to know about his heritage.

"He was a lawyer. A very successful attorney back where I grew up in Rome, Georgia. He loved the Braves and was one of the best dads that a kid could ever have." I said, feeling a tear or two spring from behind my eyes. As I spoke to my son about his grandfather, I remembered that scene in *Field of Dreams* where Ray and his long-dead father finally have that game of catch there on the baseball field out in the Iowa night. That scene always makes me cry, just like thinking about me and my own dad playing catch out in the backyard as mom made supper in the kitchen with the window open. God, I can smell the fried chicken and apple pie right now; funny how your mind goes backward sometimes.

"You guys close?"

I nodded, "Yeah, we were. He taught me how to ride a bike, throw a baseball, do math, how to shave.... He was better than I'll ever be. A very loyal man to his friends and family," I said, realizing for the very first time in my life that I paled in comparison to my father.

Somewhere I got lost, broke the connection to what life was about and I finally got it, the complexity of the meaning itself, while driving with my son to a Braves game. I had found it.

"I'd like to meet him," Davey said.

"I don't think that's a good idea, Davey. He's not all there. He doesn't even remember me. He thinks I'm a friend from his childhood named Tommy. I wouldn't want your only meeting with him to be in that state," I replied.

"I've never seen a picture of him or Grandma. Do you have one?"

I did have pictures, books and books stacked on top of each other. I hadn't thought about those pictures in years. There were perhaps images of time I'd long forgotten but would be new to Davey.

"Yeah, as a matter of fact. Your grandma was a scrapbooking fiend," I said, feeling a rush of happiness surge over me for the first time in talking about my mom and dad.

"There's no telling what's in those books I'd forgotten about."

"Where are they?"

"Back home, in Rome. They're still in the house where I grew up."

"The house is still there?" Davey asked.

"Yeah. It's still there. Man, I haven't been there since I cleaned out his closet for him to have clothes at the nursing home."

"Can we go? I really want to see this place," Davey said, looking about as happy as I felt.

"I don't know, maybe one day soon," I said. "Maybe one day."

I was putting him off because I was a little frightened to go back there and stay for any length of time, especially flipping through the old Matthews family albums. There was no telling what kind of emotional rollercoaster it would be.

"I think after the game we should go there. You know, to cap off the day," Davey said, pushing the issue.

Davey had the curiosity of a kid for sure. I think he was fascinated that he was learning new things about his family, and the prospect of knowing that there were books of pictures of me when I was a kid from a time long ago was enticing.

"Maybe," I said, not knowing what to say. "I don't know. It's another hour-plus from the park, on top of the drive from Rome to home. I don't know if I'll feel up to the drive." I said, calculating the miles and the weariness that would set in later in the day.

"I think we should." Davey nodded his head agreeing with himself. "I think we should. I really want to see what my grandparents look like. Plus, I think it'd be cool to see where you grew up, Dad."

Now why did he have to go on and say something like that? I looked at the buildings in the Atlanta skyline as they were practically on top of us as we drove in a thicket of cars, SUVs, and trucks down the multi-lane road. Davey really wanted to see the old house and the pictures. Who was I to deny him?

CHAPTER SEVENTEEN

1

The game was exciting, and as predicted, there weren't many fans there, which was typical for businessman specials. We had great seats and watched a great game between the Braves and the Reds. Davey ate three hot dogs and tried a pretzel as big as my head but couldn't even open his mouth to eat it because he was so full. On the other hand, I ate light: a burger with all the fixings, fries, and a Coke.

I was stuffed, but unlike my son, not to the point where the sight of food made me sick. In a few hours, I could've gone for something else, Davey would make a face and wave me off saying, "No more! No more! I don't ever want to eat again for the rest of my life!"

While at the park, Davey and I watched the game, laughing and talking about anything and everything, and ate. Every once in a while, I would catch Davey's eyes watching a woman two rows down from us stand up and cheer. Her blue shorts were just a little too short and just a little too tight.

Every time the Braves would do something good on the field, the blond lady would stand up and cheer, causing me and my son to just stare at her. At one point in the eighth inning, she stood up and cheered, and Davey and I looked at each other. Without saying a word, we both knew what the other was thinking: *Damn, that girl is smoking.* She was in perfect sight because there was no one sitting in the seats in front of us to obstruct our view. It was perfect. It was almost like we were there at the park alone because no one was really sitting around us unlike night games when a good team was in town.

As Julio Teheran struck out the side of the Reds in the top of the ninth with a fastball going 98 miles per hour, the crowd roared with excitement for the close 3-2 win. As the Braves all shook hands with each other on the baseball field, the fans, me and Davey included, began to turn and file away toward the exits. We lingered near our seats, watching Ol' Blue walk on by, swinging her ass side to side. She knew what she had and didn't mind showing it off. Davey and I didn't mind that she didn't mind. We stood there and watched her walk on by until she disappeared. Wow. It was one of those secret moments between father and son that a mom would never know about. It was just between the two of us guys.

2

Getting *to* Turner Field was not that bad in comparison to trying to get *out* of there during a night game on the weekend. But still trying to navigate out of the sea of vehicles that afternoon was a horrible experience in its own right. When I heard the announcement over the PA that there were 15,897 fans in attendance, I thought for sure we'd have an easier time getting out of the parking lot and onto the interstate toward home. I couldn't have been more mistaken by that notion: it was jam-packed.

My son and I didn't head directly for home. Davey poked and prodded the issue about going to the house where I grew up every five minutes as we were smack-dab in the middle of traffic. I was more focused on trying to drive us out of the storm of cars and didn't pay much attention to Davey as he talked.

I just said "yeah" a few times, not even knowing what I was agreeing to. He could have said, "Dad, I'm a dad. Yeah, I got this girl in my class pregnant and we're going to have to live at home and you and Mom are going to have to help raise the kid. Is that okay?" I wouldn't have batted an eye and nodded as I watched the cars and trucks jockey for position in the slow-moving lines heading away from Turner Field.

We had finally made it through the traffic jam after an hour and a half and were driving down the interstate at a cool sixty-five. The radio was turned on low, just like it was when we came to the park, and I began to relax. I hated downtown Atlanta, always did because of the damn traffic and rednecks that didn't know how to drive their jacked-up four-by-fours with tires too big and too wide to even be considered legal on the road. I loved going to the park to watch the Braves, but getting out after the game was complete and utter bedlam. Sometimes just watching it at home was best.

3

I was kind of tired and really could go for a nap, but I knew that I had a while yet before we got back home. Davey, on the other hand, was ready for another adventure with his old man. He had looked at me for several minutes without saying a word. I saw him out of the corner of my eye but decided not to speak because I knew what the kid wanted.

He wanted to journey to my old hometown and walk the halls of the house where I used to walk. I should've been cool with it. But I wasn't because he was making me face and talk about things that I wanted to leave shut and sealed forever. I had no desire to unlock the doors of my past.

I remember the times I had when I was growing up around my parents quite vividly. The memories hurt just as much as talking about them had. Over time I just pushed their memories into closets in my mind and locked the doors and threw away the keys. That was until Davey came around asking questions like a 1950s gumshoe.

Did I want to go home, I mean *home*, home? Not really. The last time that I was there I just dashed inside, not bothering to look around at all the décor that was still intact, just as Mom had it before she passed away. Everything was still the same inside the home, even though she was gone, decades gone.

Keeping things the same—the furniture the same way, the book that she was reading on the table with a bookmark jutting an inch out between pages 345-346, frozen in time waiting for the woman who was reading it to return. She would never return. Never. Dad never could bring himself to change anything after Mom died. I guess he saw that as sacrilege of her memory; that's why the house looked the same and even smelled the same.

I went inside the home and walked with acute tunnel vision to Dad's bedroom, which was not in the same room that he and Mom shared for years. His newer room, which he'd moved into after her death, was on the other side of the house. That sucked for me because I had to walk the entire length of the house, up the stairs past his office just to get there. And what was I there for? A suitcase full of his clothes so I could take them back to the nursing home that he'd never get out of.

I walked into his room, keeping my head down and letting the carpet be my guide, until I stood in front of the closet. I looked up and opened it. I didn't even pick and choose what clothes I thought he'd like to have. Hell, he wouldn't even care because they'd all be new to him since his mind was playing cruel tricks on him. I could have brought him a fucking clown suit, and he'd be fine with it.

I reached inside the closet and began to grab clothes off the rod and carry armload after armload over to the bed. After a few short trips back and forth, I had emptied the entire closet of clothes. They'd all be pretty much new to him. On the floor of the closet sat two empty suitcases. I reached in and grabbed them and tossed them on the bed carelessly, much like a child tosses an overused toy they're finished playing with onto the floor.

I unzipped the suitcases and began to pile the clothes—most with their hangers still on them—into the cases in no particular order. I didn't care. I just wanted to get the job done and get the hell out of that house. If I stayed too long or slowed down, I just might have heard the ghost of my mother walking down the halls or smelled one of her famous, award-winning apple pies from the kitchen. That sometimes happened. I remembered back, a few times after she had been dead, I could smell her perfume or cooking. I swear I did.

I was very robotic and quick about my job. After I stuffed the first suitcase, I went onto the other one, a green one that I'd seen Dad leave with several times when he went away out of town for some lawyer's thing. It was torn in spots, faded in others but it had character and many travel stories etched across it. I wondered if he'd even recall it. Maybe, maybe not. Half chance, I guessed.

I walked over to his dresser and pulled open the drawers, one by one, and gathered more clothes, socks, boxers, and white t-shirts. They were already folded in the drawers, so I just plopped them into the well-traveled green suitcase along with other shirts and things. Before I knew it, the drawers were empty, pulled out of their frame and I left them that way as I zipped up the cases and carried them hastily out of the house. But I swear to God, and when I say this I'm not crazy, but I could have sworn as I came down the stairs of my childhood home, I smelled her perfume and could hear faint, very faint humming. Mom always had this habit of humming her favorite songs as she walked through the house. I stood there on the last rung of the stairs and looked around and sniffed in the stale air of the house. I think she was there....

4

As Davey and I motored our way through the city limits, Davey still looked at me, daring me to turn my eyes to him and ask, "What?" I didn't. I just kept my eyes on the road and my hands on the wheel as cars passed us on the interstate like we were standing still in the road. I knew what Davey wanted but I wasn't going to start by asking him what he was looking at. I already knew.

As the buildings and the city grew further and further back in my rearview mirror, Davey's stare grew stronger and more piercing. He was going to come out and ask me eventually, but he wanted me to break the ice. I wasn't going to.

I was going to live on a prayer that he'd just give up the notion of driving to Rome and seeing the place that I called home when I was a boy. I could hope. But I knew better. "Good game, wasn't it?" I asked, hoping to dodge his approaching question.

"Yeah," Davey said flatly. "It was awesome. I'm really glad that we did this, Dad. I had fun. And I got this cool new Freddie Freeman shirt." He said, pulling at the chest of his blue Braves tee.

"Yeah, looks good on you," I said, nervously shifting my Braves hat on my head. I knew he was just lying in the weeds, ready to pounce on me with a knockout question. All our talk was merely idle chitchat, building up to the main event, the main question that was on the cusp of his lips. And then as the U2 song faded on the radio and Tom Petty's "Free Fallin'" picked up, Davey went in for the kill.

"So, are you up to going to Rome?" He knew that I wasn't planning on it, but it didn't stop him from asking. Davey had every intention of wearing me down.

I thought to myself: *Why is he so enamored with seeing where I lived, my old haunts?* The only thing that I could come up with was that he wanted to know more about me, which was cool. He wasn't a nosy reporter for a magazine, snooping around or asking prying questions for dirt on me. He was my son, wanting to know more about his dad. Could I really blame him?

I had been so guarded in the past about my folks that I had pretty much forgotten all about them until Davey began with the questions. Jennifer knew a bit about them; Marie knew a lot because of all my time growing up with her. Hell, Marie even went with us on vacations and ate dinner at my house a time or two. She was the only one of my past cast of characters who knew anything about the way things once were. But there were still things that neither Jennifer nor Marie knew about me.

Samantha had some of the same questions before, too, just like her brother. With Samantha, I told her that I didn't want to talk about it all and quickly changed the subject. She, just like Davey, kept needling the issue over the ensuing days. I eventually snapped at her, making her cry and she hasn't spoken to me about my parents, her grandparents, since. I think she eventually went to Jennifer and asked some questions, and Jennifer told her that some things had happened and that I wasn't ready to discuss them, that they hurt too much to talk about.

Jennifer knew about my mom and dad, but she didn't know how bad dad had gotten over the years since our wedding. Jennifer and I never talked about my parents, and that was okay with me. It was, as far as I was concerned, a closed case. Jennifer never prodded me, and I never shared my feelings about my parents with her. It was a mutual understanding. That part of my life I kept a secret. Even when I had to put Dad in a home, I told no one, not Jennifer or Marie. I just did it, and afterward, I locked it up in a room in my mind.

Davey had perhaps talked to Samantha at some point and Jennifer, too, about my origins. I guess that was fair. He was curious about me and wanted to know if there was more to me than what he read on the Internet. Online my life seemed like an open book; practically anything that you wanted to know was available. What Davey was looking for couldn't be found online. He wanted to know his father, and I guess he was justified. If I were in Davey's place, I'd be the same way. Like father, like son.

I nervously adjusted my Braves hat again, ready to give in to my son's request to drive northwest to Rome. "Yeah, let's go. You got to pee before we turn off the exit up here?" I asked. Davey grinned and clenched his fist in victory. And so there we went, driving for home, my home, from long ago.

CHAPTER EIGHTEEN

1

We sat in the driveway of the house that I grew up in. It, just like my and Jennifer's house, was modest, not too big or flashy, just ordinary. It sat there, in line with all the other homes in the ordinary neighborhood. It was just a house. But to me, it was home.

It was a tall, two-story home, much like the one on the TV show *Growing Pains* where the Seavers lived. Davey sat in the passenger seat looking bewildered. I, on the other hand, sat with an odd feeling in the pit of my stomach. It was nervousness, almost a nauseating feeling churning inside. I didn't remember having this feeling before, the last time I was here to get Dad's clothes. Maybe it was because I didn't look around then as I did now. Perhaps.

The day that I came home to grab Dad's clothes, I had just gotten out of the car and walked into the house. I didn't look around the place. After I was finished, I darted out, slamming the door behind me. That was it—get in and get out. Now, I was looking at the bushes and hedges that stood guard around the house as they had for decades. God, was the grass even greener than it was when I was a kid? And Christ, I marveled at the maple tree that Mom had planted out front. Man, it was huge. I remember when she planted it. It was so small, almost to my waist—I was seven or eight at the time. Mom always told me that was going to grow into a beautiful tree one day. She never lived long enough to see its full maturity.

2

Davey opened the car door, snapping me out of my trance as I looked around the exterior of the house, remembering tidbits here and there of times past. I was younger and so were my parents. And the best part was... Mom was there, still alive and smiling. I averted my eyes and saw Davey walk slowly away from the car. I got out and followed him around the back of the house.

Back there was the yard where I played as a kid. We had the biggest backyard in the neighborhood. When Dad and Mom were looking for a place to plant the Matthews flag, Dad wanted a home that had a huge backyard. And he got one. As I followed Davey into the shady back that had several towering maple trees growing there, I stopped and looked around. *My God, when was the last time I was back here?* I asked myself. I was speechless as Davey stood in the middle of the lawn. "Man, this yard is huge, Dad!" Very huge indeed.

3

Davey and I walked around the house and entered through the front door. I still had Dad's house key on my key ring. The home was cold for that time of year. I always remembered that our house was usually cool in the summer, even without the A/C on. There was no A/C on at all because there wasn't any power in the house. Davey and I walked slowly through the foyer into the living room, looking around at pictures on the wall and the décor on the tables like we were in a museum. And I suppose we were: the Matthews Museum where time ceased to exist. The 80s and 90s were still alive in there....

"Where was your bedroom?" Davey asked.

I stood at the fireplace mantle and looked up at the family photo that hung there. I hadn't seen that picture in years but I distinctly recalled the day we had it made. "Come look. Your grandparents."

Davey rushed over from the bottom of the staircase.

"Wow! You and Grandpa look exactly alike," he pointed out.

Yeah, I guess we did. I had always been told that while growing up and didn't mind because my father was a handsome man.

"Grandma was hot!"

I felt the blood rush into my cheeks as I looked down at Davey incredulously, "Davey."

"I don't mean it in a bad way, Dad. But look at her. She's awesome."

I looked back up at that picture and you know what, she was awesome. In that picture, she was thirty-something years old and would soon be dead. The picture had captured the warmth and beauty that I'd come to know over the years. Davey's observation was dead-on: She was hot. Maybe that's why the neighborhood kids always liked coming over to my house.

As we walked away from the fireplace and over and up the winding staircase, I turned back and looked back down at the living room. It wasn't that I saw or heard something in that silent home, but rather smelled something like perfume. I stopped on the stairs and sniffed the air like a hungry dog that hadn't eaten for weeks.

It was perfume, *Cool Water*, I think she called it. I was about to ease down the stairs and investigate the smell, which seemed to be coming from somewhere in the living room, when Davey yelled from the second floor, "Which room was yours, Dad?!" His voice brought me back to reality, and the smell was gone even though I sniffed the air violently. Nothing.

"Second door on the right!" I yelled as I slowly made my way up the staircase toward my son.

Davey didn't wait for me to join him as he turned the brass door knob and flung open the door to my room. It was the same as I had left it decades ago. Davey walked on inside with me following a few seconds later. By then Davey was looking around at artifacts that were on display, frozen in time. I hadn't been in there since I was nineteen years old—the day of the big fight between Dad and me. I remember the last time I was in the room. I was in there with a knapsack, gathering things that I thought I needed to leave home with—the bare essentials.

Dad and I had gotten into this hellish fight over me not going to college. I wanted to take some time off after my senior year of high school and dad didn't want to hear of it. He told me that if I took a year off, that I'd never go to college and would eventually regret it. I think a lot of the substance of our falling out back then was fueled by us not knowing how to deal with Mom's death. We were both struggling to stay afloat with the grim fact that my mother, his wife, was never coming back and how unfair life was. Sometimes you take it out on the people that you love the most. And we both took it out on each other.

When I told him that I was going to write a novel, he stood there and laughed in my face. Not just a chuckle mind you, but a full-blown horse laugh. He thought that I couldn't be serious. Oh, but I was. This was the fight that had destroyed what little was left of us after Mom died. Funny, Samantha and I met the same fate. We both believed that we were right. Where does right get you these days? Nowhere.

My dad's grand vision was for me to follow in his footsteps. I didn't want that, nor did I feel that he should have bestowed that upon me. Ernest Matthews wanted his son, with his future wide open, to merely do just what he'd done with his life. I could have, perhaps, become a lawyer. But why, when I had all this talent to write words on paper?

"You'll never amount to anything as a writer!" Dad shouted at me in the very bedroom Davey and I stood in. "You might as well become an artist selling drawings in a dime store!" Then he said my mother would have been disappointed in me. I tuned him out and packed my bag. When I was finished taking what I needed, I turned and looked at my dad and said nothing. What was there to say? He'd said it all, right? That was the last time I had been in this room, my old room. I could still hear the fight inside my head—its loud echoes bouncing around the room like a ball in a racketball court.

I had been to the house since then and had even talked to Dad several times, too. But I never entered my old bedroom. Do you want to know what I was into back then growing up? You want to know what my hobbies were in those days of my youth? You want to know what authors I was reading? All you had to do was step inside my time capsule and take the ten-cent tour, much like Davey was doing.

Speaking of Davey, he walked over to my bookshelf and thumbed through a few paperbacks that had become nothing more than dust catchers.

"Jack Kerouac? I've read this one," he said.

I was stunned by my son's taste in books. I had no idea that he read something so fragmented and dated like Kerouac.

"You read *Big Sur*?"

"Yeah, a few months ago. Felt badly for him at the end," Davey said, not paying any attention to me but instead keeping his eyes steady on my books.

"Yeah," I said reeling that he had read that book, especially at his age. Like Davey, I began to scan around my bedroom, looking at the relics of my past. There was my big tub of a TV sitting on the black wooden stand that was covered with an inch or so of gray dust. On the walls hung various items of any teenager's bedroom: baseball posters and scantily clad babes. A few shelves of memorabilia also hung on the walls and on those shelves sat a picture in a frame that was somewhat hidden by the decades of collected dust. I walked over to the other side of the room while Davey pulled books out of the shelf, flipping through them, blowing dust into the air.

On that shelf sat a small five-by-seven photo of me and Marie when we were both no more than fifteen. I was standing behind her, grinning ear to ear with my Braves hat tipped upwards like a drunk, arms wrapped around her as she smiled that million-dollar smile, wearing my favorite purple sweater. I reached up and slowly took the frame off the shelf and wiped the dust from the glass. It was clearer but could stand a spray of Windex.

I didn't recall the exact day the picture was snapped or who could have been behind the camera. But I could tell we were at her house. I knew that because in the background stood a tall pine tree that towered in her backyard. God, we were so young back then. Everything was right there to be had. My future... *our* future was wide open. I smiled a bit and placed the picture back up where it belonged.

I turned around bringing myself back from memory lane and looked over at Davey. He was standing there looking out my window out at the backyard that I used to play in when I was a kid during those endless summers.

"Huge backyard," he said without turning to me, mesmerized by the scope of my lush green yard.

"Yeah, it's big alright. Looks like the mowers came a couple of days ago," I said, walking over to him to join in gazing out the window. "You see that old board over there in that maple tree? That was where I had a tree house when I was eleven years old. A storm came through one spring afternoon and ripped it to shreds. All that was left was that board that was nailed to the tree. Dad left it there as a reminder," I said, recalling my sanctuary up in the tree.

"Yard's big enough to shag some flies, right?" Davey asked.

"Yeah, Dad and I used to go out there and play catch. He'd throw them high in the air and I chased them down like I was playing outfield for the Braves. Man, I used to be fast."

"Got a ball and gloves around?" Davey asked out of nowhere.

"Maybe. I think I might still have mine and your grandpa's somewhere around here. I don't ever remember taking it home," I said feeling something terrific and awesome come over me standing beside my son. We were going to play catch in the backyard; *my old backyard.* How cool was that?

4

I roamed the house, my childhood home, in search of two leather gloves and a baseball. The house that I was free-roaming in didn't interest me at all. I didn't stand around and gaze into the décor like Davey had. He was mesmerized by the relics of my past; me, not so much. It all might as well have been just staple background furniture and pictures from a long-running TV show.

I was checking all the rooms—closets, the attic, the basement, everywhere and anywhere for those gloves and baseball I *knew* were around somewhere. And as I went from room to room, there was that smell of mom's perfume again. I smiled a bit, thinking of her being there watching over us. I walked into the kitchen, where the smell was the strongest. There was nothing in there but usual kitchenware and appliances, but the smell was there. And I half-believed my mother was standing there looking at me. Just a feeling I got.

The gloves have to be here somewhere, I thought. When I moved away, I never took the gloves with me. The last time I used mine was when I pitched in a sandlot game at the park when I was sixteen or seventeen. I had brought it home and could have sworn I put it up on the shelf in my closet. But I had already checked there, twice.

I stood in the living room, racking my brain about where my glove and my father's baseball glove could be resting while Davey roamed around marveling at his dad's boyhood home—the home of the famous Jerry Matthews. At some point, while I was walking through the house searching for the gloves, Davey had found the photo albums in the living room and sat down in Dad's dusty recliner and began to flip through them in awe. I didn't stop to marvel at them. I kept going room to room, looking for those damn gloves and baseball.

I entered Dad's room, which was perfectly neat and well organized, much like his life had been before Alzheimer's. The bedroom itself was a mirror into the man that I called father: nothing out of order and everything, no matter how small or big, important or unimportant, was in its rightful place. Except for the drawers that I had left pulled out. They, all five of them, were still hanging empty. I immediately walked over to the bed, fell to my knees, and looked underneath it. There was a box that caught my eye, a huge Nike shoebox. It seemed so out of place there that I had to see what it was because my Dad didn't wear shoes like that.

I reached in and pulled the box out from under the bed. I had never seen the box before and wondered what the hell Dad could've kept in there. On my knees, I opened the unsealed box and looked inside. There were the gloves, his and mine, the baseball, and pictures of me and Dad and Mom. I was young and so were they— pictures of happy times, pictures of times that were forever frozen. Those pictures evoked a powerful sense of nostalgia within me. I thought of nothing but the good times.

I sat on my haunches, looking at the pictures, trying to remember those photos, when Davey came walking into the room.

"You had a neat house, Dad. Cool pics, too," he said. "What's this?" Davey joined me over at the bed and leaned down to see what I had recovered. "You found the gloves and baseball. More pictures! Awesome!" He took them from me and asked me several questions.

The first picture was of Dad and me on what appeared to be Halloween. I was standing beside him, no more than six, wearing a Batman costume, holding a plastic orange Jack O' Lantern bucket.

The next one was of Mom and me on a beach flying a kite at sunset. In the pic, she and I were holding the string but the kite was not in the shot. Just me and her smiling as we both looked up at the blue sky. The picture was so beautiful. She was so beautiful….

The last picture he asked about showed the three of us standing in front of our huge Christmas tree in the living room. Dad was on the right, I was in the middle, and Mom was on the left. We were each smiling into the camera, happy. I think I was thirteen because I was the same height as my mother, but I'm not completely sure.

Memories tend to get fuzzy as you age. And sometimes you don't remember things as they were, but rather as you would like them to have been, and that becomes the truth. Davey asked me if I had remembered when those photos were taken and I had told him a lie and said that I did. Truth was, I didn't. And it sucked that I didn't because I wanted to. I wanted to be able to say, "Yeah, that was this year and that was when we went to the beach." I couldn't be honest with Davey about those pictures because I didn't recall them much at all. It's sad when you can't remember even when the pictures are there to prove everything that happened.

5

Outside in the enormous backyard, Davey trotted out from me and he and I began to play long toss. Dad's glove smelled like a mixture of his cologne and old leather. The glove which I had never slipped on before fit me, well, like a glove. And what was cool about the whole experience was that Davey was wearing *my* glove that I used as a kid.

I had become my dad and Davey was me, just like me and my old man back in the day, playing catch, a simple game of catch. But it was much more than that, much more than just tossing a baseball around. It was something magical, something that I could never write about because there would never be any words to articulate what was going on between us that day. It was magical.

I thought that trip to Atlanta and my old home would jar Davey back to reality somehow; that maybe us bringing it all back to basics could perhaps clear the depression that was in the early stages of clouding his mind. I guess it did for a little while but our trip had to end and so did his happier mood. It wasn't long after we made it back home that Davey slipped back to where he was before Atlanta.

When we got back home, things went back to what they were beforehand. The Davey who traveled to Atlanta with me had gone back to the introverted kid who I worried about. And over the following weeks, he became a shadow in the house. At some point, and I don't remember when, I stopped trying to fix him. I thought that maybe he could pull himself out of his funk. I was wrong. I miscalculated his mental distress.

6

I stood there in the silent funeral home, in the place where they prepare the bodies. Davey lay on a table, covered halfway with a white sheet. His eyes were closed like he was sleeping, just like I had seen him thousands of times when I would go to his bedroom and turn his light off when he was a child. God, I hadn't done that in years. He looked... peaceful. He didn't look exhausted or like his thoughts were too big for him. He looked like he did back when things were good.

Jennifer stood there beside me, hand over her mouth sobbing, as distraught as you'd expect a mother to be about her dead child. Me? I just stood there, flooded with so many emotions that my head couldn't process the influx. Being numb at that point had its advantages. I stared at him lying there much like I had at the hospital, motionless, dead. For some reason, I couldn't take my eyes off of him, even as Jennifer backed away in shock and terror of seeing him, actually *seeing* him dead again since the hospital.

I wished a thousand times that I could go back in time right then and there and fix all of this. I would have sold my soul to the devil to make that happen: to fix my family, to make my son alive again.

Somewhere from behind, Mr. Conrad emerged from the shadows of the prep area and consoled my crying wife who was, by that time, dry-heaving violently. Me, I stood there towering over Davey, feeling everything at once but not knowing which feeling to hold within me. It was like the breath had been knocked out of me as I looked down at him. It was the most peaceful I'd seen him in a long, long time.

CHAPTER NINETEEN

1

It was raining at the cemetery the day Davey was laid to rest. A full day had gone by before the funeral, but the hours hadn't eased any of the pain in the Matthews home. I think the hours made things worse and made me worse.

In the hours after leaving the funeral home, leaving my dead son behind, I came home, darted straight to my office and opened the bottom drawer of the desk where I made my living. I reached in and visited an old friend that I hadn't seen in a very, very long time.

A few hours after my friend, Wild Turkey whiskey, and I got reacquainted, I sat slumped in my chair holding an empty bottle. I was numb, foggy just like I wanted to be. I even pissed myself. But the alcohol didn't take the edge off like I hoped it would. I was still hurting and hurting badly. I was mortally wounded.

Instead, the whiskey numbed my body, relaxed my mind, preparing the way for my thoughts to wrestle me down and force the emotions that I had blocked at the funeral home down my throat. Had I owned a gun I'd probably would have blown my fucking head off that night. It all came to a head there in my office.

I cried at first (so much that my eyes felt as if they had busted), saying his name over and over like a broken record. I guess I was muttering his name so much that I thought he might appear in my office back to how he was long ago: healthy and full of life. I said his name over and over, crying harder each time that I did it. And then the next wave of emotion came crashing down upon my shoulders....

I laid my head down on my desk in a blubbering heap and talked to God Himself. I offered Him several deals that I thought were great. First, I asked God that if He could send me back in time, I would fix things and make everything right. That's all I would need, a do-over. A fucking do-over. "If you're so damn powerful," I cried, "then erase this time, and I'll show you just how good I can make things. All that I need is a shot to make it right and to stop him from dying." I pleaded, "Just one chance. A do-over."

My second bargain was for God to kill me and bring Davey back to life. I begged and begged God to strike me dead right then and there and revive my son. I had heard stories about people being pronounced dead and coming back to life, and maybe that could be the case here. I wanted to trade places with my son and only God could help me.

After a few minutes of hard pleading, I lifted my head and looked at the room through watery lenses. "Fuck it!" I screamed as I smashed my empty whiskey bottle against the far wall. I went into a full rage, beast mode. I stood up from my chair and looked for something to break. It didn't matter what it was, how much it cost, or what sentimental value it had. If it was in my office, I was going to break it. And I did. I tore the place apart with my bare hands.

I tore pictures from the walls, breaking their glass frames and splintering their thin wooden frames to pieces all over the floor. All my author proof copies of every book, I raked off my bookshelf and ripped apart, hating every page. I took my computer from my desk and slammed it against the wall, shattering it in a heap of broken plastic and glass. I had so much hate and adrenaline coursing through my veins that I lifted my desk and flipped it over, spilling out all the drawers and sending its contents scattering onto the floor.

There was a baseball bat that I twirled in my hands when I wrote late into the night. I used that bat as a nervous habit, playing with it in my hands when I was lost deep in the forest of thought. The bat would be in my hands as I paced around my office, trying to come up with another idea for a scene or a subplot of a book.

The bat, a nice tan Louisville Slugger, somehow appeared in my hands and I began to swing like Chipper Jones, busting lamps off the walls, shattering the window, hitting the walls as hard as I could, feeling the vibration from the blows as I screamed out wildly like a savage in the night. I was in a drunken rage, fueled by my son's death. Most of that night I don't remember. Those were just its highlights. Jennifer was somewhere downstairs. I don't know if she even heard me or not.

2

At some point, I gave out and fell to the floor in a drunken heap. I awoke the next morning to the clap of thunder as rain flew into the room, hitting me in the face. I opened my eyes and saw the broken window. I sat up and looked around; through my headache—which pounded with every heartbeat—I saw what I had done to my office. It was trashed.

I looked down at my hands, and they were battered and bloody with a piece of glass sticking out of my right hand, between my first and second knuckle, embedded in the webbing. Perhaps it was from one of the numerous picture frames I broke in my fit of rage. I plucked it out, and it bled again.

I sat there scanning the room through my terrible hangover and saw nothing but the aftermath of a man who was so full of hate, rage, and sadness that even my hangover seemed a distant star on the outer bands of our solar system. Everything in there was broken: pictures of me and the kids, me and Jennifer, awards, plaques, golden statues of past successes and awards for my writing; all broken, smashed and scattered about like toys in a kid's room. None of it mattered.

At first, when I saw all the damage, I wondered how it all happened. But then my memory flashed behind my eyes like lightning. I didn't remember everything, except for a chunk here and a chunk there. I had been torn up over Davey and lashed out. And as I looked around the room, I wondered frantically if I had contained my destruction to just one room in the house.

Back in my dark drinking days, I had been a violent drunk, playing Hulk with anything in my path. But I never hit my wife or kids. I stayed away when I knew the thought of drinking seeped into my brain. When I got drunk, I became mouthy and physical. Sometimes it landed me beaten, left for dead, or in a hospital. The hospital incidents happened before my marriage to Jennifer. The left-for-dead parts occurred during the early days of my marriage.

I slowly got to my feet and almost fell back down. My head began to pound to the point where I could not ignore it anymore. I was woozy and felt like I had been on a rocking ship at sea for months. I staggered around and felt a sudden burst of coldness from the broken window in my office. Cold mixed with rain flew into my office and had probably been for hours. All I knew was that there was a window frame with pieces of glass edging here and there, allowing a bitter wind and rain to invade my space. The carpet next to the window was soaking, and when I stepped on it, water came above my soles.

I had seen and felt enough of the room, and I staggered across my office, stepping on things and hearing the remaining pieces of glass from the broken picture frames crack and crunch under my shoes. I had to get out of there and face the day and whatever it would bring. Still, I knew life after Davey's death would be fundamentally different from how it was beforehand.

3

I walked through the house, holding my head with my left hand, trying to push away my awful headache. I walked to the kitchen, where we kept Band-Aids and Ibuprofen in a little cabinet. I opened the cabinet door and found the bottle of hopeful relief. I twisted its cap off and shook out five blue liquid-gels and walked over to the kitchen sink. Before I could turn the tap on, I looked out the window above the sink and saw Jennifer sitting in a swing on the kids' swing set from years ago in the backyard in the storm. I dropped the pain relievers down onto the counter and dashed outside as quickly as I could, trying not to fall as I went. My headache and a strong desire to vomit made it nearly impossible.

I made it to her in the pouring rain and stiff wind. Cold rain stung my face as I stood next to her as she sat on the swing, her hands holding the rusty chains that held up the faded green plastic seat. "You gotta come inside!" I yelled over the storm. "You're going to get sick out here!" Jennifer just sat there, hair all straightened, stuck to the sides of her face, clothes soaking wet, staring off into space. "Jennifer!" I shouted. "You've got to get up and get out of the storm! You're going to get sick!" I shouted over the thunder and rain again. Still, she just sat there without even glancing at me. I knew that Jennifer was taking Davey's death hard. Hell, I was, too. But I had to try to hang on somehow, or I'd fall down a black hole of misery. I felt that it was my duty to stand when she couldn't. But that thought almost made me laugh. Since when did I care how she felt? Did I ever?

Knowing that if I just kept on talking she'd ignore me, I decided to do something to shake her from her catatonic state. I reached over and grabbed her hand. When I did that she fought me. "Let go!" she screamed as lightning flashed across the dark morning sky. "Get away from me! Leave me alone!"

"You can't stay out here!" I shouted back, wrestling with her, trying to pry her hands off the chains. "You got to get back inside!"

"Leave me alone!" she screamed again, but this time I managed to slip her wet hands off the chains and pulled her off the swing. And still, she fought me, smacking me, cussing me, trying to claw my eyes out. It was all her rage, all her emotions coming out all at once on me; much like mine had back in my office. Instead of fighting her back, I let her do her damage to me. After all, didn't I deserve it for all I'd done to her and our family?

As the rain poured down in buckets, and as the wind bent trees nearly over and thunder rattled our very bones, Jennifer punched, clawed, smacked, and tore into me. It hurt, but I let her do it. I felt it was my obligation to let her. My face was bleeding from the scratches her long fingernails made, my head rung even more loudly than before as she boxed my ears like a prize fighter and my nose, which I felt was broken, was bleeding all over before being washed clean by the rain. I held her close as she hit me time and time again.

Eventually, Jennifer began to slow down and her cries became softer. I could see she was winding down, her adrenaline spent. I gradually moved her closer to me. She laid her face into my wet, blood-spattered t-shirt and cried what was left of her tears into it. I held her close for the first time in years, and let her cry on my chest as the thunder rattled violently once again out in the backyard.

4

The funeral was surreal. I was stunned at the amount of people who showed up for my son's final act. He was lying in a coffin right above his new home and people, some I knew and some I didn't, stood all around, some seated and some not, listening to the preacher recite words from the Bible. Those words were meant to comfort, but they were of no use to me. There were no words that could make me feel right about my son's suicide. No words at all.

I sat there, Jennifer to my left and Samantha to my right, both wearing black and staring off into the distance. Van Halen could have been putting on a concert right there in the graveyard, and I wouldn't have noticed it. I was still numb about Davey's death, and I couldn't believe he was gone forever. Instead, I imagined a hundred different ways this tragedy could've been prevented. The storm from earlier that morning had given way to an overcast, cold misty rain.

"Had I been a better dad to him, I could've prevented this," I told myself time and time again in the hours before we put him into the ground. If only. The choices I made and was still making up to that point had led all of us, my entire family, to this spot in the cemetery, mourning our son who shouldn't have died.

As the preacher concluded his sermon, I looked around the gloomy, misty afternoon and zeroed in on some of the people who had shown up to pay their respects. There was Bob Windom; the old man actually thought enough of me to show up.

Then there was Curtis Phillips, my agent and best friend. He came to see my son off. Davey and Curtis, back when things were young and in bloom, used to watch the Braves play on TV for a few innings when Curtis would drop by for a visit. He was the closest thing to an uncle that my kids ever had. And although he didn't visit very often, the times he did were special. Davey loved him.

In the back were several of Davey's teachers. Mr. Beachy, Davey's history teacher, came to pay his final respects. He and I had talked a few months ago about Davey's potential for becoming a professor after he graduated college. I thought that was putting the carriage before the horse, but Mr. Beachy insisted that Davey was the most brilliant student he'd come across in years. Next to Mr. Beachy was Mrs. Whitmore, the school principal; Mr. Nelson, Davey's science teacher; and Mrs. Hudson, Davey's guidance counselor. I wondered if she knew anything about Davey's inner trauma. They came to the graveyard to see my son's eternal resting place.

Davey had a few kids his age show up to the graveside service, friends I guessed; although I never knew about any of his friends after sixth grade. Maybe he didn't have any. Maybe he died alone. I don't know exactly. I don't know how school was for Davey, but I know that things changed for the worse when he got into high school. Perhaps that was what killed him. There were a few shaggy-haired kids—skaters—that paid their respects and a girl who looked teary-eyed. She was nice looking and I could imagine Davey wanted her to be his girlfriend. The girl that I saw seemed familiar somehow. Where had I seen her? I couldn't place her.

I turned my head and saw Randy standing behind my daughter, hands upon her shoulders. I liked Randy, I did, but I wanted to beat the hell out of him for planting that stupid-ass marriage idea in my daughter's head. I know why they suddenly wanted to get hitched. See that's the part none of them knew that I knew. I wondered if Davey even knew. Jennifer sure as hell did because she helped conceal it from me.

5

Long before Davey's suicide and a little before Samantha moved out, I was milling about the house one day, talking on the phone with Heather about nothing of importance—mostly about our weekend plans. I walked into the living room and spied a pair of Samantha's shoes. I always hated when people left their shoes in the living room— just a hang-up I had. I picked them up, noticed they were a little muddy, and carried them to her bedroom while still on the phone with Heather, talking about what movies we might want to rent.

I took the shoes to the bathroom next to Samantha's bedroom instead of putting them in the tub so the mud could dry and not make a mess on the carpet. I told Heather that I was going to tell Sam about leaving her muddy shoes in the living room when I saw her. I was about to leave the bathroom when something out of place on the vanity caught my eye. I stopped and backtracked to see what it was. It was a pregnancy test stick. And it was positive. I stood there stunned and speechless at the same time. Heather said my name several times, thinking the call dropped. She hung up and called me back, snapping me back into the real world. "What happened? Your phone die?" she asked.

"No," I said licking my suddenly dry lips. "No, I um... found something in the bathroom. Samantha's bathroom." There was silence on the phone between us because I think that Heather knew what it must have been. Either a condom, a condom wrapper, or a pregnancy test box. None of the above. It was the actual stick itself.

"What?" Heather asked.

"A pregnancy test. It's positive." I remember saying with no emotion. I was rocked on my heels by this simple discovery. I stood there for minutes until I heard the front door slam and Samantha walking through the house talking on her cell phone with one of her friends. I realized where I was and quickly bolted out of the bathroom and down the hall like a cheetah trying not to tip her off.

She walked into her room and shut the door, still chatting away on the phone. I stood there at the end of the hallway trying to vanquish the butterflies in my stomach. Heather was trying to talk to me, but her words were nothing more than background noise at that point. I was lost inside my own head.

6

I looked at Randy there on that dreary, misty day at the cemetery and wanted to rip him apart. Maybe part of it was the stupid idea of them getting married and the other part was that they were pregnant and tried to hide it from me. Perhaps even some of it was because Davey was dead, and I wanted someone to hurt for that other than myself. I would deal with my daughter and her boyfriend later when everything passed.

Off to the right of the maple tree was Heather Parker sitting among a sea of mourners. She had come but stayed off to the side. She didn't want to complicate the situation any more than it had to be, and I completely understood. It wouldn't look right to have a girl a few years older than Samantha clinging to me and being paraded around my son's funeral as my mistress. Heather just stood there as a face in the crowd, keeping a steady eye on me. She wanted to be near me as I did to her, but we just couldn't. It wasn't the right place.

I sat there and looked at her and her back at me for some time during the service. I wanted her touch so badly but I couldn't. I just needed her to hold onto me so I could start repairing myself somehow. Hell, I had barely talked to her since I left her place the day Davey died. I didn't do it on purpose, not at all, but I had placed myself on an island and just sat looking around, trying to figure out how the world had gone so terribly wrong and dark. Thank God she was so understanding.

7

After Davey was slowly lowered into the ground, everyone began to spread out. I talked to scores of people, Jennifer's mother and father, Jennifer's uncles and aunts. As I walked over to the maple tree to talk to Heather, I smiled for the first time in a long time, a reaction to seeing her. I was happy to see her. We both stood there, looking at each other and talking. We wanted to be in each other's arms. But it wouldn't look right.

"I know," Heather said with hurt in her voice. I looked around and saw that people, my wife and my daughter included, were occupied with other mourners. There was no one looking at the two of us by the maple tree.

"Fuck this... come here," I said as I leaned into her and clutched her tightly. God, it was so nice to be in her arms, her heart and mine beating against each other. It was where I belonged, where I was destined to be. She felt so good. I stood there and cried for what seemed to be hours. I cried because of my dead son. I cried because I had fucked so much stuff up in my life. I cried because I didn't know what else to do. Heather just held on and let me cry under the maple tree amongst the tombstones.

After a few moments and some heavy tears, I pulled back to look at Heather. She was nothing short of an angel for standing there with her arms around me. Through all this mess with Davey, I had Heather. Thank God for that. As we talked a bit and as she wiped my tears with her hands, the young girl that I had seen earlier in the crowd approached. "Mr. Matthews?" She asked hesitantly as if she was afraid of interrupting me and Heather. She was a beautiful girl of fifteen, and I knew by the way she walked up to us that she belonged to Davey. I remembered then where I knew her from: Davey's school dance from a few years ago. He came out with her, and she kissed him on the cheek that night by my car.

Way to go kid, I thought. "Yes?" I said, letting go of Heather and standing beside her.

"I'm um... I was Davey's girlfriend, Amy Gonzalez. He was going to introduce me to you later this month," she said with a slight grin and then a quick frown as she tried to hold back tears.

I stood there shocked. "My Davey and you? Wow...I never knew anything about you. He was so... so...."

"Secretive," Amy interrupted, finishing my thought. "Yeah, he was like that. He didn't let a lot of people in." She had been crying. Her eyes were bloodshot.

I stood there with Heather and looked at her and then back at Amy, "You got a minute?" I asked. I thanked Heather for coming, and she told me that I didn't have to do that. I know that I didn't but did anyway. I told her to go on home and I'd call her later. I said that I wanted to talk to this Amy girl about my son. Maybe I could find out who Davey was, finally. Heather and I hugged one more time, both of us wanting to kiss, but we decided without words that it wouldn't be right as more and more people were walking past us, noticing the two secret lovers by the maple in the misty, overcast afternoon.

Amy and I walked around the graveyard side by side, away from the people wearing black so it eventually was just the two of us among the tombstones. Neither of us minded the thin rain that fell on us. "So you and Davey, huh?" I asked, walking alongside her with my hands in my pockets.

"Yeah, about a year officially," Amy replied.

"I wish I'd known. We could've had you over for dinner or something."

"David," she called him David, the name his mother had chosen for him after her father, "wanted to make sure we were real and not just a simple school crush. I think he was afraid of bringing people home because of you," Amy said candidly.

"Me? Why?"

"Because you're like this famous author, and he didn't want people to be around him because of that. He hated posers and he thought that people only wanted to be his friend because of his dad. It's why some of the teachers went out of their way to talk to him."

"Is that why he never had any friends?"

Amy nodded, "Yup. He didn't want people sucking up to him because of you. He wanted people to like him because of him, not because of what you are. He ended up being a loner." Her words cut me like a knife. My success and celebrity had profoundly impaired my son's life. I had no idea. I wondered if my life was one of the reasons why Davey committed suicide.

"Did he hate me?" I asked, needing to know, hoping that in some weird way knowing would ease my conscience.

Amy shook her head. "No, he loved you. Talked about you all the time, actually. He wanted to be a writer just like you but with a different name. He had a pen name already picked out: Derek Dawes. It was important for him to go his own way when that day came."

She and I walked and talked about David, as he was known to Amy, about who he was outside of the house. He was a completely different kid when out in the wild, unlike at home where he was quiet, isolated within the confines of his bedroom.

She gave me perspective about my son, stories I never thought possible about him. After hearing about what kind of person he was, and who he strived to be, I fell in love with the kid all over again, just like when I first saw him in the delivery room.

I had to bury my son to know who he was.

"Why did he kill himself?" I asked the only person who I thought would know the answer. Amy stopped and looked at me with those big doe eyes as her blond hair pressed against the sides of her face from the rain that fell. She wanted to cry but held back sternly. I could tell she had cried a lot lately.

"I don't know," Amy said. "He had just gotten sad over a lot of stuff he couldn't fix. He was getting bullied at school, and his grades were falling. He said home was bad. He just wasn't in a good place. I tried to help, but I couldn't reach him anymore. He'd gotten too far out there. But I kept trying no matter what." By this time Amy was crying. There was nothing I could do but stand there.

8

A little while after I said a long goodbye to Amy, I walked back to my family, many of whom were leaving. Samantha said bye to her mother and glared at me. Our old grudge about her getting married was beginning to resurface, and Davey had not even been in the ground for thirty minutes. Little did she know, I knew about her pregnancy. Maybe I was looking for a fight. Maybe I was looking to blow off some steam. Perhaps both were correct.

I know that the graveyard where we had just buried my son wasn't the right place to start a fight, but man I was raw from head to toe, especially after talking to Amy. She had confirmed what I already knew: My letting our family fall apart was one of the causes of Davey's suicide. How could I ever get over that? Unbeknownst to me at the time, I wouldn't live long enough to come close.

I approached Randy, Samantha, Jennifer, and her parents as they stood next to the line of cars parked on the paved path in the cemetery. I stood there and felt Samantha's coldness, and I'll be damned if she was going to look at me like that. Not today, I decided.

"So, when is this marriage going to happen?" I asked, putting everyone on the spot. Jennifer looked at me and so did her parents and Samantha. Randy, that pussy, lowered his head and wasn't man enough to even look me in the eye.

"Hardly the time," Samantha shot back.

"Oh, I think it is. Why not? So, how long were you going to hold onto that secret of being pregnant, kiddo?" I glared at Jennifer. "Were you in on this? You didn't think I needed to fucking know?!"

"What are you talking about?" Samantha asked.

"I saw the pregnancy test in your bathroom a while back! Don't lie to me! You all knew about this, and you wanted to hide it from me?! Fucking conspiracy," I said, getting hotter by the minute.

"I'm not pregnant!" Samantha shouted and then Randy looked up and at me. He wasn't scared like I thought he'd be. Either he knew nothing about it, or he had the guts of a burglar. I wasn't sure which.

"Don't fucking lie to me, bitch! You ain't nothing but a whore! Like mommy dearest over here!" I shouted. By this time, Jennifer's dad stepped in front of me and tried to calm me down, but I pushed him to the side and kept my eyes fixed on my daughter.

"Fuck you! I'm not pregnant!" Samantha said, bucking up to her old man.

"So who's pregnancy test did I find in the bathroom a while back? Davey's?!" I said as Jennifer's dad tried to put space between me and Samantha. Good thing too because I was ready to strangle her right then and there. I could tell I was slipping off into that beast mode that I had gotten into in my office. The small rational part of my mind was scared.

"It wasn't mine! Don't you accuse me of getting...."

"So that's why you came into my office that night, spinning me that tale about how you and Randy love each other! You knew you were pregnant the whole time, and you tried to hide it from me! What a stupid bitch you are!"

I was full throttle now, trying to get into her face. I had become Ernest Mathews, and she was me back in the day up in my bedroom where I left my dad. I wanted to slap the hell out of her, I did. I never in my life hit any of my kids, but dammit, I wanted to beat her down there in the graveyard.

"You're just a kid yourself, and you want to have a kid?!"

"Stop it!!" Jennifer shouted, shutting me and Samantha up. It was the first thing Jennifer had said all day. "The test wasn't hers... it was mine."

I stood there ready to hit my daughter with clenched fists as the blood drained from my face. Samantha stood there with her mouth gaping eyes fixed on her mother. Randy had the look of freedom, and Jennifer's parents stood there like the rest of us, stunned.

"What?" I asked quietly. The fight had fled out of my tightly wound body.

"It's mine, okay?" Jennifer said, tears coming down her face. She stood there for a moment and looked at us before walking away. Samantha followed, leaving me to stand there to look at her parents and Randy in the now-pouring rain. What a day.

CHAPTER TWENTY

1

The events of my life, in every person's life, serve as a timeline of sorts. I view it in full-blown retrospect as things around my life had crumbled before me. I had lost it all: my marriage (lost that one a long, long time ago), my first true love only to be replaced with Heather, my dear son, and my daughter. To me, there was nothing left to hang onto but Heather. Had it not been for her, I would have allowed the horrific times of my life to consume me; they almost did regardless. I actually pondered following in my son's footsteps and killing myself.

The road to hell has a toll, they say. And that toll levied upon me was enormous. I paid in full with the heaviest price of all: Davey. It had been weeks since he had killed himself, but time did not ease my pain, not one single bit. Did I expect it to? No, to be honest, I didn't know what to expect or how I was going to carry on. I was never the same. None of us in the family were going forward.

Davey's blood was on my hands, and I riddled myself with guilt for hours upon hours, wondering if I had killed him. Deep down I knew that I didn't, not literally, but my past actions had. I had destroyed our family for selfish reasons. I wrecked everything. It was me behind the wheel, no one else. The totality of my past sins was now in full bloom. I hated seeing them in all their glory. Davey paid in full for the sins of the father.

I told myself, time and time again, that Davey's mind was weak. Why else would you take your own life, right? But that was a generic cop-out answer to something that I was trying to avoid. The fact of the matter was that I had caused and added to the pain that eventually led him to end his own life.

Tough thing to realize, knowing that you perhaps were the one that was the tipping point to your son's death. His fate was sealed the day Jennifer and I were married. From there, future events created a sad reality that put Davey in its crosshairs. And the one who ultimately pulled the trigger was me and my carnival of bad decisions. Sure, Davey had killed himself, but it might as well have been me who had shoved the pills down his throat.

I guess I always thought Davey would be there; his breathing and being alive was something that I had taken gravely for granted. I always assumed too much in my life. Assumptions are nothing more than mere hopes when you strip them down. And that was my life, always assuming and hoping. I never allowed myself to evaluate the situations realistically. I always thought that things would just turn out in my favor. They never did until Heather came into my life.

My children witnessed my coldness over the years and both reacted to the dysfunction within the Matthews home in different ways; ways which led Davey to his death and Samantha to walk away from home with Randy denouncing me forever since our heated exchange in the graveyard. My writing career went south because I assumed it would always be there. It's hard to make it in the publishing industry, but I realized it was even harder to stay there.

2

All the prices that I had to pay to be with Heather were markers on my timeline. Everything had its cost, every decision that I made cost more than the last. Life is a gamble, and I was never a gambling kind of guy. However, I gambled my life away basically when I held out hope for years that Marie and I would end up together. The gambles that I made didn't pay off, causing me to lose everything in the process. I should've folded and gotten away from the table years ago.

But I couldn't do it. Had I been able to, maybe my life would have turned out for the better. If only I could go back and undo the things that I did. I wasted so much time on wishful thinking.

But we all make decisions and defend the roles we play—each of us, every day. The funny thing was, that I was not defending my role anymore. I knew what I had done to myself and my broken family. How could I defend the choices I had made? I couldn't, so I didn't. There weren't any excuses. There was no one else to blame. It was all on me; everything was, in the end.

It's crazy, I know, but when I started drinking days after Davey's death, I saw things much, much clearer than previously. It was like I had been looking through life with an opaque plastic bag over my head, and when I started drinking again in earnest, that bag was removed and I could see.

The power of the drink gave me an insight that I used to have long ago, back when things were manageable. But things changed so much along the way that I got lost. A wrong turn there, wrong turn here, and *bam!* There I was, lost with no direction home. I did it to myself, the entire time, and cannot blame anyone but *myself.* I started the effect by toppling over the first domino, and then from there it was impossible to stop. The momentum of the bad choices was too much to stop as each domino toppled over the next. And in the end, nothing was left standing, not even me.

It was simple cause and effect. I set into motion stuff that I could not reverse, even if I wanted to. It's funny how one can trace the origins of when things first went wrong. I can *and* have. I own everything that I did not to just Jennifer, but to Samantha and most importantly, to Davey. And it all was over a woman, a true love I thought who made me do the things that I did. Wasn't her fault; it was mine in believing in the lies that I told myself every night. I had kept the thought of me and Marie being together one great day in my head for so long that I sacrificed my marriage and family. And look at what it cost me. Everything, in the end.

3

The only reason I didn't take a shotgun and blow my head off was the simple fact that I had Heather in my life. She was my touchstone, my rock to lean up against. Had it not been for her, my ruined life would've surely ended. Trust me, I wanted to kill myself—just lie someplace, bleeding onto the floor as the images of my life flashed before my eyes in one quick moment. Who would've known that's how things would eventually go down with me?

The power of the drink had taken over like days of the past, and it nearly cost me my future with Heather. I'd just gotten bad for a while after Davey and sought refuge in the bottle. I had started pushing Heather away like I had all others over time. Thank God for Heather's stubbornness. She stayed and brought me out of the bottle and into the bright light of sobriety. From what I can recall, it was a dark several weeks.

I thought after my writing career tanked and Marie left my life, that I was home free. But when Davey killed himself, everything about the way I lived and saw the world changed. And what I realized was just when I thought that I had lost everything, I discovered I could lose even more. I did.

I pretty much shut down after Davey died. I sat in my office, door closed at my desk with a half-full bottle of liquor daily. I didn't really think about one thing in particular—just random thoughts that filtered in and out of my mind. I closed everyone off. Of course, Jennifer had been closed off for years, but I locked the door and threw away the key when it concerned her. Looking back, I shouldn't have because I know that she was hurting just as much as I was when our son passed. There was nothing else between Jennifer and me. I didn't care about hardly anything after Davey was in the ground.

Jennifer was devastated by Davey's death. She cried, questioned God, cursed Him and herself, too, for what had befallen our son. Of the two kids, Davey was closer to her because he was the baby, the only son, her last kid to raise. She and Davey had had a connection that I often longed for but never got with him, not like he had with his mother.

My connection with Samantha mirrored a profound relationship Jennifer and Davey shared. It was like their roles were reversed: Davey was a momma's boy and Samantha was a daddy's girl. Instead of Jennifer taking Samantha on a shopping date or to get her hair done, she was taking Davey shopping for clothes and out to lunch. It was completely topsy-turvy. That isn't to say that Davey and I didn't have our moments. We did, but just not a lot of them. The ones we did have I remember fondly.

I was not envious of what my wife and son had. I was good with it. Did I want a better relationship with Davey? Of course, what father doesn't want a better relationship with his son? We did stuff together sometimes, like go to the driving range to hit golf balls, watch the occasional baseball game on TV, go to the movies, and watch some of his favorite comic book superheroes. But it was not the same as the time he spent with Jennifer.

Jennifer, days after Davey was put into the ground, would walk around the halls of the house and cry, carrying his picture in her hand. Sometimes she would sit alone in his bedroom and just cry. She walked about mostly in a daze, and I really don't think that she knew where she was most of the time. I would sit up in my office, the door closed tightly getting drunk while listening to Jennifer cry and moan like a ghost that was haunting our home. Her life was fucked up, too. Her son had died, and her daughter had moved away. Plus, she was pregnant, and her husband was on his way out for good. I tend to forget that Jennifer had some problems, too.

4

In the days after her revelation that she was pregnant, carrying another man's baby, I hadn't mentioned it since the burial. What was the point? I had done things, too, over the years. Who was I to condemn her? I let it go because I didn't care anymore. As far as I was concerned, she and I were finished a long time ago. We were finished because I had burned us. She and I could have been a happily married couple. But I didn't want that because all I wanted and needed was Marie Evans.

I had been able to handle every tragedy lately: My writing career turning into a memory of what used to be, my walking away from Marie, Samantha running away from home, and a crumbling marriage that finally crashed and burned. However, Davey's death was something I couldn't handle. I don't know who could. I certainly couldn't. Davey's death made everything else very, very heavy.

With the sting of Davey never coming back home battering my mind into oblivion, I began to drink and drink and drink until I didn't feel anything anymore. I drank myself numb while sitting at my desk, thinking about nothing reasonable and ignoring Heather's texts and voicemails. I wanted to be left alone for a while. I wanted to slowly drift into the unknown and never be found. Fade to black.

In my drunken stupors that went on for weeks on end, I let myself go completely. The only time I exited my office was to go to the bathroom. I hadn't changed out of my funeral clothes, nor did I brush my teeth, shower, or shave. I didn't feel like doing anything but sit there and wither away.

We all dealt with Davey's suicide in completely different ways. I was no different. I cut myself off from my family members when they needed me the most. It was another glaring example of how out of touch I was with home and how much I had grown apart during the years that had gone by. In truth, they didn't need me. Samantha had left and Jennifer was really never there at all. They had gotten used to me being away for so long that it was the natural order of things for me not to be accessible.

I could have come out of my office, cleaned myself up, and called Samantha to try to make amends. I should've and I know that now, but I thought that she'd come around and see the errors of her ways. She never did, and I left this world with the lasting memory of the last time me and my daughter had talked: Davey's burial.

I could've been a good human being and grabbed Jennifer up in my arms and dealt with Davey's death as grieving parents should. But I choose not to. I choose to hide and sink lower into my abyss. I could've been the man who held us all together, but then again I could've done that years—even decades ago—but I elected not to.

5

The choices that I made years ago had set into motion the events that would define my life. That November, my life as I knew fell apart, and Heather was the only glimmer of hope amid the wreckage. She pulled me out of the emotional damage eventually and got me to safety, where she cleaned me up and brought me back to life. I could've used my ninth life to pull my estranged wife and daughter to safety with me, but I allowed them to suffer.

Jennifer should've been given a better hand in life. I guess she thought that getting married to me was a step in the right direction. In her marriage to me, she would have two kids, one who killed himself and the other who ran away from home. She had a husband who had pushed and pushed and pushed her away, eventually into the arms of another man.

I knew that Jennifer had found love somewhere else, but I didn't care. She needed it. But I care that I put her through all that I did. All I had to do was just pull the plug on our marriage and wash my hands of it and go our separate ways. Jennifer wasn't a bad person by any means. I was bad enough for both of us.

The kids were the reason I held the shambles of my life together. They were always one of the excuses I had to stay in the same house as Jennifer. I didn't want to put them through any undue stress, but I'll be fucking damned if I didn't do just that. In trying to spare them the pain and agony of divorce, I helped cause Davey to commit suicide and Samantha to leave home. All I wanted to do was save them. And in the end, I caused them all more pain than I ever thought possible. Had Marie called me up and said, "Let's get married," I'd bolt for the door and left them all. The lie I told myself was that I stayed for the kids, but in reality, I stayed because Marie wouldn't have me. That's the real and the raw of it... and I hate myself for it.

If I had just forgotten about Marie and focused on my family, maybe we'd all be in better shape. Davey would be alive, hopefully, in better sorts, Samantha would be home thinking about what college she was going to, my writing career would be soaring, and Jennifer and I would've been that great married couple down the block that everyone wanted to be. If only I would have allowed it to happen.

It was so simple, yet so complex. All of this began over a woman who I never would have. If only I could've allowed Marie to go gently into the night a long time ago, I could've saved us all. If only I was brave enough to never answer her phone calls.

God, how I wanted a do-over—a reset to go back in time and fix things.

I wanted a family, always did, but with Marie. Jennifer was a consolation prize if you could call her that. She was a placeholder until the day that Marie would accept my marriage proposal. But that day never came, and the placeholder status I held for Jennifer became a full-blown first prize by default.

I never wanted Jennifer to feel bad about anything that happened between us. She was intelligent, funny, outgoing, and alluring, and any guy would've been lucky to have her. I had her, but didn't want her, not how I should've and not how she deserved.

Jennifer could have walked out years ago and found a guy with ease. But she stayed with me, even though I treated her like trash. She stuck around all these years, and her doing so made me wonder. Could it have been the lifestyle of having everything she wanted that made her stay? Perhaps. If so, she was no better than I was.

During the first few years of our marriage, she tried in earnest to garner my love. She knew that I didn't love her as much as I should have. I hadn't bothered to conceal it. I mean, I guess for a few years I fooled myself into playing the good husband for her. I did make her happy and we did have some good times, enough of them to fill some scrapbooks. But I was not invested in the marriage emotionally, not like I should've been. My mind was always somewhere else, longing to be with someone who didn't take me seriously.

Over time, I'd become more and more self-absorbed and thought about my place in life. At around thirty, I looked at myself in the mirror one day while I was shaving in the bathroom. I had everything a guy could ever want: fame, fortune, a beautiful loving wife, and two wonderful children. But the thing that was missing was Marie. She would always be the missing link in my existence before Heather. That missing link caused me to behave badly toward Jennifer and sink our marriage. But who was I kidding—our marriage was sunk like the Titanic from the moment we both said, "I do."

Honestly, I should have just walked away from Jennifer long ago and set her free. But I didn't. At first, I didn't want to be alone, and then I told myself I didn't want to put our children through a divorce. That had become the standard in our home. I was just there, Jennifer was just there, and so were our kids. It was like we were all playing out some stupid game that was winding down in the final stages. We all knew what the score was, but no one wanted to say it aloud. It was the worst best-kept secret of our lives. I'd lied a lot, but the best lies were the ones I told myself. Those were the ones I needed myself to say so I could hear. And you know what? I felt better after I lied to myself every day. It got easier.

6

After some time, Jennifer finally walked away. I never expected her to continue fighting a battle she was never going to win. It was like me fighting to win Marie. It was a lost cause and so was Jennifer winning my affection. We both had lost our respective quests.

Over the years, I saw less and less of Jennifer until I hardly saw her at all. She had become a ghost in the house, haunting the place from time to time. She made herself show up for our children, but when it came to me, she disappeared from the home and out into the world. I didn't care because I was too wrapped up in my failing writing career and thinking of Marie and *our* future.

I never really missed Jennifer during those miserable years of our marriage. I know that I should've and I'm a bastard for doing the things that I did to her. She was never the same after she realized I was not invested in our marriage. After she stopped trying, Jennifer evolved into an entirely new person: a harder, colder person who had walled up her feelings and emotions. She had become an island.

I'd burned her severely over the years, and the men who she would later be with would pay dearly. They'd never be able to power through her fortress that she'd spent years building, with my help, of course. I hated myself for a lot of things, but after reflecting on my life, I think I hated myself the most for the way I treated Jennifer. It was all because of Marie, but *I* was the one who killed our marriage, not her. And that, in turn, killed the rest of my family.

Before our marriage got to the point of no return, I could've won Jennifer back and repaired the burned bridges of our past. But I didn't. I could've done a lot of things, but I didn't. I could've made our home happy. But I didn't. I burned everything in my path for a woman I couldn't have. And in that waiting, I lost myself; I lost track of what was important. And by the time that I saw the light and error of my ways, it was too late. I'd lost Davey before I could *fully* realize what I had done. It had taken his death for me to finally *feel* the consequences of my actions over the years.

Meeting Heather was a turning point in my life. It could've been Davey's death, Samantha's running away from home, or any number of things. But Heather made me realize my errors, the flaws of my life. She made me do an entire self-evaluation to see reality. And what I found was that everything that had ever happened to me was all my fault. It seemed that my fate was because of all my actions; my family's fate was determined by the sins of the past.

7

As the year came to a close and the start of a new year began, I made some decisions about my life and how I was going to try to move forward. Much of that was me and Heather deciding that we were going to buy a place and move in together. There were a lot of loose ends I needed to tie up at my home before I made my escape to go live with Heather like we planned. Those loose ends were Jennifer and Samantha. Sometimes loose ends are all you have....

I had been trying to call Samantha for weeks but she never answered and never responded to my voicemails or texts. I really tried with her, I did. So, I wrote her a big, 30-page letter and mailed it to Randy's house. I didn't think I was going to get a response so I never checked my mailbox. There was no need. She was finished with me.

I never knew if she received the letter and certainly didn't know if she even read it. I left this world never knowing. I never saw or spoke to my daughter again. That, much like Davey's suicide, devastated me.

Jennifer was another story. She was at home, but she wasn't the same person she was before Davey's death or even before when she first thought she was pregnant. She was still at home, physically. But mentally? She'd checked out. The pills she was on helped with that, I guess.

She and I had not talked at all since her pregnancy admission at the cemetery. We hadn't talked much at all beforehand either. But I felt that it was time to air out some things and begin to heal the wounds that had scared us both throughout our marriage. I wanted closure, wanted to give her some piece of mind and some valuable insight into why our marriage went sideways and out of control. It was never her. I wanted her to know that.

It had been a long hard winter at home and an even harder Christmas without the kids. But a new year had flipped the calendar, and I was on my way out of there for good. Before I left, I wanted to leave my estranged wife with some final words. As if words could help anyway, right?

8

I had returned home from Heather's place around six o'clock that evening to find Jennifer's car in the driveway. That was rare in general but especially so during those days. She and I were hardly ever home to begin with, but after Davey's suicide, she was a ghost. Where she went, I had no idea. I surmise it was to be with the man with whom she was pregnant. Our home might as well have been empty, filled with trinkets and pictures of times past, a prop home used in a film or TV show, much like my childhood home in Rome.

I pulled into the driveway and parked my car beside Jennifer's and just sat there for a moment. I didn't want to go in there and see her, see the product of my years of negligence on her face. I didn't want to see how Davey's death had destroyed her. I didn't want to see how Samantha's running away tortured her. So, I sat in the driveway for an hour, contemplating whether or not to go inside. *Maybe a clean break is best*, I thought for some time out there.

My initial plan was to go inside and up to my office to grab my belongings—or, rather, what was left of them—and leave. Over the last several days, I'd been steadily moving my stuff to Heather's apartment where she and I were living until we finalized the deal on the house we were eventually moving into. The only reason I came back home was to get my backup laptop, some more clothes, and my extra pair of glasses. I guess, in some small way, I was hoping to run into Jennifer. There were some things I wanted to get off my chest that I had to do in person.

This was the last night and time that I'd ever be back home, and I was hoping to run into Jennifer. I didn't think it'd happen because I hadn't seen her in a while, but when I saw her car there, I was shocked. I was also, admittedly, nervous. Seeing her meant that I had to tell her everything. It's one thing to do something behind one's back, but to admit it face-to-face is something altogether different.

I unlocked the front door and entered the warm confines of my home. It was dimly lit, warm, and inviting. I experienced a sense of comfort that I had not felt in a long time. It was strange. I took off my coat and hung it on the rack and walked into the living room from the foyer and saw that the TV was off. I walked down the hall, into the kitchen, where the lights were on and there sat my estranged wife. Her elbows were on the table, hands holding her head up propped under her jaw. She looked so devastated, so tired.

I was taken off guard by how awful she looked. Her eyes were droopy, with black underneath them from a lack of sleep, and her hair was a mess. She wasn't wearing any make-up. By the looks of it, she had lost a lot of weight, looking like a sickly version of herself. I stood in the doorway, looking at what was left of my wife. She was a shell of what she once was. I had taken away a bunch of the life she had and what she had left had been burned away by Davey's suicide and Samantha's leaving.

I stood in the kitchen, looking at the finality of my previous life. It was me and Jennifer in the same room, looking at each other and not knowing what to say after years of marriage. It shouldn't have been that way, but I had made it so. It had come to pass by my actions. I had broken her down and when the bad times came, they broke what was left of her spirit. I saw firsthand how my actions had broken her. I was not good with that and hated myself for what I had done to her over the years.

"You okay?" I asked, looking at her sit there looking back at me with her red and tired eyes.

"I don't know," Jennifer replied after a few quiet moments.

I couldn't believe that the same woman who I had married decades ago had been reduced to what sat before me. And it all was made possible by me. I felt like a prick. It had been nearly two months since Davey's suicide, and Jennifer still looked as though it had just happened. I was not much better because I felt the sting of his loss, too. The only thing that I had was a support system in Heather otherwise I wouldn't have been standing.

"You look bad. When's the last time you ate?" I asked.

Jennifer sat there for a few moments to think about what I had asked. "I don't know." There was silence between us in the kitchen. Not like the usual silence we've had, but a different kind of silence; the silence of not knowing what else to say. It was like there was nothing left to speak about because everything had already been spoken. Too much damage had been done, I guess.

"Samantha call?" I asked, already knowing the answer to that silly question. I guess I was trying to keep the conversation running.

Jennifer looked down at the table. "I don't think so. I think she's gone for good." I lowered my head and looked at the floor as if there was some magical healing potion lying there for me to fix what I had fucked up. "We really messed these kids up, didn't we?"

"Listen," I began as I raised my head to look at my wife. "I'm sorry for everything. All of this... is my fault. Everything. It was never you. It was me."

It was the most honest thing I had ever said in my life. And telling the person I needed to tell it to made it feel even more significant.

"I screwed things up so badly that after a while I didn't know how to even fix them anymore. So I let them go. And then I let you go."

My words rang true. Jennifer looked up at me from the table and stared at me without saying anything. She didn't need to, though; I knew how she was feeling. I knew that the pain I had caused over the years compounded with the loss of our children, destroyed any prospect of her being happy.

Jennifer gave a small, low chuckle of disbelief and shook her head. "Don't bother. Too late."

"I know," I replied. She didn't care anymore, didn't care about anything anymore. And who could blame her? "I just wanted you to know that all this is on me. I never meant to do this to you."

Jennifer sat there in the kitchen, seemingly considering what I had said as I posted up against the doorway, looking around in the silence. Words, I knew, would never help ease the pain I caused her. I don't even know why I ever tried. But something pushed me to do it when I saw her sitting there. "Then why did you?" she asked.

I stood there, knowing full well why I did the things that I did over the years. And I wrestled with telling her the truth. But if I was ever going to exorcise my demons, I had to come clean and be honest, no matter the damage that was to soon follow.

"It's hard to explain, really. I, um… I was never fully invested in our marriage. I always had this thing for a girl who I was with in school. I thought she and I would always be together. And when it didn't happen, I got this sinking feeling that I was going to be alone for the rest of my life. Then I met you and felt like we could make it work. But I was still in love with her. I never gave us the chance that I should have because in the back of my mind, I figured she'd call me and we'd be together. I didn't want to love you because I thought it would be harder on you when I left to be with her. I saw us as temporary."

Silence. Jennifer sat there, emotionless. Maybe it was because my explanation was too late, especially in light of recent events. Maybe she didn't care. Or perhaps she was too numb to feel anything else. And I knew that those words, the truth, were like jagged edges of glass for her to swallow.

"So you used me so you wouldn't wind up alone?" Jennifer managed.

"Yeah… basically," I said.

I hated telling her the truth, but she deserved to hear it after all the time that had passed. And I had to take the internal beating that I was going through at that moment. It made me sick to express my actions out loud, but it also brought me some measure of relief.

"It doesn't matter anymore," she said. "So much has happened… I couldn't care less about us." Jennifer responded the only way she knew how: honestly. I knew that's how she felt, but I wanted to hear it from her mouth. I wanted to know that she felt nothing so I could move on. I had to make sure she didn't love me anymore.

"I figured," I said. "For what it's worth, I am sorry. I never meant to do this. I never meant to hurt you over and over again. If I had my way, I would have left you a long time ago so you could've been happy. You deserved it."

"Then why didn't you?" Jennifer asked.

"The kids. I didn't want the kids to have to see us divorced and have to go through that. In trying to spare them, look at what I caused. Plus, I didn't want to end up alone."

"Better choices could have saved… Davey's life," Jennifer said coldly.

"I know that," I replied.

"Was it worth it? Worth all the bullshit you put me through? Put this family through?" Jennifer asked, holding back her tears.

"There are no winners here, just losers," I finally said, speaking as honestly as I could after thinking about her question.

Jennifer sat there at the table, looking off into the distance of the kitchen before speaking. "I should have left you a long time ago. I should have packed my bags and moved away, taking the kids. Because if I had then Samantha would still be around and Davey would be alive."

"Why didn't you?"

There was a momentary pause before she retorted.

"I loved you. I always thought we'd work it out. But now I know that you were never in love with me from the beginning. Such a fool I was."

"I tried," I said honestly. "But my heart belonged someplace else."

"Why are you telling me this? Why now?" Jennifer asked, looking over at me as I stood, feeling exposed and vulnerable.

I stood there for a few moments and thought about whether I should say anything or tell her the full truth. I had spoken fragments of truth up to that point and saw no reason to turn back now. Words had begun to pierce her heart as I spoke, so why hold back now?

"You deserved to know. You deserve to know why I was so cold and distant over all these years. It never was you. It was me, entirely me."

Again, silence engulfed the kitchen. We looked at each other without speaking. What was there left to say? She didn't go into a violent rage like I thought she might. Jennifer had too much going on inside her mind at that moment. I did, too.

In retrospect, I probably should've just let her be at the table. I should've just gone inside, gotten what I needed, and left for good. But I felt, deep within me, that I had to set the record straight. Did it matter, in the end? Not really. She didn't care, one way or the other. Her son had died, her daughter had run off to live with her boyfriend, and she was pregnant with another man's baby. What was an explanation for a doomed marriage? Nothing. It amounted to nothing in the grand scheme of things. A mere afterthought of what was.

After I left my home for good, that was it. The next thing was a divorce—a real one—from Jennifer. The papers were signed in February, and I gave her the house. Heather and I planned to buy a house together in the future. Besides, my old home was a house of horrors anyway, and nothing lingered there but bad memories.

CHAPTER TWENTY-ONE

1

Heather and I sat on her couch, looking through the immense bay window in her living room as the rain came down, spattering upon the glass and obstructing our view. Despite the raindrops that came rushing, streaking down the window in thousands of small creeks, we could see the forest off in the distance as their backdrop.

She and I sat on her couch, each holding onto a cup of hot cocoa and listening to Bob Dylan's *Highway 61 Revisited* album. For a younger girl, Heather had taste in really good music that was way before her time. Hell, even before my time.

When I first arrived at her apartment, she and I talked a bit and held each other close. And then we kissed, and our passionate kisses led us to her bedroom where we had sex. It was phenomenal—every time was better than the last. I think it was great because we loved each other, really loved each other. It wasn't like it was with Marie or Jennifer. That was just sex. With Heather, it was something more profound, like we shared an incredible connection.

We sat on the couch and looked out the window, not saying much. Our relationship had taken another huge step forward. She was there for me when Davey died. She was amazing and just what the doctor ordered.

"I talked to Jennifer," I said slowly as "Desolation Row" came on her stereo.

Heather put her cup up to her ruby-red lips and sipped the cocoa. "How'd that go?"

"I don't know... weird. Sad. Wasn't what I was expecting. But then again, I didn't know what to expect. I guess I thought she'd be a little more upset."

"She's probably got too much going on inside her mind than to fight with you," Heather replied. "Something you gotta realize is that she's been through the wringer. Maybe she just didn't care about you anymore. Ever thought about that? Maybe she was done, too, a long time ago," Heather said wisely.

"I don't know, maybe you're right. But I told her everything. I told her why I treated her the way that I did. I thought I'd feel better about being honest with her...."

"But you still feel badly. Because getting everything off your chest, to her, was more about you feeling better than it was telling her the truth, right?" Heather finished.

I nodded. "Yeah. Maybe you're right about that." She was right.

"You feel bad because what you did to her was wrong. You should have pushed Marie away a lot earlier and given Jennifer and your family all your energy." I sat there and looked out of the window as the rain smacked harder against the glass. She was right. All I needed to do was denounce Marie Evans a long time ago, and maybe my family would've been perfectly fine.

And then I think about Heather. Had I pushed Marie away, Heather and I wouldn't have met. That's it; we never would've happened. And as I sat there looking at her, something hit me: I would've traded Heather any day and any hour of the week just to have my family back again; back when times were good, back when we were all young.

Before I could feel badly about that thought, I knew that Heather would've been fine with it. She would've understood. I know that to be the truth. I didn't know what I had until they were all gone forever, and it hurt like hell. I wanted to go back and erase the last ten years and fix everything. I wanted to go back....

CHAPTER TWENTY-TWO

1

My newest book, *What Is and What Will Never Be*, was my comeback novel. I published it independently online. After I put out a media blitz with the help of Curtis, I found the sales for my newest and perhaps finest work were profoundly low. I guess the days of Jerry Matthews being a household name had run their course. My run as a best-selling author was complete. It was time to retire.

My fans, as I read on numerous blogs and critics' columns, had pretty much fed me to the wolves, saying I was out of good ideas and that my time in the sun was finally over. And it was. My career in writing was down for the count, and there was no getting up again.

I had written the best piece of fiction my brain had ever produced, and it didn't get back what I had lost. I had alienated so many fans, took them all for granted by writing shit for so long, that eventually it all caught up to me. That book was the best thing I'd ever written, but fans and critics hated it.

Sure, I had some hardcore fans who loved the book, and on some websites I was hailed as being back in the saddle. But for every good review and pat on the back, there were six bad ones from people who hated it. But hey, what did it matter? I was still cashing checks from Windom and would be for as long as I would live. I could still write from time to time if I wanted, just to appease myself and my small fan base. One thing I've learned: A writer writes, no matter what.

CHAPTER TWENTY-THREE

1

Heather and I decided to buy a home out in the suburbs and start over so to speak. I needed to recover from all the wreckage of the last several months. I wasn't in great sorts: I still battled the urge to drink and fought nightmares of seeing my dead son's body under the white sheet in his bedroom. Through it all, Heather was there to lift me up, dust me off, and set me right again.

Things were going about as well as they could've been heading into the summer, given the circumstances. Heather and I had talked about getting married, but neither one of us was in a hurry to do so. Heather had taken a vacation from school. But I knew what that vacation really meant. She wasn't planning on going back. I was fine with that. That would give us more time to spend with each other. I was still on the mend from Davey's suicide and Samantha's vanishing act. Months had rolled by, and winter turned to spring and spring to summer, and I still didn't hear from her. I left *this* world never hearing her sweet voice again.

I wanted to talk to my daughter to tell her I was sorry for the things I had said at Davey's burial. But I couldn't find her. I trolled social networking sites looking for her, but turned up with nothing. I called, texted, and emailed her. I know she's out there somewhere, doing just fine.

Sometimes I would lie in bed late at night and think of her as a little girl running around in the backyard or through a sprinkler on a hot summer day. I thought of Davey, too, laughing and playing with his imaginary friends or playing tag with his sister, maybe rolling that red fire engine he loved so much around on the living room floor. That was back when things were wonderful. Back when everything was still young and still at that point where I could've prevented all our misery from happening. If only I had the sense to do so back then.

I was so haunted by seeing Davey's body in the casket at the funeral home that I'd have panic attacks when I thought about it too much. The same thing would happen when I thought about my heated verbal exchange with Samantha on the day we laid her brother to rest. I wished that I could take back those words, but I can't. I'd have to learn to deal with that and most of all, live with it.

2

As I started my new life with Heather, after the divorce papers were signed, I didn't think much about Jennifer at all. Hell, I never did when we were married. I did hear through back channels that she had a miscarriage and the guy who'd gotten her pregnant left town.

As far as I know, she's alone in that house with the ghosts of our memories. I suspect that Samantha has visited her a time or two; which is good because after all the things Jennifer had gone through, she needed someone in her family to lift her up again. It might as well be Samantha. Hopefully, they patched things up. Maybe their hatred for me is a tie that binds them into getting their relationship back on track like it once was back when things were good.

The weeks and months leading up to my impending death were just as they had been since Heather and I made the bold leap to move in together. I had given up a chunk of money and a percentage of future royalties to Jennifer in the divorce, but I was still living well off other royalties from movies based on my novels and short stories. Heather and I had nothing to worry about.

Jennifer didn't take me to task like her lawyer wanted. Instead, I gave her a pretty damn good parting package. She got the house, and a percent of my book royalties: fifty percent of what I received. I wanted her to be okay and never to have to worry about money. That was the least I could do for the decades' worth of damage I did in our home. Best atonement I could offer her.

Unlike the suburbs I lived in during my first marriage, Heather's and mine were private, meaning that no one knew who I was or what I used to do for a living. And that was good by me. I was just a part of the rows of houses that lined our neighborhood; just another face on the street.

I could go outside and mow the lawn and not be stopped a dozen times and asked for an autograph as sweat rolled down my face. I could be completely unknown, and that was a slice of heaven if there ever was one. I was just that new guy in the big blue house on the corner with the hot girlfriend. My new life was okay.

Suburbia suited me just fine and so did it with Heather. We both lived life and did what we wanted to do for those months. We had no obligations to anyone or anything. Heck, on Saturday night, her parents would come over and play card games with us. They were good people, her parents. And they didn't seem to mind our age difference. I don't know if that was because they didn't care as long as their daughter was happy or if it was because of my former fame. Either way, I didn't care because I had Heather Parker.

My life had been almost perfect after I left home. I didn't fool myself into thinking that leaving would free me of all the trauma of my past. No matter where I went, Davey was still dead, Samantha was still out of my life for good, and my ex-wife was carrying on the best she could. No matter how good my life appeared to be on the surface, deep down in the shadows where no one but Heather and I saw, I was still fucked-up goods. I left this world as fucked-up goods.

That's the hard thing about the past, especially ones that really drive you into the ditch. If I had lived and not died earlier than I expected, I still don't know if I'd have made it all the way through. In other words, I'd still be damaged, no matter how much better my life was with Heather. Sometimes you just can't come all the way back.

I think Heather did her absolute best in helping me. She did. She loved me with a freighting fervor that Jennifer had for me back in our good ol' days. I had seen it before and was happy to see it again. The difference this time around was that I didn't it push away. I embraced Heather's love with arms wide open. And I loved her passionately back every day. Like we both said a while back: We were soul mates, destined to be together, and the events of our lives led us down roads and forks that caused us to make what we thought were choices of pure calculation. But those choices were meant to be made, good and bad alike.

3

Everything, I mean *everything* had to happen for Heather and me to meet and spend the rest of our lives together. It made me sick at times that Davey had to pay the price. My family paid a heavy toll for me being me. And that wasn't right, but it happened. I can't change that. Alone on the front porch sometimes, when Heather is visiting her parents or when she's out shopping, I have time to reflect.

I reflect on things that perhaps never should've been, pondering alternate realities. I think of what life would have been like in one such alternate reality: Marie and I would've been married, her a college professor and me still a potent world-class wordsmith. We would've had two children: a boy and a girl, much like Davey and Samantha. We would live in a nice two-story home, on a quiet street where we could be as happy as larks.

In a different alternate reality, Jennifer and I were living like she wanted us to when we first met. In this world, there was no Marie to twist my mind around. There was no holding out until Marie gave me the green light for us to be together. I would love my wife immensely and show her that every day; not freezing her out or driving her away and sinking our family like I had in the real world. Things in this second alternate reality would've been fantastic. Plus, Davey would be alive, happy, and prepared for a career like his old man, and Samantha would be an astute student, looking at the waiting world as hers. Things would've been great in this world. They could've been great if I'd have let them.

I know that neither of those worlds involved my sweet and beautiful Heather. I know.

I sometimes ponder a lot on how my second alternate reality would feel and taste if Marie had simply gone away.

Marie was the ultimate road to nowhere, and I drove on it for decades with my family as unwilling passengers. Would I trade my current state for a shot to live my second alternate reality? Yes, but I would never admit that to Heather. It would kill her. It would be a secret that I would take to my grave. I just didn't realize how early I would get there....

CHAPTER TWENTY-FOUR

1

I sat there on the swing of our front porch on a summer afternoon, just thinking. I never saw him walking up the road. He wore a plain black baseball cap pulled down. He was average-looking at best. Nothing remarkable about him. I never noticed him at all until he turned from the sidewalk and up our walkway, which connected the two pathways from across our front lawn.

When I did see him, he had both his hands in his pockets. I knew that this guy was the bringer of death. Don't ask me how I knew, but I knew. I watched him approach my yard and then up the porch steps in slow motion. I watched all of this happen and couldn't move. It was as if he had put me into a trance. A strange witch's spell. But how? How did this guy do that to me?

Before my scattered mind could focus, this guy leaped onto the porch landing, standing over me, and pulled his hands out of his pockets. I knew that he was going to kill me. I just watched as he did it, not once trying to flee from the porch swing.

At that moment, I was completely frozen. In one of the hands was a potent stun gun he jammed into my ribs, electrocuting me out of my swing and onto the porch floor. I sat there horrified and watched it all happen, able to do nothing about it. I didn't even put up a fight. I wonder why. It was like I just sat there and let him do whatever he wanted to me.

My body shook violently and my thoughts were scrambled like the eggs I had earlier that morning. All I could see were the boards of the floor and the boots of Paul Hanson, Heather's abusive psycho ex-boyfriend. He was wearing the blackest boots I'd ever seen. He knelt and whispered something into my ear, but I couldn't register it.

I was fried. Paul rose and no doubt looked around the neighborhood to see if anyone was watching us. Apparently not. Paul had seemed to stop time and slip into that summer afternoon, unnoticed, as he killed me. He gathered my legs in his arms and dragged me back into the house, through the front door, and into the living room.

I wanted to fight at this point, I did, and I thought I could take him because he wasn't a hulking piece of work. He was about as average as the next Joe. At best, he had twenty years on me. I could've taken him if not for the shock he had put on me. Besides, I was in and out of consciousness between the dragging and being tied up to a chair. Yeah, he tied me up in a chair in the living room—the next step of his diabolical plan.

At some point, I raised my throbbing head. My face stung and felt numb. I knew my nose was broken and saw blood on my shirt. My mouth had the stout taste of copper. Oh, how I desperately wanted to just hold my aching nose with my hands, but they were tied together behind the chair I was sitting in. The rope was so tight that I had lost all feeling in my hands.

Paul Hanson sat across from me on a table in the living room, looking at me like a baseball player on the bench, waiting to get the call to go into the game. "Who are you?" He looked like a garden variety nice guy, but those are the worst, right? The ones you never seen coming from miles away until they're on your front porch, shocking the fuck out of you and tying you up in your home for some sort of murder adventure.

"You already know, Mr. Fancy Writer Man," Paul said. "You've been with my Heather so long now, and I'm sure she's told you about me. You know who I am."

"What do you want?" I asked, wincing in pain. Paul had worked me over pretty good while I was out.

"Just what is mine. You see, Heather and I are meant to be together, chief. Her and me, and I'll be damned if you're going to come in between us. Took me a long time to find you guys. But I did," he said as he laughed. He had a maniacal laugh, the kind of laugh that turned your blood cold.

"She doesn't want to be with you... you abusive prick," I said dreamily, feeling the effects of all that had just happened.

"Well, when she gets home, I'll let her decide that," Paul replied. I could understand how Heather was afraid of this guy. He had that certain coldness in his eyes. He wasn't coy about it either. There was a murderous side to him. I've written enough books and characters to know an unstable psychopath when I see one.

"Why don't you leave her alone, man? She's been through enough," I said weakly, knowing mine were empty words being spoken to an empty man. Blood trickled out of my mouth and nose.

Paul grinned like a hungry shark at me. "It's me and her in this life. *Together.* It's always been like that and always will be. Life or death." Life or death? I wanted to laugh in his face if I could open my jaws all the way. What did this fucko know about life and death? I knew all about it, read the book about it, and lived the movie based on the book, so to speak.

We both heard a car pull into the driveway. It was Heather's car. Oh God! My mind perked up and it took every strained and hurting muscle and broken bone for me to try to wriggle out of the thick twine Paul had me tied up with. I began to rock side to side in my chair like my life depended on it, like Heather's life depended on it. I was not going to let something else bad happen to someone I loved.

Paul had seen me try to rock out of the chair. He frantically looked outside through the living room window and then back at me. I think he made a choice right then and there to eliminate the risk. He took out his hunting knife that had been sheathed to the side of his jeans in the waistband underneath his shirt and came for me.

I tried to wriggle free and felt my eyes widen with fright when I saw the sliver-jagged edge of the blade in his hand. Before I could scream to warn Heather about Paul being in the house, he grabbed me by the hair violently, slung my head back and cut my throat deeply. Blood, *my blood*, gushed in an instant.

I remember shaking so violently and twisting from side to side with such excruciating pain that I fell to the floor, still tied to the chair. That fall would've hurt badly if my neck hadn't been bleeding out. I couldn't feel anything but blood, could even taste it coming from my wound and pouring from my mouth. My head was on the floor and I saw the approaching river of crimson slowly inch its way to my face.

I was dying and as I lay there, I heard Heather's approaching footfalls on the porch before she got to the front door. I was fading fast. I couldn't hear well, nor could I see anything but the couch legs and the pond of blood coming toward my face. I tried once again to scream, to warn her about Paul, but it was no use. It came out as a wet gurgle.

Right before the lights went out and as my heartbeat slowed to a faint thump... thump... thump..., I heard something that would have surely haunted me if I had lived any longer. I heard Heather open the front door and a few seconds later scream, although it was muffled because I was fading further and further down a dark road. And then I died... at least I think I did.

CHAPTER TWENTY-FIVE

1

I opened my eyes and saw myself standing in the backyard of my old house. The kids' swing set was there, as was the back deck I built years ago. I looked up and saw clouds in the sky, birds flying, and the sound of a lawn mower from one of the neighbors, probably Mr. Jenkins out working in his yard. I saw the sun and felt its warmth on my skin. It was a typical summer afternoon, or at least it felt that way when I looked around.

I reached up and felt my face. It didn't hurt. I ran my fingers across my nose. It wasn't broken anymore. Then I timidly ran my fingers across my throat. The gash Paul sliced into my neck was gone. My mind raced frantically. *Where the fuck am I?*

Am I dead? Am I back home? I asked myself frantically these questions as I saw Samantha, maybe six years old, come dashing out of the house from the backdoor with a three-year-old Davey closely behind. My God, *Davey*, chasing behind her laughing. They were both... so young. *What the hell is going on here?* I wondered as I watched them. My heart raced and nearly leaped out of my chest. I could feel the banging against my chest. It was as though I was having a heart attack. No, that wasn't right, maybe a panic attack. All I knew was that all the wiring inside my body was going haywire at the moment when I saw my children.

I was mystified. How in the *fuck* did I end up here? The last thing I knew was that I was bleeding out on my living room floor. Just how did this happen? I stood there in the yard, watching my kids play like I was watching it all in a home movie, I wondered if I was dead. And then Samantha came running up to me, "Daddy, come play with us. You can be *it!*" She ran back into our backyard with Davey, both waiting for me to join them. And you know what? I did. I can't explain it, but I ran out into the backyard and chased them as they laughed and screamed with excitement. It was amazing and scary at the same time. I had no idea what was going on there; still don't....

After about an hour or so of laughing and running with the kids, I stopped and decided to walk into the house to cool off. (Was this Heaven? Was I a ghost? What the hell had I stepped into?) Man, it was hot out there. I walked into the house through the back door like I had in all the times past and there I saw Jennifer in the kitchen making lunch; ham and cheese with a side of chips for everyone with a tall glass of Coke for me, Davey, and Samantha. I had seen this scene before. I was sure of it. Had I traveled back in time?

I stood there looking at Jennifer bewildered; like I didn't belong. She wasn't the devastated mess that I last saw after Davey had died. She was radiant and beautiful just as she was back when our marriage was young and growing. She was happy, too. Had I indeed traveled back in time, back to when our marriage was young and our kids were still kids?

Or was I dead? I mean, after all, I just had my throat slit by a maniac sometime before. Not too long ago, I calculated. I won't hesitate to tell you that I was scared to death. Not knowing where you're at is a frightening moment.

"Jennifer?" I asked with reserve.

She turned and gave me a million-dollar smile. "Yeah? Taking a break from your book to play with the kids? Nice day out there."

I stood there in the kitchen, still feeling that overwhelming sensation of shock and disorientation. I honestly didn't know what to say. "Yeah, nice day to do something like that," I said almost in a robotic voice as I was still trying to figure out where the hell I was. It felt wrong but right at the same time. I even dug my fingernails into the palm of my hand to make sure I wasn't dreaming. The nails hurt and brought a few patches of blood to the surface. No dream. At least it didn't seem to be.

"Well, The Weather Channel said it's going to be gorgeous all week. Hot, too. Here, I made you a sandwich." Jennifer showed me on the counter. I smiled. God, she hadn't done that in years. I mean, she used to, but I never cared as much as I did right then. For some reason, things felt… right; they felt good.

"Thanks," I said, standing there looking at her oddly as I heard the kids laugh and play out in the backyard. To her, I must have appeared to be high or something. She had no idea that I was either dead or had just been murdered or just did a bit of time traveling. I had no idea either. But I was there in the kitchen. Me and Jennifer.

"Are you okay?" Jennifer asked.

I stood there and didn't know how to answer that question. I didn't know if I was okay or not. I mean, I was back home, that I knew for sure. When? I didn't know. But I was back when things were still manageable with my family, right before I let it all rot. Was I given a second chance? Could that be it? Is that even possible? Was this that alternate reality that I was thinking about on the porch right before Paul Hanson killed me in my living room? Was that *even* real? *What's real anymore?* I wondered wildly as Jennifer gazed at me.

"I think I'm okay. What year is this?" I asked sounding dumb to my wife.

Jennifer looked at me for a few seconds and then laughed incredulously but noticed I was dead serious, "You're serious? Are you drinking again, Jerry? I've told you about how much I hate that." She was about to get angry over the possibility of my return to the bottle.

"No!" I exclaimed. "No, no drinking at all." I looked over to the side and saw a calendar hanging on the kitchen wall. I immediately walked over to it and was horrified and elated all at once when I saw:

July 15, 2004, Tuesday

I stood back and smiled and ran my trembling hands through my hair. I was back! How could that be? I was left for dead with a slit throat just moments ago, and now I'm here. I shot a look at Jennifer and smiled. I probably looked like a madman standing there in the kitchen, excited over something small like a calendar. I don't know if it was more of a surprise or relief or both that I was back in the year 2004. I was back to where I could save it all.

My wife stood there, hands on her hips, looking at me and wondering what the hell was going on inside her husband's head. What was going on was that... and I say this with clear sanity right now... I had been sent into what I called my second alternate reality, or maybe I was back in time. Whatever you want to call it, I was back in 2004. Back to where I could change the outcome of everything; fix *everything* that went wrong. How? No clue but I felt that I could.

How I got here, I don't know. Still don't to this very day. But here I am. Perhaps God took pity on me and sent me back. Maybe He heard my pleas back when Davey died. Maybe he gave me a deal. Whatever it was at work, I don't care. I'm back early enough in my marriage to repair things: to save my marriage, save Davey, and keep Samantha from leaving. I can save it all. In the back of my mind, I wondered if I was dead and this was an illusion that my dying mind was showing me. I wondered a lot of things and I still do.

I walked over to my wife quickly and kissed her for the first time in what was decades to me. It was sweet, it was dreamy, and it was right. That kiss had a lot of passion built behind it and Jennifer could tell as I pulled my lips from hers and looked into her hypnotic eyes.

"I love you. Things are going to be better... I swear. I can fix it." I said with butterflies infesting my insides. Tears welled up in my eyes.

She smiled and looked at me curiously. "What's gotten into you? Fix what?"

I stood there with my arms around her waist looking into her eyes. I hadn't looked in them for that long before, and I remembered how good we could have been together if Marie wasn't hanging around in my head.

"Nothing... just glad to be here. Glad you're here with me. Glad Samantha and Davey are here. Things are going to be better. I swear. I love you, Jennifer."

2

Later that night, after a family dinner with all of us sitting together in the dining room, I went to my office. I slowly opened the door and expected the room to still be a mess from when I destroyed it after Davey committed suicide. Everything was intact. It looked neat and organized like it had in the past. But what was the past? Was I *in* the past?

On my desk was my old boxed-style computer, not the laptop that I had been using in the later parts of my life. I sat down behind my desk and marveled at the time trip I was in, and then, suddenly, my cell phone rang. It was sitting on my desk next to the computer. It was an old one, a flip phone, well perhaps not old in 2004, but old from where I had come from, a relic. I remember it from long ago, but I guess "long ago" is now. Time, I was realizing, is relative and most of all, fluid.

I picked it up and pressed the green send button, "Hello?" I said, knowing full well who the number on the screen belonged to. Some numbers you never forget.

"Well, hey there," Marie said in a sexy voice. A voice I had known all too well over the years. Her voice made gooseflesh pop up on my skin.

"Marie?" I asked, not believing it was her again.

"How've you been lately? I called last night but you never picked up. Everything good?" Marie asked, sounding a little concerned. My God, it was her.

I looked around my office and my perfect life—the life I had before but let it go to hell.

"Yeah... never better."

I ended the call right then and there, putting the phone down on the desk. A few seconds later, it rang again. Instead of answering my doom like I had in the past, I took the phone and threw it violently against the wall of my office, breaking it, and silencing it forever. No more Marie. I was done. I had gotten a reprieve from someone or something. I didn't know which, but I had my suspicions. I was not going down that road anymore. I had learned my lesson. I was a new man.

3

For some reason, it appeared that I was given a second chance and I wasn't about to let it slip through my fingers. I was cognizant of the consequences of my choices and actions before and now I was back in 2004, back when things could be turned around. My marriage was in a good spot and that was plenty of time for me to be the husband and father that I should've been before in my last life... or whatever it was. A dream perhaps? Was my life a dream? And had I finally woke up after Paul murdered me in that dream?

I came down later that evening from my office after thinking about where I was and what had put me here. Hell, I had the rest of my life to figure all of this out and try to piece together how I got here. The big question was: Where is here?

I entered the living room where Jennifer was sitting on the couch doing a crossword puzzle book. Davey was rolling a huge red fire truck around on the carpet and Samantha was reading a book while listening to her headphones. I seemed to be at an ideal place in time: a place where I could keep Davey alive, Samantha at home, and Jennifer from getting pregnant by another man. I could be the husband she deserved and the father the kids needed. I was back to a place where I could fix it all. It was all that I ever wanted.

I stood in the archway between the kitchen and living room and watched my family members—young, alive, and perfect—go about their activities, not knowing that I was watching them. I could have watched them forever just like that, just as they were. Things were going to be different this time around. I was given something that scores of people on this planet never get: A second chance.

Tears began to trickle down my face. And then my mind quickly wandered to Heather Parker. And then it hit me. I would never see her again. Right now, she was nine years old, a playful child with her whole life ahead of her. I wondered quickly if I should warn her about Paul Hanson.

I then thought about how that would sound years later when she was a teen and a famous writer came to her to warn her about that monster. Would she even believe me? Was that monster even real or was it all a dream? I decided that I would deal with that later. And I would, too, because if I had a chance to save my family, I had a chance to save Heather, too. I could change her future. I could stop Paul dead in his tracks and spare Heather the immense heartache she was destined to have at the hands of that monster. And I would. Right now, the *here and now*, I had other things on my agenda...to put right what I had destroyed in whatever reality I was in.

4

As the days turned to months, months to years, and years to decades, my marriage to Jennifer became stronger and stronger. We were very happy. Very rarely did we fight and when we did we were able to patch it up before it poisoned our future. I'm happy to say now she and I now are celebrating our thirtieth wedding anniversary. The kids threw us a party for that, which included Samantha and Randy and their two kids: Marty and Max; Davey and his wife, Amy, and their three kids: Jack, Jason, and Jasmine. It was such a fun time to be with all my family. I looked back and marveled at how I made it to 2004 when I was murdered in my and Heather's home by her crazy ex-boyfriend. I still don't understand it or how it happened.

Over the years I've had a chance to examine what happened. I've studied time travel and even spoke at length to college professors and other giants of the science world. I told them I was doing a new book— using my fame to gain access to most of them who were more than eager to speak to me about the subject—and that I was conducting research for it, that's why I was asking about such things. Most of them were pretty firm in their belief that it wasn't possible. A few said that there was a faint hope that it was plausible. I still don't know if time travel is possible after the decades I've spent on the subject even with all the knowledge I've received.

I even went as far as consulting men of religion over the decades since I went back in time. Not about time travel but of the work of God and His power. Was it possible, I asked all of these clergy, for God to grant wishes and make deals with mere mortals, much like the ones I wished and tried to make with him when Davey died in my other life? All of them said no, that God didn't work that way; he wasn't a genie that granted wishes or a tradesman that made deals.

However, one priest did say, never to discount the mystic power of God's miracles. He told me that God performs thousands if not millions of miracles a day; some we see and some we do not. But it was very possible that if I was true of heart and asked God for something and if God saw fit He would allow it. I walked away from that priest with a better sense that maybe what I had received that had brought me back to my family was a gift from God, one of those miracles, and not time travel.

I've never spoken about what happened to anyone. Who'd believe me anyway? They'd think it was some sort of new book plot I was writing. Come to think of it, it sounds like a really neat idea.

5

My writing career never suffered in this second chance. I didn't allow my writing to fall to garbage like I had before. Why? Because I wasn't drinking and thinking about Marie Evens all the time. I wasn't preoccupied with her. I was a new man with straightened-out priorities. I was a man, a writer, who was still producing novels and short stories that were still on best-seller listings all over. I won a few more awards for my writing and eventually was presented with the Presidential Medal of Freedom. I inked a six-book deal with Bob Windom which made me one of the richest writers in the industry ever: Made Windom happy, too. With that money, I banked what I thought all my family would ever need in the future and the rest I donated to schools and hospitals and needy families around the community. I was a new man with a renewed sense of purpose.

6

Now onto Heather Parker and Paul Hanson. This was by far the most difficult thing I've ever had to do. Murdering wasn't in me; especially a kid. I didn't arrive at killing Paul quickly, mind you. I did consider numerous other options but when I actually sat down and thought about how that was going to sound coming from me, I knew that it wouldn't work. I thought about getting Heather's parents involved, Paul's parents, and even the police. But how was that going to sound coming from a famous writer? It would sound crazy and they would have me fitted for a straight-jacket. Paul was bad, this I knew for sure. But still, killing a kid in cold blood wasn't something I jumped at the chance to do. I had choice-less choices in the end. I tried other options and ran them in my head over and over.

Ever since I came back to 2004, I had made plans to stop that monster from ever putting his hands on her. But every plan I made seemed to have more holes than a piece of Swiss cheese. So, I had to ask myself in front of the mirror in the bathroom one night if I was ready to take the life of a thirteen-year-old boy. I was because I knew what he would grow up to eventually be: A monster. And if you could stop a monster before they got started, wouldn't you?

I wasn't too clear on approximately when Paul and Heather started a relationship. All I knew was that it was when they were both thirteen and lived down in Atlanta. I knew from Heather that they both went to Hanbee Junior High School where Paul was a quarterback for the team. From there he would have the same position for the high school in the same area of Atlanta. God, there were so many junior schools in Atlanta. My best bet was to catch Paul at a junior high football game one night. But that meant stalking him for a few games. In turn that meant that I had to lie to Jennifer, which I hadn't done since I was brought back to 2004, about where I was off to.

I went to three home games and watched him on the field. And most importantly I watched him after the games and got a sense of what his activities and movements were afterward. They were always the same: after the games, he would give his football equipment to his parents, they would leave and Paul would stay and help clean up the sidelines. Good boy Paul, always there to lend a helping hand, and a coach, I think they were coaches, always gave him a lift home after everything was said and done.

The night that I killed Paul, I traveled to Atlanta for the final time to watch his final game. I wasn't nervous. I was ready. I was doing it for Heather. If I was able to fix everything that I broke in my life, I could fix everything in hers. It was the right thing to do. It was a correction of the universe as I saw it.

I sat up in the stands that cold night with the rest of the people watching a junior high football game. You'd think it was an NFL match-up the way those people carried on. At any rate, I knew how the night was going to go. I knew what I was going to do. Was I afraid of getting caught? Nah, not really. The way I saw it, I was playing with house money and I was given a second chance by something to put things right. And I believed that *then* as I do *now*.

After the game was over, with Paul's Rams winning by ten, the crowd of people had slowly dispersed and only a handful of fans remained on the field cleaning up. Paul, right on cue, had given his helmet and shoulder pads to his dad and kissed his mother and off they went. In the stands where I was walking away, a couple of people stayed after the game to pick up food wrappers, cans, and other such debris. Me, I pulled my black hat down low around my eyes and walked slowly towards Paul who was carrying a bag of trash to the big blue trash cans over by the concession stand.

"Hell of a game tonight, kid," I said.

Paul stopped and smiled.

"Ah, man it was a team effort. I'm just glad we won. Barely but we did. That team was tough," he said putting the trash in the can.

"I hate to ask, but can you help me with my car hood? I tried starting my car and I think there's something wrong under the hood but I can't open it because of this sling." I showed him my arm was in a sling under my jacket. I thought being "wounded" would give that psycho a false sense of security. And it worked. Under that sling was a lead pipe.

Paul looked at the sling and nodded, "You got it. Happy to help you out, sir. Lead the way."

We walked outside the football gate and down the street a bit to where only a few cars were still parked. Those cars were empty because the owners were the ones still at the football field cleaning. The football field itself was located on the other side of the school and the street we were on was in a small neighborhood with only a few houses dotting the landscape. Paul and I were the only ones on that dark narrow side street. I went to the driver's side and opened the door and popped the hood latch under the steering wheel. Paul felt for the latch under the narrowly open hood and found it. He raised the hood and propped it up on the thin metal stand. And when he turned to me with that boyish smile of a job well done, I clocked him with that lead pipe right across the head.

Sometimes late at night, when I'm trying to sleep, I can still hear that ping of the metal hitting Paul's head. Sometimes I can still feel the vibration that the pipe had given off in my hand.

I hit him so hard that he fell. He didn't even scream out it happened so fast. I looked around and made sure that no one was watching. I was in the clear. I knelt down and continued to beat the kid until I could no longer feel a pulse. After a few long minutes, he was dead. I rolled him into the nearby ditch beside the side street.

I closed the hood in a hurry. I didn't turn the lights on until I got a mile down the road. I headed for home.

A few days later, I read online and watched the news on TV about what had happened to this innocent star football player. The details were sketchy of course. The police had zero leads and nobody saw anything. His death was a mystery and a mystery that remains to this day. A true cold case. I hated it for his parents, I truly did. They didn't deserve this. But Paul had to be stopped. It was the only way.

7

As Heather Parker had gotten older, I sent her a friend request on one of the social media platforms when she got into college. She was so stoked about having a famous writer following her. I was one of her favorite writers, she told me, and one they were studying in her college Lit course. We became fast friends and she and I and Jennifer met regularly for dinner with her boyfriend and future husband, Rich. She went to college and became a social worker right after she graduated. When she got married, me and Jennifer were invited to attend—which we did happily. It was beautiful. She was beautiful. Her husband is a really nice guy. I'm happy for them both. I'm happy that Heather was able to live a normal life free of that maniac.

I have to admit it was really awkward having Heather in my life as a friend at first because I knew what we were in another time. But eventually, the more and more we talked the less awkward it felt. I filled into the new role as a friend. It made it immensely easier that I was in love with Jennifer and that Jennifer and Heather had become friends as well. Jennifer was like a second mother to her. Samantha, Heather, and Davey also had a special relationship as well. It was like it was meant to be or something and we were one big family. As the years rolled by, years turned into decades. I was complete.

One night, not too long ago, me and Jennifer, and Heather and Rich all went out to Atlanta to have dinner to celebrate my sixtieth birthday. After it was over, Jennifer went to the car to call Samantha who had called her earlier; something about the kids. Rich ran into a guy he knew from school and hung back to talk, and me and Heather walked side by side out of the restaurant.

"I got to tell you this really funny dream I had," Heather said laughing as we walked out of the restaurant. As I looked at her from the light of the outside of the building, she didn't look to be forty-two. But the years had surely rolled by.

"Okay, lay it on me," I said standing there looking around at the parking lot.

"Okay, so in this dream, I was going into this bookstore and you were coming out and I smashed your face with the door when I pushed it open. You fell backward holding your nose and mouth. And all these people were staring. It was crazy. I looked like I was in my early twenties I think and you looked like maybe in your forties. It was so strange." I looked at her. I felt like a ton of bricks had been dumped on me from above. That wasn't a dream, that had actually happened! So how did she know about that in *this* time?

"What else happened in this dream?"

Heather stood there, "Nothing. I woke up because of the alarm. Crazy dream. But it seemed so real, you know? What's wrong? You seem like you're not feeling well."

I stood there trying to process what Heather had told me. She told me a precise moment in time when we met in another time, another life. But how? How was that possible? "I'm good," I replied, half smiling. It wasn't authentic, but I was trying for it to be.

"Well okay, then. I'm heading to the car to wait for Rich. Who knows how long he'll be. Tell Jen I'll text her later. Happy birthday." She grabbed my hand and squeezed it and walked away.

It was the first and only time that my previous life and current one ever crossed paths. And how that happened I have no idea. To my knowledge, Heather never had another dream about the other life where we were together. If she did, she never told me or Jennifer about it.

I stood there in the night air and looked around trying to figure out how I felt about what I was told. I saw Jennifer in our car talking on the phone to Samantha and I waved. I saw Heather walking across the parking lot towards her SUV. I stood there and wondered, like I did in 2004, how in the hell did I get here. Where *is* here, exactly?

Author's Notes

This novel is a tragedy at its core. There's nothing good about it and all the characters are flawed to varying degrees. A lot of people have invisible struggles that people never see and those struggles spur emotions within themselves that cause actions; mostly bad. As much as this novel is a tragedy, it's also a book about redemption and second chances. At the end of the day, a second chance is what people want the most. Sometimes we get that elusive second chance but most times we don't. When we don't, we tend to spend that time in regret wishing that we had never done what we did or said what we said. It's wired into our DNA to fuck up just as it is wired in our DNA to want another shot.

I wrote this novel several times with several different endings that never really seemed to fit. For a long time, it seemed I was trying to fit a square peg in a round hole. Eventually, I just stopped writing this novel and decided that I would go back to it when I had the time. When I did finally get around to it back in 2015, I saw a story in it. So, I did what any good writer worth their salt does; I blew the dust off of it and revamped it with an ending that I was good with.

Does this ending work? Only the readers can answer that. Where is the narrator at the end of this story? Is he dead? Is he in an alt-reality? Did he really go back in time to fix things for a better future? I don't exactly know. What I can say to you, the reader, is that whatever you decide, you're not wrong. It does make for a great conversation piece, doesn't it? Isn't that at their core what books are supposed to do?

One more thing before we part: Thank you for reading this novel. I hope that it was time well spent. See you in time!

—Matthew McConkey,
June 24th, 2021

Acknowledgments

I would like to thank God for giving me the ability to read and write and have a way of seeing the world in a different way.

Thanks to Dennis Hicks, a teacher, who in my senior year showed me a better way. I only had him for a semester but his imprint upon my life was everlasting.

I like to thank the owner of The Village Book Shop back in 2007 for taking a chance on me and putting my very first book in her store. Who would have thought something so primitive would have sold a hundred copies in a week.

Patty Walker from Postnet Publishing who published that very first collection of shorts back in 2007. What a run we had.

My late Uncle Warren who got me my first typewriter back in 1992; an Underwood 315. I typed at least a million words on those old ribbons late at night in my bedroom.

My parents for putting up with my constant yammering about books and writing.

My high school sweetheart Rene Barker-Jamerson who read everything that I wrote back in my teen years when things were really clicking. I never forgot those late-night conversations under the stars talking about everything. Thanks.

Frankie Cline who pushed me to write because she could see what I could do even though I could not.

Thanks to my best friends new and old: Daniel, Dusty, Justin, Corky, Mitchell, Travis, and Derrick. Thanks for the good times and love you all.

To my daughter Macy and stepson Cameron. Being a dad was the best job I ever had.

Special thanks to Casey Jones for getting me straight on this book.

The Katz family.

And last but not least, Lisa Elliott.

THE AUTHOR

Home Again is Matthew McConkey's first novel. He has since published two additional novels, *Summerland* and *Maple Lane*, and two collections of short fiction, *Everything Fades in Time* and *Scarecrows and Shadows*. He lives in Tennessee.

www.ingramcontent.com/pod-product-compliance
Lightning Source LLC
Chambersburg PA
CBHW032234310726
48973CB00008B/2137